M000281176

THE EvoAngel

Ellen King Rice

ELLEN KING RICE

This is a work of fiction. Names, characters and incidents are a product of the author's imagination. Any resemblance to persons living or dead is unintended and coincidental.

Cover, formatting and book design by Damonza.com
Art by Duncan Sheffels

Paperback ISBN: 978-0-9969796-0-3

Epub ISBN: 978-0-9969796-1-0

Mobi ISBN: 978-0-9969796-2-7

PDF ISBN: 978-0-9969796-3-4

Library of Congress Control Number: 2015918167

Parasola plicatilis

artifact:

ar - ti - fact

noun

an item, structure or behavior left from a previous time

Note to readers:

This is an adult book. Sex, reproduction and evolution abound throughout.

It is my hope that this story will affect how you see your body and our Earth. We are at a point in history where we no longer ask if offspring are more affected by nature than by nurture. Everything influences us and provokes a response. Sometimes the response is explosive.

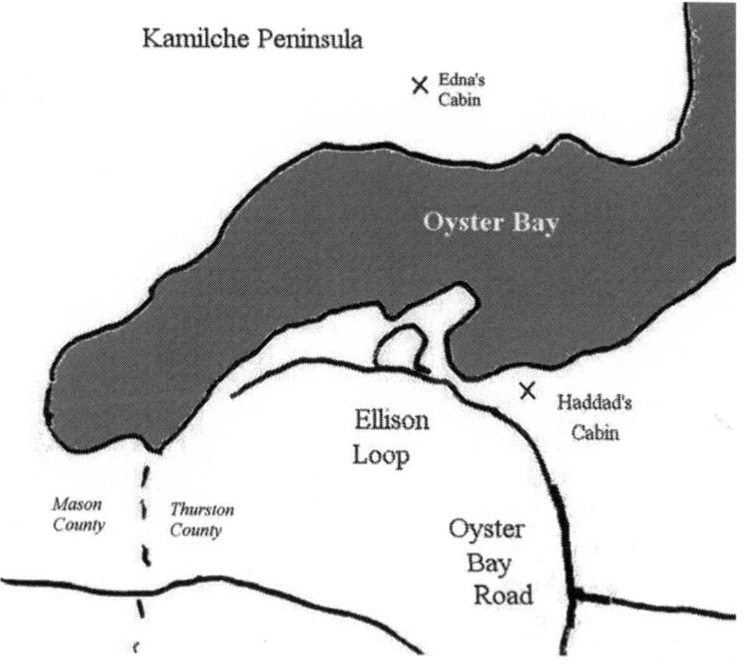

Oyster Bay, South Puget Sound, Washington State

"Once the mushroom has sprouted from the earth, there is no turning back."

—Luo proverb from Kenya

Chapter One

Tuesday morning, September 15, Kamilche Peninsula, Olympia, Washington

SHE WOULD POISON Dr. Band. She knew which mushroom to use.

Edna's hands trembled as she lifted the latch on the door to her cabin. She ached for a cup of chamomile tea.

She would collect the mushrooms after the tea.

Edna crossed her narrow living room, navigating carefully at the edge of the rug. At her age, she didn't need a fall.

She allowed herself a grim smile. She could use an invading species to do the deed. A landscaper had dumped a load of bark chips near a school bus stop and that action had introduced *Amanita phalloides* to her neighborhood. Even if the deadly species happened to be growing in a mixture of edible fungi, as mushrooms often do, the death cap would stand out to her. Eighty years of mushroom hunting was good for something. She knew her fungi.

Edna made it to the kitchen where she rested her hands at the deep enamel sink. The geraniums on the windowsill needed watering. Edna blinked back tears. She had bigger challenges now. Her hands continued to tremble as she filled the teakettle.

A death cap mushroom signaled its presence with a bright white stem erupting from an egg-shaped sac. There was the white ring on the stalk, the white spores, the unattached white gills, and the elegant profile that all said *Amanita phalloides* just as clearly as a nametag.

For handsome looks, she liked the spring season destroying angel, *Amanita ocreata,* with its dazzling white cap.

Edna sighed. Death caps and destroying angels were too dramatic. With her expertise there was no need for a poisoning cliché.

She would choose a small brown mushroom, *Galerina marginata.* It contained the same amatoxins as the Amanitas, but lacked a dramatic appearance.

As the flames from the propane burner licked the bottom of the teakettle, Edna's nerves steadied. She should think this through.

Amatoxins were not affected by heat. Cooked or raw, they poisoned. Surely a brownie would be better than a salad. Who gave a gift salad?

Her mind skittered through the details of cooking up a pan of brownies with minutely diced *Galerinas.* It would be a four phase poisoning. First there would be a latent span of quiet hours. The arrival of the second phase would be signaled by stomach pain and diarrhea. This would pass as the third phase unfolded as a quiet rebound day. The horrible Dr. Band would feel much better. It would be the following day when the gruesome fourth phase started. That was when the kidneys and liver would fail.

She should frost the brownies. That was always a special touch.

Edna lifted the squealing kettle off the flames and poured the boiling water over a teabag. She made her mind take a step back from such destructive thoughts. Mushrooms were her life.

There was also the reality that a locally experienced ER doctor might read blood tests shrewdly and provide the correct supportive treatment. If poisoning were suspected, then leftover brownies might be tested.

She sighed. Poisoning by mushroom wasn't fast enough.

Edna blinked back tears again as she sipped her tea. She could kill things. She had slaughtered more than a few chickens in her day. A human being was different. Dr. Band was no chicken.

She thought of dear Dr. Patel. None of this was his fault. She had made the appointment with him, trusting that her odd condition could be discretely discussed. It was high time to tell someone about her changing body.

She had not known there was a visiting doctor working at the clinic. Dr. Band was tiny and intense. She had the gleaming eyes of a predator.

Dr. Band terrified her.

Edna knew, of course, that an old woman should be sprouting chin hairs, not feathers. A narrow feather had emerged on her sternum a month ago and now that odd emergence was adding little friends. Dr. Patel had been kind and soothing. Then Dr. Band had walked in and spied Edna's chest.

When Dr. Band's hand went snaking into a pocket after a smartphone, Edna had leapt off the examination table and fled from the clinic. There would be no photographs of her chest. Not if she could help it.

Edna had raced home to her dear cabin where she knew her jumbled thoughts could soothe into a plan of action.

She considered her options. She could get a dog - a large dog with large teeth - and a *No Trespassing* sign. Her daughter, Lena, would think these were fears of old age sprouting like mushrooms after fall rains. Her granddaughter, Piper, would love a dog and would, no doubt, spoil the beast into delivering wet kisses instead of growls.

Edna's mind skittered around the idea of her daughter and granddaughter changing as she had.

What she had, they might have next. There was a distinct and lengthy heritage of odd women in the family.

Lena. Piper.

Edna groaned.

She picked up a frame from a kitchen shelf and studied the picture of her daughter. Lena was so precious and in so much danger from the modern world. Thank goodness Lena's husband was such a good man. Piper, now eleven, had the family cunning to go with the family oddities.

Edna kissed the glass of the picture frame, steering her lips to the glowing halo of blonde hair fringing her daughter's perfect face. Edna's stomach swooped down with a wave of worry, then stabilized as the chamomile did its magic.

Her jangled thoughts began to settle. There was a better way.

She would protect Lena and Piper by doing what wild creatures do. She would hide. She would also forge a back up plan in case she needed a speedy weapon to stop Dr. Band. Speedy meant no mushrooms.

Edna exhaled. There was no need to betray the mushrooms that had sustained and enchanted her all these many years. She would get out of the cabin and into the woods.

If she had to do any poisoning, she would choose something fast acting.

Edna made her decision.

She would collect the most poisonous plant in the northwest woods. She would walk down to the marsh and hunt in the shadow of the trees for poison parsnip.

Galerina marginata

"From the oyster to the eagle, from the swine to the tiger, all animals are to be found in men..."

Victor Hugo, poet, novelist
(February 26, 1802 – May 22, 1885)

Chapter Two

Tuesday afternoon, Westview Condominiums, #15B, Tacoma, Washington

DR. THEODORA BAND sat at the desk in her home office, tapping a well-manicured nail against her lips. Her sleek desk sat devoid of clutter, in odd contrast to the shelf on the wall that sat crowded with teddy bears.

She had driven home from the rural clinic on autopilot, weaving in and out of traffic with finesse. It had taken the entire drive to process what she had just seen.

She had fought doing the community service hours. Patel's tiny clinic was beneath her to a degree that was laughable. Theodora's attorney had managed to tamp down her assault charge to a no contest plea agreement. The judge handed down two days of service with a frown that had Theodora whipping out an agreeable smile that fooled no one.

Now Theodora smiled with a twisting smirk. This was one time community service paid.

A smoking hot trail to fame and fortune was opening before her. She had to research what she had seen. She needed to reconnect with that old woman to investigate further.

Theodora inhaled. She must keep her interior lava under control.

Theodora leaned back into her desk chair, recalling with some satisfaction the moment of her discovery. She had pushed into the exam room of the seedy country clinic because that dolt, Patel, had told her to wait in his office. His next patient was shy, he'd said.

Theodora did not wait for anyone.

If Patel didn't want her to see the next patient, then of course she would interrupt. How stupid of Patel to think otherwise.

Theodora had amused herself by scarring a doorframe with a paper clip as she listened at the door. She had heard a firm voice report a skin condition.

"Let's look," Patel had said. Theodora slowly counted to five. She had clasped a clipboard to her chest and marched into the exam room while speaking rapidly, "Dr. Patel, I'm sure you didn't mean…"

The look of horror on their faces had been priceless. Theodora had thought, just for a moment, that she had caught the two in an embrace. It was far more interesting than that.

Patel turned shades of scarlet and began to sputter. It was too late.

The old woman had feathers.

The granny had bolted out of the room before Theodora could snap a photo. The old woman was surprisingly nimble, grabbing her sweater and darting out the door. Patel blocked Theodora's effort to follow. The old woman had raced out of the clinic to an ancient Volvo station wagon that fired up with a roar. Theodora had not been able to capture a single image of the woman.

Theodora endured a lecture from Patel because it bought her time to think.

Patel could go on, as he had, about an unfortunate skin condition. While Patel had babbled, Theodora was thinking of the usual list of genetically originated skin disorders. There was nothing like this.

Feathers. Why not? They were made of protein, just as hair and fingernails were. Somehow the crone's DNA had been triggered into a different pattern of protein building.

There were traps everywhere. As usual, the stupid people of the world could cause any number of headaches.

Theodora's eyes narrowed as she sat, hating the world.

Control. She had to take control. That meant she had to leash her rages, at least for now. She'd done it many times before. She must do it again. She must move from fire to ice. The volcano inside had to stay dormant until she had control of Edna Morton.

Theodora opened a desk drawer. She took out a screwdriver and turned to the shelf behind her desk.

She had begun collecting teddy bears when she was eight. It was a useful cover.

Theodora selected a small teddy bear. She thought of Dr. Patel. He had touched her. He had put his hand on her elbow and steered her out of the clinic, his eyes flashing with disapproval. As the memory filled her with rage, she inhaled deeply. She drove the screwdriver into the stomach of the bear. Again and again she stabbed the bear. Stuffing swelled out of each rip. Small polyester pellets came pouring out to bounce down to the carpet.

Theodora took a cleansing breath. She dropped the eviscerated teddy bear into her wastebasket and returned the screwdriver to the drawer. Her cleaning lady could deal with the pellets on the carpet.

Theodora ran her hands through her impeccably highlighted hair and took a second cleansing breath.

It was time to learn about feathers.

What happens when he's your Prince Charming but you're not his Cinderella?

Chapter Three

Tuesday morning, Summit College, Olympia, Washington

"LET'S BEGIN," SAID Dr. Anderson, "by meeting some beautiful mushrooms."

Biology of the Northwest Woods looked to be a popular course and this term's lecturer was sheer eye candy. Dr. Milo Anderson stood at a lectern in lean, magnificent, six-foot-four, mahogany curled glory.

"You know this mushroom," Dr. Anderson waved at the screen. "You've seen the characteristic red cap and white blotches in illustrated books for children, and you've seen this mushroom portrayed in ceramic in garden shops. You've also met this mushroom while playing video games with a guy in overalls." A ripple of laughter flowed through the room.

Dr. Anderson added, "This mushroom is poisonous. It contains the chemicals muscarine and ibotenic acid."

Dr. Anderson's voice dropped to a growl. His words came out in a deep, careful staccato. "Please know that just because it's handsome, it doesn't mean it's for you."

In the last row, Grace Mossler blinked. As the new graduate student assigned to assist Dr. Anderson, she had not thought through the challenges a handsome speaker faced as mentor to so many students. Dr. Anderson had just laid down territorial lines to any smitten coed in the class. Fascinating.

Anderson added, "You'll be responsible for reading on the course website about the eight poisonous compounds that can be found in mushrooms and their methods of action. You'll be making spore prints of gilled mushrooms in the lab. It would be wise to look up spore prints before the lab, unless you particularly like that clueless feeling that comes with being unprepared."

This garnered a small chuckle from the students.

Dr. Anderson continued in a warmer voice, "I met my beautiful wife, Lena, because of this mushroom. I was seventeen and was scouting a location for a service project."

Grace inwardly sighed. Service project? Was he a lottery winner too? Handsome, knowledgeable, and now charitable – yes, he could be a magnet for fantasies. Grace smiled as she thought, *He just told us about his beautiful wife. Get a life, girl. Get a life.*

Dr. Anderson put up a photo of a forest-rimmed meadow. He leaned on the podium and said, "I was near here. I passed two little girls setting up a picnic with dolls."

Anderson turned to look at the picture on the screen. "You can see the 'fairy ring' of *A. muscaria* growing in a circle in the meadow. We'll discuss the mechanisms of ring development later, but for today, let's just observe the beauty and charm of such a circle. It didn't occur to me that the girls might add mushrooms to their tea party. When I returned from my walk, the girls were gone. A young woman was kneeling right where the mushrooms had been. She told me, "I think those little girls picked mushrooms."

"I could tell she was worried. If the kids ate wild mushrooms, they could be very sick before long. How sick varies by the species consumed."

"Some mushroom species can cause a headache. Others can cause stomach cramps followed by organ failure. This can make a mushroom diner very nervous. Although it can be embarrassing when we learn that a particular gastric upset is due to a person finally having some fiber in their diet."

A nervous ripple of laughter swept the room.

"Now, were these children in peril? The red-capped *Amanita muscaria* is actually not one of the most seriously poisonous mushrooms. However, the amount consumed and the size of the victim matter. In this case we had two small girls, and they had mowed through a large arc of mushrooms known to be somewhat toxic."

He continued, "The lovely young woman in the mushroom ring said to me, 'We've got to find the girls.' At that moment, I'm a seventeen-year-old nerd who had never had a date, so I'm liking the 'we' part."

More laughter.

Dr. Anderson said, "I gave her a hand to help her to her feet. She reached out with her other hand and grabbed a specimen to take with us. That was a smart move."

Anderson's voice intensified. "We got to the family at the trailhead as they were loading their car."

Dr. Anderson stopped to sip from the water bottle on the podium. The students sat silent as he recapped the water bottle.

He cleared his throat and finished. "The kiddy picnic basket was stuffed with *Amanita muscaria*. Some had nibble marks. My new friend showed her matching specimen, naming the species and explaining that *Amanita muscaria* could make the girls ill."

"The parents didn't hesitate. They called 911 and the girls were taken to the hospital where they got supportive treatment."

Dr. Anderson paused and frowned. The entire auditorium

remained hushed. Anderson leaned into the microphone and insisted, "Don't ever eat it unless you are certain – truly certain-that you know what it is. And never hesitate to call for help. If you have second thoughts after eating something, don't hesitate to call for help. There's time to turn things around if you get help."

Grace felt the collective whoosh of agreement as students responded with grins and some chatter.

Dr. Anderson clicked a new photograph onto the screen. A lean woman of astonishing beauty sat on a moss-covered log. Her white blonde hair glowed against a background of dark shadowed woods. Her hands were out in front, cupped and filled with golden mushrooms. Anderson fetched out his stunning smile again. Grace could feel the students respond like flowers rotating to follow the sun.

He said, "So, guys, there I was, left in the parking lot, watching the ambulance leave. That's when I realized that I was still holding hands with this gorgeous woman. So, men, know your mushrooms!"

Laughter rippled across the room.

"This is my wife, Lena. In this photo she's holding *Cantharellus formus*, also known as 'the Pacific golden chanterelle.' It is a delicious edible mushroom that we will seek on our weekly field trips. However, please know this mushroom has a near twin, named *Hygrophoropsis aurantiaca*, or false chanterelle. Another orange mushroom is *Chroogomphus tomentosus*, which has black spores. You'll see all three in the lab. You'll be responsible for learning to tell them apart."

Dr. Anderson looked over at Grace. She nodded and stood up. He'd said to circulate samples of oyster mushrooms as soon as he started in on varieties of local mushrooms. She should fetch the trays now.

He's teaching on so many levels, Grace thought. Visually, tactilely, emotionally. *He's very good*, she decided. There was opportunity here to learn a great deal.

Grace was at the table of samples at the back of the room when she heard the creak of the exit door opening beside her. She saw a thick hand move to hold the door open. The pudgy hand was hairy. *An adult male*, Grace mused. She had seen that heavy gold pinky ring before. *Where? Why didn't the listener come in to the lecture hall?*

At the front of the auditorium, Anderson was moving on with his slide show.

Grace hefted a tray loaded with paper bowls of oyster mushrooms. She balanced the tray carefully. She wanted to time her movements so she didn't distract from the lecture.

Dr. Anderson said, "We're only just beginning in the world of look-alikes. In California, there is another mushroom that looks similar to the delicious chanterelle. It's the Jack O' Lantern mushroom or *Omphalotus olearius*. The Jack-o-lantern is bioluminescent. The whole mushroom doesn't glow – but the gills will appear green in low light. That's because of a special enzyme called luciferase.

Dr. Anderson grinned with boyish delight. "It is a luciferase enzyme that gives a Midwestern firefly it's glowing hind end."

Dr. Anderson put up a picture showing two brown mushrooms. "Two different species growing together. They look like the same thing, but they're not."

"Before we get into the anatomy of the mushroom," he said. "Consider this: Small details constantly make a difference, particularly in human/organism interactions. Mushroom production is a good example of this. It is details that make biological work a success or a failure. Have some patience because we are going to spend some considerable time on details."

Dr. Anderson's eyes twinkled with good humor as the next slide popped up on the screen. It showed a pair of homely camels nuzzling each other. "Successful sex is pivotal to successful biology, so these details may not be all that painful for you."

A cheerful "Yee-haw!" came from the back row, and the classroom rippled again with laughter.

Grace needed to get the samples moving. As she passed the first bowl of mushrooms, she thought back to the brief staff meeting on Monday. *That hand and ring*, she decided, *belongs to Dr. Yousef Berbera, head of the Biology Department.*

Grace didn't have time to think deeply but she knew there were biological behaviors that repeated. A habit of observation was one of them. Secrecy was another.

Catharellus formosus

"How ludicrous and outlandish is astonishment at anything that happens in life."

Marcus Aurelius, Roman Emperor
(April 26, 121 – March 17, 180)

CHAPTER FOUR

Tuesday afternoon, September 15, Summit College

GRACE'S MORNING OF work unfolded into an afternoon of more work.

Grace and Dr. Anderson were reviewing the drawers of ornithological specimens in the northeast corner of an enormous storeroom when Grace kicked something that rolled under a heavy specimen cabinet.

"That was a roll of coins!" she said.

"Huh. Maybe there was a copy machine in here at one time." Milo Anderson peered around from the end of the shelving. "I can't see anything from this angle. Do you want it?"

"Sure. Could be coffee money."

Milo Anderson laughed at her eagerness. He said, "Okay. Here's my penlight. You look from below. I'll turn off the overhead lights. That might help."

Grace turned on the small flashlight as the storeroom plunged into darkness. She lay down on the floor to peer under the cabinet's legs. "A roll of quarters! Lunch money! Can you hand me something so I can roll it out?"

"Here, let me. I've got long arms." Milo Anderson strode back to the corner and lay down on the floor next to Grace. He reached under the shelf while she held the light beam steady.

The door to the storeroom opened and the overhead light went on. Milo and Grace froze, both horribly aware that no assistant professor should be lying on the floor of the storeroom, in the dark, with a graduate student.

"How did Anderson do today?" said a female.

"He's good. We're lucky to have picked him up," replied a low baritone.

"How did that happen, anyway? I thought he was a golden boy up in Seattle."

Milo and Grace stared at each another in dismay. The baritone sounded like Dr. Berbera, the department head. The female sounded like the formidable Dean of Students who had recently returned from a sabbatical. Milo extended a finger to his lips. Grace needed no coaching. Lying on the floor with her mentor was an embarrassment she didn't need. She wouldn't even risk the click of turning off the flashlight.

Berbera answered, "Anderson's wife went off the deep end. Beautiful woman. Named Lena. One day she went tearing through the campus, screaming and crying. She ended up perched in a cherry tree blooming on the quad. It took the paramedics a couple of hours to coax her down. That episode cooled Anderson's rise in the department."

Grace heard the metal rasp of a key being inserted into a lock.

Dr. Berbera continued, "Lena's mother is a mushroom collector - lives out on Kamilche Peninsula. Sounds like she's more stable around her mother, so we got a call asking if we could use him. They've got a cute little girl, about ten or eleven. Must of married really young."

The Dean replied, "So the wife is fragile. Anything else? Do I have to worry that Dr. Golden Boy has an overly sympathetic gal grad student this fall?

Berbera gave a bark of laughter. "Inappropriate grad school sex is a Dean's constant worry. We're okay this time. Steady sort. You'll see her. Short. Round face. Grace something from New Mexico State."

"Oh, yeah. Black hair. Kinda chunky? Navaho. Not the seductress type."

Grace was rather charmed as Milo Anderson frowned, then silently extended his middle finger up in the air on her behalf.

Dr. Berbera's voice echoed through the storeroom. "Here you go. Two sets of binoculars."

"Thanks. I'll get them back next week."

The light switched off and the door pulled shut.

Grace stood up so fast that she felt dizzy.

Milo reached under the shelving and retrieved the roll of quarters. He stood up and handed the roll to Grace, saying, "I'd say that was a scary way to earn ten dollars."

"Wow. No kidding."

"She didn't have to be so insulting." Milo moved down the stacks to the light switch to turn the light on.

Grace shrugged. "I am chunky - and if you're a native from the Southwest, you must be Navaho. It happens all the time. Only my mom's Apache and my dad's from the Kamilche area. He's a native too."

"West coast guy and Apache gal? How did that happen?"

"My folks met in the Air Force. My mom was adopted out and grew up in Texas. Dad grew up here but ran away from home. The family stuff is one of the reasons why I came out to Summit College. I'm going to try to connect."

Milo's jaw came forward in a rigid line. "Family is important," he agreed.

Ah, still tough times? Grace thought. She decided to investigate. *I should offer my story first. Submissive action.*

Grace shoved an errant cabinet into alignment. "I went to meet some of my mother's family while I was in New Mexico. That didn't go so well. I totally screwed up. I said the wrong things and… it was awkward."

She shrugged. "You can't just show up and announce you're a member of the tribe."

"It can take some time," Milo agreed. "I grew up around here, but I've been gone for more than a decade. It's been a little tough to re-connect."

Milo exhaled a huff, halfway to a sigh. "Berbera's right – my wife has been ill. Even with her mother here, she's had a tough time re-assimilating. You have to put some time into it."

Grace replied, "You're right. I didn't take time. In New Mexico, I went into a riff about being an impoverished student. They thought I was looking for a handout." Grace tossed the roll of quarters in the air and snagged it on the downward arc. "I am a poor student, but I'm not a leech. This time I'll handle it better."

"My mother-in-law teaches some classes on Kamilche peninsula," Milo said. "Her name's Edna Morton. I'll bet she could introduce you around. Would it help to talk to her?"

"Sure! I want to put my toes in the family waters slowly this time."

Milo slid a specimen drawer open. "Let me talk to her then."

Grace nodded. "That'd be great. I'll take all the help I can get."

"Hey, you're nice. They'll like you." Milo picked up a stuffed puffin and moved toward the door.

Stepping in behind him, Grace saw how Anderson's blue oxford shirt did little to hide his wide shoulders and a strongly muscled torso.

Get a grip, girl, she scolded herself. Handsome, but not available. She couldn't keep back a quick grin. She would bet a lunch that no besotted grad student had ever been lying in the dark with the delicious Dr. Anderson.

Let's see if you can hang on to some dignity here, she silently chided her wayward brain. *Prioritize. Behave. Let's learn stuff, get the degree, meet Dad's family with some decorum and try really hard not to get into a jam with some bat shit crazy wife in the attic.*

Grace shoved the roll of quarters into her jeans pocket. As she pulled the storeroom door shut, she decided that Milo Anderson's wife was Milo Anderson's problem.

She's a few feathers short of a whole duck.

CHAPTER FIVE

Tuesday afternoon, Edna's Cabin, Kamilche Peninsula

EDNA SAT AT her computer. She had a document file open, a large font chosen and her tea mug sat on the coaster just to the right of her mouse.

She made herself start.

"I, Edna Morton, being of sound mind and body… " Edna stopped typing. She missed her typewriter. It had been so satisfying to see the ball rotate to strike the letters onto the page.

Edna sighed. Missing her typewriter was not the real problem. She had to untangle her mess and give her family both history and options.

Hide. Not attack. Predators could be avoided by hiding. She would hide as long as she could - and she would tell Piper and Lena things they needed to know.

Her body had been activated in ways she had always feared possible. She had ducked the responsibility of explaining the family heritage to her daughter.

"Ducked." Edna groaned. "I'm just ducky."

Edna firmed her lips into a sour line. She needed to get on with this.

It didn't help that Lena was a nervous sort - beautiful, ethereal and so susceptible to emotional upheaval.

Edna leaned back in her old swivel chair to think. She couldn't blame Lena for her own shortcomings. It had been her own fears that had kept her from communicating with her daughter.

Edna put her fingers back on the keyboard. She had avoided educating Lena. She had dawdled and allowed herself to be distracted by the work and play of each day. As time went on, she had to admit, she skipped educating Lena altogether, with a plan to tell Piper. That had been a convenient approach as she told herself that Piper was much too young. There was time yet.

No longer true.

The Internet and the regional library changed her thinking. She knew things her mother hadn't. She had a better idea of the biology at hand.

Edna deleted her writing and began anew. It was time to warn her family.

She typed.

Dear Piper,

There is a difference between a snake's scales and a bird's feathers. Scales are flat plates, while feathers are tubular. One clever writer has compared scales to a folded napkin and feathers to a straw. Scales, like a folded napkin, have the same surface on top and bottom. But a feather begins as a hollow quill that rotates and opens- with this unfurling, a new surface emerges. It is complex biology.

The difference, dear Piper, is important because you,

your mother and I all have the world's weirdest goose bumps. Mine started to emerge at the armpit when I was 53 and pregnant with your mother. I was an ancient mother! By the time your mother was born, I had a dozen rows of bumps, running in an arc from my armpits, across the tops of my breasts to meet in a ridge on my breastbone. I also have several rows across my back. Your mother had this same goosebumps when she was born and I know you have it as well. You called it 'my funny freckles' last year. I should have said something to you then.

My goosebumps have been nothing more than funny spots all these years. This spring we lost Grandpa. The stress seems to have triggered my bumps into action. I am one hairy old lady. Actually, I am a downy old lady. I am not the first, and I will not be the last in the family to be this way.

You know that I was raised in the woods and that I was alone, with my parents, for most of my life. I have never told you why my mother was so reclusive. She knew that children from our strange family could be in danger. This has been true for centuries and may still be so.

I met James in 1982. My mother had just passed away. For the first time in my life I was free to do as I liked. I looked up my father's family in Ballard. I was fifty years old. Fifty! James was sixty-two. We thought we were too old to have children so we married and began to socialize. We had such fun! On the summer solstice of 1984, filled with happy mushrooms and blackberry wine, we…

Edna stopped typing. What did Piper know about sex? Did

any child ever want to know about the history of a parent's conception? Was the date of Lena's conception important?

Edna closed her eyes and sank into memories. Solstice. Mushrooms. Wine. Aging but infatuated lovers. Cousins. What had set the stage?

The pregnancy had begun normally. She hadn't had the big skin pores then. It was three months later that the pores emerged. If she were honest, she had to own that it wasn't the solstice. It was silly to suggest such a thing.

Edna's lips firmed into a grim line. It was the mushroom extract for respiratory distress that triggered the goose bumps. She should have been more careful when she cooked up that recipe. It was unfortunate that she had made as much as she had. She was responsible. Not the phase of the planets. Mushrooms activated human DNA. Shamen and healers used mushrooms for a reason. Fungal medicines initiated anatomical changes.

The sound of a car door shutting galvanized Edna into closing her word processing file. How feather-brained she had become. Normally she heard a vehicle as it came up her long gravel driveway. No one could sneak up on her when she was young. Now she was old and not nearly as alert as a wild creature should be – and this was no time to be complacent.

"Thank goodness we don't get all the government we pay for"

– bumper sticker

Chapter Six

Tuesday, National Security Agency, Fort Meade, Maryland

A BROAD BELLIED MAN in a blue polo shirt and wrinkled khaki slacks carried two cups of coffee through a vast government cubicle farm. He turned right when he reached the unit labeled 2478 Ito.

Harry didn't say "Hello." He said, "What do you know about mushrooms?"

Ken Ito massaged his very tired eyelids. "I live in this cubicle box and digest too much bullshit, so I must be one?"

Ken yawned. "Sorry, Harry, I am not up to speed today."

"Magic tournament? Dungeons and Dragons meet? What fantasy event did we attend this last weekend?" Harry held out the cup. "Coffee. Black."

"Thanks."

Ken yawned again and rubbed his eyes with the heels of his palms. Ken had large hands for a small man. His pale ivory face floated between a drooping spill of straight black hair and a black shirt. His dark shirt and tailored black slacks blended into his black leather office chair.

"Space Film festival. Beef Wellington."

"Beef Wellington?" Harry blinked in confusion.

"Mushrooms go into Beef Wellington."

"Great. You know it's Tuesday?"

Ken gulped coffee and nodded. "The festival was north. Got stuck in Boston because of thunderstorms. Why do we care about mushrooms?"

"Because the North Koreans care," Harry said. "Lots of traffic over the weekend. They're shopping Internet sites, books, online journals. All on mushrooms. And you're our go-to fun guy."

Ken groaned. "Fun-gee. It's pronounced Fun-gee. My Ph.D.'s was on yeast. Not mushrooms."

"Yeast is fungus. Right?"

"Yeah, Harry. Fifteen hundred species of one-celled fungi. That's yeast. Just remember that I was twenty-one years old when I started my grad schoolwork. My interest in yeast was an interest in mastering the fine art of brewing great quantities of beer. I did a lot of math and charts on yeast population growth while brewing vats of beer. If you want to know about hops and worts, I'm your guy - but mushrooms are a fruiting body of a mycelium fungus."

Harry nodded. It was time to kick Ken into gear. "Sounds like you know a hell of a lot more than most of our analysts," Harry said. "What do you know about mycoremediation?"

Ken slurped coffee and said, "Mycoremediation. I actually do know something. I went with a Granola Girl to a talk. Let's see. Mushrooms are decomposers. Mushrooms can concentrate heavy metals. That's why they don't let people collect mushrooms around the Chernobyl site."

"Ah. Are the Japanese keeping an eye on mushrooms after the tsunami nuclear mess?

Ken slurped more coffee and yawned again. "Absolutely. Phosphorus bonds. That's what I remember. The mycelium – that's like the mushroom root system – has all these enzymes it can put out. Some can degrade phosphorus bonds. There's research using mushrooms to clean contaminated soil - like when someone dumps out their motor oil."

Harry jumped in, "Phosphorus bonds! There are phosphorus bonds in sarin gas, and in soman and VX. You don't get any more toxic than that. What the hell are the North Koreans up to? Are they dumping stuff or tweaking stuff into something weirder?"

Harry gestured towards Ken's computer. "I sent you a bunch of files. There's high interest in DNA methylation too. What does that mean?"

"A methyl group is a carbon atom with three hydrogens attached. I used to know more, but it's too early in the morning for my brain to retrieve biochemistry lecture material."

Harry grinned down at him. "You'll figure it out."

"I guess." Ken sighed, "That's why you pay me the not-so-big bucks."

Ken set down the coffee cup and typed in his computer password. "The Granola Girl dumped me. Big time. Uber-nerd strikes out once again. I haven't been very keen on phosphorus bonds since then, but I'll see what I can find out about mushrooms and DNA methylation."

Harry said, "I know you're thinking this is another day chasing shadows, but in this business you never know what nutty thing will end up being true."

"Yeah, yeah. Mushrooms end the world as we know it."

Harry smiled. "It's always the sneaky little guy you never saw coming."

"I am the wisest man alive, for I know one thing, and that is that I know nothing."

Socrates, Philosopher (469 BCE – 399 BCE)

CHAPTER SEVEN

Wednesday morning, National Security Agency, Fort Meade, Maryland

"THERE IS AN inverse relationship between CpG methylation and transcriptional activity." Ken massaged his neck as he digested that thought.

He called Harry and said, "Methyl groups constipate the system. When there is a lot of methylation, genetic transcription halts."

"That's good, right?" It sounded like Harry was talking around a sandwich.

"Depends. If you stop a fat cell from filling, that's sometimes good. If your pancreas stops producing insulin, that's bad. It depends on what the DNA section activates. Failure to properly methylate may play a role in some cancers. If you switch off the cellular garbage collectors, you can get tumors growing."

"What else you got?"

"In 2012, the world shifted, DNA wise."

Harry audibly swallowed and said, "And?"

"We used to think that mammals had a lot of junk DNA. We thought it was evolutionary leftovers in the form of DNA wrapped around protein spools called 'histones'. When the DNA is all wound up, enzymes don't get in to read the DNA. We thought there was a lot of leftover baggage."

Ken continued, "The 2012 ENCODE project showed how much DNA is regulatory. Switches on or off and structures appear or disappear. We don't understand it all. A change in the environment or in diet can cause a DNA strand to unwind, go to work and then goes back into storage. Gene regulation is more complex and interactive than anyone had guessed. It's a whole new science. Epigenetics."

Ken took a breath and added, "Over 80% of human Cytosine-guanine sites are methylated. Harry, there's just tons of stuff that we have the directions for, but don't use, or only use once in a while. Fungi are at the other end of the spectrum. Fungi only have a tiny portion of their DNA methylated."

"And why do the North Koreans care about methylation and mushrooms?"

"Hard to say," Ken answered. "Cancer cures, weapons degradation, water purification or just healthy stuff to eat are all on the table at this point."

Ken sat up, his voice crackling with excitement. "Whoa. I just made a connection. Harry, mushrooms are part of traditional Asian medicine. Hell, they're part of indigenous medicine everywhere. Maybe the North Koreans are connecting certain mushrooms to certain genetic switches. That could be huge."

Harry wasn't impressed. "Yeah, yeah. Weaponized shiitake ravioli makes us all stupid. Somehow I'm not seeing that as a threat to America. Can you add in some reading on blue green algae and anatoxin-a? The North Koreans are fishing on those topics too."

"Anatoxin-a? As in the Very Fast Death Factor?"

"Afraid so. If they are planning to weaponize algae, that could be really bad."

"It's also stupid," Ken argued. "It doesn't target just humans – and it would target all humans. We already have many weapons that do that. You'd want something that…" Ken's brain was firing rapidly. "You'd want something for your team that turned on or off the right DNA switches. Anatoxin-a causes constant stimulation of muscle cells, which then causes rapid respiratory failure. You want something that doesn't let that happen."

"Can mushrooms do that?"

"I have no idea."

"In words are seen the state of mind and character and disposition of the speaker."

Plutarch (46 -120)

Chapter Eight

Wednesday afternoon, Westview Condominiums, #15B

THEODORA INHALED A centering breath before she began composing her request. She exhaled and began keyboarding.

Dear Uncle David,

You said to send along any clever topics for consideration and I've come across a terrific one. It is a great fit for the quick response NIH research fund. I'll work up the full proposal for you soon. I anticipate taking over the supervision of the described patient within the next few days.

Theodora paused. She must not overreach. It was important

to start with well-documented terms before leaping to explore the riveting possibilities represented by Patel's odd patient.

She needed a brief history and a stellar grab for attention. It was always a challenge to tease a jaded reader.

Theodora wrote *Geneticists have identified master body building genes that are consistent throughout the animal kingdom. The Pax-6 gene is the master gene for eye development for everything from fruit flies to elephants. The Distal-less gene regulates limb development in people and in spiders. The Tinman gene regulates the development of the heart.*

These are shared DNA sequences that regulate on/off states during embryonic development. We now know that the same sets of genes control the formation of body parts in thousands of species.

We all have nearly the same "genetic toolbox." We contain the same DNA instructions. It is the activation of the instructions that drives diversity.

Bodies have repeated modular parts such as vertebrae or extremities that may present as a hand, a paw or as a flipper. The vast majority of activation happens as an embryo develops.

An exception to this is cancer, which is the epitome of post-embryonic activation. In cancer, normal cellular regulatory constraints fail and a DNA signaling pathway goes awry.

I have identified an elderly female patient whose genetic toolbox has been activated into a novel morphology. Her chest has a row of skin pores that have developed filoplumes, or rudimentary feather like structures.

Post-embryonic DNA activation is of immense

importance to medicine. I therefore request an immediate allocation of $250,000 to initiate examination and analysis of this unusual patient. I will research her family for similar traits and collect biological samples for analysis and identification of the activating homeoboxes.

Theodora clicked "send" with a surge of satisfaction. She didn't need the full power of the U.S. Government to be flowing through her hands. She only needed a piece.

"He was a bold man that first ate an oyster."

Jonathan Swift
(November 30, 1667 – October 19, 1745)

CHAPTER NINE

Thursday evening, Twin Cedars School cafeteria, West of Olympia

BY THURSDAY EVENING, Grace felt she knew Milo Anderson. She could see how he thought and where he wanted to take his students. His pace and organization were impressive.

Now Grace sat in a grade school cafeteria, poking at the lump on her plate with distinct feelings of reservation. The texture alone deserved some scrutiny.

"Don't analyze it. Just eat it!" Her freckled and pig-tailed companion demonstrated by popping a fried oyster into her mouth.

Piper Anderson clearly had no food shyness. Grace grinned at Milo's slender daughter in her pink overalls. "You sure are free with the advice! Why don't you eat the broccoli salad?"

Piper grinned back. "It's more fun to boss you."

Piper's oak brown braids nearly dipped into her plate as she leaned forward to shovel in more oysters. She tossed one braid over her shoulder with dexterity as her mother gently moved the second braid back.

"I've never heard of spaghetti with oysters." Grace stirred the pasta. The noodles and sauce looked like the gelatinous masses she remembered from school lunches. The fried oysters were nothing like meatballs. They were sea-flavored nuggets with an odd squishiness.

The cafeteria echoed with voices and the clatter of trays and utensils as families crowded in.

"It's okay," came softly from Lena Anderson. "The oysters are donated and come straight from the boats. It is a special blessing. Family night does take some getting used to."

Lena Anderson took some getting used to as well. It wasn't just the long, lean form in jeans and a T-shirt or the bright, near white, blonde hair – there was an aura of tension interwoven with sweetness. *She's like a bunny who knows there is a fox nearby*, thought Grace. *She's not crazy, just nervous.*

Lena Anderson turned heads. Her beauty unnerved, making plump housewives grimly nudge husbands and star-struck teens into passing.

I feel like I should be asking for an autograph, Grace mused.

Milo came weaving through the packed school cafeteria with a plate piled high with fried oysters.

"No fair," cried Piper. "How come you didn't get the spaghetti and salad?"

Milo winked as he sat down. "I have connections."

Lena turned a radiant smile on her husband. "Mary Margaret O'Reilly was serving?"

"Yep." Milo turned to Grace. "She was my Den Leader. She's the most terrifying woman on the planet. I can't believe she's still here, serving oysters."

"Earth to Milo," teased Lena. "She has a girl in Piper's class."

"Oh. Right. Her Late-in-life baby." Milo gave Piper a hug. "To bookend our early-in-life baby."

Piper shrugged, "Mrs. O'Reilly isn't that bad. The principal is worse."

"Sez you!" Milo laughed.

"Thanks for bringing me along," Grace said. "This is an amazing event."

"Yep. Of course it's a huge event so that doesn't help you find your relatives."

Grace snorted her bass laugh. "Actually it does. I've had a couple of people read my nametag and give me a look. I know my dad is homesick. He always talks about this area like it was heaven. I wish I could get him back here."

"Why wouldn't he come?" Piper's eyebrows rose with the question.

"He got into some trouble with his family and left. He never told me what it was. Something embarrassing, I guess. "

Piper swung a tennis-shoed foot up and under her rump to boost herself a bit higher. "Tell me about the other family. I don't get what happened."

Grace was glad of an excuse to leave the oysters. She propped her elbows on the table and turned towards Piper.

"History. That's what happened. Followed by my ignorance," Grace said. "When she was three years old, my mom was taken from her family under a program called the Indian Adoption Project. That happened a lot in the '50s. She was sent to a white family in Texas. My mom grows up, joins the Air Force and meets my Dad. Eventually they have me and I've also got two younger brothers."

"And German Shepherds"

"Yep. Our dogs are Air Force retirees."

"That is so cool."

"Thanks. Anyway, I went to college at New Mexico State. I

went to meet some of my mother's birth family. When I got there, I just kept saying and doing the wrong thing."

"Were they mean to you?' Piper's face scrunched with worry.

"No. They were really polite. Super duper polite."

Lena reached out across the table and touched Grace's arm. "You knew they were uncomfortable?"

Grace picked up a paper napkin and began shredding it. "Yeah. I met them at a resort restaurant. It was very upscale and that made me nervous. I kept babbling. I showed them the snake-skin boots I'd found at a yard sale. Basically, I didn't learn anything about my cousins because I just wouldn't shut up."

Piper nodded. "Cassy O'Reilly is like that. She knows as much as the teachers. She can't shut up either."

Grace dropped the napkin remains and picked up a fork to stab the spaghetti. "And people can't stand her, right?"

Piper shrugged. "Sometimes. It's funny when we have a substitute teacher. They don't know what to do with her. She's very confident."

Milo reached down the table for a saltshaker. "Did the cousins say anything to guide you?

"No. I..." Grace looked up at the ceiling. "That's not what they would do. At least, I don't think so. I think it was hard on them too. It's an ugly past. After my cousins left, the waitress mentioned my boots. When she explained there is an aversion to snakeskin, I was mortified. There was even a sign in the place. 'Please be culturally sensitive.' Gack. I had the sensitivity of a sledge hammer."

Lena laughed in sympathy. "I like you, Grace Mossler! I am so clueless about social boundaries."

"Lena was raised under a toadstool," offered Milo.

"My mother will know who you should meet," Lena said. "She lives out in the woods, but she seems to know people from all over." Lena shifted her weight on the hard bench. "She's better at connecting than I'll ever be."

"Grandma's cool," confirmed Piper. "She'd make you eat mushrooms with your oysters."

A tall middle school boy bearing a tray stopped at the end of the table. "Dessert, anyone?" he asked. His eyes hung on Lena.

As Lena and Piper looked at the desserts, a barrel-chested man in worn brown workpants and a gray I-heart-Oysters T-shirt came down the aisle bearing a loaded plate and a drink. He stepped slowly between the tables, looking for space for his family. A stout woman and a small dark-haired boy in jeans and sweatshirts followed him closely.

Milo waved an arm, indicating that there was room at their table. "Suck it in, ladies. Let's get these folks a spot."

The couple sat down next to Milo. "Thanks. Joe Harbo. My wife, Daylene. And this here is Little Joey." As the adults shook hands, the small boy put his plate on the table next to Lena. He touched her arm.

"Joey, don't bother the lady," rumbled his father.

"It's alright," Lena said softly. "He has something to tell me."

Piper rolled her eyes. "Little kids have a thing for my mom," she told the Harbos.

Grace watched silently. The boy didn't fit the parents. He was dark-haired, dark-eyed and very slim while the parents were hefty with the red faces and blue eyes of Caucasians. Was this child a repeat of her mother's life? Grace frowned. *Easy. Let's not jump to conclusions,* she thought. *What did this kid want from Lena?*

The little boy whispered long and hard into Lena's ear. She listened, and said, "It's okay."

Lena dug into her jeans pocket. "I want you to take my ticket. The door prize is a mountain bike."

Lena continued with her soft voice oddly carrying the length of the table "You will find more people wish you well than ever wish you harm. I forget that myself, but it's good to remember."

Little Joey took the ticket and threw his arms around Lena's neck. She hugged him back and set him down. Joey galloped back to show the ticket stub to his mother.

"Well, that's a kindness for sure," Daylene told him. "You are old enough to ride a bike. If you don't win, we should look for one anyway."

"I'll win! I know it!"

"We'll see," his father rumbled. "Don't get your hopes up."

Lena smiled. "He will win."

Grace stared at her. It was an odd thing to say. 'He will win'. Not 'He might win.'

Lena blushed and started spooning up her dessert.

"By the pricking of my thumbs, something wicked this way comes."

Witch in Act IV, Scene 1, Macbeth
by William Shakespeare (April 1564 – April 23, 1616)

CHAPTER TEN

Friday morning, Edna's cabin, Kamilche Peninsula

ON FRIDAY MORNING, Dr. Patel drove out to see Edna.

"I wasn't sure I had the right driveway," he told her. The small cabin was hidden in the Douglas fir trees until the last turn of the graveled tracks.

"It's not so hard to find," Edna responded as she opened the screen door to the porch. "On Tuesday I had a dinner truck come up the drive! I had no idea we had such services out here. He stood right here on the doorstep and sold me Chicken Cordon Bleu."

Edna realized she was babbling with an odd country girl twang, a sure sign of her nervous state. "Come on in. I'm glad you're here." *And*, she thought, *please tell me about Dr. Band. Was the plan to hide the right one? Would Dr. Band be coming here?*

Dr. Patel stepped into the cabin. Edna smelled garlic, ginger and turmeric as he entered her living room. He smelled healthy.

He was agitated today. He declined her offer of coffee and sat at the edge of her worn orange sofa, smoothing the fabric of his trousers with small strokes. Edna sat down in her rocking chair.

"I am so very sorry, Miss Edna, for my colleague's rude intrusion the other day," he began. "I lectured her so very sternly. I have waited these past few days to see if she would return. All is quiet." Dr. Patel seemed to be convincing himself as much as Edna.

"Who is she, exactly?"

Dr. Patel rolled his eyes skyward. "She is a disaster. Dr. Band is an M.D. who loses her temper. She slapped a lab assistant and was facing assault charges when her attorney negotiated for her to do some community service hours at our poor clinic. This is not help I need."

Patel said, "I know you have some concerns about Dr. Band, and I should hear them. But, first, how are you feeling today?"

Edna squirmed.

Dr. Patel put the palms of his hands together and inclined his head gently. "Do not worry. I promise you, Miss Edna, your secrets are safe with me."

Edna took a breath and rushed out with, "The popping out seems to have settled down. I'm just a funny old woman."

Dr. Patel smiled. "You are a fine woman."

"Why doesn't my condition worry you? Some doctors would ship me off to a zoo somewhere, but I just knew you were going to be, well,... discrete."

"Ah," Patel's head bobbed, almost as if it were unattached to his frame. "I am from India. There is much there that cannot be explained by western science. That is why I took your mushrooming class. Mushrooms are part of native health care around the globe. There is much to be learned outside of our textbooks. Recently I am reading about consumption of turkey tail mushrooms to treat breast cancer. "

Dr. Patel added, "I am, of course, interested in your condition. Does this run in your family?"

"There's oral history. My mother was intensely secretive and very protective. She did tell me stories. She said the women in our family tend to turn odd at times. Two were burned as witches. One was tossed into a pond with rocks sewn into her apron pockets. That one drowned. The drowning supposedly revealed she wasn't a witch, but I'm not sure that was a comfort to her."

Edna worked to keep her voice calm and professional. "Mother had a heightened fear response. She would say that a woman who could live independently in the woods triggered fear in others. It wasn't enough that we had to find our way. We had to be invisible too." Edna was surprised to find tears welling up.

Edna inhaled and burst forth with, "I lived an invisible life for many years. We didn't have friends. We didn't meet up with my father's family. It was a very isolated life."

She rocked forward, saying, "It's rather awful to say that my life got better after my mother died, but that's the truth. Then I met my cousin, James, and I was just too full of life to be invisible any more."

Edna slipped a tissue out of the cuff of her cardigan and dabbed at her nose before continuing, "My father was a quiet man. Mother managed him completely. He was killed in a logging accident in 1970."

She added, "Some of my ancestors have been ugly women. Our women are given to hooked noses, large hands and black hair. I got lucky and took after my father. I was a brunette before I went gray. Mother said that was fine. The family has brunettes occasionally. But once in a while there will be a girl who is dangerously different. She'll be blonde. My mother said if I ever had a blonde baby girl I should, oh, my. "

Edna stopped. She couldn't speak the words.

Dr. Patel nodded. "I understand. In India too, we have those who don't want a baby girl."

Edna's hands clasped together tightly. She said, "My father adored little girls. He loved me so much. He told me I'd make a good mother. When Lena came along, I decided Dad was right. I kept her. "

Edna leaned forward in the chair to finish. "Mother said it was the forest foods that make us different. We know mushrooms. We're generations and generations of forest women. From Russia and Romania. From Poland and Germany. Some live in the United Kingdom. We're all mushroom eaters and we're all related, like a giant mycelium. Some perceive the future. They call that the second sight."

She added, "I've got that. Sometimes I know things. I can look at a woman's hand, and I know what will happen to her. Maybe that's the mushrooms too."

Dr. Patel made no argument.

Edna took courage from his easy acceptance. "Dr. Patel, it's not just my feathery fringes. My daughter, Lena - she's... different in other ways."

Dr. Patel's cell phone ring shattered the moment. "I'm so sorry," he said. "It's my clinic staff. I must take this now."

Edna fell silent, both relieved and unsettled by the interruption.

Patel frowned as a tinny voice came through the phone. "I'll come now."

He tapped the phone off and said, "Miss Edna, there has been vandalism at my clinic. I must go."

Patel held up his hand and started counting by holding up his thumb. "One. Don't worry about Dr. Band. She is gone." Dr. Patel held up his index finger. "Two, I would be glad to look at your daughter." The next finger popped up. "Three. For you I am seeing an interesting development but nothing inflamed that calls for immediate treatment. We can run some lab work when you are ready."

Dr. Patel brought up a fourth finger. "Finally, our medical records are private. No one will see."

"Thank you. I do feel better." Edna suddenly felt a bit silly about bolting out of Dr. Patel's clinic. "I'm sure there's no reason to worry."

"Okay, boys. Let's go make a withdrawal."

John Dillinger, Bank Robber
(June 22, 1903 – July 22, 1934)

CHAPTER ELEVEN

Friday, lunchtime, Summit College

"WELCOME TO THE Biology Department's lunch time short stroll." Milo Anderson addressed a crowd of students and colleagues at the edge of a parking lot.

"Today we are going to be talking about associations. I am also going to be talking about robbery. Those of you going out with us this afternoon on the Bio 121 field trip will have an entire afternoon devoted to sex."

A cheerful rooster crow came from the back of the crowd.

Milo said, "Our stroll is short. We start with an ornamental birch tree."

He led the way to a large white-barked tree. "Here, at the base of the paper birch, we have a special sort of mushroom, the birch bolete. The mushrooms and the tree are living in an association. The mushroom puts out "hyphae" – a mushroom root-like system. These hyphae push their way through the soil gathering nutrients."

"This is an ectomycorrhizal fungus, living in symbiosis with the tree. Other kinds of mushrooms are saprophytic, which means they eat dead or dying stuff. If you want to do in your professor during finals week, make sure you know which sort of mushroom you'll use to get rid of the body."

Grace grinned as a light ripple of laughter rose from the group.

Milo continued, "Enzymes are released from the hyphae. Like animals, fungi use enzymes to eat. Here the enzymes are secreted outside the hyphae to break down the organic matter, so we have digestion without a stomach. But," Milo paused dramatically, "there's so much more."

"We have a symbiotic relationship between the mushroom hyphae and the tree roots called a 'mycorrhiza.' As the mushroom enzymes go to work, the hyphae pick up sugars. The mushroom gets to eat. Meanwhile our tree gets nitrogen, phosphorus and potassium from the hyphae – the same chemicals you buy at the garden center to give your veggies a boost. Now the tree is having a happy lunch… and… there's more." Milo patted the tree trunk. "The mushroom may protect the tree from some pathogens. The tree gets lunch and health care."

Milo held up his thumb and index finger with a sliver of light showing. "The fungus along the tree root tips is only one cell thick. The fungus can work its way into places that the root tip can't reach. Basically our tree and mushroom make a highly successful bank robbing team."

Milo smacked the tree trunk. "You've got Al Capone here working with his little mushroom henchmen, and they are sucking up the nutrient goods out of the neighborhood."

Milo ran his hand down toward the roots. When he got to the ground, Milo kept going, kneeling to follow a root out into the dirt.

He said, "A similar sounding word is 'mycelium.' The mycelium is the name we give to the mass of hyphae that make up the body of a fungus. There is a giant mycelium in Oregon that may be the world's largest living organism. It covers over two thousand acres and may be as much as two thousand years old."

Milo slid a pencil out of his pocket and used the pencil to lift up rich dirt beside the root. "See the white hyphae strands running through the dirt? A cubic inch of forest soil may hold a mile of hyphae. Myceliums make up huge interconnecting webs in the forest. There is a strong similarity between the architecture of mycelium and the architecture of hurricanes and of spiral galaxies in space. We are foolish if we ignore the repeating structures found in nature. So many times the very small things - like rain drops and fungal spores – connect or grow to become powerful entities."

Milo stirred the dirt with his pencil. "This white rot fungus produces an enzyme called 'peroxidase' that is effective in breaking hydrogen-carbon bonds. We're learning that white rot fungus can break down oils, herbicides and pesticides into carbon dioxide and water. Myceliums can destroy toxins before they enter the food chain."

Milo stood up. "There was a time when plastics was the career of the future. I'd say today's young graduates should consider enzymes. And fungi! We need to move, onto a commercial scale, more of what we know from our science projects."

Milo threw his hands wide to emphasize his next word. "Power. This birch is like a gangster. He depends on lots of little guys to be his muscle." Milo waved at the tree. "It comes down to the power of alliances. In this case, we have physical magnificence made possible by mushrooms."

"Whoa," chirped a shaggy student. "Physical magnificence made possible by mushrooms. I could sell mushrooms on the internet with that tag line."

Milo agreed. "There's a growing industry on line doing just that. I need to stop at this point as I do have an afternoon field trip dedicated to the very odd sex in the great outdoors. That is a commercial for our *Biology of the Northwest* class. We try to be alluring." The group laughed and applauded.

God, I love biology, Grace mused. *This afternoon is going to be totally hot.*

"An alibi can be a lie by which a criminal escapes punishment."

Anonymous

CHAPTER TWELVE

Friday, Westview Condominiums, #15B, Tacoma

"THEODORA! WOW. WHAT a surprise to hear from you!"

Theodora adjusted the laptop on her desk and plastered on her most charming smile. She needed an alibi for the afternoon. This was it. She said, "Hi Ginny. I wanted to catch up with my old classmate."

"Great. Let me just get Robbie latched on here."

Theodora worked hard not to grimace as her former classmate exposed a breast and inserted herself into the gasping mouth of a doughy baby. Theodora made her voice casual. "Take your time," she said. "Skype is so amazing, isn't it?"

"No kidding. What's new?"

"Got an older patient with an odd skin condition. I was wondering what you knew about genetic switches."

"Gosh. Tons."

"Give me a quick start."

"You took basic med school genetics, right?"

"No, actually. I took the second semester of pharmacology." Theodora skipped over the fact that she had taken a full year of genetics as an undergraduate. Ginny liked to lecture. Theodora could use that.

Ginny said, "We've got lots of DNA we use only occasionally. It's like snow pants."

"Snow pants?"

"Yeah. Kid's snow pants. If you don't want a side zipper to come down while they're out sledding, you can park a safety pin across the tracks of the zipper. The zipper head will work down to the pin and stop. Same way that messenger RNA reads DNA – that is until it hits a genetic switch that says, "Stop here. No need to go ahead." The RNA stops its work. Things stay closed until you remove the safety pin. Once the pin is removed, you can slide the headpiece of the zipper down and open things up – or you can remove the genetic repressor and the DNA opens up for replication."

The baby made gulping sounds that came clearly through the speaker. Theodora repressed a wave of nausea.

"The math is impressive." Ginny clearly was unfazed by the creature sucking her dry. "Say you have 600 DNA genetic switches in a critter. That would be like 600 diaper pins in a bowl. Any one can be open or closed, so that would 600 X 600 or 360,000 combinations of sequences. You add in boosters and repressors that can amplify or reduce how strongly a characteristic is expressed, and "voila!" You get amazing potential diversity."

"Take bone switches," Ginny continued enthusiastically, "Things switch on and off as an embryo develops. You get nose cartilage, knee cartilage, and ear cartilage. You get ribs and femurs and so on. It's all the same process with different stop and go signals make sure you don't get a tail bone on your face or a nose on your ass."

"What about post-embryonic genetic switches?"

"Tougher country. Some work on fungus is happening. Everybody would love to turn off the characteristics of aging or cancer. You say you have an older patient, so I can see where you are thinking of post-embryonic switches. What's going on with your patient?"

"Just some weird skin patchiness."

"There's a patient in the news who has growths of fingernail-like keratin coming out of her hair follicles. Is your case that odd?"

"Oh, no." Theodora now had her alibi and some confirmation of her thoughts on genetic switches. It was time to move the conversation elsewhere. "How's the family?"

"Same old, same old. Marko works like mad, but he's been good about taking weekends off. Emma is five. Robbie here is six months. I'm trying to keep my hand in some public health work. How's your handsome brother these days?"

"Fine. He's down near Olympia, doing a little errand for me." Theodora stood up and picked up the laptop. "Let me show you the view from my balcony. You can see tugboats working. It is such a clear and beautiful Friday afternoon."

"You've got it made, Theodora. Research. Hot singles space. Friday afternoon off, and no diapers!"

"I am enjoying things, yes." Theodora soon said her goodbyes. *And now*, she thought, *I am here and Patel is history.*

"Don't worry. It only seems kinky the first time."

—Unknown, but verifiable.

CHAPTER THIRTEEN

Friday afternoon, Mud Bay, west of Olympia

NINETY MINUTES OF constant sex was enough to put Grace's brain into a maelstrom. Milo Anderson's stamina was impressive. He had lectured, nonstop, from the moment the students had gathered at the edge of the estuary until the group completed a two-mile prowl through woods, fields and gravelly beaches. Now, finally, there was an end to the sexual marathon.

Grace sagged against a cedar tree. Nearby two shirtless males jousted with pencils. Grace knew immediately that the students were reenacting flatworm sex.

Milo had said, "Flatworms are hermaphrodites, having both male and female organs. Two flatworms fence with their extended penises. When one spears the other, the victor injects sperm, making the loser the mother of the next generation."

"Grace, can you help me?" came from a body sprawled in the shade.

Grace recognized the sweaty blonde. "Sure. Meghan, right?"

"Yes." Meghan struggled to sit up. "What's left of Meghan. My God, what a field trip."

"I know. Who knew that Pacific oysters are born male and then become female?"

"Got that one. Protandic hermaphrodite."

"Good job! I'm still trying to get my head around the notion that the garter snake has two penises," Grace grinned.

Meghan giggled. "And they alternate which penis they use!"

"Or that a barnacle has an inflatable penis that's fifty times longer than its body."

Meghan laughed again. "I'm going to have nightmares about that one."

"Me too. What's your question?"

"I got confused on the plants. The mycorrhizal mushrooms and the trees?"

"That topic I know. Only the trees are in the plant kingdom. The mushrooms are in a separate kingdom. The Fungi."

"But they are interdependent?"

"Right. Symbiotic. All conifers depend on the fungus on their root tips for nutrient uptake."

"Which ones mate with themselves?

"Some fungi are homothallic. Dr. Anderson spoke about the fungi imperfecti like the blue cheese fungus and the athlete's foot fungus. Mushrooms are different."

Meghan nodded. "The mushroom is the gonad of the fungus. But there are virgin mushrooms, like the ones in the grocery store."

"Right. Its spores have two nuclei so the spore doesn't have to find a partner."

"What was the 'siren of foreplay'?

"A fungus. It has sex in two ways. The fungus can release haploid spores into the environment via the mushroom structure. That's the fruiting body. Two spores meet up on something like a wet log. They combine to make a diploid cell and off you go. The second path is through the hyphae. The 'roots' of the fungus can meet up with other suitable hyphae roots and the hyphae roots combine cells. Sometimes the nuclei hang out together for months before they unite. Siren of foreplay."

Meghan exhaled noisily. "I had no idea all this was going on."

"Yeah. Fertile place, the world. Scary how much is going on."

Milo clapped his hands. Grace and Meghan rose to their feet and turned his way.

"Nice field trip. To finish up, go to the class website. There's the sixty-five vocabulary words we covered this afternoon. Fair warning, any of those sixty-five terms can show up on the exam in two weeks' time."

There was a group groan but no follow up complaints. Grace observed with some amusement that Milo Anderson was continuing to lay down territorial boundaries.

Milo's cell phone rang. As he tapped his phone he said, "Grace, my oil light came on when I I arrived. Can you give me a lift back?"

She nodded and watched for left belongings as students departed.

Milo finished his phone call, looking grim. "I need to ask a favor," he said.

"Sure."

"That was a call from Lena. Piper's in the principal's office, and the principal wants to see us. Lena will ride her bike over. Could you give me a lift out to the school?"

"Of course." Grace unlocked the doors to her aging Civic. "Is Piper alright?"

"We'll see. Remember Little Joey? Some kids were tormenting him on the playground, and Piper clocked one of the little snots."

"Good for her." Grace threw her daypack into the back of the car. She waited until Milo had folded himself in before adding, "That's a military brat's perspective. We tend to be pragmatic and fierce on the playground."

"I don't think the principal would agree." Milo sighed. "Piper may get a suspension."

"Piper's a good kid!"

"She is." Milo agreed. "But even good kids can find trouble."

"Evil is easy, and has infinite forms."

Blaise Pascal, Mathematician and Philosopher
(June 19, 1623 – August 19, 1662)

CHAPTER FOURTEEN

Friday afternoon, Shelton Best Health Center, west of Olympia

DR. NEELADRI PATEL sighed as he put the mop and bucket away. The clinic still stank. He should wipe down the walls again.

Kaylee, the receptionist, discovered the vandalism in the morning when she had opened the door to the clinic. Rotten egg fumes sent her staggering back onto the front step.

Kaylee called Dr. Patel and then braved the stink to grab the daily calendar. By the time Dr. Patel had arrived from Edna's, Kaylee was sitting in her car using her cell phone to cancel patients.

Kaylee took no part of cleaning the clinic.

"Sorry, Dr. P. I can't breathe in there. I tried three cleaning services, and everyone is booked today. Can't we just leave it until tomorrow and let the pros handle it?"

"No. It is best to remove the egg immediately," Dr. Patel had insisted. "Protein decays aromatically."

"Yeah, but my asthma can't handle that air."

Dr. Patel understood. Kaylee left as soon as she finished the cancellation calls.

The nurse, Estella, was made of sterner stuff and had begun to wipe down the walls and floors. After an hour, she complained of a headache. Dr. Patel sent her home.

"For this I went to medical school," said Patel to himself as he picked up another roll of paper towels.

An orange-headed deputy had arrived at noon to ask many questions. Dr. Patel was stymied as he gave careful and complete answers. He could think of no motive for this juvenile nastiness. He did not do abortions. The majority of the clinic's patients were elderly or low-income people who seemed glad to have his services.

He was, he told the deputy an immigrant, arriving two years ago on a special program to provide M.D.s to rural communities. He had arrived to find a clinic stuck in the past, with paper records and an ancient carbon copy billing system.

Despite the need for modernization, no one had complained to him about his services.

"Shelton has been a nice community," he said. "No one has been hateful."

The deputy had looked at him skeptically. "Treat any beaten wives?"

"Ah." Dr. Patel admitted. "Yesterday. We are told that she is clumsy, but the bruising concerns me. I am a mandatory reporter and have been drafting the report."

"Can you give me a name? We'll figure out where the husband has been today."

Dr. Patel paused. "Let me finish the report. We must do this correctly."

The deputy departed, leaving Dr. Patel deep in thought. Maybe the bastard husband would end in jail. With that cheerful thought, Patel returned to cleaning.

The second wipe down diminished the sour smell significantly. Dr. Patel opened the back door to the small clinic and propped the door open with a rock. "Ah, How dumb of me. I should have done this sooner."

Dr. Patel could feel the air move thorough the clinic now. Another hour or so with the front windows up and the back door open and he might have the smell vanquished.

Dr. Patel sat down at one of the clinic's computers and typed in his password. He pulled up the name and address of the beaten woman. He should finish the report at once.

He would need to make up an extra full staffing schedule for the next week. With some luck they could catch up in two days. Dr. Patel paused to load an on-line radio station and went to work to the sound of an NPR jazz show.

Dr. Patel did not hear the quiet arrival of a man entering through the open back door. He knew nothing until his hair was seized and yanked back, which thrust his neck forward as his chair swiveled to the left. Before he had time to cry out, a scalpel sharp knife severed his left carotid artery and arced through the wind-pipe. By the time the right carotid artery was severed Dr. Patel had a moment to know that he was dead.

"Knowledge has three degrees – opinion, science, illumination."

Plotinus (204 -270)

Chapter Fifteen

Friday afternoon, National Security Agency, Fort Meade, Maryland

HARRY RUBBED HIS eyes and read Ken's report. "Cancer always originates with an alteration of the DNA. There are three typical paths: a) an inherited variation or b) one triggered by exposure to a carcinogen or c) an error in DNA copying during cell division. All three paths originate in epigenetics, where methyl and acetyl groups start or stop gene action. Methyl groups as gene regulators are likely to also have a role in diabetes, hypertension and in the development of Alzheimer's disease. Two DNA-demethylating drugs, based on fungal extracts are currently being tested."

Harry raced through the rest and said, "Wow. Fungal extracts."

Ken nodded. "My traffic analysis shows this is the point of origin for North Korean web searches."

"We don't know if their interest is specifically the cancer treatment or in the de-methylating agents."

"They may want to copy the fungal extract process. That might be the piece they're after." Harry's eyes flicked back to the computer screen. "Why do you want to go to Olympia?"

Ken drummed his fingers on his desk. "The FBI should investigate domestically, but their fungal expert is on maternity leave. I'm the next best thing. There's a commercial specialty mushroom growing operation out there that I can tour, and I want to follow up on that blog posting about a mushroom extract counteracting an algae poisoning."

"Good luck on that one. A 1999 reference to a 1983 event."

"I know. 'Mushroom Edna' may be long dead and buried." Ken sighed, "I am so burned out."

Harry smirked. "I found a cool story that says that some large dinosaurs had feathers. It was titled 'Fluffy and Fierce." More on gene activation in conjunction with environmental changes but nothing there on fungi."

"Feathered dinosaurs? Sounds like Mrs. Goldstein at the facilities desk. She's got that fluffy shawl thing and she hunts for parking violators like a velociraptor.

"Ah, come on. She's sweet."

Ken rolled his eyes. "Definitely a predatory dinosaur. You gotta keep an eye out for predators, Harry. They'll pounce on you."

Chlorophyllum olivieri

"The righteous are like carvings upon stone, for their smallest act is durable."

Horace, Poet
(December 8, 65 BCE– November 27, 8 BCE)

CHAPTER SIXTEEN

Friday afternoon, Twin Cedars School

GRACE DROVE MILO Anderson out to the sprawling beige brick school.

Lena was at the window of the hatchback the moment Grace pulled into a visitor's slot.

Grace strove to be positive. Her window down, she called out, "Delivery of one Professor, as requested."

Lena blinked.

Ouch, Grace thought. *I'm too flippant.*

Lena said, "Grace. Please. Will you come in too?"

"Me?"

"Yes. Grace. Piper asked for you."

Milo leaned over with a frown. "I'm sure we can manage."

Lena's eyes filled with tears. "She asked for Grace. It's in the school rulebook. She can have an outside advocate. Please."

Milo's eyes swept from his wife to Grace. He said, "Do you have time?" There was neither warmth nor coolness in the question.

He's embarrassed, Grace realized. *His wife is fragile.* Those thoughts decided her. "If it will help Piper, I'm yours," she declared. "Strength in numbers!"

Lena's pale face regained some color, and Grace felt she'd said the right thing.

"Thanks," Milo said. "Piper thinks you're cool."

"I'm usually better with dogs than people." Grace climbed out of the Civic, certain that her hair lay lank with field trip sweat. Her mother's voice popped into her head, *Sometimes being present is a present.* If Piper wanted a pal, then Grace would be one.

Piper was easy to find. She was sitting on a mauve modern chair outside the principal's office with her knees curled to her chest and arms hugging her knees. When she saw her father, she unfolded and launched herself into Milo's arms. She began to sob.

"Shh. Shh. Let's take a look at you," Milo murmured.

Piper sniffed and stood straighter. One pigtail had lost its closing bauble. Her face was mottled with tear tracks. "Boys are pigs," she declared.

"Hey." Milo brushed her cheek with his thumb. "Some boys. Some days. Let's be specific."

"Dylan Kushner and Jason Feinstein are complete toads." Piper wiped her nose down the back of her hand before looking up at Grace. "Thanks for coming, Grace."

"Sure, kiddo. Strength in numbers."

"Mr. and Mrs. Anderson," came a cool voice from the doorway. "Thank you for stopping by."

"Good afternoon, Mrs. Sheehan." Milo rose gracefully to his feet. "This is my associate, Ms. Grace Mossler. She is a family friend. Piper asked for her."

Grace did her best to look dignified as she shook hands with a tall, gray-haired woman whose dark tailored slacks and cashmere sweater set did not look like they had been tramping through woods and fields for an afternoon.

"Do come in. Piper can tell her story and then, perhaps Ms. Mossler can sit with Piper shile we confer."

Grace's fingers curled automatically to make fists. There was no "perhaps." Ms. Sheehan was a dictator with an exterior of good manners. Grace made herself breathe carefully as they entered the conference room.

Mrs. Sheehan indicated with an open hand that they should sit. Piper chose a chair next to her parents. Grace sat down across from Piper while Mrs. Sheehan took a seat at the far end of the oval table.

"Piper, please tell us what happened today."

Grace lifted her chin. She felt for Piper. Grace worked to channel serenity as her own mother would do.

Lena was not calm. She clutched the edge of the table with the tips of her fingers, pressing so hard that the nail beds went rosy with the stress. Milo put a hand on her shoulder.

Piper looked at Grace. Grace made eye contact and raised her shoulders up and back to a soldier's ready stance. Her animal training parents knew how to communicate nonverbally, and Grace had long practice with her brothers. Now was the time for control. Piper nodded, took a steadying breath and began.

"We met Joey last night. He's a nice kid."

"Yes. Go on."

Grace gave a near imperceptible nod, and Piper took another breath.

"He won the door prize. The bike. He's so happy. He was on the playground, pretending he's riding the bike. He's only in first grade, and kids do that. He's pretending."

Mrs. Sheehan said, "Continue."

"Dylan and Jason came over. They tell him he's too stupid to ride a real bike because his parents are tweakers. Well, his parents are nice people. We met them. But Dylan and Jason won't shut up. They tripped Joey and yelled "Tweaker, Tweaker." Piper turned to her father. "What's a tweaker, anyway?"

Milo said, "Someone who uses the drug methamphetamine. It's a nasty drug that makes people jittery."

Milo put an arm around his daughter. "I don't see Joe and Daylene being involved in that. "

"Joey is a recent adoptee," said Mrs. Sheehan. "His birth parents were… troubled. Piper, if you heard this rudeness, why didn't you tell the playground monitor?

Piper snorted. "Ms. Consequences? She tells you to have a thick skin and to ignore stuff. But Joey's a first grader, and Dylan and Jason are in fifth grade, like me. How can you ignore someone nearly twice your size when they are pushing and yelling at you?"

Mrs. Sheehan ignored the question. "Speak respectfully about our staff," she instructed.

Milo's eyes blazed, "Even if the staff member is not doing her job?"

"This will be discussed with her. Meanwhile, Piper, what did you do?"

"I yelled at them to knock it off. They didn't stop. I ran over there, and slapped Dylan. He grabbed my hair. I grabbed him back and threw him on the ground. Jason jumped on my back, and I flipped him off. Then he grabbed at my hair, so I punched him in the face. And I'm not sorry."

"That's where we have a problem," said Mrs. Sheehan. "When you hit someone, it is called assault. You may not assault people at school. Ever. You can be suspended or expelled from school for assault." Mrs. Sheehan held up a hand for silence before Milo could leap in with a defense.

Mrs. Sheehan said, "At this point, Piper, please go outside

with Ms. Mossler. Sit where you were earlier. I have a few things to review with your parents."

Milo gave Piper's shoulders a squeeze. Piper stood up and trudged out the door. Lena's chalk white face carried two blazes of rose on her high cheekbones. Grace felt her own face flush as well. Poor Piper!

Grace followed, taking her time pulling the door closed. She heard Mrs. Sheehan say, "You have a darling girl there."

Grace's tension melted away.

Piper flung herself into the mauve chair. "It's not fair!" she wailed.

Grace smiled at her. "Hey, I think you're going to be fine." She leaned over and whispered, "Sheehan was just saying you're a darling girl."

Piper stared at her.

Grace grinned. "It's territorial dominance. She's got to show she's boss – but she can root for the good guys. She has to be careful. She doesn't want you busting chops all day." Grace put an arm around Piper's shoulders. "Tell me about the guys you creamed."

Piper produced a small smile. "I did cream them. Jason is okay. He just wants to do what Dylan does. Dylan is… a mess."

"Smart or dumb?"

"Dumb. He makes terrible grades." Piper flipped a pigtail over her shoulder. "I don't know that he's really dumb," she admitted. "More… choosing to be difficult."

"Ah. Oppositional. Making a career out of being a villain?"

"I guess." Piper looked over at Grace. "What will happen to me?"

"My bet is your parents are getting an earful about horrible consequences if you keep belting kids. You get a major lecture about problem solving with words. Lay low for a couple of weeks. Don't give Sheehan a reason to remember you."

"You're good at this!" Piper surprised herself with a smile.

"Air Force brat, two brothers." Grace grinned back at her. "But your mom has a tough time with stuff like this, doesn't she?"

Piper nodded.

The door to the conference room opened. Mrs. Sheehan led the Andersons out. Milo looked better. Lena looked bleached with worry.

"Piper," Mrs. Sheehan said, "You may go home with your family. Your parents will discuss your behavior choices. You will write an essay on your options when confronted by a similar situation in the future. You are on probation for three weeks."

Milo put his arm around his daughter, pulling her into a hug. Piper blossomed with a smile of relief.

Mrs. Sheehan crossed her arms and looked down at Piper. The principal said, "You should try out for the middle school track team next year. Coach Hernandez saw you run across the playground. He says you can really fly."

Milo was focused on his daughter. It was Grace who saw Lena go white, and it was Grace who caught Lena as she fainted.

"My manner of thinking, so you say, cannot be approved. Do you suppose I care?"

Marquis de Sade, Politician and Libertine
(June 2, 1740 – December 2, 1814)

CHAPTER SEVENTEEN

Friday evening, Westview Condominiums, #15B, Tacoma

THEODORA DRESSED CAREFULLY. She started with a lacy bra followed by a blue shirt that complimented her eyes. She peeled off her underpants and tossed them in a hamper. She added a calf-length floral skirt. She fastened a light silver chain around her right ankle. Finally she switched out her pearl earrings for long dangles.

Theodora applied a pink lipstick and returned to her computer.

She read a paper on the human genome project. Lies should begin in fact. Lies could be convenient. All one needed was to remember what one had said.

Theodora's memory was exceptional.

At six o'clock a key turned in the lock. Theodora leaned back in her desk chair to watch as Kurt entered. He set down a daypack, and then turned to relock the door behind him. Her brother always remembered to lock away the world.

She smiled as she took in his height and the broad chest that tapered down to a tight waist. The military haircut suited Kurt.

He stopped to look at her. She saw the gleam of approval in his eyes.

"You're beautiful," he said.

"Thank you. Is it done?"

"Absolutely. It was a real joy." Kurt eyes sparkled with delight as Theodora mirrored his smile.

Kurt crossed the small living room and knelt at her feet. He reached up to caress her calves and to urge her forward. Obediently, she slid her bottom to the front of the chair and spread her legs open.

Kurt flipped up the foamy skirt as he slid his large hands up her bare thighs. He nuzzled open her labia and began to lick. Theodora ran her hands through Kurt's short hair and urged him on with her moans. Theodora wrapped her ankles around his neck and slid further down the chair as his hands slid up to caress her breasts.

She sighed with satisfaction as he sucked on her clitoris, and she arched her back when his tongue entered her. Kurt paused and with his right hand he tweaked the nipple of her breast.

She knew what he wanted. She peeled off the T-shirt and removed her bra. Kurt continued to lavage her clitoris as his hands massaged her breasts and gently rolled over her nipples.

He stood up. He scooped up topless Theodora in her skirt and placed her on her desk. She waited patiently as he slipped off his shirt, shoes, jeans and boxers. She reached down to stroke his jutting penis.

"My God. You are so gorgeous."

Kurt pushed her back onto the desk. She lifted her knees and drew back the skirt while he used one hand to guide his shaft into her. He crashed into her with force. She met his every thrust with enthusiasm, running her hands up his arms and across his shoulders as they rocked together. They climaxed together with the precision of practiced lovers.

Kurt rested his hands on her waist and kissed Theodora's neck as the flush of sex subsided. "Can psychopaths love?" he asked.

"Sociopath," She corrected. "Or perhaps we are a blend. As to love," she kissed him back. "The psychologists say no, but I think we just see the world a bit differently. You've always been there for me."

"And you for me. I brought you presents."

Theodora playfully pushed against his chest. "Let's see!"

Kurt withdrew from her. Theodora sat up and saw he had a knife sheath strapped to his right leg. "A knife. That's what you used?"

"Yep." Kurt pulled out the knife and said, " Nice quality. I like the balance."

Theodora reached for the blade, but Kurt held it high. "Don't. You don't want your fingerprints on this."

"Is his blood still on it?"

"Maybe. There was strong arterial spray. It's easy for blood mist to get in under the tang. I'll clean it again and get rid of it, but I wanted to show you first."

Theodora wrapped her arms around her brother's waist. "Thank you. You were careful?"

"Of course. I wore latex gloves and changed clothes after. I tossed everything in a dumpster in Olympia." Kurt nuzzled her neck. "I'll make sure of the knife too."

Theodora knew she owed him, so she cupped his buttocks and purred, "Can you stay the night?"

Kurt still held the knife in one hand as his other caressed her breast. He kissed her hard, driving his tongue into her mouth possessively. She leaned in with anticipation, but he withdrew. "No. I need to get back to Fort Lewis. Why don't you go shower, and we can go for some dim sum." He nuzzled her neck. "Maybe dim sum and some nookie for dessert before I head back."

"Sounds fantastic. I'm starved. I'll shower fast."

Kurt nodded. He knew she would. She was always efficient.

He dressed, returning the knife to its sheath. He waited until he heard the shower start before moving to his daypack.

He unzipped it and brought out a second knife, wrapped in plastic and tape. This was the knife he had used on Patel.

He knew his sister. She would ask to see the blade again before he left. He would again show her the innocent knife strapped to his leg.

The actual murder weapon was a problem. It was difficult to destroy a high quality knife. It was better used as a motivator. Kurt stood up, surveying the condominium.

He extracted a shoelace from a side pocket of the daypack. He tied a loop around the handle guard of the knife.

Kurt moved over to a flat screen television mounted high on a wall. He tied the knife to the mounting bracket at the back of the television. He stepped back and evaluated. The knife was hidden.

Kurt smiled when he heard the shower stop.

Theodora could call the shots as long as she provided fun assignments and shared her fine body. Like a bonbon, his sister was delicious and disposable. When the fun was over, he'd move on.

Amanita phalloides

"I am on the edge of mysteries and the veil is getting thinner and thinner."

Louis Pasteur
(December 27, 1822 – September 28, 1895)

CHAPTER EIGHTEEN

Friday early evening, September 18, Kamilche Peninsula

"THANK YOU SO much for delivering my family," Edna put her arm around Grace's shoulders and gave a strong squeeze.

"It's nothing." Grace blushed at Edna's praise. Grace liked this short and colorful woman of the woods. Edna's denim overalls and striped knee socks were adorable. There was something both earthy and maternal with her tight hair bun and her creased face.

"Take this." Edna directed Grace to a steaming mug of soup. The two carried mugs to Edna's kitchen table.

"I love your house," Grace said. "It's so peaceful out here. The firs and the ferns are so huge."

"I like it too. Particularly since the indoor plumbing was installed!" Edna's eyes twinkled. "I married my husband, James, in 1982 when I was fifty years old. When we learned we were going to have a baby,

James insisted that we needed a real bathroom and a real kitchen sink. You may think a trip to Paris might be more romantic, but I was over the moon with the improvements."

Grace laughed. "If I lived with an outhouse, I'd pick the plumbing over Paris too."

"Milo gave me a computer and internet service a few years ago. I like that almost as much."

"The sandwiches should be hot now," chirped Piper. Under her Grandmother's careful eyes, Piper donned oven mitts to pull a tray of sandwiches out of the oven.

"Dinner! I am starved." Grace paused. "Should we wait for Milo and Lena?"

Edna shook her head. "Lena fell asleep while you were ferrying Milo to the sick car. And Milo may need some minutes to rest now. It always hits him hard when she's not herself."

Grace bit into a sandwich. "Wow. This is incredible."

Edna smiled. "A little deli mustard, a slice of sharp cheddar and a slice of ham. Grill in the skillet and then heat in the oven."

Piper plowed through one sandwich and slurped her soup. She paused eating to ask, "Grandmom, why did Mom faint? She just keeled over. Is that because I'm in trouble?"

"What was said?"

"That Coach Hernandez had watched me run."

"That you could really fly," added Grace.

Edna went very still. "You can't fly. My body is unusual, and so is your mother's, and yours may be as well." *God*, thought Edna. *Is now when I tell her?*

Edna was saved by Milo's voice from the doorway. "Piper, sweetheart, I don't think it's a good idea for you to run track."

"Why?" Piper wailed. "I might be good."

Milo walked into the small kitchen, wiping his eyes. "Whew. Musta dozed off a minute. Keep it down, short stuff. Let me eat something, and I'll tell you."

He looked at Grace, then inhaled and committed himself. "Grace, you seem to have fallen in with us. My gals like you. I'd like you to hear this too. Maybe your quick brain will see some things we missed." Milo pulled out a stool from under the kitchen table, sat down and reached for a sandwich.

"Piper, you know how I met Mom, right?"

"Yeah. At Jarrell Cove."

"Yeah. There's some stuff we haven't told you. I was starting my senior year in high school. She had paddled a kayak over to the park, but she told me where she lived. I came over the next day."

Edna smiled, remembering. "I told him to go away. We were busy with home school."

"Your Grandmom ran me off several times. In the spring I came back and asked if Lena could go with me to senior prom."

Edna looked at the ceiling. "When I said "no," Lena had her first ever teenage drama scene. She said I was keeping her from living a life. I was horrified at that thought, so I changed my mind."

"Did you get married then?" Piper was wide-eyed.

"No," Milo said. "When we went out to prom, your mom had a half a beer from a friend of mine. She proceeded to throw up for almost an hour. We had to call the paramedics. Mom's body can't handle alcohol."

Edna nodded. "I was glad that happened. I thought maybe all that vomiting would turn her off dating you."

Milo leaned back on the stool, clasping one knee with both hands. "It was a tough date. I brought her back home. A couple weeks later I graduated and went to work as a camp counselor. I was all set to go down to Stanford in the fall."

Milo's eyes suddenly took on a cool look. He turned his head to Grace and said, "In late July, my parents went out one evening to buy blueberries. They were on a roundabout when a logging truck rolled. They were killed. I got the news and came home from camp. I was in a daze. Next thing I know, Lena is at the door. I don't know how she got the news, or how she knew where I lived, but suddenly she was there."

Edna reached out and took Piper's hand and held it. "You know in our family, we often have premonitions and insights. Mushrooms lead to visions. Your mother got her bike that night and rode out like a rocket."

Milo nodded. "Lena moved in. I was so numb, that I couldn't function. One of my aunts showed up from Cleveland and tried to run Lena off, but she wouldn't leave."

"I was frantic with worry," commented Edna. "I knew Lena would do anything to help you with your grief."

Milo grinned wryly. "She did. So, Short Stuff, by the time it was the middle of September, your mom said she was pregnant with you. Against everybody's wishes, we got married and headed to Stanford. We were eighteen years old."

"Wow. Mom would kill me if I did that."

"Yeah. I wouldn't be happy with you either. I've been meaning to tell you all this for a while. You're old enough. It's just been a crazy year. There's more. We moved into married student housing. Fall term was a blast. Winter quarter was fine. In March, there's a spring break. Your mom was seven months pregnant. She didn't want to go anywhere. So we hung out."

Milo continued, "One morning we're up really early. She couldn't sleep, so I suggested we go over to the Stanford track and run some laps. This is like, five in the morning. The place is a ghost town."

Milo reached out and snagged another sandwich. "Your mom ran the socks off of me. She's seven months pregnant and she flies like the wind."

"She's athletic?" asked Grace.

"No. She's unreal. No one runs that fast."

"I don't get it," pouted Piper.

"Me either. There was one other guy at the track that morning. Dr. Mohan. He was a retired physiology professor who had cancer.

He couldn't sleep that morning either, so he was out for a walk. He had some theories."

Grace shifted in the kitchen chair. "What did the professor think?"

Milo turned to Grace and said, "He felt Lena has a genetic change in her actin or myosin fibers." Milo set down his sandwich. He splayed the fingers of his large hands and held them up so the fingertips of each hand touched one other. He carefully offset the fingers and pushed his hands together slowly, so the fingers rubbed one another in passing.

"Muscles work like pistons with a ratcheting system. The myosin fibers ratchet themselves along another protein fiber called actin. A myosin head docks onto the actin. It pulls the actin along. There are very few variations in how actin works. Human actin and yeast actin work essentially the same – about 95% identical. That means this is a very crucial pathway that just works one way. It limits how fast a person can go. Lena may not only have a change, but a change that also works well. Dr. Mohan was very interested."

Grace was fascinated. "Did Dr. Mohan take some samples?"

"No. He died about six weeks later. I did a little reading about muscle types. It may be that Lena simply has a higher proportion of fast twitch fibers. We didn't pursue finding out. We left it alone. Lena doesn't run all out if people are around. She keeps a lid on the bike speed too."

"I can't run because I've got a mutant mom?" Piper looked aghast.

"Easy there. You've got a year before middle school. Your mom just had a freak out today because Dr. Mohan warned us that real speed draws major attention. Speed means big money in sports. Next thing you know, it'll be 'Piper for President,' and we'll have paparazzi out here photographing everything including my nose hairs."

Piper giggled.

Edna reached over to pat Piper's hand. "Your mother has always been a bit shy."

Milo added, "Fear can be a survival trait. Your mom has a big dose of it."

He went on. "We can time you while you're running and see what you've got. You want a race to be a fair thing." He turned back to Grace. "You can see, can't you, that I don't want the family to seem too weird?"

Grace nodded. "You are re-connecting here. People need to know you a bit so they won't reject you."

Milo agreed. "Something like that, yeah."

Edna said to Piper, "You run privately. No drawing attention to yourself until you know."

Piper protested, "I played peewee soccer in Seattle. No one said anything."

Milo pulled a pigtail. "I played with you before we signed you up. There was nothing remarkable. We watched like a pair of hawks that first few weeks of soccer. When the coach had you run laps, you ran while talking to your friends. The rest of the time you played goalie or were looking at the mushrooms sprouting on the fields. You never really pushed yourself. You said it made your side hurt."

Edna smiled down at Piper. "I do remember that you found some nice mushrooms."

"Yeah. But this is now. I want to run track!"

"You're growing up. Your body's changing. Let's be careful."

Grace said, "There'll be lots of middle school choices. I saw dog and horse club posters at the spaghetti feed. I'm sure there's even more to do."

Piper's head swiveled like an owl's. "Dad, could we get a horse? And a dog?"

"Ohhhh, kiddo. Those are big commitments. Let's talk with Mom first."

Edna swooped in to give Piper a kiss. "That is not a 'no,' so don't pout. I've been thinking of getting a dog myself. Maybe we will share."

Grace stood up and took her plate to the sink. "Do you need a ride tomorrow to pick up the car?"

"Thanks, no. The mechanic is an old friend. He said he'd drive it out here in the morning. We'll bunk here with Edna tonight."

"Before you go, Grace, I have two things for you." Edna was on her feet and taking the plate from Grace's hands. "Your aunt has an ethnobotany lecture at the cultural museum tomorrow morning at ten."

"My aunt?"

"Yes. Very knowledgeable. Esther Mossler."

"Thank you! I will go. Laundry can wait."

Piper moved next to Grace. "Grandmom's going to tell your future."

Edna shot a look at her granddaughter. "How do you know that?"

Piper shrugged. "Just do."

Edna sniffed and picked up Grace's hands in her own. Edna narrowed her eyes and hummed. Then she smiled. "You'll marry a red-haired man and have three children. You will be a leader all your life."

"Wow." Grace worked to sound appreciative. "That'd be great. Any stock tips?"

Milo laughed. "Keep that scientific skepticism going." His eyes went soft and kind. "Thanks for being there for us. You've been super."

Grace would have sacrificed her beating heart for him and his family at that moment. She chose to be outwardly casual. "I'd better get going home. I hope you're right, Edna. I could use a date. All I see in my future is laundry and a thesis."

Edna put a hand to Grace's face to give a farewell pat. "I am glad to have you in my home – I think everything will be fine if we can just have some peace and quiet for a bit."

"Tut, I have done a thousand dreadful things as willingly as would kill a fly, and nothing grieves me heartily indeed but that I cannot do ten thousand more."

Titus Andronicus by William Shakespeare
(April 1564 – April 23, 1616)

CHAPTER NINETEEN

Saturday morning, Shelton Best Health Center

AT TEN A.M. on Saturday morning Detective Rodger Raposo surveyed a gore sprayed computer and desk. The victim's body, a small adult male believed to be Neeladri Patel, was on its way to the morgue.

Raposo thought the killer had held his victim's head back as the blood had begun to spurt to make a wide arc pattern.

Dr. Patel's body and desk chair had been rotated to the left, like steering a water cannon. It spoke to an enjoyment of the act. There were no footprints in the gore. The weapon was gone.

Detective Raposo stepped carefully around the perimeter of the room, stopping frequently to study the site.

Raposo was not yet forty. He looked older. With his large ears and prematurely sagging jowl line, he knew he looked like a rumpled hound. The look suited the hell out of him. Prosecuting attorneys loved him to testify with his slow, deep voice.

Courtroom theatrics would wait. This was the time to collect details.

Raposo used a mechanical pencil and his Rite-in-the-rain journal to take notes and make sketches. He didn't trust his laptop. Not for this. He would not let a killer walk because of a crashed computer or smeared notes from a little or a lot of wet. Mason County had a lot of wet.

"Premeditated and by experienced hands," Raposo muttered. Why the hell did he, Raposo, have a small, dead doctor on his hands?

The lean deputy waiting outside was sharp and aggrieved. "I don't know, Sir. Yesterday there was some vandalism - a busted window and rotten eggs. The doc and I talked it over. We thought it was going to be a guy who had slapped his wife and then got peeved she'd come in for treatment. Jesus."

The deputy's orange eyebrows hooded gray eyes that were haunted with regrets. Raposo liked him for that. "You're new," he said.

"Yes Sir. Don MacRae. Don. No nickname."

Raposo nodded, "Don it is. Patel was to call you?"

"Yes Sir. He said he'd finalize a report and call. He was also supposed to call his receptionist last night. She tried his cell phone this morning. When he didn't pick up, she called it in, and I came over."

"Everything was open?"

"Yeah. Front door, windows, back door. Doc's car in the parking lot."

"Okay. Will you canvas down the road and see if anyone saw or heard anything?"

"Sure. Ah, Sir?"

"Go ahead."

"The computers were off when I got here yesterday. The vandalism had happened during the night. It was stinking of rotten eggs when the staff arrived." MacRae spoke rapidly, "I remember the receptionist saying that she was glad she didn't have to come inside to start up the computer because it's slow to wake up – but when I found Dr. Patel, the computer was on. It still is. There's also a message that indicates a USB drive was removed improperly. That would be recent - since the computer was last shut down."

Raposo studied Deputy MacRae. "Good catch." He thought for a moment. "We've got spatter on the keyboard. No fingerprints in the spatter. I'll ask the techs to process the mouse."

Raposo sucked in his lower lip then released it with a pop. "Maybe the egging was meant to get the other staff out of the building. Maybe our killer handled the eggs."

MacRae produced a grim smile. "I'll follow my nose out back and see if I can find the trash."

"Genetics loads the gun and the environment pulls the trigger."

Geneticist saying

CHAPTER TWENTY

Saturday morning, Westview Condominiums, #15B

THEODORA OPENED THE email with high expectations.

Teddy,

Good to hear from you. The NIH does have some limited funds for immediate uses. However, the criteria for tapping those funds are very specific. Your project doesn't fit.

I suggest that you get a blood draw from your patient. Have a specialty lab sequence the transcriptomes.

See if your patient is willing to work with a Personal Genome Project. They will work up a personal genome for her if she completes and passes their screening regimen. They do a good job of walking people through the ramifications of knowing one's DNA.

Many times people decide that they would rather not know, particularly if certain information might impact employment or heighten anxiety among relatives.

All this takes time, of course. I'll look for an update from you after the first of the year.

All the best, David.

The first of the year? Theodora clenched her fists. She would make progress now. Not in four months. Now. Theodora stood up and hurled her coffee cup against the wall. The coffee dregs splashed across the white paint. Theodora stared at the brown streaks. She would dock her house cleaner's pay if the wall didn't scrub clean. She sat back down at her desk.

Uncle David was right to mention the transcriptomes. Transcriptomes gave the instructions for which proteins a cell should make, and feathers, like reptilian scales, were made of beta keratin protein.

Transcriptomes, she knew, could vary in response to environmental conditions. They provided a road map to which DNA sections were currently active. Theodora poked her tongue between her front teeth and bit down. Pain led to focus.

A blood draw from Edna was essential. A single drop of blood could provide eighty thousand white blood cells, each with Edna's entire genome.

The challenge wasn't in the sample size needed. The problem was collecting and properly transporting a sample to the lab. For best results she needed Edna's cooperation. That meant soothing Edna. Theodora bit down on her tongue harder.

With her lips compressed into a hard line, Theodora inserted the flash drive from Kurt. He had assured her that he had captured all the patient's files that had begun with M. Edna Morton's records should be somewhere on the drive.

Five minutes later, Theodora slammed her fists on her desk. Edna's file was a joke. There was no address. No phone number. There was no social security number or health insurance number. It showed only one previous visit.

Theodora rechecked the miniscule record. Edna had first seen Dr. Patel the previous year for a pilonidal cyst. An abscess on the tailbone could have simply been an ingrown hair. Could it have been a filoplume? Theodora saw no record of a sample sent to a lab for analysis. The only other record was for the recent 'skin condition'.

This was insane. What elderly woman had only two visits to a doctor? Where were the rest of Edna's medical files? The next of kin was listed as Angelena Anderson, a daughter, but there was no phone number anywhere in the file.

Theodora stood up. She would go to Olympia. She would track down Edna, get the blood sample, and she would, by God, do the same for the daughter.

Theodora smiled.

She would tell them it was what Dr. Patel had wanted.

"The apple doesn't fall far from the tree."

Proverb known in at least 42 languages

CHAPTER TWENTY-ONE

Saturday morning, The Coastal Arts Museum

GRACE OVERSLEPT. SHE dashed through a shower and then discovered her last clean shirt was too tight. It announced that she had no waist. Round face, thick trunk, and short legs, she reviewed her body with dismay. She was getting married someday? With this body?

Grace muttered, "He'll love me for my brains. He'll have to." She grabbed a blueberry toaster pastry and dashed out the door.

Grace drove west of Olympia. She was in luck. The museum was easy to find.

She heard an introduction to the lecture as she pushed open the glass door to the museum. Grace purchased an admission ticket and moved quietly to the rear of a crowded seating pit.

In the center of the arena was the sort of woman Grace ached to be. The speaker had a glorious ripple of dark hair that spilled over her shoulders. She wore a sheath of steel blue silk that fell gracefully to just below the knees. There was a matching secondary layer with sleeves that ended properly at the wrist.

Grace knew those sleeves were tailored because the woman was short and close to Grace's circumference. Clothes in her size usually had sleeves that draped over her knuckles. The speaker wore accessories that flashed like birding marks. There was a scarf with a Pacific Northwest primitive motif in black, white and steel blue. The woman's earrings were tribal strands of liquid silver. Her lip-gloss was the perfect, understated pink.

The elegant woman stood in front of a huge screen with a PowerPoint slide labeled "Ethnolichenology. By Dr. Esther Mossler. Yale School of Forestry."

Yale School of Forestry? Grace felt her mouth open like a landed trout. This was her Aunt Esther?

Dr. Mossler clicked on a control unit to bring up a photo of green blotches on a rock.

"Lichens," said Dr. Mossler, "are a symbiotic partnership between algae and fungi. Many are tiny, and many are also long lived. Some artic species may be as much as 4000 years old, which makes them among the oldest living things on our planet."

She clicked again. This time the blotches were bright orange.

"There are some 20,000 species of lichen worldwide. There are about 1,000 species here in the Olympic Mountains. The Pacific Northwest is particularly suited for lichen growth. Today I am going to speak about the historical uses of lichens and how lichens may serve us in the future. Lichens can save lives and perhaps even save the Earth."

Grace blinked. Her aunt sounded sincere.

Dr. Mossler brought up a picture of a tangled mat of gray and green threads. "This is *Alectoria sarmentosa,* which we know as witch's hair. We see this magnificent lichen on Douglas fir trees throughout the Olympics."

"The dominant partner in any lichen is the fungus

component. Lichens have been described as fungi that have discovered agriculture."

"The fungi protect the algae from becoming dehydrated and dying. The alga has chlorophyll. The algae photosynthesizes and provides nutrients to the fungus which then grows and spreads."

Dr. Mossler clicked up a new slide.

"I like the neon green of this one. It is poisonous. Historically, our coastal ancestors used this wolf lichen, *Letharia vulpine*, to make a yellow dye."

Dr. Mossler put up a slide of a muscular Scot in a kilt. Grace thought this might be a redheaded man that she would consider dating. Was that hunk of manhood a colleague of Aunt Esther's? Were introductions possible?

"In Scotland, lichens were used to make the browns and reds that were incorporated into tartans. Many indigenous people use lichens. They can be important to human and animal survival."

Dr. Mossler brought up a slide of a doe browsing lichens.

"We have low soil nitrogen levels in the Pacific Northwest, which can limit plant growth. Lichens with cyanobacterial partners fix nitrogen from the air and can make a form of nitrogen that is available to plants when the lichen dies. Deer and elk will eat nitrogen rich lichens."

The next slide featured greens resembling wilted lettuce.

"The real power of lichens may be in their medicinal and pollution remediation abilities. It's estimated that fifty percent of lichen species have antibiotic properties."

Dr. Mossler changed the lettuce picture for one of a large woman in a red and black blanket cape standing at a deep-fried ice cream stand.

"We have become, I am sorry to say, a polluted nation. Instead of eating for free from our lands, we pay for sugar water and sugar treats. Eating from the woods takes time, walking and knowledge. We now have gaps in our knowledge and frantic days that keep us from the woods. Obesity rates are up across the country, and Native American populations are especially impacted."

Grace suddenly regretted the breakfast pastry. She could have added a banana.

"By relearning how to eat traditionally, we may be able to address the obesity epidemic and reverse the onset of diabetes that wrecks havoc in our people."

Grace made a mental promise to eat a healthy lunch. It was a promise that she would remember days later when she worked to recall her last tranquil morning.

Down in front, Dr. Mossler put up another colorful slide, and Grace slid into a happy haze of biology.

"A cold lasts seven days without treatment or a week with medicine."

Mother

CHAPTER TWENTY-TWO

Saturday morning, Reagan National Airport, Washington D.C.

KEN ITO STARED at his laptop screen with aching eyes. *Forget sarin gas*, he thought. *The North Koreans can kill our will to live with a fucking cold.* He leaned his head back against an airport lounge chair that seemed diabolically engineered for discomfort. He tried not to moan out loud.

He was making progress on his research today, despite the head cold and being in a public space. He found a list of classes on Olympia area fall mushroom collecting, including one that touted, "Instructor: Edna Morton. Edna is a lifetime resident of Kamilche Peninsula and a well respected mushroom expert."

Ah. This could be the "Mushroom Edna" from the blog find.

Ken sneezed. He was going to load up on decongestants, crawl on the plane, and see if he could telephone Edna Morton once his plane landed in Phoenix.

Maybe she knows the mushroom recipe to cure the common cold, he thought. *If she can save people from algae poisoning, why can't she save people who feel like death already?* He coughed and groaned and ached as his flight was called.

"Nothing is so strong as gentleness. Nothing is so gentle as real strength."

Saint Francis de Sales
(August 16, 1567 – December 28, 1622)

CHAPTER TWENTY-THREE

Saturday morning, Steamboat Island Peninsula, Washington State

AS HE KNOCKED on the emerald green screen door, Detective Raposo felt fifteen years old again. It was the same door he had rapped on as a teenager assigned to help with a Cub Scout den. Mary Margaret O'Reilly was still the one who answered.

"Rodger!" Here she was, beaming approval as if he was the greatest sight on Earth.

"It's grand to see you." Mrs. O'Reilly may have been seeing a man in the place of the teen, but Detective Raposo saw the same Den Mother. She was tall, with a formidable bosom and a trim waist. Her hair was gray now with white feathering at the temples.

"I didn't see you at the spaghetti oyster feed," she scolded.

"No, Ma'am. I took Brooke out for oysters instead."

"Did you now," Mary Margaret's eyes sparkled. "Is there an announcement coming soon?"

Rodger Raposo grinned. "We're talking."

"She's a lovely gal and a talented teacher."

"That she is. I actually came to talk to you about someone locally."

"Come on back to the kitchen. If it's gossip you want, you should come when my daughter's home. I swear my Cassie is a sponge."

Rodger followed Mary Margaret to the back of the sprawling house. It seemed strangely silent, but then, in his days here, there had been the constant near riot of the four O'Reilly boys. It had been the most fun house in the district.

"Is it different raising a girl?" he asked.

Mary Margaret poured two cups of coffee and set them on the kitchen table. "Night and day. So is being a mother at twenty different from being a mother in her fifties and sixties!" She efficiently set out a creamer pitcher and a sugar bowl, and added, "She's been a surprise every step of the way - but that's not why you're here, is it?"

"No, Ma'am." Rodger took a seat at her direction. "Do you know Dr. Patel?"

"Sure." Mary Margaret sat down and poured cream into her coffee. "Small fellow. Runs the Shelton Best Health Center."

"He was murdered yesterday."

"My God!" Mary Margaret set down her cup. She squared her shoulders. "How can I help?"

Rodger could have kissed her. This was the Mrs. O'Reilly he knew and loved.

"We're looking at his computer. We're working through files, trying to figure out whose information was compromised. One of the files belongs to an Inger Edna Morton. No address. I'm trying to figure out who this Inger Morton is, and how we can contact her."

"Ah, she's an odd bird, that one."

"You do know her."

"Yes. She was very kind when I learned Cassie was coming. She said being an older mother was fun, which I doubted at the time. But, Rodger, you know her. She goes by her middle name. Edna Morton - the mushroom lady out at Kamilche. Near Hurley Cove. You should have asked at the fire department. All the paramedics know her."

Rodger groaned. "Mushroom Edna. I didn't make the connection. And it's not like the world is full of Ednas. He shook his head. "God, I feel stupid."

He smiled at Mary Margaret. "I knew you'd help me figure out who she was."

"Her granddaughter is in my Cassie's class. Piper Anderson."

"Who are the Andersons?"

"You know them too. Milo Anderson was about ten years behind you, in your brother Caleb's class. Remember his prom night?"

Rodger sat back, feeling the crossbar of the wooden kitchen chair bite into his spine. He winced and straightened. "Caleb's prom night. Of course I remember. That was my first week as a deputy. I got called over to the high school. The paramedics had a vomiting skinny blonde. My brother was the one who gave her the beer."

Mary Margaret patted his hand. "Rough night all around. You handled it well."

"No, my sergeant handled it well. He was the one that decided not to file charges because Caleb and… Milo. Yeah, Milo, had called for help." Rodger shook his head. "I was ready to throw the pair of them in the drunk tank for a month. What idiots."

He looked over at Mary Margaret. "They were terrified out of their minds."

She smiled. "The puking kid was Lena Morton. Now Lena Morton Anderson. She's Edna's daughter."

"Why don't I remember her from around here? I remember Milo. Tall guy. Basketball player. Went off to Stanford, right?"

"Yes. Lena was home schooled. Beautiful girl. If she hadn't been projectile vomiting, you would have noticed her beauty. She's remarkable. Very odd family though. I remember Edna's mother – Lena's grandmother – from when I worked as a teen at the farmer's market. Edna would come with mushrooms to sell. She always wore a long skirt and her hair up in a bun. And any time you saw Edna, you saw her ugly and very scary mother dressed the same."

"The old lady still around?"

Mary Margaret shook her head. "Oh, no. This was decades ago. Edna's in her eighties herself. Her mother died ages ago. Ghastly woman. So very sour." Mary Margaret set down her coffee cup, lost in remembrance. "Her husband was a handsome man. We swore she was a witch who had a prince under her spell. We were sure she'd enchanted him with a mushroom stew."

Rodger Raposo shrugged. "Maybe she did."

"That which does not kill makes us stronger."

Proverb

CHAPTER TWENTY-FOUR

Saturday morning, Edna's cabin, Kamilche Peninsula

MILO WAS RELIEVED to see his wife dig into her breakfast. A night in her childhood home had revived her. Her sweet smile popped out when he caressed her hand. "Better?" he asked.

Lena said, "Yes. I feel rather silly. I have no idea why I get so wound up about things."

Edna joined them at the table. "You have always been a nervous child. It is just the way Nature made you."

Piper came clattering into the tiny kitchen with an armful of old books.

"Now this one," Edna said, hugging Piper, "never has had a worried day in her life."

"That's not true! I worry about lots of things." Piper set the books down and slid her slender, pink pajama-ed rump onto an old stool. Her braids were fuzzy from sleeping. She unclipped one end and began to unbraid.

"No hair management at the table," her father said mildly. "I think Grandmother means you aren't frozen with worry. You manage to keep moving."

Lena groaned. "Unlike me. I just run away or freeze and pass out!"

Piper nodded. "There are goats that do that. Fainting goats. I saw them on online. It's called 'myotonia.'

Milo stared at his daughter. "By God, you're right. Myotonia may have to do with acetylcholine deficiency to myosin and actin filaments. Wow." Milo sat back and ran his hands through his hair and then stared at his wife. "I hadn't put together your speedy muscles differences with your psychosis."

Lena blinked her azure eyes and sweetly said, "psychosis?"

Milo winced. "Sorry. You have a…clear fear response. Makes you a fascinating woman."

"Good save, professor." Lena scooted over next to Piper. "Into ancient reading?"

"Just checking out what Grandmom is doing. See? She bookmarked this one."

Edna splayed her fingers on the tabletop. Maybe now was the time to talk to her family about her filoplumes. Edna peeked at Lena and was reassured by Lena's calm aura.

Piper said, "I know this recipe. We're learning about paralytic shellfish poisoning in science class, and Mr. Torres told the class about Grandmom saving the dairy cows from the algal bloom with her recipe. That's this recipe." Piper's finger pointed to the page.

Edna asked, "I'm surprised he's talking about that. It was almost thirty years ago."

Piper shrugged. "He does. He told me he got interested in microclimates after he heard about you and the cows."

Piper looked up at her grandmother. "Can I use this recipe for my science project?

Edna shook her head. "Sweetie, that's not a good idea. That

recipe was one of my mother's. She was very secretive about it and for good reason. It's very powerful."

Edna's inner voice added, *'like the poison parsnips I wanted for murdering witches.* She squelched that thought and said, "There's also the ecological aspect. One of the ingredients is a very rare mushroom. If everyone goes and makes the recipe, then the species might not survive in our area. You don't want a gold rush on these things."

Edna's inner voice leapt forward with her mother's constant refrain of "*ignorant, eager people are very, very dangerous to women of the woods.*"

Edna brought one hand up to cover her mouth. She had marked the recipe with a pink glittered bookmark. Of course it drew Piper's attention. It was time to be honest about the real consequences of using a particular small mushroom.

Milo saw Edna's worried face and tried to referee. "Why don't you get the assignment sheet? Let's see exactly what the science fair requires. Maybe there's a way to do the project and have Grandmom be comfortable too."

Piper's eyes widened. "My bag! It's in Grace's car!

"Let me text her. If she's at her aunt's lecture, she'll be driving close by after."

Before Milo could get the text started, his phone rang. "'Lo. Okay."

He clicked off and the phone rang again. "'Lo. Sure. Let me check." Milo turned to his wife. "First call was Bill. He's bringing the car out. This is Joe Harbo. He's taking Joey and the new bike to the park. He wants to know if we want to come watch the first ride."

Lena beamed. "Terrific! Maybe Grace could catch up with us there."

Milo spoke into the phone. "We'll be there in about an hour."

Milo started his message to Grace.

Edna stared at the ancient recipe book opened on the table. Milo had no idea how odd she had become – or how a simple mushroom extract had changed everything. If she was going to quit keeping secrets, then she needed to quit keeping secrets.

Edna set the cup down with a thump. "Before everyone takes off, I have something to say."

Amanita muscaria

"Educating the mind without educating the heart is no education at all."

Aristotle (384 BCE – 322 BCE)

CHAPTER TWENTY-FIVE

Saturday morning, The Coastal Arts Museum

THE LICHEN LECTURE finished to enthusiastic applause. Grace stayed in her seat, digesting all that she had heard.

A small woman came down the aisle to speak to Grace. "Would you be able to stay and speak with Dr. Mossler?"

Grace looked up. "Oh! I would be honored. Where should I wait?"

"In the museum area. She can find you there." The woman turned her eyes to the crowd milling around Dr. Mossler.

Grace followed the look and knew the woman was communicating, "See for yourself how long it will be" with a silent humor.

Grace wandered through the museum, marveling at tiny baskets woven from pine needles. Her stomach started to rumble just as Dr. Mossler arrived.

"It's almost lunch-time, isn't it? Thank you for waiting. I am your Aunt Esther. I am so glad to meet you."

Grace blinked. Her heart squeezed with joy and relief.

"I loved your lecture!" Grace managed. "It was incredible!"

Dr. Mossler responded with a gentle smile. "There is so much to share. There never are enough hours in the day. I am scheduled to have a lunch with the Governor, and I must go now or risk being late. Could I take you to dinner this evening?"

Grace laughed. "An easy 'Yes'!"

Grace agreed to a suggested time and place. She was pleased when the elegant lady pulled her into a hug. As Aunt Esther glided off, Grace felt her cell phone buzz. Milo's text read "Piper bag in your car. We @ 41st park soon. Passing by?"

Grace typed, "Will bring" back. She was starving. She should find a nibble before heading to the park.

The museum guide was able to direct her. "That road will take you to the Taylor Town convenience store."

Grace hesitated. Pastry for breakfast. Chips and pop for lunch. Dinner out.

I'll order the fish tonight, Grace thought. *Grab junk food now, deliver daypack, conquer laundry, and go to dinner. The perfect plan.* Grace slid into her worn Civic and fastened her seatbelt.

"I've even got a roll of quarters for the laundry," she mused. "I'm getting my life together."

Ramaria abietina

"As the twig is bent, the tree will grow"

Proverb

CHAPTER TWENTY-SIX

Saturday mid-morning, Edna's Cabin, Kamilche Peninsula

AT EDNA'S CABIN, all eyes were on Edna. She said, "Lena, you were conceived at the summer solstice of 1984. I don't know if the solstice matters."

Piper stared at her, confused. Edna reached out and patted her hand. "There is a lot you need to know. People know that my mushroom cream helped some cows, but they don't know the whole story. It starts with that recipe."

Edna folded her arms across her chest. "We had a September heat wave. Then we had a week of rain. Hard rain."

Edna closed her eyes in remembrance. She said, "We had a flush of fall mushrooms, including a tiny brown mushroom my mother used to call "Witch's Friend." You don't see them every year, but that year they were out."

"My mother was… so strong willed. Even though she was

gone, her voice was in my mind every day. Her voice said, "When Witch's Friend is all about, it's time to get the kettle out."

Edna opened her eyes and looked around the table at her family. She saw she had their attention. "Grandpa had gone fishing, and I was getting bored with the garden work, so I thought I'd try my hand at the Witch's Friend recipe. It's an oil for respiratory distress. It requires salmon heads, and I had some, fresh, from a Nisqually trip. Tribal people use salmon head soup to help with respiratory ailments. The recipe also takes royal jelly, from bees."

Lena chimed in. "You saw this on that nature show, Piper. The bees feed certain larvae the royal jelly, and only those larvae grow into queens."

Piper rolled her eyes. "You are what you eat. Got it, mom."

Milo tapped Piper's wrist. "Be respectful. The royal jelly affects the methylation of certain genes. Genetic switches are turned on or off. It's not magic. It's science. Go on, Edna."

"I spent the better part of three days making up the recipe. Everything had to be perfect. The little mushrooms had to be heated, just so. There was an alcohol extraction. I had to fetch *Hericium abieti*. The directions were very specific that it had to be collected off a Garry oak tree. That combination is nearly impossible to find because it likes conifers, but I knew a spot."

Piper picked up a spoon and traced a design on the tablecloth with the spoon handle. She asked, "Is *Hericium* fungus the one that looks like a white waterfall?"

Edna beamed. "Yes! There was a *Ramaria* in the recipe too."

"That looks like coral." Lena murmured.

Heartened by their understanding, Edna plunged on. "We had more hot weather. It even was hot through the night. I made a beautiful oil."

"At dawn one morning my neighbors called and said one of their cows had a bit of labored breathing. They were worried about cattle emphysema and wanted to know if I could identify the weed, perilla mint, which can trigger pneumonia. I could, so I said I'd come over."

Edna continued. "I put a jar of the oil in my vest pocket and went to see my friends, Glory and Cloud. They had a small Guernsey herd and they sold raw milk. No one has Guernseys these days. They are such sweet cows, but small producers."

"Grandma!"

"Oh, sorry! This is hard." Edna took a breath and plowed on. "We went out to the barn. Glory let the cows out to go down to the pond for a drink while we looked at the one sick cow. Suddenly their border collie started barking and barking. She was going wild. We heard the cows bellowing. We ran down to the pond, and there are the four cows, staggering and falling down. They were frantic. They were all struggling to breathe. The pond was covered in green scum."

"The algae?" Milo contributed.

"Yes. One of the cows collapsed in front of me. I reached in my pocket, got out the jar and opened it. My hands were shaking." Edna's face was solemn, and her eyes wide. "I started smearing oil on her udder."

"Her udder?" Piper echoed.

"Very vascular," her father explained. "The skin is your largest organ."

Edna agreed. "I smeared oil all over the udder, and, within seconds, she seemed better. I ran to the next cow and smeared her, and the next."

She sighed. "For some reason, Cloud was furious. He said I didn't know what I was doing. Glory argued that the water had poisoned the cows, but Cloud just got angrier. He screamed, "It's not the water! It's the mint!' and he ran into the pond. He started scooping up the scummy water, and drinking it."

Edna paused, and stared out the window, lost in memories.

"Mom! What happened?" Lena jiggled Edna's elbow.

"Oh. He turned blue. He couldn't breathe. So I smeared oil on his chest too."

Piper beamed. "You saved him!"

Edna sighed. "He did start breathing again. We took the cows back to the barn. That night their milk was off. It was bitter tasting. It never was the same. Somehow they were changed cows. Cloud was furious with me. It was the end of their raw milk business."

"You saved lives!" Lena argued.

"And I changed lives. I tried to keep quiet, but Glory didn't. My goodness, she was a talker. She wanted to understand the biology of things."

Edna brushed a toast crumb off the tablecloth and smoothed the cloth flat. She said, "They couldn't sell the milk. It didn't seem safe. Cloud was so angry. I sure didn't want to say anything. It was very awkward."

"What happened to Cloud and Glory?" asked Milo.

"Oh, they bickered for weeks. One day Cloud called the knackers in a fit of rage and had the herd slaughtered. Glory was furious. A few months later she divorced him. Last I heard, she was a booger in the Bay Area."

"Blogger, mom. It's called a blogger."

"I don't get it, Grandmom. You did your best," Piper said.

Edna looked down at her granddaughter and said, "It was a scary day. A recipe should have predictable outcomes. You want to know, ahead of time, what will happen. This one clearly says to use just a drop or two and work it into the chest of someone with congestion. I used it to treat a poisoning…" Edna paused, "off label."

"That does happen," Milo said.

Edna persisted. "But this had permanent consequences. I had it all over my hands and I was pregnant. The baby,… Lena… started moving after that. Really moving. She kicked and kicked." Edna took a deep breath. "That's when my skin pores enlarged."

There was a banging at the front door of the cabin. "Helloooo! Anybody home?"

Milo called. "Come in, Bill."

The mechanic came in accompanied by a dark haired girl, who greeted Piper with, "You're in your pajamas? Aren't you going to the Quiz Bowl practice?"

Piper jumped up. "I forgot!"

Lena said, "Thank you, Paola, for reminding us. Piper, you need to get dressed. There's clean clothes in our visiting box. Scoot."

Milo looked at his watch. "We're meeting Joe at the park. Thanks for bringing the car out."

"It was an easy fix," Bill said. "Gema will be here in a minute to pick us up. We can take Piper to Quiz Bowl."

Lena gave her radiant smile. "That would be a big help." She stood and carried cups to the sink. "Mom, as usual, you saved my life. I feel so much better. I'll wash these up and we'll scoot too."

Edna gave up. Between Milo speaking with Bill in the living room, and Piper and her friend chattering in the bedroom, there was no hope of showing her feathers now.

Sushi: known to the rest of the world as "Bait"

CHAPTER TWENTY-SEVEN

Saturday morning, Interstate Five, Southbound from Tacoma to Olympia

THEODORA STABBED THE radio button off as she steered her Lexus through heavy traffic.

"Vernalization." Theodora had not known the term. The gardening show host had discussed plants moving into winter dormancy. The host said, "Many plants need a cold spell to activate growth in the spring. In winter dormancy certain plant genes add in methyl groups, repressing the flowering sequence until a long chilling season resets the genetic switches."

Methyl groups. Theodora's thinking returned to Edna. Perhaps de-methylation had activated the construction of beta keratin.

There had to be enzymes at work, Theodora mused.

So what was the need, the trigger for Edna's filoplumes? Was she in optimum conditions? Was this a stress response? Now that the filoplumes had emerged, what was next?

Theodora floored the Lexus to dash to the front of a merge

lane. She ignored an angry honk and thought of the receptionist at Patel's clinic. Kaylee, Patel's receptionist might know where Edna was.

Damn. Kaylee had seen Edna flee the clinic and surely Kaylee had heard Patel's angry lecture. Theodora clenched her jaw. Getting Kaylee to help might be a challenge.

"Call Kurt," she ordered her in-car phone.

"Yo." Kurt picked up on the second ring.

"I'm headed to Olympia. I've got more fun."

"Yeah? Do I get to play with my prey this time?"

Theodora smiled her most feral smile. "Sure. Can you get some tools? For one female, Young. And one female, Old."

"On it."

"I'll be at the Red Hawk Inn in Olympia."

"Sushi for dinner?"

"Yeah. Raw and wild."

Kurt chuckled. "That's how I like them. Raw and wild."

"Pleasure in the job puts perfection in the work."

Aristotle (384 BCE – 322 BCE)

CHAPTER TWENTY-EIGHT

Saturday, Chad's Sporting Goods, Olympia, Washington

KURT LINGERED OVER the knife display. He flirted with a petite shopper while looking at filleting tools. He wasn't surprised when the woman pressed a note into his hand that said, "Call me!" along with her phone number. His height and fit body attracted women, but not every woman was suitable prey.

The women who fit his hunting parameters were smart, gentle and optimistic. He liked righteous women who felt they were good judges of character. He would spend a time grooming his target with long phone calls that slowly escalated into dinners and movie dates.

The payoff came when he had her trust. A night of rape and terror would end with his signature; he'd use a razor above her knee, deep enough to scar, but not deep enough to require stitches. He liked the above-the-knee scar because then he knew his victim would see the scar every time she was on the toilet.

As the blood welled up, he'd grab her hair tightly and hiss in the woman's ear, "You tell anyone – anyone – about tonight and I'll do this to your mother, your grandmother, your sister and your little brother. Nod to show me you understand." The head nod was important. If she made the physical act of agreement, she was more likely to do what she had agreed to do. Kurt loved the power of habits. Predictability worked well for him.

Intelligent women hated the embarrassment of making a mistake. They were his specialty. This shopper was not bright enough to be embarrassed. He would toss her number.

He turned to the task at hand.

He chose a Bird and Trout knife and a "magic fish scaler" that looked like it would be a fun tool for abrading pubic hair. He paid cash.

As he strode out of the store, he surveyed the parking lot. He was pleased to see two dark Tundra trucks in the parking lot. He strolled by each truck, taking a cell phone photo of their license plates. Pocketing his phone, he thought about gaining access to Kaylee.

He had the most fun when agony followed hope.

"This changes everything"

Occupy Wall Street meme

CHAPTER TWENTY-NINE

Saturday late-morning, County Park, Olympia

JOEY LIKED HIS bike. The first ten minutes had been wobbly. There was one big wipeout. He jumped up, righted the bike and started over. His father cheered him on. "Atta boy, Joey!"

Grace drove into the lot and parked at the far end.

Milo called, "Joey's doing great!" Grace waved and turned to pull Piper's daypack out of the back.

"Oof. She's got lots of books." Grace slipped on the pack.

Milo and Lena applauded as Joey pedaled by.

"Get some speed up!" Milo cheered.

The asphalt strip of the lot was perfect for the beginning bicyclist. The lot was almost deserted.

The only other visitors were three middle school boys who were practicing touch and go landings with a radio-controlled airplane. One of the boys had a video camera mounted on a tripod, and he was directing the action. "Next time take it up and to the right. Take it across the field of filming for the phugoid."

His friends understood, and the boy with the controller taxied the plane down the asphalt.

Joey saw the toy plane taxiing. He changed course to parallel the plane. As the little plane accelerated, so did Joey. The plane lifted into the air at the entrance of the parking lot. Joey turned underneath it. He removed one hand from the handlebars to wave at the plane.

"Show-off!" beamed his father.

Joey crossed the far end of the parking lot, clearly intent on turning back to join his fans.

A black pickup, high on two-foot leaf springs, came roaring into the park. Joey was peddling across the road, concentrating on his turn.

There was a blur, followed by a horrible squealing crunch as the bike disappeared under the right front wheel of the truck. Joe Harbo and Milo sprinted toward the disaster as the truck came to a screeching halt. Grace came thundering behind, the heavy school bag pounding her back with every stride.

A young man with headphones on came tumbling out of the truck, pale and frightened. He peered under the truck, yelling, "Are you okay?"

Milo reached the truck ahead of Joe Harbo. Instead of looking under the truck, he swerved and flung himself to the right embankment where Lena sat, cradling little Joey in her arms.

Joey was quivering and had his head buried in her shoulder.

Joe Harbo came lumbering up, heaving for air. Gasping, he reached down and pulled Joey up into his arms. "You all right, son?"

Joey gulped and nodded. "My bike!" he wailed.

Joe Harbo hugged the little boy tight. "Kid, we can get another bike. We can't get another you." Joe looked down at Lena, still sitting on the grassy slope. "You okay?"

Lena rubbed her face and exhaled. "I'm fine. I think I will sit here a moment." Milo sat with his arm around her shoulders.

Grace finally made it to the group. She could see lines of exhaustion in Lena's face. Lena was so pale she seemed translucent. Her white blonde hair glowed in the midday sun like a radiant halo.

The young truck driver came stumbling up, "My God. Is he alright?"

Joe Harbo swung around, fury on his face. "This is a park - where kids come to play. What the hell were you thinking?"

The young man showed his open hands. "I wasn't. Man, I am so sorry. I was here a couple of days ago and the place was empty. I came back today and, man, I just wasn't thinking."

"It's Saturday," Harbo growled.

Milo still had his arm around Lena as he watched the red color build on Joe Harbo's neck. "Joe," he called, "Let's get these two home. Lena is in shock. Joey could use a hot drink too."

The young man helped by saying, "I'll clean up the bike. I'll get a new one. Just give me an address."

Joe Harbo waved him off. "Stay the hell out of my life, and slow down."

Joe turned to Lena. "Thanks." With that he stalked off towards his car, carrying Joey, whose face was snuggled in his father's massive neck.

Lena whispered. "Joey and I aren't the only ones feeling shocky."

Milo pulled his beautiful wife into a hug. "I don't know how you did that, but I am so glad that you did. Let's get you a shower and a hot drink."

"Piper," Lena said, leaning into Milo. "Bill and Gema said they'd drop Piper here after the Quiz Bowl practice. We need to wait for her." The words came slowly, as Lena struggled with the enunciation.

Grace interrupted. "Let me help. I'll wait and bring her out to your house. She can tell me the way."

Milo looked up. "Super. Only we're going back to Edna's. Lena, sit here with Grace. I'll go get the car."

Lena gave a weary nod. Grace sank down on the grass next to her, and put her arm across Lena's shoulders. "Got her, boss."

Milo sprinted to the station wagon. He didn't pay attention to the radio-controlled plane trio. The boys were crowded around the video camera, watching the video replay on the tiny screen. One of the boys said, "I am so posting this!"

"A little knowledge is a dangerous thing."

Anonymous.

CHAPTER THIRTY

Saturday late-morning, Airport, Phoenix, AZ

KEN ITO SNEEZED and blinked. He sneezed again. His cold was getting worse.

He scrolled through an on-line phone directory with his eyes aching and his nose running. He had ninety minutes before the Seattle bound plane departed. He wanted to telephone Edna Morton if he could locate a number.

So far he was coming up with a number of Mortons, but no 'Edna' or even 'E' Morton. He closed his eyes and leaned back on the pseudo leather of the lounge seat. "God. If I get much sicker, I'll have to call for the paramedics."

Ken suddenly sat up and searched the Government pages for Olympia, Washington. He came up with the volunteer fire department number for the Kamilche Peninsula. Moments later he learned that, yes, they knew Edna. Yes, they had her number.

Ken paused to get an expensive soda from a surly vendor. He sat down in the lounge and dialed Edna's number.

"Hello?"

"Edna Morton?"

"This is she."

Ken clenched a fist in victory. "Hi. Ken Ito here. I'm with the N.S.A. I'm calling you from the Phoenix airport. I'm headed up to Olympia. Could meet with you sometime in the next few days? I'd like to hear about your experience with anatoxin-a."

"Anatoxin-a?"

"Blue green algae poisoning?"

"Oh. For heaven's sake. We were just talking about that at breakfast." There was a sigh. "I suppose. It's time to share a bit."

"Super. When can we meet?"

Edna heard the sound of a vehicle coming up her driveway. She peered out the window and saw a Mason County Sheriff's sedan.

She said, "Just a minute, please. Someone's just driven up."

Edna carried the phone with her to the door as Rodger Raposo came ambling up the walk.

"Ms. Morton, I'm Detective Raposo. I need some help on a case I'm working."

Edna unlatched the screen door. "Please come in." To Ken, on the phone, she said, "Someone just arrived at my door. Could you call me when you arrive in Olympia? "

Edna gestured to Raposo to enter as she said good-bye.

"Got a visitor coming?" Raposo asked.

Edna sighed. "The N.S.A. thinks I know something."

"The N.S.A.!"

Edna said, "Oh, I'm mostly known for mushrooms, so it may seem odd that the National Shellfish Association wants to talk to me - but I've been around a long time. I can tell you that oysters don't like algal blooms."

"Algal bloom? Huh." Raposo's quivering detective antennae switched off. He pulled out his small yellow notebook to begin his interview.

"Oh what a tangled web we weave, when first we practice to deceive."

Sir Walter Scott
(August 15, 1771- September 21, 1832)

CHAPTER THIRTY-ONE

Saturday late-morning. Edna's cabin, Kamilche Peninsula

"THANK YOU." RODGER Raposo accepted a cup of coffee. He was pleased when Edna placed a plate of cookies on the table. In Raposo's experience, anyone who had gray hair in a bun was likely a champion cookie baker.

"Ms. Morton, do you know a Dr. Patel?" he asked.

"Do call me Edna. And, yes. He's my doctor."

"I'm sorry to inform you that Dr. Patel was killed yesterday afternoon." Raposo watched her face as he delivered his news.

Edna sunk down into her kitchen chair like a butter brick melting in a microwave. "My God."

"He was murdered," Raposo added.

Edna turned large, pained eyes on him. "Murdered!"

"Yes Ma'am. His throat was cut. We're trying to figure out who would do such a thing."

Edna clasped her coffee mug tightly to stop her fingers from shaking. Surely this had nothing to do with her. It had to be a crazed patient or drug addicted youngster responsible.

Edna croaked out, "How can I help you?"

"Certain patient files were downloaded at the time of Dr. Patel's death. Yours was one of them. Is there any reason that someone would want your medical records?"

"Me?" she quavered. "I'm sure there's some mistake."

Raposo sipped his coffee. "When did you last see Dr. Patel?"

"On Tuesday. I have a little skin condition. He said to watch it – it's fine." Edna spoke in a rush.

"Anything unusual at the clinic?"

"No. Well, yes. There was a visiting doctor. Dr. Band. I think she's gone now." Edna tried to be as guileless as possible as she raised her eyes to Raposo's.

Raposo calmly picked up a cookie. "Tell me about her."

"Not much to say," replied Edna. She shrugged. "I didn't care for her – a bit forward, that's all."

"Anything strike as odd while you were there?"

"No." Edna's eyes darted around her kitchen, like twin flies looking for a spot to settle. She made herself stop and focus on Detective Raposo. He was watching her as he finished the cookie.

Raposo said. "I'll leave my card with you. It has my number on it. Please call me, any time of day or night, if you think of something."

Edna accepted the card. "I hope you catch whoever did this."

"We will. Thanks for the coffee." Raposo finished his coffee with a gulp. He stood up and pushed his chair in, like a properly brought up lad. "I'll see myself out."

Raposo ambled out to his sedan. He felt, to his most cellular bloodhound level, that there were things that Edna knew. Those eyes that blinked and moved when discussing the doctors were telling him something.

"*What*," he wondered, "*is that nice granny hiding?*"

Raposo was fastening his seatbelt when he became aware of a car racing down Edna's long driveway. He waited. He was curious to see who was coming to Edna's at such speed.

A green Subaru station wagon came to a gravel-tossing stop next to Raposo's sedan. A grim faced man shifted into park and got out. He came around the car, nodding to Raposo as he passed. He didn't stop to chat. The driver was focused on a white blonde woman who sagged against the passenger side window.

Raposo watched as the fellow opened the car door and assisted the woman out. That's one ghost white woman, Raposo observed. Milo and Lena Anderson?

Raposo tabbed down the sedan window and called, "Need any help?"

"No, we're fine." Milo was curt and focused on his wife.

The pale blonde did not look fine. She stood with help but looked close to fainting. She rallied enough to plant one foot in front of the other while clinging to her husband to complete the short journey to Edna's screen door. Edna pushed open the door and hustled her daughter inside.

Raposo frowned as he turned the ignition key to start his unit. He didn't know what the hell was going on, but he'd added a liar and a beautiful woman into the mix.

"The cause is hidden. The effect is visible to all."

Ovid (March 20, 43 BCE – 17 CE)

CHAPTER THIRTY-TWO

Saturday late-morning, U.S. Airways flight to Seattle.

AS THE AIRPLANE attained cruising altitude, Ken Ito felt better. His original dismay at having a mid row seat disappeared when he found he had the row to himself. He flapped out his elbows and began to read.

It was time to understand DNA methylation better. He knew that standard methylation occurred when a carbon/tri-hydrogen cluster or "methyl group" attached to the fifth position of a cytosine base in a DNA strand.

Of particular importance were those spots in the DNA where a cytosine base existed next to a guanine base. The "Cytosine-phosphate-Guanine" or "CpG" sites were the on/off switches for most of the human genome.

Once the methylation occurred, the changed status of the cytosine base could then be transmitted through future cell divisions to daughter cells.

DNA methylation was important because it stopped DNA

transcription. When methylation failed, DNA "reading" began. A cell could move towards cancer or toward expressing other genes. Given that any human had up to 80% of her DNA methylated or silenced, there was strong evidence that the tiny methyl groups were as important to geneticists as corks were to wine makers.

It boiled down to enzymes. "Methyltransferases" were the enzymes that added methyl groups. When a tumor-suppressing gene got hit with methylation, it ceased to do its job and abnormal cell proliferation began.

Ken scrolled down to a publication on the fungicide vinclozolin. If the chemical killed fungi, what did it do to mammals?

The study on rats showed that the vinclozolin changed DNA methylation. The DNA changes persisted into the next three generations.

A single exposure to the fungicide changed the brains and metabolism in rats and in their descendants. The grandsons were fatter and more anxious.

Ken paged through the rest of the report. What happened in one generation could make following generations more susceptible to stress. There was a possible link to the development of post-traumatic stress syndrome.

Ken wiped his running nose. Killing off grape fungus in a vineyard could trip off bad effects in mammals. Poison here, consequences there. He closed his aching eyes and murmured a prayer for war veterans everywhere. How many had terrors because of their genetics?

God only knows what monsters we have inside us, he thought, as his virus-ridden sinuses demanded that he rest. *It'd be great if old Edna has something for us.*

"The Gods have sent medicines for the venom of serpents, but there is no medicine for a bad woman. She is more noxious than the viper, or than fire itself."

Euripides (480 BCE – 406 BCE)

CHAPTER THIRTY-THREE

Saturday mid-day, Bagel Boys Deli, Olympia

THEODORA FINISHED HER sandwich. She bit into the crisp pickle that garnished the lunch. She liked pickles.

She'd leave the plastic basket and crumbs for the counter girl to clean up. She didn't like the girl. Maybe it was time to spill some coffee.

Then again, security cameras were everywhere these days. Destructive acts gave such a lovely adrenaline surge, but she had work to do. She should be discreet.

Theodora barely remembered her early years. She remembered a cold, gray room with hard floors. She remembered Kurt putting his arms around her as they huddled for warmth. She owed him her life. She rewarded him when she could.

Sipping her coffee, Theodora surveyed the stores nearby. Lover's Passion blinked in pink neon from a small storefront, giving Theodora inspiration. She'd pick up a little something for the evening. Kurt would like that.

She thought again of her target. How to manage Edna? Her first preference was to charm Edna into giving a blood sample followed by formal analysis and reporting. That path would give her the most options. She could play this one out for years.

How much could she indulge in her passion for destruction without getting caught? Quite a lot, if she stayed clever. Earning the M.D. was a great step. Managing a breakthrough research project would take her to a whole new level of opportunities.

She had to be mindful that Edna might not cooperate. That would be… infuriating. Then again, she and Kurt had not amused themselves with a granny before. That, too, could be a new frontier. "Cooperate or don't cooperate. I win either way," Theodora mused. She took another bite of the pickle. The pickle was cold and crisp with a biting finish. *Like me*, she mused.

"When a dog bites a man that is not news, but when a man bites a dog, that is news."

Charles Anderson Dana
(August 8,1819 - October 17, 1897)

CHAPTER THIRTY-FOUR

Saturday mid-day, County Park

GRACE WAITED AT the park until Piper arrived and cheerfully climbed into the car.

"Mom forget something?" she asked.

"No." Grace hesitated.

Piper squirmed in alarm. "Did my mom go wonky?" she asked.

'Wonky' covered a lot of territory.

Grace gave it to her in a rush, "Your Mom saved Joey's life. He was riding his bike when a truck came peeling into the park. It totally smashed the bike – but your Mom managed to grab Joey off."

Grace turned onto the main road, trying to accurately report what she had seen. "I don't know how to describe it. She was so…

fast. It was a blur. She was tired after that. Your Dad took her to your Grandmother's."

Piper looked down at her lap and nodded. "Okay."

Grace flicked her a glance and saw a fat tear drop. "Hey, no tears! She's fine. Just tired."

Piper sniffed. "Sorry. My mom was really sick in Seattle."

Piper began to chew on the corner of a fingernail. Around her finger, she asked, "Did you hear about her?"

"I don't know the specifics."

Piper switched to the next finger. "There wasn't a diagnosis," she mumbled. "My Mom has a friend named Georgia. Georgia was taking a class my dad taught. Her husband was overseas. They were expecting a baby."

"One day my Mom knew – she says she just knew – that Georgia's baby had died inside and that her husband had stepped on a land mine. An I.E.D. My Mom knew this before Georgia knew. Mom was screaming her head off. She ended up sitting in a tree."

"I'm so sorry," Grace said.

Piper scowled. "My family is so weird."

"Special. You guys are special." Grace tried for a light tone. "Now my family? We're half dog. I mean it. When someone asks my mother how many kids she has, she always says, "Six. One girl, two boys and three German Shepherds."

Piper looked out the window. "I'd like a dog."

Grace talked dogs until they arrived at Edna's. Piper bounded out of the car and into Edna's cabin, leaving Grace behind with the school bag.

Grace hoisted the bag and started up the walk. She made it to the cabin steps when Edna opened the screen door and beckoned Grace in.

"Thank you, once again, Grace. We need to talk." Edna put her hand on Grace's arm and pulled her into the cabin.

A wan Lena was stretched out on the sofa with a quilt over her long legs. "Hi," she croaked.

Piper knelt next to her mother. Lena stroked her daughter's hair. "I'm just a little tired. Grandmom is making brownies. That will help."

Piper gave a tiny nod and slid under the quilt to snuggle close to her mother.

"Grace was telling me about her family dogs," Piper mumbled. "They sound awesome."

Edna said, "Come on in the kitchen, Grace. I'm thinking about getting a dog soon. I could use some advice."

Surprised, Grace went the few steps into the kitchen that smelled fantastically of baking brownies.

Edna patted the back of a kitchen chair. "Come. Sit. Let me get you a cup of tea while we wait for the brownies." Edna's eyes looked weary.

Grace didn't know whether she should mention the action at the park, so she asked, "What kind of dog would you like?"

"A Rottweiler."

"A Rottweiler? That's a serious dog." Grace accepted a mug with a submerged tea ball. "You'll want a dog that is very well socialized. Aggressive dogs are dangerous and a big Rotty can pull you off your feet."

Edna put out a honey pot and spoon. "Oh. Dear. What about a German Shepherd?"

"They're herding dogs with lots of energy. If you don't keep them busy, they can be destructive." Grace swished the tea ball in her mug. "Edna, are you worried about security?"

Before Edna could answer, Milo walked into the kitchen. He said, "I've always been a bit worried about you out here, Edna - but I can't picture you with an attack dog."

The oven timer chirped. Edna bent over the open oven door and extracted a pan of brownies that filled the kitchen with the smell of melted chocolate. Grace felt her mouth watering. Edna briskly set the hot pan on the oven top and closed the oven door. "We'll let these cool a bit."

Grace's stomach rumbled. Apparently the chips and soda had not been an adequate lunch. She tried to focus on Edna. The smell of the brownies had her saliva glands overriding her brain.

Edna joined Grace at the kitchen table. "Honestly, I don't know what I want."

She sighed. "My doctor, dear Dr. Patel, was murdered at his clinic yesterday. It's terribly upsetting."

Edna put up a hand to forestall questions. "I don't know any details. I really don't. I've thought about getting a dog for a while now. I think I'd feel safer."

Grace pulled the tea ball out and set it on a saucer. "Piper definitely likes the idea of a dog," she agreed. "They can be great. Why don't you take it slow and visit a few animal shelters and talk over some options?"

Milo snorted. "If Piper visits a shelter, we're coming home with a dog. I can foresee that one without Edna's talents."

Edna turned to Grace. "I'd like to take you with us. You could help us make a wise choice."

"Sure! Just say when."

"Not today. Lena is too tired. Tomorrow? Or would you rather rest on your Sunday?"

Grace was tickled by the notion that graduate students might have a day of rest. She smiled and said, "Tomorrow would work."

She directed her next question to Milo. "Will Lena be alright?"

"I think so. I just did some reading on-line and I'm increasingly convinced that her muscles are different. I don't see any other explanation for what we saw."

Grace agreed. "That was so amazing. I'm still not fathoming how she could have gotten to Joey that quickly."

"I just found some stuff on-line about a gene called

ACTN3-577R that enhances sprinting ability. Everybody has slow, fast, and super-fast muscle fibers, but sprinters have more of the super-fast fibers; they move fast but then they tire out and can't keep up the pace."

"She's certainly tired," Edna agreed. "Are you sure everyone has super-fast muscles? I'm certainly not fast at anything these days."

"It's like a chicken, Edna. Even a mature hen has 'white' meat in the breast. That's fast twitch fiber. The 'dark' meat of the leg and thigh is slow twitch muscle. Cheetahs have 80% or more fast or super-fast fibers. "

Grace jumped in. "But you said you thought Lena has different muscles. Do you mean she just has more of what most people have or do you mean she has something altogether different?"

"God, you're sharp." Milo picked up a knife from the kitchen counter and cut into the still hot brownies. He deftly cut a square and popped it onto a small plate to give to Grace.

He lifted out another brownie and said, "Professor Mohan suggested that hers might be truly different. Something on the cellular level. To find out would mean a biopsy."

"Good luck with that," Edna said. To Grace she explained, "Lena is shy. I'm not that keen on doctors myself, but Lena has a real fear."

"I can hear you, you know," called Lena from the living room.

"Me too!" sang Piper. "Are the brownies ready?"

"I'll bring one to Mom," Milo answered. "You come get your own."

"Okay." Piper scrambled out from under the quilt. "I think it's great that we're getting a dog."

"Let me tell you the secret that has led me to my goal. My strength lies solely in my tenacity."

Louis Pasteur
(December 27, 1822 – September 28, 1895)

CHAPTER THIRTY-FIVE

Saturday afternoon. Mason County Sheriff's office

RAPOSO SAT IN his cubicle, talking to Don MacRae. They were making progress. They knew that the clinic had been professionally cleaned on Wednesday night and egged by Thursday morning. Estella and Dr. Patel had cleaned surfaces again after the egging.

Deputy MacRae zeroed in on the men's room off the clinic's lobby, hoping the killer washed up. The forensics tech turned up a print near the sink and, even better, the print was in the system.

"Only the one?" Rodger tried not to sound greedy.

"The tech is speculating that our perp wore multiple layers of latex gloves and just rinsed his knife. Sometimes a big hand in a glove is such a snug fit that the fingerprint ridges will push through. The lab has the egg shells that I collected from the trash."

"Our one print so far comes back to?"

"Kurt Otsoa. Army Ranger out of Fort Lewis. Originally from Kankakee, Illinois. Six four. Blond. Blue."

"Ahh. And why is an active duty military guy washing up in a country clinic?"

"One does wonder."

"Does Kaylee recall six four, blond, blue as a recent client?"

Deputy MacRae produced a smirk at the memory of the answers he'd gotten to that question. "She assured me that their male clients are 'dumpy, not hunky.' No Army Ranger anytime in her memory."

"An Army Ranger would know how to use a knife. Good work. Great work, in fact."

MacRae's face flushed deep pink, which contrasted oddly to his orange crew cut. "Thanks, sir."

"We need to navigate carefully. He's a county over, on a military base. We have to respect the territorial boundaries."

Rodger leaned forward, "I'll give the chief an update and give Fort Lewis a call. They'll pick up Mr. Kurt Otsoa and hold him for us. What's your schedule like?"

MacRae didn't hesitate. "I'm working tomorrow and off on Monday and Tuesday. I'd like to see this through, no matter what the schedule."

"Good man. I'll call you in once we know Otsoa is in hand."

"I'll be waiting." Don sketched a salute and departed.

Raposo leaned back in his office chair. One fingerprint. Not much of a trail. Raposo flicked a finger at the bloodhound bobble-head toy that Brooke had found for him. The toy dog's head swayed up and down. Not much of a trail. Then again, he wasn't one who needed clashing cymbals to start a parade. He wasn't in the parade business. Raposo set his fingers on the computer keyboard. It was time to learn a little more about Mr. Kurt Otsoa.

"You don't make mistakes. Mistakes make you."

Anonymous.

CHAPTER THIRTY-SIX

Saturday evening, Totten Bay Café, Olympia

GRACE SLID INTO the restaurant booth at six. Despite the afternoon brownie break, she was, again, starving.

Esther arrived, wearing sleek jeans and red polo shirt, this time accessorized with turquoise earrings.

Grace stared at her. "How do you do that? You've got my body shape and my face, but you look terrific."

Esther smiled at the compliment. "It took me years to figure it out. Find a great hairdresser. Don't be afraid to talk to a tailor. I'll give you some brand names that fit me."

"Okay!" Grace beamed. "Now, who's the hunky guy in the kilt in your slide show? Him I want to meet!"

To Grace's surprise, Esther blushed crimson. "Alasdair. That's Alasdair. The photo is about thirty years old."

"Auntie, am I detecting a wee crush on this Alasdair?" Grace teased.

Esther bubbled with laughter. "Busted. He's a visiting

professor of Ecology at Yale. I met him this last year. I came out to tell the extended family about him. We're getting married this winter."

"Wow!"

"Wow, indeed. We've both been married before, so we were both wary. Recently we decided to go for it." Esther acknowledged the waiter with a nod and said, "Crab cakes for me, please. With the coleslaw."

Grace grinned. "Make it a double, we're celebrating."

"Two plates, crab cakes," the waiter chirped and moved on.

"Grace, I am so glad to connect with you. We have all missed your father. How is he?"

"He's fine," Grace said. She picked up the cloth napkin and began creasing it into tight pleats. "Well, not totally fine. His problem is that he smoked for years and he has a spot near his heart – Stage I lung cancer. They won't do surgery if they can get the tumor with the radiation. He's quit the cigarettes and that makes him grumpy."

"I am so sorry," Esther replied.

"It's a bummer. He acts cool on the outside, but when I was home last time he sat out with the dogs a lot. I think he's terrified."

Esther reached across the table and patted her hand. "Some of the best cures to cancer come through ecology. Mushrooms and lichens have a lot to offer. Have you done some reading on how to help him?"

"That's one of the reasons why I'm here," Grace agreed. "To be the Queen of Ecological Knowledge. Also to meet Dad's side of the family tree."

The waiter returned with steaming plates, and the two women fell silent as the food was placed. Grace, however, had a question burning inside.

"Aunt Esther, why did my dad leave?"

"He never told you?"

He says, 'They don't want me, and I don't blame them.' Then the topic is closed."

Esther sighed. "A good bit overstated. Give me a moment with dinner, and I'll try to make it concise." With that she placed a napkin in her lap and picked up her fork.

The two women ate in companionable silence.

Eventually, Esther put down her fork and cleared her throat. "Rob was eighteen. I was away at college, so this is all second hand. He had just graduated high school. Raymond, our little brother, was a year behind. One of our cousins had a new truck that he drove to the convenience store at Taylor Town."

"Taylor Town. I bought chips there today," Grace said.

Esther continued, "Alvin left the truck running while he went in."

"He left it running?"

Esther made a wry smile. "Rural western Washington. It still happens. Rob and our brother, Raymond, thought it would be hilarious to move the truck. They jumped in, and drove the truck up the road."

She said, "As I understand it, they were just going to drive up the hill a bit - but here comes Alvin out of the store. He's running after them, yelling. My brothers think this is hilarious, and Rob accelerates. He's watching Alvin in the rear view mirror. He doesn't notice that the road is curving, so he drives the truck over the edge. It rolls and slides into a tree. No seat belts on."

"Oh, my God."

"Rob smacked his head and had some bruises. Raymond put out his arms to brace himself and ended up with double compound fractures. He was a mess. The truck was totaled."

Esther added, "Raymond was a high school wrestler - the crash put an end to his sports career. My parents were devastated." Esther leaned back and allowed the waiter to take away her plate.

Esther continued, "Rob went off to the military recruiters.

He signed with the Air Force because they could take him immediately. He left within two weeks of the accident and has never come back."

"Is Raymond still angry?"

"No! He never was. He says it was just two guys being goofy that got out of hand. Our father was furious for a long time. Dad passed away ten years ago. Mom eight years ago."

"Where's Raymond now?"

"On Kamilche. He's a plumber. He's married with two girls. He coaches softball and spends a lot of time in the tribal woodworking shop. He's an amazing carver. I know he'd love to meet you."

"I'd love to meet him too." Grace set down her fork. "I'm so glad that Edna Morton told me about your lecture."

Esther smiled. "Edna is a natural healer. She knows that community is everything. We are all so very inter-connected, and our hearts are ripped open when we lose a member of the community. Our connections are so important."

"You sound like Dr. Anderson," Grace teased. "He's constantly lecturing about how the mycelium network of fungus in the forest floor is structured like other things. The Internet. The cosmos. Everything connects."

"Are we singing Kumbaya next?" Esther cheekily responded.

"Yeah. And you'll make me sing harmony," Grace zipped back.

Aunt and niece dissolved into laughter.

Five miles away a thirteen-year-old boy checked his video posting of a long-legged blonde racing to grab a child off a bike. It already had registered five thousand hits. The boy shouted for his family, and, with his mother's urging, the boy forwarded a link to a Seattle television station.

Sacrodon imbricatus

"While the fox is chatting with you, keep an eye on your chickens."

Basque Proverb.

CHAPTER THIRTY-SEVEN

Saturday night, Red Hawk Inn, Olympia

KURT PARKED THREE blocks from the hotel. One serial killer was known for his Volkswagen and another for a white corvette. Kurt smiled. He was smarter. He would be known for… nothing.

He avoided the staffed lobby. The trick was to find someone exiting a wing of the hotel while appearing as if he had a key card. It didn't take long.

An elderly couple pushed open a wing door. Kurt, playing the gentleman, jumped forward to hold the door. He smiled at their thanks. Once inside he sent a text: "Room?"

The response was, "204."

The staircase was on the right. Kurt took the steps two at a time.

He passed an Asian male near the drink machine at the top of the stairs. The guy gave a hacking cough as a bottle of orange juice clunked out of the dispenser.

Kurt knocked on 204 and Theodora opened the door. She wore a saucy pink corset, a garter belt and black fish net stockings. She gave her brother a hug. "I know you like me in pink."

Kurt picked her up while elbowing the door shut. "Hot pink suits you." He carried her to the bed and dropped her onto the mattress with a small bounce.

Kurt stripped. He un-strapped his knife and sheath and tossed them on his pile of clothes. Naked, he turned to the waiting Theodora.

"You're gorgeous," she said.

Kurt winked at her. "Not so bad yourself, kid." He lazily stroked her leg, up and down knowing that she was impatient. She wiggled and opened her legs for him.

"Not so fast," he murmured. "Remember our first hitchhiker?"

Theodora's eyes shone with delight. "I'll never forget. She thought we were so nice to give her a ride."

"Mmm." Kurt knew the reference would make Theodora wet. He ran a finger inside her panties and found her damp. He liked that she had put the panties on over the garter belt. It meant he could remove the panties and leave the stockings.

He peeled off her panties, and then he returned to stroking Theodora's legs, this time from the knee up to the crotch on the inside. Theodora moaned and brought her knees up. Kurt slipped a finger inside her and stroked gently.

Then he stopped.

Theodora hissed and opened her eyes. He laughed at her and pulled her off the bed, dumping her onto the floor. "Earn your keep, sis."

There was no one else on the planet that could interrupt her without painful consequences, but Theodora took the interruption from Kurt.

Obediently, she knelt between his legs and began to caress him.

Kurt ran his fingers through her hair and groaned. He tapped her shoulder and she stopped to look up at him. Kurt patted the mattress. "Up," he said.

A moment later Kurt grabbed the bed pillows and lifted her hips, placing the pillows underneath. He inserted himself and began to move. "Slow?" he asked.

"Slow, then fast," Theodora commanded.

Kurt went for a slow count of three lingering strokes and then picked up the pace. When he felt Theodora convulse, he smiled. He held her waist and poured himself into her.

Later, in the shower, he ran soapy hands over her chest and back. Kurt stuck his head in the shower spray and let the water pour down around his head and shoulders while he massaged Theodora's body.

"How sick are we?" he asked.

Theodora shrugged. "We have our own normal. We take a little pleasure where we can."

Her eyes lit with pleasure as she said, "I keyed my neighbor's van this morning. They'll know it was me, but there's no proof. If that pimply loser whines at me again, I'll call the police and say he tried to sexually assault me."

Theodora went round-eyed and brought up a shocked voice. "Officer. It was awful. He pushed me and grabbed me. I'm so lucky to get away."

She smirked. "I love my M.D. It's like a license for happiness."

Kurt turned the shower off. "Dry me off, Dr. Band" he said. And she did.

The two moved back to the bed and slid under the covers. A cell phone jingled. Kurt leaned out of bed and fished his phone out of his clothes.

"Yo!"

Theodora watched as rage flew into Kurt's face.

"When was this?" Kurt barked. "Thanks. I owe you." Kurt slapped the phone off.

"Problems?"

"Maybe. A buddy on base says MP's came looking for me. When he told them I was on leave, they said they'd be back."

Kurt picked up the television remote to scroll through the on-screen guide. "We should watch the news"

The siblings gave unblinking focus to the screen when the local news began.

An anchorman looked into the camera and said, "Mason County sheriff's deputies have identified a person of interest in the killing of Dr. Neeladri Patel. The lead investigator indicates that the killer was knowledgeable in the use of a knife, which might indicate military training."

"Shit," Kurt growled.

"That's not much," Theodora protested.

"They never release everything to the reporters. I'm not liking this, Teddy. This time they may be getting close."

"You wore gloves, right?"

"Of course. I threw out the clothes miles away - even the shoes. I had a ski cap to keep hair in too. It was supposed to look like local revenge."

The news anchor was onto the next story.

"A stunning rescue in Olympia today. Ms. Lena Anderson was at a park west of Olympia this morning when a child on a bicycle was moving into harm's way. Just watch this amazing run."

The short clip showed Joey and the truck followed by Lena as a blur. The co-anchor jumped in with, "That is amazing. How fast would you say she's going?"

"We did a little math. She covered about seventy yards in about 3 seconds."

"That's impossible!"

"So you would think. That is one lucky little boy."

"He sure had an angel watching him today. We'll be posting this clip on our website. Send us your comments!"

Theodora muted the TV. "Anderson. Edna Morton's next of kin is an Anderson." Theodora eyed Kurt. "It was the contact name in the medical record. The first name was, what?" Theodora thought for a moment. "Angelena. The reporter said Lena Anderson. "

"Could be the same. What do you want to do?"

Theodora slid out from under the covers to reach for her laptop. "I'll go out to the clinic tomorrow to talk to Kaylee. Maybe she knows if Edna is related to this Anderson. And let's see if we can find an address for this Lena Anderson. You could reconnoiter. It may be we want samples from both women."

Kurt grinned. "I love the two-fers. The two sisters we did were excellent. A mother - daughter pair could be lots of fun."

"Rumor grows at it goes."

Virgil
(October 15, 70 BCE – September 21, 19 BCE)

CHAPTER THIRTY-EIGHT

Sunday morning, Seven a.m. Apple Town Apartments

GRACE STRETCHED AND yawned. Seven a.m. on a Sunday was a brutal time to be awake, but she had so much to do.

There was reading for her seminar on Monday. She'd promised Edna and Piper to be a dog-shopping guide and that should be followed by more class prep. At least her laundry was done. Grace exhaled. The clothes were clean. According to her now beloved Aunt Esther, all wrong in color, make and size.

Grace started coffee and tried a few yoga stretches. "Yoga gives you long, lean muscles," Esther had told her.

"Gotta take a class," Grace mumbled. Esther had landed in her life like a thunderbolt. They had discussed gene therapy, Kermode bears and melanocortin-1 receptors. They had also discussed men, haircuts and the lack of coverage on low-waist jeans.

Yawning again, Grace carried her coffee to her desk. She

popped open her laptop, pulled up a desk chair, and had her first surprise before she sat down.

Her email in-box showed sixty messages. "Spam!" she grumbled.

A few moments later, Grace was wide-awake with the coffee forgotten. The emails were from across the country.

Grace, isn't this out your way?

Yo, sis. Is that you with the daypack in this video? Whoever it is runs like a sad cow. Do you know the blonde? I could be available. Your ever-loving brother, J.

Grace, Did you see this?

Grace, Do you know Dr. Anderson? This clip is going viral.

Honey, call home. Dad and I are worried about you.

Grace, I'm trying to reach Milo Anderson. He's not answering his phone or email. Do you know his whereabouts? Y. Berbera. Department Chair, Biology, Summit College

Ms. Mossler, I'm a reporter for KIRI 3 news in Seattle. I'd like to interview you about the recent viral video posting from Olympia. Please call me.

Grace clicked on a link and watched in rising horror. Not only was Lena's run documented for all the world to see, but the boys doing the video had also added in identification. "That's Piper Anderson's mom. Her name is Lena. She's the fastest mom ever. And the hottest."

Grace groaned. Piper would be mortified. Grace thought furiously. Milo wasn't answering his phone. It was early. Perhaps he'd just turned it off for the night.

There was a good chance the Andersons were still at Edna's.

Grace fired off an email to her parents. *I'm fine. A lot going on. Had dinner with Aunt Esther last night. She's great. I'll call soon. Grace.*

Grace closed the laptop, ignoring the other emails. She'd grab a shower and head to Edna's. 'Auggh,' she grumped. Breakfast would be another cold toaster pastry.

Coprinus comatus

"Beware what you wish for."

Anonymous advice

CHAPTER THIRTY-NINE

Sunday morning, Seven a.m., Red Hawk Inn

KEN ITO FELT better. The cold was retreating.

Today he'd meet with a manager of a local mushroom production facility. The manager had offered to give a Sunday morning tour.

"I'm really looking forward to meeting you, Dr. Ito," she had emailed. "Our production crew will not be operating, but there's still much to see."

Ken seized the offer. He'd call Edna Morton after the tour.

He rolled out of bed, stretched, and glanced out the hotel window. The street was quiet. An elderly woman walked a schnauzer and a tall, lean man with a military crew cut strode down the walk, moving away from the hotel.

He sure got lucky, Ken thought. That was the same tall guy who had been greeted by the bombshell in a pink corset. The door had only been opened for a moment, but it was an eyeful that Ken wouldn't forget anytime soon.

I wish I'd meet someone like that. Ken stretched and made for the shower.

"The willing, Destiny guides them. The unwilling, Destiny drags them."

Seneca (4 BCE – AD 65)

CHAPTER FORTY

Sunday morning, Eight a.m., Edna's cabin, Kamilche Peninsula

EDNA LET GRACE in. "I heard your car coming up the drive. Goodness, you're up early for a student." Edna was dressed in her usual denim overalls, striped socks, and running shoes. Her gray hair was in its tight bun anchored with a tiny daisy topped hairpin.

"I see Milo's car is here. Are they still here?" Grace whispered as she stepped up to the door.

"Yes. They're here. Piper too. She's asleep. The rest of us are in the kitchen."

Grace and Edna stepped through the living room where the back of Piper's head could barely be seen at the end of a quilt burrito on the sofa.

Milo and Lena were at the kitchen table.

"Good morning!" Lena chirped. She pulled back her long legs

to make room for Grace to pull out a kitchen chair. Lena smiled asked, "How are you today?"

Grace had a minimal smile in return. "Sorry to be here so early," she said, "You are in the news."

"Me?" Lena's rosy color faded to pale pink.

"The kids with the radio-controlled airplane at the park yesterday were videotaping. They posted a video of you on-line."

That comment elicited three vary different responses. Edna looked confused. Lena alarmed and Milo… looked furious. "Shit," he said.

"Young man!" Edna scolded.

"Sorry, Edna. This is a problem." Milo replied.

Grace had to agree. "The clip has a million hits. It was on the late night news. There's also an email to me from a reporter."

"How did they find you?" Milo asked.

Grace threw her hands up in wonder. "The early part of the video pans the parking lot. You can see our cars. Maybe a license plate?"

Lena asked, "Do they know my name?"

"The kids say you are 'Piper Anderson's mom,' and your name is 'Lena.'

"Good enough," Milo growled. "Damn."

This time Edna did not admonish him. "People won't really care about Lena," she argued. "The little boy is safe. That's what is important." Edna's voice came out strained.

Piper, in pink pajamas, spoke from the doorway. "The video has been seen a million times, Grandmom. That's a lot. When a video goes viral, the whole world cares."

Grace added, "Dr. Berbera emailed me. He said you weren't answering your phone or email."

"It's Sunday morning, for crying out loud," Milo growled. "Not your fault, Grace. Thanks for warning us. Shoot. We may have reporters at the house."

Lena took a deep breath. "What if we just ask them to go away? We could say I'm sick." She was looking paler by the minute.

Milo disagreed. "We have to show you. We have to be dull, not intriguing. Piper, you can stay here with Grandmom. Get your homework done. Lena, you can do a quick wave and get inside. I'll talk to anyone who shows up. Heck, I can lecture. I'll suggest that maybe the boys did a little video editing to spice things up."

"You'd lie?" Piper squeaked.

"Damn straight," her father retorted. "Your mom doesn't need public scrutiny." Milo softened as he saw Piper's distressed face. "Mostly, it's re-direction. Middle school males get blamed for everything under the sun. If Mom is there, and I'm boring, things should quiet down fast. I hope."

"Why can't we just tell the truth?" Piper insisted. "Mom's weird. So what?"

Edna patted the empty kitchen chair on her side, inviting Piper to sit down. "Public scrutiny can be intense," she answered.

Lena leaned in. "Piper, I'm just a nervous sort. I wouldn't do well being on television." She shuddered. "I'm too shy."

Piper plopped down on the kitchen chair defiantly. "You should get over it. You made Dad take me for all my shots."

Lena winced. "I almost didn't let the midwife in when you were born, but Dad insisted. Sorry, honey."

"You're fast," Piper groused. She crossed her arms and glowered.

"I'm fast," her mother agreed.

"There's more," Edna said. She looked around the kitchen table and committed to her confession. "I've been growing feathers for a while now. I am concerned it may be a family trait."

"You have feathers?" Milo echoed.

Edna unhooked her overalls, slid down the front, unbuttoned her camp shirt and slipped the shirt off her shoulders. From shoulder to shoulder she displayed a fringe of grayish-brown feathers. The feathers nearest each shoulder were short and fluffy.

The feathers dangling from Edna's breastbone were several inches longer and had a distinct center rachis and an iridescent brown shimmer. There was a second and third row of bulging, dark dots that ranged down her chest to disappear beneath a practical white bra. The dots signaled more feathers were coming.

"Whoa," gasped Grace.

"I don't want you to be a bird," wailed Piper. "I want a dog!"

"The further one goes, the less one knows."

Lao-Tzu (Sixth century BCE. Or possibly later.)

Chapter Forty-one

Sunday morning, Eight thirty a.m., Edna's cabin, Kamilche Peninsula

GRACE COULDN'T HELP it. She laughed.

Edna smiled too. "I've been so nervous about telling," she said.

Milo, however, looked thunderous. "Life is not all about you, Piper. Your mother and your grandmother have some real challenges here. Forget the dog!"

Piper burst into tears. She leapt up from the table. "We had to move because of Mom. I can't run track. I can't have a dog. I can't do anything normal. I hate you!" She ran to one of the bedrooms, sobbing, and slammed the door.

Milo started after her, but Lena put a hand out to stop him. "She's right," Lena said quietly. "Give her time to process."

Milo sat down. He ran his hands over his face and sighed. "Grace, you are seeing the Anderson-Morton clan in all our glory."

Milo looked over at Edna's feathers. "Jesus, Edna. What the hell happened to you?"

Edna re-buttoned her shirt. "Stress. Age. I'm not sure. I do think it began years ago when I was pregnant with Lena. I noticed the big skin pores after the cow episode. Lena had these pores when she was born. And you've seen them on Piper."

Milo sighed. "She was such a perfect baby. Hardly ever cried."

Milo exhaled again. "I showed a remarkable lack of curiosity about my own child's biology."

Lena disagreed. "You taught yourself embryology and all sorts of things. When she started preschool, you read about animal territoriality."

Grace couldn't stop another nervous snort of laughter. "Sorry. My mother did the same thing. She said preschool was all about dominance behaviors."

Milo went to the sink and refilled the teakettle. He set the kettle on the stove and took down an extra cup. "Tea, Grace?" he asked.

"I'd love a cup," Grace accepted. "You have the same pores on your chest, Lena?"

Lena nodded, "And on my back. They were always there. I tried an astringent when I was fifteen but the pores didn't shrink."

Milo sliced banana bread and made tea. He made a graceful pirouette to set a plate in front of Edna, earning him a sweet smile from his wife. Piper could be heard wailing down the hall. There was a thud. Then there was silence.

Lena arched an eyebrow. Milo shrugged. "You're right again." Milo turned to Grace. "The storm just passed. Piper loves her books. She feels bad after she throws one."

They all heard the sound of the bedroom door opening.

"It's got to be some sort of phenotypic plasticity," Milo said calmly as he finished serving banana bread. "An environmental change makes for a physical response. I'll bet we all have the genetics for this, but, somehow, in Edna, it's been activated. "

"Like our hair going gray because we get older?" Lena asked.

"Maybe a little different," Milo mused. "We go gray because the pigment making cells in hair follicles start to die off. Men go bald because some of us produce too much dihydrotestosterone, which kills off hair follicles. In Edna's case, I don't think anything is dying or halting. I suspect something is starting."

"There's more," Edna continued, raising her voice. "You'll want to hear this." She dropped her voice to near normal as they all heard Piper shuffle down the hall.

Edna said, "I went in to see Dr. Patel."

Edna sipped her tea, and said, "While I was disrobed at the clinic, a visiting doctor came in. Dr. Band is an evil woman. I don't use that word lightly. I ran away from the appointment, but she knows about my feathers - and now Dr. Patel is dead. He was killed at his clinic on Friday."

"That's why you want a big dog," Grace interjected.

"Yes." Edna agreed. "I'd like a dog. I've been looking on the Internet, but I don't know how to search for dogs."

There was the sound of a loud, soupy sniff from down the hall. Edna said, "It's important to make a good choice."

"Grandmom. I can help you search on the computer."

Lena opened her arms wide. Piper came around the corner and into her mother's arms. "Sorry, Mom."

Lena kissed her daughter's forehead. "I'm sorry we're so awful."

"Come here, Short Stuff," Milo growled. Piper walked around the table to give her father a hug as well.

"Sorry, Dad."

"Points for drama, kid. Banana bread?"

Piper nodded. She looked up at her father. "There's a girl who has fingernails growing out all over her body. There's someone who looks like a werewolf. Hairy face and everything."

Grace jumped in. "I've seen those pictures. The fingernail lady may have had a reaction to a medication."

Lena pinked up a shade. "So maybe Mom and I are just this week's flash in the pan."

Milo disagreed. "This is headline biology. If you think Lena's gallop across the parking lot is getting Internet hits, then wait until someone films Edna. We'll have the world on our doorstep."

Edna turned a level look at Piper. "Sweetie, I've told you that my mother was hostile to the world. Do you understand that she may have had some reasons?"

Piper nodded. "We had a school assembly on it. Being different can mean you have a target on your chest." She added, "Dylan Kushner would go to town if he saw me sprouting feathers."

She pulled her pajama top away from her front and looked down at her chest. "Nothing there. No feathers, no boobs."

Lena smiled. "The bosom will come," she assured her daughter. "Eventually."

Milo pushed on, "I think we should stick with my plan. Lena and I'll go home. If there're any busybodies at our house, I'll talk to them on the lawn. Lena can go in through the garage and be out of sight. I'll be chatty and bore them to death. Piper, you stay here with Grandmom until we know what's up."

Piper looked mulish until Edna said, "Grace is here. We can see about getting a dog."

Piper's face lit up instantly. "I looked online yesterday. There's a no-kill shelter that is open on Sundays. I can print off the map." She crammed the rest of the banana bread into her mouth and ran down the hallway.

Milo watched his daughter go. "My world is totally rocked, and she's just thinking about getting a dog." Milo turned to Edna. "Are you sure you want the complications of a pet right now?"

Edna arched an eyebrow just as Lena had done.

He winced. "Okay. You know what you're doing."

Milo looked at Grace. "I'm not sure what we're seeing, but we're definitely seeing something. Is this getting too crazy for you?"

Grace set down her tea mug carefully. "Boss, I wouldn't miss this for the world. I don't know how I can help, but I will do everything I can."

She met his eyes steadily. "The safety of Edna, Lena and Piper come first. I get that. I'm honored that Edna feels she can share with me here. I won't let any of you down."

Milo gave a short nod of approval. "Thanks. I'd like to avoid public scrutiny until we can figure out the biology."

He groaned. "I'm not ready for lectures this week. This is going to take a ton of research to even begin to know what questions we should be asking. The timing on this stinks."

Edna reached out and patted his hand. "Life rarely comes with perfect timing. I know one thing," she said as she gathered up tea mugs. "Birds usually have feather lice. I don't seem to have any, so I am going to count my blessings."

"Perseverance is a great element of success. If you only knock long enough and loud enough at the gate, you are sure to wake up somebody."

Henry Wadsworth Longfellow
(Feb. 27, 1807 – March 24, 1882)

CHAPTER FORTY-TWO

Sunday morning, September 20, Ten a.m., Mason County Sheriff's office

RODGER RAPOSO WAS not happy. Kurt Otsoa was proving elusive. He wasn't at his listed address in Lakewood.

The company executive officer said Kurt drove a dark truck. Washington vehicle records were not coming up with any vehicle registered to a Kurt Otsoa, which could mean the truck was registered under a previous owner.

Raposo tried the police department in Otsoa's hometown. The dispatcher in Kankakee, Illinois didn't know a Kurt Otsoa.

He bit back a snarl as he clicked off his phone in frustration. He was scowling as Deputy MacRae walked by.

"MacRae!" Raposo barked. "Any bright thoughts on how I find out the dirt on our Kankakee lad on a Sunday morning?"

Don MacRae reversed and came into Raposo's cubicle. "PD poop out?"

"Got nothing. Fort Lewis MP's have come up with bupkis. We're not even sure what he drives. We do know he's on a week's leave."

Raposo threw his pencil down on his desk. "I'm thinking that an Army Ranger probably was a high school athlete, but I can't track down high school staff until tomorrow."

Deputy MacRae said, "Midwest time now is noon. Church should be ending. A church office lady knows a small town."

Raposo broke into a feral smile. "Damn, you're good. You headed out?"

"Yeah," MacRae said. "I'm supposed to meet the receptionist at the clinic. Then I've got some papers to serve. Sunday is good for that."

"I've done the same. I'll be here. Let me know if anything twitches your nose at the clinic."

"Sure." MacRae sauntered off, and Raposo started an Internet search on Kankakee churches. "It's the Midwest. Two dozen churches for a town of twenty thousand," he grumbled. Still, it was a thread to tug.

Parasola plicatilis

"He has the deed half done who has made a beginning."

Horace
(December 8, 65 BCE – November 27, 8 BCE)

Chapter Forty-three

Sunday morning, September 20,
Ten a.m., Near Ellison Loop

KURT STUDIED THE map. Theodora had used an online directory to find "M. and L. Anderson" on Ellison Loop. It was up to Kurt to verify.

Kurt turned the truck down a dirt road winding through the trees. He was across a wide cove from Ellison Loop. He wanted to study the terrain before driving by the Anderson home.

He was blessed. The long dirt driveway led to a cabin perched over the sound. Kurt parked in front of the cabin and waited. There was a heavy dusting of Douglas fir needles on the walk and an empty bird feeder near the window. When no one emerged to ask his business, he began a reconnaissance. All was quiet.

Kurt got his spotting scope out of the truck and made himself comfortable on the cabin deck. If anyone showed up, he'd plead a passion for bird watching.

He could see that Ellison Loop was a road at the very foot of Puget Sound with expensive waterfront homes on the outside of the loop and more modest homes on the inside of the loop. The neighborhood was thick with huckleberry bushes. Giant sword ferns grew under soaring Douglas firs

He had an unobstructed view across a waterfront neighbor's tennis court. The scope gave him a detailed look at the Anderson home on the cheap side of the road. The enhancement was clear enough to show a scratch in the garage door and a small hole in a window screen.

Kurt saw KIRI 3 and KOJA 9 news vans in the Anderson driveway. Two cameramen were shooting footage. Kurt watched as a reporter hammered on the door.

He looked up from the scope to see a green Subaru station wagon turning off the main road. Kurt followed it as it turned by the news vans. He returned to the scope to study the two occupants of the vehicle. The passenger had shoulder length white blonde hair. She wore sunglasses and a ball cap.

Kurt watched as the garage door swung up, and the station wagon pulled in. The two competing reporters and their cameramen legged it into the garage before the garage door could close. Kurt smiled. He enjoyed observing predators.

A tall man walked out of the garage, swinging his arm in a beckoning fashion. The reporters reluctantly left the garage as the cameramen remained inside the garage. A tableau ensued for several minutes as the tall man stood patiently in the front yard and the blonde remained in the car.

Kurt could respect the tactics employed by the Andersons. The reporters and cameramen were being denied an interview with the blonde, but they were clearly being given access to someone in the family.

Eventually, both reporters went for the half loaf offered. The cameramen emerged from the garage to focus on the man on the front lawn. The garage door came down. Kurt assumed the blonde was now moving into the house.

The interview went on for a good ten minutes. Kurt had ample opportunity to study the profile of Milo Anderson. *Six four, like me* Kurt mused. Dark brown hair, muscular physique. *Pretty boy. I could take him.* Kurt classified M. Anderson as an athlete but not a warrior.

There were handshakes happening now. The cameramen loaded equipment and the vans were pulled out of the driveway. Kurt stood up from his spotting scope. He was convinced he had the right Andersons.

Kurt packed the scope in its case and stored it in his truck. While he had the driver's seat pushed forward, he flicked through a half dozen magnetic signboards that were leaned on the floor well of the jump seat.

He flipped past "Good Gospel Property Management" and "Good Samaritan Home Repairs" with the Christian fish motif that he often employed. He pulled out one that read "Eco-Loving Lawn Care." Kurt smiled. The bunny was a nice touch. He set the sign onto the driver's side door.

Kurt used his fingernail to scrape off the Fort Lewis parking sticker. He had paid cash when he bought the truck. Now he didn't want anything connecting the truck to the military base.

Finally, he flipped through his cell phone pictures of Toyota Tundra truck license plates. He pulled a roll of navy blue duct tape from the glove box of the truck, and, using the scissors from his tool set, he clipped narrow strips. It took a few moments of careful work to alter 11 to an H and a 3 to an 8. Kurt studied the end result carefully. He couldn't afford to be sloppy in this detail. He repeatedly checked his cell phone picture before deciding that he had the look he needed.

The truck finished, Kurt moved to test the doors of the summer cabin. He needed a place to do his work. This might do.

"Nature alone is antique, and the oldest art is mushroom."

Thomas Carlyle
(December 4, 1795 – February 5, 1881)

Chapter Forty-Four

Sunday late morning, The Mushroom Farm

KEN ITO WAS reconnecting to the power of Mother Nature. He stood in awe of the rows and rows of sawdust-filled trays sprouting mushrooms. The trays lined both walls of the room like layered bunk beds for elves. More racks ran down the center of the unit, and the unit extended back as far as a double football field. His brain was not really grasping all that his eyes beheld. "Wow."

"Yes!" The farm manager was named Carys Kidwelly. The lovely Carys said, "We start with a superior mushroom that we wish to develop. We work to keep the exact genetics of that specimen going. The challenge is to increase the mycelial mass from a small beginning. It takes a great deal of mycelium to produce fruiting bodies, or what we call 'mushrooms.'

She added, "We begin with small amounts of the mycelium. We grow it on agar in a Petri dish. You can really see when molds or bacteria contaminate the sample."

She continued, "Once the Petri dish is covered with mycelial growth, we can transfer our mycelium over to sterilized sawdust or to grain in mason jars."

Carys waved a hand toward the rows of trays. "We can repeat that step, and then move the expanding mycelial systems to the trays."

"I shouldn't be surprised. Brewers go through tons of yeast. I just hadn't thought about growing fungus."

"We take a tremendous amount of care to make sure we don't have contamination," Carys said, "because that can quickly move us away from the line we want to produce."

Carys pointed to her rubber boots. "That's why I asked if you had showered today, and said to step into the disinfectant tray."

Carys had a fabulous dimple that kept appearing regularly. The dimple and the curly brunette mop of hair went well with her slender frame. Ken's eyes danced between the racks of mushroom culture and Carys' fine rump as she led the way to the exit.

"The structure of the room is important," she called over her shoulder. "Rectangular rooms work best. We also like a curving, high roof to bring the water back down to floor level where it can evaporate and re-humidify the room." Carys moved briskly between the towering racks of mushroom trays.

"I read your article on historical yeast," Carys turned to give a sparkling smile. "I loved that you brewed beer from the yeast found in an ancient amphora."

"You really read the article?" Ken was stunned. "You said on the phone that you knew my work - but you actually read *The Journal of Yeast Research*?"

"Absolutely. I have a subscription."

"I think I'm in love," Ken whispered.

"Excuse me?" Carys stopped and looked at him.

"Nothing. Today's turning out different than I expected." Ken felt a momentary pang of guilt that he hadn't yet called Edna Morton. That twinge was quickly forgotten when Carys said, "We all have lots of recipes for cooking with mushrooms. Can you stay for lunch?"

"Said the cunning Spider to the Fly, "Dear friend what can I do, to prove the warm affection I've always felt for you?"

in The Spider and the Fly by Mary Howitt
(March 12, 1799 – January 30, 1888).

CHAPTER FORTY-FIVE

Sunday, noon, Shelton Best Health Center

THEODORA WAS NOT pleased to see a lean deputy on the porch of the health clinic speaking with the receptionist. Theodora made a point to exit the car with a smile.

"Hi. I came to see if I could help." Theodora strode up the short walk to the entrance. She said, "I'm Dr. Band," to the deputy and a warm, "Hello, Kaylee," to the receptionist.

Kaylee didn't ooze warmth in return. She crossed her arms and gave a sullen "Hi."

I'll deal with your snotty little ass later, Theodora thought. Her mind added, *Where on God's Green Earth, did you get those cheap fishing lures you call earrings? You tasteless moronic twit.*

Outwardly, Theodora made herself present a sympathetic face. "I am so very sorry for your loss. How can I be of assistance to you and the clinic's patients?"

Kaylee thawed under the charm onslaught. "I'm getting the appointment book. You could help me call the patients."

Theodora's eyes narrowed as she thought, *Hell will freeze over first.* She sensed the deputy watching and regrouped. "Sure!" she said.

The deputy removed the crime scene tape from the door. Kaylee unlocked the door, and they stepped into the quiet clinic.

Kaylee's eyes began to overflow as they moved to the receptionist's workspace. She pulled out a tissue. "He was such a sweet man," she sobbed.

Whatever, Theodora thought. *Dry up already.*

Kaylee unlocked the receptionist's area and went in for a ledger. "This is what I need, Don," she said.

The deputy looked at the ledger. "It's a paper log?"

"I know. It works. We've been moving the medical files to the computer first. Dr. Patel was shopping for scheduling software." Kaylee's eyes filled with tears. "He wanted to get the right product. He was fussy that way."

Don MacRae patted Kaylee's shoulder. "It can hit you hard," he told her.

Theodora worked hard to keep her face compassionate.

MacRae asked, "Will you need the computer?"

Kaylee chewed her lower lip. "Not immediately. The most important thing is to cancel the people who have appointments next week."

"Good," the deputy said. "We need to notify the forensics techs before you turn on any machine."

Kaylee nodded and followed the deputy out, locking the receptionist's door behind her.

Theodora clenched her fists in an effort to keep from screaming. She needed to find Edna Morton. Theodora needed her complete medical history. She needed to get on the clinic computer.

"I'll leave you ladies to it," the deputy said. "Call me if you need anything."

Kaylee moved a hand in a desolate goodbye. Theodora graced the deputy with a radiant smile of appreciation that disappeared as soon as the clinic door shut behind him. She ditched the smile and came up with a worried look.

"Kaylee, there's one patient that concerns me. Her name is Edna Morton. She had a nasty wound."

Kaylee took a seat in the waiting room and opened the appointment ledger. "She's fine. Dr. Patel drove out to see her. I remember Dr. Patel saying he should update her file after we finished cleaning."

Theodora went still. She moistened her lips and said, "Let me update her file. Does the computer have a password?"

Kaylee looked up, alarmed. "We're not supposed to turn on the computer! Why don't you just make a note for the in box?"

"I'd rather review her file. It was important enough for Dr. Patel to drive out and see her, so we need to make sure we don't miss anything. I need her full record."

Kaylee shrugged. "We've been working on e-files for months now. Her old file might be in one of the filing racks in the break room. I guess I could let you in there."

Theodora made herself smile. "I'd feel so much better if I could take a look."

Kaylee sighed but moved to unlock the break room. Medical record racks lined the back wall beyond a small table and chairs. Theodora moved forward, pushing past Kaylee.

Kaylee rolled her eyes and went back to the waiting room to start her calls.

Theodora found the "M" section of the filing racks. She raced through the folders. There was no Morton. Theodora paused to work through the A's, looking for any Andersons. Three Andersons. An elderly couple and a man. No young woman.

Frustrated, she slammed the break room door, causing Kaylee to look up in surprise. Theodora stomped back to the waiting area, and stood, tapping her foot, as Kaylee finished a call.

"Kaylee, there's nothing. Nothing on Edna Morton at all."

Kaylee shrugged. "I don't think you need to worry. She'll call if she needs something." She gestured to the appointment book. "I could use some help here."

As fast as an adder, Theodora's hand snaked forward to grab Kaylee's dangling earring. She yanked hard on the earring, making Kaylee yelp in pain and surprise. "Listen, you worthless, brainless little piece of trash. I need Edna Morton. Where do I find her phone number?"

Tears of pain welled up in Kaylee's eyes. "I don't know," she gasped.

Theodora gave a quick tug on the earring. "Where does Edna Morton live?" she hissed.

"Stop this!" Kaylee wailed. "I don't know! I swear I don't know!"

Theodora ripped the earring through the lobe of Kaylee's ear. "Bitch!" Theodora screamed. Theodora flung the earring across the room as she marched to the clinic door. Theodora grabbed the doorknob, and then turned to sneer, "You're fired." Theodora opened the door, stomped through and slammed the door shut with a crash.

Dazed, bleeding and weeping, Kaylee made her way to the bathroom off the waiting room where she washed her ripped earlobe and used paper towels to make a pressure compress. Holding the paper towel wad against her ear, she made her way back to the waiting room.

She sank down on a chair and reached down, one-handed to rummage through her purse. She extracted a business card and thumbed the number, her hands trembling with shock.

"May I speak to Deputy MacRae?" Kaylee sniffed and tried to stabilize her breathing. "Will you please have him call Kaylee Kovacev? He has my number. It's important. Thanks."

Kaylee tapped off the call and took a deep breath. She needed to warn that dear old lady. Whatever Dr. Band wanted, it could not be good.

Kaylee focused on the appointment book lying on the floor. She picked it up, sniffing back tears. She produced a watery half smile and turned the pages back to a previous week. With still shaking hands Kaylee began tapping the number for Edna.

"Truth is confirmed by inspection..."

Tacitus (56 CE -117 CE)

Chapter Forty-six

Sunday, Noon. The Anderson Home, Ellison Loop

MILO HAD A dozen tabs open on his computer. He rapidly moved between web pages. He now knew that there were several types of feathers, each with its own function.

The simplest feather was a simple, straight filament. Then there were downy feathers that were fluffy and branched.

Next came feathers with a central stem or 'rachis.'

The most developed feathers had a central stem and interlocking barbs.

Milo closed his eyes and worked to visualize what he had seen on Edna's chest. Definitely some downy feathers. Those would be for insulation. There had been some straight, poky things and those would be the Stage One feathers. The long, brown feathers dangling from her sternum could have been contouring feathers. What he hadn't seen were any asymmetrical feathers. That made sense, in a biological way, because the asymmetrical feathers provided lift used for flight.

Count your blessings, Milo thought as he opened his eyes and returned them to the screen. Flight was off the table. Edna showed no signs of the enormously developed sternum required for flight. She'd have to have hollow bones, like birds, to become airborne, and a different respiratory system to support the oxygen demands of flying. There was an entire host of physiological barriers between feathers and flight.

"Finding anything?" asked Lena from the doorway.

"Tons. Too much. It's hard to know what is really important. My working theory is that we all have the DNA instructions to make feathers, and, in your mother, these instructions got activated."

"And my muscles?" Lena came into the tiny home office. She leaned over Milo's shoulder to look at feather display on the computer screen.

"Same thing. We probably all have the directions, but in everyone else those directions are packed away in unused DNA strands. Somehow, someway, the map is out in you. Every track coach in the country would like that map, so maybe it's not all bad."

Lena moved around Milo and sat down in her husband's lap. She lay her head on his shoulder and asked, "and Piper?"

Milo put his arms around her. He gave his wife a gentle squeeze. "Let's not borrow trouble. Let's stick with what we know and what we see. We'll work through each detail, and work, really hard, not to terrify ourselves with scary thoughts."

Milo nuzzled Lena's hair. "We could always go to work as a carnival exhibit. I could sell the tickets."

Lena sighed. "As long as we had a dog in the show, Piper wouldn't mind."

Milo ran his hand up his wife's back. As he neared her shoulders, he frowned at a rough texture he felt under her shirt. He made an effort to speak gently. "Lena, let's take a look at your back."

"Grief teaches the steadiest minds to waver."

Sophocles (496 BCE – 406 BCE)

Chapter Forty-seven

Sunday, Noon, Happy Paws No-Kill Shelter

"THESE PLACES CAN be depressing," warned Grace. She was in the passenger seat of Edna's faded Volvo. Piper sat in back.

Grace added, "The dogs will be barking. You'll want to take them all home."

Piper bounced and wiggled. "We could get a bunch of Dalmatians. Gran has room."

Grace snorted. "Dalmatians are coach dogs who need constant exercise – and remember, there's poop collections every morning."

Edna pulled into the shelter's gravel parking lot and parked near the entrance. Chain link kennel runs branched out behind a dingy stucco rectangle. A front door showed "Happy Paws" in a lime green arc. A long dead geranium poked out of a plastic pot near the door.

The clamor of barking dogs rolled and echoed around the station wagon as a cell phone started a heavy metal ring tone.

"Grandmom, that's your phone."

"It is?" Edna fumbled in her sweater pocket.

"Remember, you said I could put in something more modern."

"Oh dear. I mean, thank you." Edna sighed, and Grace burst out laughing. Edna finally produced the phone. "Hello?"

The car fell silent as Edna's face sobered. "Are you going to be alright?" There was a moment of reply. Edna spoke with worry on her face. "Are you sure?"

Grace and Piper listened in, hearing the tension in Edna's voice. Edna ended the call, saying, "I deeply appreciate the warning."

"Everything okay, Grandmom?"

"No." Edna's rested her hands on the steering wheel. "That was Kaylee – Dr. Patel's receptionist. She tells me that Dr. Band was looking for my medical records. When she objected to Dr. Band using the clinic computer, Dr. Band grabbed her earring and ripped it through the ear lobe."

"Ouch!" chorused Piper and Grace in unison.

"Ouch, indeed. Kaylee said she's reporting this to a Deputy MacRae, but she also wanted me to know that Dr. Band is hunting for me."

Edna's mouth firmed into a grim line. "We need a dog. A big one."

Grace opened the car door. "Let's look. There's someone coming."

A tank of a woman came out the shelter door. Dark hair roots clashed with the remains of a long-ago effort to be blonde. A key lanyard ran down between pendulous breasts, and a nametag over the left breast proclaimed the proprietor as "Bambii."

"Come for a dog?" she called.

"Yes!" Piper scrambled out of the car. "Do you have Golden Retrievers today? I'd like a movie star!"

Bambii laughed, showing bright teeth. "Got a dozen pit bulls with attitude problems. We're a no-kill shelter. We've got all sorts. Come on in. Maybe we have a pooch for you."

The small reception area echoed with barking and smelled

slightly of dog urine. As Bambii unlocked the door to the back, the dogs began barking hysterically.

Piper put her hands over her ears. Edna's hands went to her throat as they stepped out to the kennel runs. Grace, more accustomed to dogs, knew the cacophony was normal for dogs slowly losing their minds. Still, she was saddened to see some sixty kennel runs, each with an occupant. The closest dog was a huge brindled pit bull, who lunged at the fence, snapping.

"Down, Bruno!" Bambii shouted. "This way," she directed her guests.

Bambii led the trio down one lane of gravel, shouting tidbits about each dog that they passed. "Daisy bit a child, but the kid was tormenting her, so she ended up with us. Charlene there has cataracts. Mopsy got dropped off after he killed a cat. Sugar and Spice were chained to a stump outside a meth lab. They're not socialized at all."

The encyclopedia of misery went on.

They reached the end of the first row and crossed over to come back down the next walkway when Edna wobbled a bit. Grace put out a hand to steady her. "Edna, are you alright?"

Edna shook her head. "I need to sit down a moment."

Grace saw an old picnic table on a small rise behind the runs. "Can you make it up to the table?" she asked.

Edna nodded, but Grace kept her arm. They made their way to the picnic table with Piper anxiously trailing. Bambii puffed up the slope behind them.

"Take your time," Bambii advised, breathing heavily. "We're not going anywhere."

Edna sank down onto the table's bench. "Sorry, dears. That was just so horrible that I had a moment."

Piper sat down next to Edna, while Grace took a seat opposite. Bambii slid in beside Grace, tilting the picnic table precipitously.

Piper turned grieving eyes to Grace. "You're right. I want to take them all home."

Grace reached across the table to give her arm a pat. "I know. Let's agree that the aggressive dogs are out. Those take professional work and lots of it."

"The dog with cataracts might not be much of a guard dog," Edna mused.

"Oh, you'd be surprised," Bambii said. "Her nose and ears work fine."

"This may not be the time to address a lot of health issues," Grace said. "Family life is… active."

Edna frowned in concentration. "I don't think I could stand constant barking - and you're right. I couldn't handle an aggressive dog. I need a quiet sweetheart."

Piper agreed. "A romance novel hero. Big, handsome and quiet."

Grace stared at her. "Aren't you a little young for romance novels?"

"Nope. Grandmom has stacks of them behind her couch. They're fun."

"Bambii, do you have any suggestions?" Grace asked.

"Big, sweet, not too barky. Sounds like what you want is a bird dog." Bambii offered.

Grace met Edna's eyes, and they both shook with laughter. "Sorry," Edna finally gasped. "Family joke. A dog that likes birds. We've been learning about birds. Oh, dear me, too funny. Do you happen to have an old bird dog? A sweetheart? One that I could manage?"

Bambii studied Edna. "You home most of the time?"

"Yes. I go into the woods a great deal. The dog would go with me."

Bambii stood up, causing the picnic table to pop up an inch. "He's not truly a bird dog, but he might work. I keep him on the far side in a double run. I don't show him to everyone. It's a special case. Let's go take a look."

"A suspicious mind always looks on the black side of things."

Publilius Syrus (about the first century, BCE)

CHAPTER FORTY-EIGHT

Sunday, Noon, Mason County Sheriff's office

RODGER RAPOSO STRUCK gold calling at Saint Christopher's of Kankakee. Her name was Betsy Lancaster and she had been the church secretary for forty-five years. She knew Kurt Otsoa.

"I'm not surprised to hear from you, Officer." Betsy's booming voice could have directed a hockey camp. "The military straightens out some young men, but that one is rotten to the core. His so-called sister too."

"So-called?" Raposo leaned forward in his office chair. He pulled a fresh legal pad into writing position.

"Theodora. Theodora Band. She has a different last name. Jim and Josie Band adopted her. Poor Dears. There are times when good deeds go awry. They most certainly do."

"Is she a half-sister?"

"Who knows? They came as a pair from Romania. Muriel Otsoa saw some kiddies in an orphanage on TV, and she just had to have one. About drove her husband to death with all this 'do the right thing' twaddle. Funny how we Christian folks can get when we want something. We're so into asking and receiving that we don't always think about what we're asking."

Betsy plowed on, "They mail-ordered a kid through a Chicago adoption agency. They could have gotten one here! This must have been, oh, 1991 or so. Muriel gets a phone call saying that the company has a two-for-one special, and can she take another child? Well, John Otsoa said 'no way', but Muriel never heard a 'No' in her life, so she talked Jim and Josie Band into taking the little girl. Never a moment's peace then, God rest their souls."

Raposo knew when he was on a full vein. His computer calendar chirped, but he ignored it to tell Betsy, "Anything more you can tell me would be deeply appreciated by my department."

"I am glad to assist our officers of the law," Betsy leapt in with barely a pause. She boomed on. "Those kids showed up one November. Skinniest kids you ever saw. Everyone was feeling so sorry for them and their rough start."

Betsy's voice dropped a musical third as she added, "Real quick it became clear to everyone that those two were sick. Sick in the head. Cats started disappearing. A puppy went missing from Tad Greenlaw's litter, and then it was found, in pieces, behind the Dairy Queen. This sort of thing went on for years."

She added, "Those two would always be around when something awful happened, with these big, innocent eyes. Their mothers swore they were angels, but I'm swearing that they were little devils. The cat killings only stopped when those two left town."

"Were the families members of your church?" Rodger asked.

"No!" Betsy boomed. "The Otsoas and the Bands were Methodist. But everyone in town knew those kids. Theodora turned into the prettiest little thing. Very athletic. She seduced anything in pants from the time she was eleven. She went to medical school."

"And Kurt?" Raposo persisted.

"Army Ranger. Every time I saw one of those news reports about that torturing at Abu Ghraib, why I just wondered if Kurt Otsoa was there. He would like that sort of thing. He set fires too."

"So are Kurt's parents still in Kankakee?"

Betsy made a tsking sound. "Muriel's brain-dead in a nursing home. The brakes failed on their motor home. Her husband, John, was killed."

"And the Bands?"

"Dead of a fire from a gas leak in their lake house. And you know what?"

"What?"

"I do believe Josie Band was finally starting to wake up about the nightmare that she called her daughter. The sheriff's secretary, Eileen, told me that Josie ordered a surveillance camera on-line the week before she died."

Rodger Raposo listened, but he had what he needed. Otsoa was a person of interest in Patel's killing. Training and mindset were there.

After he finished hearing Betsy, a call came in from the forensics lab.

"We found a print on the eggshells collected by Deputy MacRae," the tech reported. "Kurt Otsoa."

"Thanks." Raposo clicked off his phone and sat thinking. He typed in the number for Deputy MacRae. MacRae was in his patrol car and answered.

"Good work on the eggshells," Rodger told him. "They found a print of Otsoa's. I just spoke to a church secretary in Kankakee. Otsoa has an ugly history."

"What's the connection to Patel?" MacRae drawled.

"Don't know. I'll put out an APB on Otsoa. We need to get him picked up." Rodger started to tell MacRae about Otsoa's sister, when his computer chirped again. He looked down and saw the reminder. Damn. He was supposed to be meeting Brooke at her parents for a late lunch.

"Ah. MacRae, I'll get back to you." Raposo clicked off the phone. He tapped a text message to Brooke as he stood to leave.

MacRae waited a moment. There was nothing more from Detective Raposo. There was, however, a blue Camaro hurling past at ninety miles an hour. MacRae turned on his lights and pulled out onto the road.

"Speak to the earth and it shall teach thee."

Job 12:8

CHAPTER FORTY-NINE

Sunday, 12:30 p.m. The Mushroom Farm

KEN ENJOYED WATCHING Carys' slender fingers as she tore mushrooms and slid them into a skillet for sautéing. The break room kitchen was hospital clean and hospital white. Ken found Carys added all the color he could desire.

"Heat activates and lets the nutrients of the mushroom become available," Carys lectured. "Eating raw mushrooms gets you nada, nutrition wise. We get better taste out of shitakes when they are torn instead of sliced. For this recipe I'm using shitakes grown here in our buildings."

Ken knew he'd muff small talk. He went with, "How many species do you grow?"

Carys' marvelous dimple appeared. "A dozen species in production. More in testing." She stirred the cooking mushrooms. "There are constant challenges. Our outdoor beds can end up sprouting wild mushroom species, and our indoor racks are susceptible to molds."

“It looked like some of the outdoor beds were being dug up. Contamination there?”

“Not necessarily. We do have to replace the bed substrate regularly. We inoculate the fresh bed with plugs of mycelium called ‘spawn.’ The details are extremely important. You have to have the substrate be the right sort of wood chips, and they have to be the right size.”

Carys stirred the mushrooms as she said, “The spawn inoculation rate has to be right. We wet down the beds and then they have to be monitored so they continue to have the right amount of shade and water. When we get it right, voila! Tons of mushrooms and money in the bank!”

Carys beamed, showing a dimple on each side of her lovely face. “And that spent substrate gets bagged and sold as mushroom compost. We’re extremely eco-friendly.” She said, “The mycelium grows all through the bed. It has to keep expanding. The expression we use is *keep the mycelium running*. When the mycelium reaches the limits of its sustainable habitat, it has a die back and you get less fruiting bodies. The mycelium is a bit like a shark – it has to keep going.”

The frying shitakes smelled earthy and wholesome. Ken’s mouth began to water as Carys added chopped shallots and broth. “Grow any truffles?” he asked.

Carys rolled her eyes. Truffles! Everyone wants truffles!”

Sensing he had put a foot wrong, Ken put up his hands in mock surrender. “Ignorant here. Educate me.”

“Truffles are great, don’t get me wrong. They’re also very rare and expensive, so when everyone thinks ‘mushroom farm’ then they think ‘must farm truffles for lots of dough.’ But truffles are finicky. For any mushroom growth, there has to be the right substrate, the right inoculation, the right moisture and the right temperature.”

Carys picked up a bread knife and began slicing into a long, crusty baguette. "We've tried truffles. We failed repeatedly."

Carys wagged the knife. "I don't like to fail! Sometimes you have to say that Mother Nature has some tricks that we can't match. For truffles you have to have a site free of competition. No ectomycorrhizal trees, like Douglas fir, on the site. You put in your inoculated nut or oak trees and hope for mild winters. It's too hard to do here, so we just focus on less sexy fungus."

Ken worked to keep a straight face. He had never thought of the lumpy truffle as sexy.

Carys pulled out soup bowls. "My favorite project here is the turkey tails. They are beautiful mushrooms and they save lives." She layered the baguette slices along the bottom of the two bowls and spooned mushroom soup over the bread. "Here," she said, passing a bowl to Ken. "Tell me what you think."

"I want to see what a beautiful mushroom looks like." Ken picked up a spoon off the counter. "After I eat this fabulous lunch."

Carys beamed. "*Trametes versicolor* really is a colorful mushroom. I'd be glad to show you some of our products too. The turkey tail mycelium supports human immune systems and is helpful in treating some cancers."

She frowned, erasing the marvelous dimples. "Not all cancers respond. It depends on which genetic switches are involved."

Ken was half way to swallowing as she spoke. He began to cough.

"Soup's fine," he finally croaked. "I should make a phone call after lunch." He coughed some more, and rasped, "Do you happen to know a lady called Mushroom Edna?"

"What mask was there, what a disguise!"

John Milton
(December 9, 1608 – November 8, 1674)

CHAPTER FIFTY

Sunday, One p.m., A Summer Cabin near Ellison Loop

"AWESOME FIND, BRO! This is excellent." Theodora whirled in a circle around the generous living room of the summer cabin that faced the mudflats of Oyster Bay.

"The key was over the door sill," Kurt told her. "The power is on, we even have cable TV."

"Who owns this place?"

"A Dr. and Mrs. Haddad, who kindly marked the September calendar page with notes on their busy little lives. The Haddads, dear sister, are traveling this week and in New York for a wedding next week." Kurt leaned against the kitchen counter and gave his wolfish grin. "The freezer has salmon and steaks and there's a wine bar." He paused and winked, "and a very excellent kitchen knife collection."

Theodora grinned. "Where are the Andersons?"

"I'll show you. I set up a spotting scope." Kurt unhooked the screen door and stepped out onto a long porch. "We've even got deck chairs."

Kurt moved to the spotting scope. "They're across the bay. See that house with the tennis court? The Andersons are in the little house across the road from the court."

Theodora studied the landscape. "Their house is teeny. That waterfront home must be four thousand square feet. Did the Andersons get the gardener's squat?"

Kurt shrugged. "That's a converted summer cabin. If you look around the bay, you see a mix of small old with big new. Look at that understory growth. I could take a whole Ranger unit through that neighborhood and no one would know."

"You're sure that's the right house?"

"Bright haired blonde, TV crews. It's her."

Theodora rested her hands on the deck railing, eyes narrowed as she thought through her next steps. "I'm not sure which way to play this," she said. "I'd like to get to Edna and do a legitimate blood sample. If I can get lined up as her doctor, I can get to the daughter through her. That would make it a long running play." She tilted her head towards her brother. "What about you?"

Kurt shrugged. "I won't go back to Fort Lewis. My next rotation is stateside, and that's dull. Besides, the heat's too close. I'm thinking I'll stick around here for as long as we're having a good time, then grab a boat and sail to Canada."

His eyes lit up. "Maybe crew on a luxury boat. Be interesting to be out at sea where you don't have to worry about anyone hearing some screaming."

Theodora trilled an impressed whistle. "You are so inventive!"

She stroked Kurt's arm. "Will you do Kaylee for me?" Theodora tilted her head back to look up at him. "I lost my temper. Again. Now she's really a loose end."

Kurt pulled her into a hug. "People are such morons. It's no wonder they upset you. Sure, I'll take care of it. You had her in mind for me, so why not? I was thinking I'd deliver some flowers."

Theodora's eyes sparkled. "How charming. I'll get my laptop and find an address for her."

Kurt looked out over Oyster Bay. "I need a couple different looks – I'll look for some gardening tools out back. But it'd be good to have a basketball and a team shirt."

"What's your thinking?"

"That I can walk around that neighborhood working as a landscaper or bouncing a ball like I'm on my way to a practice. No one will think anything of it."

"Smart! I've got to pick up a few things in town tomorrow. I can get the sports stuff."

"Great. I'll track down a bionic ear. It's a listening device. They sell them at bird food stores and home security places. But if you're at a box store, can you get some hair dye?" Kurt's eyes narrowed as he thought. "Best to hide in plain sight. Get me that wine red color. I'll dazzle."

"We should grill." Theodora leaned on the deck railing and gazed out over the water. "Grilling is such a nice way to celebrate."

"Hope is the thing with feathers that perches in the soul."

Emily Dickinson
(December 10, 1830 – May 15, 1886)

CHAPTER FIFTY-ONE

Sunday, One p.m., The Anderson home, Ellison Loop

LENA SAT IN the bedroom closet with her back against the wall. She wrapped her arms around her knees and sniffed a nose running from tears. "I am such a freak."

Milo came into the bedroom bearing a cup of hot chocolate. He knelt down and handed the mug to his wife. "That's Piper's line. She gets to have it because she's an adolescent."

Lena gave a watery laugh. "Thanks for the sympathy. Tell me again what I've got."

"I'm seeing three lines of enlarged pores with filaments protruding. That's your back. You've seen your front, it's got just the double row."

Lena took a slurp of cocoa. "The feather tips look grimy. Mom's feathers are brown. Do you think mine are going to go darker?"

"I think we're seeing a bit of an outer layer of keratin that may slough off as the feathers emerge and uncoil. Judging from the base, yours may be lighter. "

"Ugh. Dingy blonde? Guess I'll have to wear lipstick so I don't fade into the wallpaper."

Milo patted her knee. "That's the spirit. How long are you going to sit in the closet?"

Lena sighed. "Until my feathers fall off? Do you suppose I could shave them away?"

"I'd rather you didn't. Let's work to figure out the biology. I am finding some fascinating feather archeology. A lot of dinosaurs had feathers. The speculation is that the feathers were initially for warmth."

"I'll trim the family budget by not needing sweaters."

"Maybe. The gene that's involved in feather construction is the famous Sonic Hedgehog gene. It's found in most animals – even hookworms. It's a signaling gene that says 'stop', or 'go', or 'go slowly.'

Milo stroked Lena's arm. "Sonic hedgehog genes are important in embryonic development, and, sometimes they activate a cancer in an adult. That terrifies me more than a little, because we don't know what else is going on besides the feathers. I'm thinking we need to have you looked at by a doctor."

Lena said, "Look what happened to Dr. Patel when Mom got seen."

"We have no idea what was going on with Dr. Patel."

"When do I start flying around the room?"

Milo snorted. "That question I can answer. You don't. You'd need hollow bones, a different respiratory system, different musculature…" his voice trailed off.

"I have different muscles."

"Shit. I'm slow. So are the muscle switches and the feather switches connected? Why doesn't Edna have muscle changes?" Milo rocked back on his heels. "My instinct is the two developments are connected. But how?" He looked over at his pale wife and quickly added, "It doesn't matter. Flight is way, way, way down the road."

"That's good." Lena sniffed. "Because we both know I'm afraid of heights."

"The only cure for grief is action."

George Henry Lewes
(April 18, 1817 – November 28, 1878)

CHAPTER FIFTY-TWO

Sunday One p.m., Happy Paws No-Kill Shelter

"IS HE SICK?" Piper studied the large, dark blob in the far corner of the kennel run.

"Depressed," offered Grace. "Dogs can be depressed, just like people."

"You got it," Bambii agreed. "This guy is a sad case. Fourth of July there was a mom with a kid in a stroller. They got hit in a crosswalk. This is their dog."

Edna swayed slightly. She steadied herself by putting a hand onto the chain link fence. "I remember hearing about that. How awful."

"The family didn't keep the dog?" Piper was aghast.

"The husband couldn't handle everything. There is a special needs child at home. The husband is adamant that the dog needs a country life. I think he's avoiding a family member who wants the dog. Sometimes there's a gut feeling that a stranger is a better bet than a family member with a short attention span." Bambii's assessment made a shrewd sense.

She said, "We've had him about eight weeks. He needs to start eating more or he'll be in trouble."

"May we have him out of the run?" Grace asked.

Bambii opened the run with a leash in hand. "Come on, big boy. You got visitors."

The big dog lay still, with his head on his paws, staring out at the gate as Bambii knelt down, snapped the leash on, and gave an authoritative tug. Slowly, the giant dog came to his feet.

"My goodness," Edna squeaked. "He's huge."

"Newfoundland. He's awfully skinny. I think he's down to about 110 pounds. He hardly eats for me."

The big dog tottered forward. Grace touched Piper's arm. "Bend down and put your hands on your knees, like this. It's called a 'play-bow.' It signals you're ready to play with him."

Piper bent over and cooed, "Here, doggy. Here doggy." As the giant dog came to the kennel run gate, he made eye contact with Piper. "Hi, Gorgeous," she chirped. "Want to live with us?"

The big dog hesitated, and then gave a slow, tentative wave of his tail.

"Go ahead and pet him," Bambii ordered.

Piper started with a tentative pat, but soon was chest to chest with the dog, delivering an enthusiastic massage. The dog sighed and put his massive head down on Piper's shoulder. Piper hugged him and said, "Gran, he's just a great big teddy bear!"

Grace looked up to see tears streaming down Edna's face.

"We'll take him," Edna managed.

Bambii beamed. "This is why I do this job. Some days are good days." She handed the leash to Grace, and said, "We might get him to eat now. I'll get a bowl of kibble."

Edna sniffed and wiped her face. "Can we get him out of that awful jail?" she whispered.

"Come on, Piper. Let's try a little walk." Grace doubled the leash in her hand, ready for a strong pull, but the big dog ambled out quietly. "Looks like you have a winner, Edna. Someone has spent time training this guy."

Piper and Grace walked the dog over to a grassy area, where the dog urinated with obvious relief. "Wow," Piper said, "How could he hold that much?"

"Most dogs don't like to potty in a kennel run," Grace told her. "It's like going to the bathroom in your living room. You'd only do that if you had no other choice."

Bambii returned with a bowl of kibble. She set it down, and the big dog launched into his meal. Bambii smiled. "That's good to see."

"Can we give him seconds?" Piper asked.

"Not until this evening. You'll want to pick up some good quality dog food. Don't shut him in the car while you shop. Any dog can overheat and these giant breeds overheat even faster."

"Physics," Piper agreed. "Large bodies conserve heat."

Grace laughed. "Where did you learn about thermodynamics?"

"Discovery channel."

Edna gave the dog a smoothing pat. "His coat feels just dreadful. What can we do about that?"

"Good nutrition," Bambii instructed. "We have to feed cheap stuff. A dog shampoo will help too - but Newfies have a rough coat."

Bambii bent over to give the dog a scratching between his front legs. "This guy is seven years old. That's getting old for a giant breed. He may age rapidly. You're looking at one to five years with this one."

Piper looked up at her grandmother. "We can still have him, right?"

Edna nodded. "We'll make the most of what time we've got."

Piper threw her arms around the dog and hugged him close. "We can call him Teddy Bear."

Grace noted the card on the kennel run gate. “His name is Drew!” she called.

“Actually,” said Bambii, “There’s an ‘L” missing. His name is ‘Drewl’.”

A large goober dripped down on Piper’s shoe.

"Life is really simple, but we insist on making it complicated."

Confucious (550 BCE – 479 BCE)

CHAPTER FIFTY-THREE

Sunday, One p.m., Island Reserve

DR. ESTHER MOSSLER stepped out of the canoe onto a gravel shore. She felt as she did as a child and had first come to this Puget Sound island. The soaring firs and cedars with the thick underbrush of salal and ferns made city life seem far away and foreign.

This was the natural world, and she was one with it. Her ancestors had fished and collected oysters here for thousands of years. Now she was here to continue the family story. Esther took a deep breath of the air, heavy with tidal smells. The air was a complex perfume of local life. It smelled sweet and dear to her.

The traffic signs of nature were everywhere. A tiny handprint in the fine gravel signaled that a raccoon fished here. An iridescent blue feather on a rock said a Steller's jay lived nearby.

Her brother, Raymond, stepped out of the canoe and lifted the canoe bow up onto the gravel. He secured the canoe's prow rope to a weathered log before lifting out a daypack. As he shouldered the pack, he watched his sister stop and just breathe.

Raymond smiled. "Nice, eh?"

"You have no idea."

The siblings walked along the gravel beach to a driftwood log. Silently they each took a seat, facing the water. Raymond opened the daypack and took out a battered metal thermos and two metal mugs. He poured two coffees and handed one to Esther. She sipped the steaming coffee and watched the water. They sat for a long time.

"What's she like?" Raymond asked. "Our Grace?"

"Smart. Really smart. A kind and decent heart too." Esther paused, then added, "but not confident. She doesn't know her own value."

"Ah," said Raymond. "Like you at that age."

Esther chuckled. "Touché."

They sat a while longer, then Esther asked, "Would you like to see Rob?"

"Yes."

"Things should have been healed years ago."

Raymond gave a nearly imperceptible nod. "Do you remember when you got the letter to go to college? Your first college?"

"To Dartmouth? Of course. I couldn't believe it was real."

"That next morning, after the letter, we were eating breakfast. You kept asking Mom and Dad if it was real or a joke. And they didn't say anything. Remember?"

Esther shrugged. "I think they were letting me make up my own mind."

Raymond shook his head. "I think they didn't know what to say. They were embarrassed that they did not know. So they said nothing."

Esther blinked. "I hadn't thought of that."

"You had to fill out a postcard to say what freshmen activity you wanted."

"Freshmen trips. I'm surprised you remember that!"

Raymond produced another quiet smile. "Little brothers watch everything." He emptied the dregs of his coffee cup out onto the gravel. "You had the scholarship for school, but the freshman trip was extra. Mom and Dad didn't know how to value that. No context. So they were quiet." He looked out over the water. "Then Uncle came in."

Esther laughed. "I'll never forget that. I swear I had no idea he had money. Ever."

Raymond chuckled. "Normally he didn't. But he had just sold that carving. I remember him picking up the postcard. Then he asked you why you should go east to hike and canoe."

"And I said it wasn't the hiking or canoeing," Esther recalled. "It was making friends at the new place."

"Then he says, 'Having a good tribe is worth an investment,' and he takes that roll of money out of his overalls. Fifteen hundred dollars!"

"It paid for the trip and my books. It was a wonderful gift." Esther asked, "What made you think of all that?"

"Dad and Mom didn't know how to reach out to Rob either. They didn't know what to say, so they said nothing. Rob is the same. When he doesn't know what to say, he says nothing. Twenty-six years have passed. Maybe that's enough of saying nothing."

"What do you want to do?"

Raymond stood up and stretched. "Maybe you and I, together, can be the next Uncle. We let Grace know this tribe is worth having - and we get Rob a plane ticket to come see us."

"I must be a mushroom. They keep me in the dark and feed me bullshit."

American office poster.

CHAPTER FIFTY-FOUR

Sunday, One p.m., Seattle, WA Channel 17 KBRN News Station

THE KBRN PRODUCER'S office was cold, cluttered and grimy.

"How the hell did we miss this?" The news producer slammed a hand down on her desk. "A beautiful woman saves a little boy's life. There's video of it, going viral, and we miss it."

Her assistant, Soo Min, waited for instructions. Soo Min wasn't about to say *We miss stories all the time*, even as the thought did a screen crawl through her mind.

In her mind, "Blonde saves Boy" was on the 'medium to filler' end of the news spectrum. Soo Min took a peek at her boss. This story wasn't big news in her boss's mind either.

It's getting scooped that hurts, Soo Min thought. If there was a terrific story of a local rescue, they wanted it.

"There's the video clip," the producer mused. "KIRI and KOJA didn't broadcast an interview with the kid's parents, so that's an obvious step for us. KIRI and KOJA also only got the blonde's husband. They didn't get the blonde. Let's get her on the air for six o'clock."

Soo Min swung into action. "Dave's up north, Maria's downtown, covering the protests."

"Which protests, again?" The producer groaned. "Never mind. Doesn't matter. It's Seattle, so someone is protesting something. And Aida is sick. We need an Olympia stringer. Give Savio and Vico a call."

"The Carlevaros? Are we still using them?"

"They are aggressive, I'll give you that. But Savio is good in front of camera, and charming with the ladies. Vico knows how to catch his brother's angles. Vico. What a hunk."

Soo Min nodded, trying not to let on that she, too, had a weakness for a certain cameraman. "Savio and Vico to cover the rescuing blonde. Anything else?"

"Check in with Maria. See if she can come up with a new angle on the protest. It'd be good to show something more than screamers and signs." The producer looked up at the wall clock. "Let's talk again in twenty. Maybe we can give Weather an extra thirty."

Soo Min knew "twenty" meant twenty minutes and "thirty" meant thirty seconds broadcast time. If she was going to research the blonde, contact the Carlevaro brothers, and call Maria within twenty minutes, she needed to move.

"On it!" she said.

"If you wish to eat a mushroom, you cannot consider what the mushroom fed on."

Igbo Proverb (Nigeria)

Chapter Fifty-five

Sunday, One p.m. The Mushroom Farm

LUNCH AT THE Mushroom Farm had skittered to a halt.

"Of course I know Edna!" Carys beamed, showing double dimples. "She's marvelous!"

Ken set down his soup spoon. "Tell me about her. Everything. It may be important."

Carys blinked in surprise, and said, "I think of her as a 'Wise Woman of the Woods.' You find such women globally. They are gatherers, healers and nurturers. They begin gathering food and medicines from nature when they are just toddlers. By the time they are grandmothers, they have decades of experience in micro-climates. They know when and where to find certain plants, animals and fungi. They can pull off health cures that can be astonishing. It's not magic, but they have been called witches by some."

"How old is Edna?"

"Eighties. She looks great."

"Edna knows mushrooms. As much as you do?"

Carys set down her baguette slice before answering. "Edna's knowledge base is different than mine. I'm in production. We work to have consistency in our products. We need to get the same outcome as we go."

Carys continued, "Edna and women like her know the woods. The color, the texture, the substrate – even the smell of a mushroom can tell her a great deal about what's happening in that microclimate."

"For example, mushrooms are heavy metal accumulators. It's a tough gig and you'd want to experiment with a robust specimen. We're experimenting with some bio-remediation of oil-contaminated soils ourselves. Mushrooms secrete cellulases and lignin peroxidases."

"Got it." Ken shot back. "That's what can break down the cellulose of fallen trees, but those enzymes can also break down petroleum products and toxins."

Carys face lit up with delight. "Yes! The trick is to get the right sort of mycelium running through the substrate, and that's not always easy. Another species can get a start first. It can be insects, molds or bacteria. If something else gets the jump, then you may never get your mycelium going strong."

Carys earnestly added, "Someone like Edna knows how to find a good candidate. She knows where to look. When she finds a cluster, she'll examine each specimen and choose the particular fruiting body or mycelium section that suits her needs."

She added, "It's part knowledge, part experience, and part intuition. She's not trying to produce great, consistent quantities, but she's an amazing resource when we want to try something new – which we do, constantly."

Carys smiled the double dimple smile again. "We have Halloween next month and that's when I love to see Edna in action. Teens show up at the Mycology Society wanting to know where they can find psychoactive mushrooms for Halloween partying. Edna's awesome."

Carys said, "She'll sit down and show *Psilocybe stuntzii*, which is definitely psycho-active, and then she'll set out the similar looking *Galerina marginata,* which is toxic as hell. Edna's not judgmental. She starts talking about seeing the mushroom as part of the ecology – where you found it, what was around it, what it looks like, what's in the air – the list goes on and on. She talks about location, location, and location. She's like a real estate agent for fungus. The kids get hooked on the ecology and get more careful about their experiments. Good thing."

"Ever hear a story about one of her recipes saving some cows?"

Carys immediately sobered. "1983, right? Algal poisoning?"

"You do know!" Ken split between incredulity and relief.

"It's a bizarre story. I didn't hear it from Edna. In fact, I was told that she wouldn't want to talk about it. One of the older Mycological Society members told me about it."

Carys sighed. "In this business, you hear lots of odd things. We have so much traditional lore. We're way behind in examining mushrooms scientifically, so I work to keep an open mind. Sometimes lab research strongly supports the historical usage, and sometimes it doesn't."

Carys tucked a dark ringlet behind one ear. "Edna's rescue remedy. It was supposed to be respiratory relief oil. The sort of thing that you use a drop at a time. Supposedly she slathered it like mad on these poisoned cows. They kept breathing, but they weren't ever quite the same. The milk was bad."

Carys looked away, through the window. Ken felt there was more.

Ken reached out and took Carys' hand. "I hope you'll tell me everything you heard. It could be important."

Carys blew out a big breath. "The old biddy who was filling

my ears added some vicious gossip." Carys dark eyebrows winged together in outrage. "Edna's a bit odd. Her daughter is odd too. Who cares?"

"What was the gossip?"

"Ms. Ugly Yapper said Edna's respiratory cream was teratogenic."

"Edna was pregnant at the time of the cow incident?"

Carys shrugged. "So the story goes."

"How did this manifest in the daughter? Does she have disabilities?"

Carys produced a small dimple. "She's a blonde goddess. Tall and slim. She has a nervous temperament. Shy as a deer."

"Mentally ill?"

"No, not that." Carys frowned in concentration. "She just seems… flighty."

Psilocybe stuntzii

"Truth and roses have thorns about them."

Henry David Thoreau
(July 12, 1817 – May 6, 1862)

CHAPTER FIFTY-SIX

Sunday, Two p.m., The Kovacev Home, Olympia

KAYLEE PULLED A suitcase out from her closet and threw it on her bed. She wiped her nose. It kept running. Tears of rage and pain threatened to overflow yet again. She was glad that her parents were out of town. They would be horrified to see her torn ear.

Kaylee mopped up her streaming nose with a tissue and thought about her next step. She was supposed to care for the cat while Dr. and Mrs. Kovacev attended a tennis competition in Portland.

"Fuck Felix," Kaylee sniffed. She'd pile up some kibble, rake out the litter box and call it good. She'd head up to Seattle for a few days. Her parents weren't due back until Friday night. If she came back Thursday no one would know she'd skipped out. Felix would still be his cantankerous self on Friday no matter where Kaylee spent the week.

She threw a handful of colorful panties and bras into the suitcase. She stopped for another tissue. The box was empty.

Kaylee swiped her hand under her nose. Her ear hurt. Dad had some oxycodone in the family safe. It was for emergency purposes. Damn it, this was an emergency.

She'd just take a few tablets. If she took one tablet now and split the others, she should be able to get through the next couple of days. When Dad saw her ear, he'd understand.

Kaylee went to her parent's bedroom. She took down her graduation photo that hid the wall safe. She really needed to talk her father into a better combination. Using her birth date for a safe hidden behind her picture wasn't the brightest security choice. She keyed in the numbers, opened the door and peered in the metal cave. Medicines were in the back.

Kaylee pulled out a pile of envelopes and set them on her parents' bed. She pulled out two small, heavy boxes and set them on the bed as well. Finally she could see the medicine box.

The trill of the doorbell made her jump. Kaylee slammed the wall safe shut and scuttled out of the bedroom. "Coming!" she yelled.

Kaylee paused at the front door to peer out the sidelight window. A man stood holding a bouquet of red and pink roses. He had a cap on that said "Love-a-Dove Floral".

She didn't hesitate. She pulled the door open and crowed, "Are those for me?"

"Yes, Ma'am. But the bottom is awful wet. Do you have a paper towel?" Kurt sounded completely apologetic as he stepped up to the doorway. Drops slipped between his fingers from the water he had pooled into his gloved palm.

"Just a sec." Kaylee did as Kurt had anticipated. She left the door open and dashed to the kitchen to fetch toweling. Kurt stepped into the foyer, allowing more water to drip from his palm onto the tiles of the entryway.

“I’m so sorry, Ma’am.” He moaned as Kaylee returned.

“No problem.” Kaylee bent down to drop a paper towel square. Kurt slammed the door shut. He dropped the roses, grabbed Kaylee and flung her up against the wall. Her head snapped back and whapped the wall with a satisfying crack.

Kurt lunged in and throttled her with his right hand. Kaylee’s dazed eyes went wide with terror. Kurt latched onto her breast with his left hand. “We’re going to get to know each other.” Kurt squeezed her breast and twisted the nipple. “You’re not going to scream. You scream, you die. Get that?”

Kaylee nodded. Kurt smiled. “I’m very sporting,” he whispered. “Let the games begin.”

"Don't judge a book by its cover."

Your Parents.

CHAPTER FIFTY-SEVEN

Sunday, Two p.m., The Kovacev Home

"THERE'S MONEY," KAYLEE croaked. "You can have it." She had always thought that she would fight to get away from an attacker, but this monster had a vise grip on her neck. She struggled to breathe.

"Oh, yeah?" Kurt squeezed her neck and enjoyed having her hands come up to grab his arm. "Shh," he crooned as she gasped. He marginally relaxed his hold. "Where's the money?"

"Bedroom. In my parents' bedroom."

"Is there a safe?"

Kaylee gave a minute nod. Her father had coached her on this. Everything in the safe was replaceable. She started to cough.

"You know the combination?"

Kaylee cleared her throat. "Yes. Please. I need my inhaler."

Kurt studied her. Her lips were turning blue. Her breath was rapid. He could hear a rattle and wheeze at the end of each breath.

Kaylee coughed again, then began to claw at his hand. She twisted and gasped.

"Combination," he demanded.

"0515" Kaylee wheezed. "My birthday." Her lips were changing to a purplish hue. "Please," she whispered.

Kurt laughed.

Kaylee erupted in a flurry of motion. She flailed against Kurt's arm and kicked at his shins. Kurt kept her pinned against the wall, his elbow and forearm digging into her sternum, not squeezing but not giving ground.

Kaylee scratched at his arms and kicked harder. Kurt held firm, laughing at her as Kaylee beat against his chest. Her lips were darkening to navy blue. Suddenly the pupils of Kaylee's eyes dilated and she collapsed.

"Shit." Kurt lowered Kaylee's body to the floor. She lay still.

Kurt crouched down, studying her body for several minutes. A brown stain appeared on her bottom. As the stain spread, a fecal odor rose from the body.

"Huh." Kurt stood up and surveyed the entryway. The dropped roses littered the tiles.

Kurt cocked his head and moved his eyes from the roses to Kaylee's now stinking body. It could be read that Kaylee had an allergic reaction to the flowers. Satisfied that he didn't need to change the scene, Kurt strode down the hall. He passed an elegant living room and a well-appointed kitchen.

He moved on to the master bedroom. He saw the envelopes and boxes on the bed. He used his ankle knife to slice open one envelope, and was pleased to see wads of currency. Kurt teased the lid off one of the small boxes and gave a whistle. Gold Krugerrands lined up in a stately row. He counted twenty Kugerrands in the box. The next box held the same.

Kurt did a little multiplication in his head. "Own gold," he said with a smile. "Great advice."

Kurt turned his attention to the wall safe. A picture of Kaylee leaned against the wall at his feet. Concentrating, he used a gloved finger to type 0515 on the keypad. The wall safe opened smoothly.

"Huh," Kurt grunted. She hadn't lied. He peered into the gloomy bin and saw two more coin boxes and a small plastic bin. Kurt pulled each item out. The plastic bin had three prescription vials and three syringes. "Oxycodone, lorazepam, Valium. And what do we have here? Nembutal, Ketamine and Propofol. My, my. We are prepared."

Kurt strolled through the house and turned into a bedroom. It looked to be Kaylee's room. A cat rocketed off the bed and dashed under an antique dresser. Kurt ignored the cat and picked up a denim daypack.

Kurt returned to the master bedroom and loaded the envelopes and coins into the pack. He shut the safe and rehung the picture.

He had to step carefully around the strewn roses in the foyer. He peeked out the front door to survey the street. It was quiet.

Kurt stepped out of the house, closed the door, and strolled down the street to his truck. Once inside his truck, he stripped off his vinyl gloves and tossed them into the litterbag dangling from the cigarette lighter.

"Give a hoot, don't pollute," Kurt giggled. Now, in the peace of his truck, he could enjoy his adrenaline surge. God, he felt alive!

Kurt started the engine. He carefully pulled away from the curb. Kurt grinned. He'd tell Theodora about the meds. She'd know if they were useful. The money he'd keep to himself.

He smiled again. The money meant freedom and flexibility. He could crew on a boat later.

Kurt turned the truck onto a wide street. He should find a Christian bookstore and pick up some preachy T-shirts. He'd set himself up as an evangelical landscaper, and work some nice neighborhoods like this one. He could specialize in bored upscale matrons.

Kurt thought of all the money in the daypack. He threw back his head and laughed. Hell, he'd buy a whole raft of doo-dads. "I wonder if they have Christian athletic socks?" he said out loud. He braked for a pedestrian entering a crosswalk. He waved politely as a young mother pushed a stroller across the street.

"An angel of God never has wings."

Joseph Smith, Jr.
(December 23, 1805- June 27, 1844)

CHAPTER FIFTY-EIGHT

Sunday, mid-afternoon, The Anderson home on Ellison Loop

LENA HELD THE phone to her ear, treasuring the lilt in Piper's voice. It was such a relief to hear her daughter be so happy.

"He's great!" Piper said, adding, "Drewl, Grandmom, Grace and me went to the pet store."

"Drewl, Grandmom, Grace and I," corrected her mother.

"Whatever. We bought a brush, shampoo, coat conditioner, a leash, bowls and dog food. A lot of dog food."

"Sounds like quite a shopping list."

"Mom, can I stay at Gran's tonight? Puhleeeze!" Piper didn't wait for an answer. She ploughed on with "Drewl needs me. We're bonding. Besides, Grace and me are giving him a bath, and that will be a big job!"

"Grace and I will give Drewl a bath." Lena droned.

"Grace and I will give Drewl a bath. That means I can stay, right?"

"Alright." Lena gave in. "Do some homework after dinner. I mean it!"

"Sure. I have my bag. Love you. Bye."

Piper was gone before Lena could say her farewell. Lena hugged the moment to her heart as she tapped off the phone. Her daughter was happy. This blessing mattered.

Lena pulled down her shirtfront to study the V-shaped rows of feathers on her chest. Earlier the feathers had been odd bits of fluff protruding from hard, hollow straws of keratin. Now the feathers had pushed out of the keratin straws and were fluffing out.

Lena moved to examine herself in a mirror. The top two rows were snowy white. A wider V of darker feathers was emerging lower, between her breasts. Lena could see those feather tips shimmered blue.

"Blue and white," Lena murmured. "That's a new look." Lena decided she'd better show Milo the latest.

Lena peeked into the tiny bedroom that Milo used as a home office. He had earphones on. Lena could see half a dozen tabs open on the computer – all bird related. Textbooks lay open across the desk. She did a quick survey. Anatomy. Physiology. Evolution. Ecology. Genetics. Geology. Chemistry.

Lena withdrew. Her husband was working as hard as he could. It was best to leave him alone. Lena stood in the hallway, thinking. Part of her wanted to run, hide, and not face what was unfolding. She could shave the feathers. Pluck them.

"Don't weenie out this time!" Lena lectured herself. "Be brave!"

With another peek at her emerging feathers, Lena made up her mind. "I'll try a shower. Let's see what happens when I get wet."

She strode down the hall to the bathroom

Lena began the pre-shower routine mandatory in the old

home. She slid the window open for ventilation, and she started the water in the shower. It would be several minutes before hot water emerged.

The running water obscured the knock on the front door. Milo heard nothing over his headphones.

At the front door, Savio and Vico Carlevaro exchanged a look. A peek into the garage window revealed a station wagon. There were no fences, no gates, and, even more important, no signs saying "No Trespassing" or "No Entry." There wasn't even a "No Solicitations" sign by the door.

Savio knocked again. The brothers listened carefully. No barking dog, - another good sign - but there was the sound of running water.

"Let's take a look around the back," Savio directed. Vico hoisted his camera and followed his brother.

Inside, Lena peeled off her clothes, dropping them in a laundry hamper. She knelt down to slide open a door under the counter to retrieve a fresh towel.

She saw that Piper had crammed in the towels when she had put away the clean laundry. "Augh!" Lena grumped. Lena removed the cascading towel wad and began refolding and stacking the towels. Behind her the shower began to steam slightly.

Lena reached up and put one towel on the countertop. She slid the cabinet door shut and turned as she rose to her feet. She was nearly six feet tall, totally naked and facing the open window. Looking back at her were two men, peering through the window.

Lena froze in disbelief.

"Get this!" Savio hissed. His direction was unnecessary. Vico knew a money shot when he saw one.

Lena grabbed up a towel and began to scream.

"It has sprung up like a mushroom."

Latin saying

CHAPTER FIFTY-NINE

Sunday, mid-afternoon, The Anderson home

LENA FLUNG OPEN the bathroom door and ran down the hall to Milo. She pulled the earphones off his head with one hand while clutching her slipping towel with the other.

"Men!" Lena gasped. "Video! At the bathroom window."

Milo erupted out of his chair and ran for the bathroom. No one was at the window. He pivoted and sprinted for the front door. As he pulled the door open, a car door slammed. He saw a silver sedan reverse down the driveway.

Milo ran after them, shouting, "Hey!" The sedan reached the end of the drive, careened into a reverse turn and roared away.

Milo raced back to the house. He found a pencil and scribbled down what he had seen on the car door. *Got Breaking News? Call or text Car... Brothers at 360-838-* . Milo closed his eyes to visualize the license plate. He opened his eyes and wrote BLM 9?? He called 911.

"911. What's your emergency?"

"I'd like to report trespassers." Milo's pulse was pounding. He was surprised at how hard it was to speak.

"Are they on your property now?" asked the operator.

"No. They were looking through the bathroom window at my wife. They had a camera."

"Can you identify them?"

"I saw their vehicle and got a partial license plate number."

"I'll send a deputy out. Will you please confirm your address?"

As Milo recited the street address, he heard Lena turn off the shower. Moments later he hung up as she came down the hall, dressed in jeans and a turtleneck sweater. "You okay?" he asked.

Lena shook her head 'no'. She said, "The feathers have really popped out. I was going to take a shower to see what they looked like wet. Those guys had a big video rig. Like a TV news camera. They had to have gotten a good picture."

Lena turned and kicked the wall. "Stupid! Stupid! I stood there like a stupid, frozen goose. They got a hell of a look."

Milo gathered his wife into a hug. "A deputy is on his way. Maybe he'll sling those bastards into jail."

"Great. Now it'll be official." Lena leaned into Milo and wept.

"Instinct is the nose of the mind."

Madame De Girardin
(January 24, 1804 – June 29, 1855)

CHAPTER SIXTY

Sunday, mid-afternoon, Mason County Sheriff's Office

DEPUTY MACRAE TRIED Kaylee's cell phone number for the fifth time. She still didn't answer. MacRae drummed his fingers on his desk, worried.

Raposo strolled by, coffee cup in hand. MacRae raised a hand, signaling for a conference.

"What's up?"

MacRae said, "I got a message from Kaylee Kovacev, Dr. Patel's receptionist. She wants to talk to me. I've tried calling her back five times now, and she doesn't pick up. She strikes me as the sort who lives on her cell phone, so I'm getting uneasy."

"Do we know where she lives?"

"I just looked that up. There's a Kovacev that lives off Sunset Beach road. Waterfront house."

"Maybe her parents, then? Definitely Thurston County."

"Yeah."

"Let me give Thurston County a call. We'll ask one of them to drive by."

"Thanks, boss."

"Nothing to it. Give me a minute."

Raposo had the Thurston County Sheriff's Office on speed dial.

"We're slammed" the desk sergeant told him. "I don't have a unit available for a well person check. Not anytime soon."

"Mind if our Deputy MacRae wanders over to Sunset Beach to check on his caller?"

"Wander away."

"While I've got you," Raposo continued, "I'm looking into the histories of Inger Edna Morton and her daughter, Lena Anderson. Any history with you?"

The desk sergeant started typing. "Anderson sounds familiar. I think I've got a call pending to an Anderson. Give me a mo."

Raposo tried to relax. He found his fingers tightening around the phone.

"Yeah, Detective. We got a call from a Milo Anderson that someone was photographing his wife, Lena Anderson, through a bathroom window. The perps are gone. I should have someone out there within the hour."

"Sergeant, I'm on a homicide case and this may be pertinent. May I go take that report?"

"You'll get back to us on it?"

"Of course."

"Okay then. You want 759 Ellison Loop NW. I'll put you in the system as the responding officer."

Raposo scribbled down the address. His luck was turning.

"From so simple a beginning endless forms most beautiful and wonderful have been, and are being evolved."

'Origin of the Species' by Charles Darwin
(February 12, 1809 – April 19, 1882)

CHAPTER SIXTY-ONE

Sunday, midday, The Mushroom Farm

"THE MAILBOX IS full. Please try your call again later." Ken tapped his phone off and frowned. "Edna's not picking up. Does she have another number?"

Carys said. "I doubt it. She's a very simple lady."

Her eyes twinkled. "What if we take a fast walk through the farm so you have an idea of what's here. After that we could drive out to Edna's together."

"Great!" Ken liked the idea of spending more time with Carys. "Lead on, dear lady!" he invited.

Carys blushed a darling rose. Both dimples appeared as she moved towards the door. "We'll do the *Pleurotus citrinopileatus* house first. You mentioned research – I have to tell you that almost everything we grow has a medical application. We're looking at reductions in blood sugar with the *Pleurotus*."

Moments later, Ken walked through a warm building that was hung with dozens of punching bags, all a bright sunny yellow. Closer examination showed that the long bags were plastic bags stuffed with wood chips. The bags were covered with yellow mushrooms.

"Column method of growing mushrooms," instructed Carys. "These are the Golden Oyster mushrooms. It has a nice nutty flavor, but, alas, this one doesn't ship well. We pack the perforated bags with hardwood sawdust. You have to have the right substrate for the species."

Carys moved rapidly through the high peaked building and stepped out of the door at the far end. "We also use column bags to grow pink oyster mushrooms, which are quite attractive. There's a blue oyster mushroom too."

Ken's eyes moved to a window on the next low building. "What is that?"

Carys double dimpled with great enthusiasm. "That's what the Japanese call Enokitake."

Ken moved to the window, bracketing his eyes with his hands to get a better look. Inside the building there were rows of silver metal shelves. The metal shelves held hundreds of milk bottles sprouting small, white, long-stemmed mushrooms.

"It looks like space alien heads sprouting antennae."

Carys smiled. "If you think that's funky, just wait." She led him to the next building and pointed. "Lion's Mane. I think it should be called "Snowy Waterfall." Ken peered into the gloom of the building and saw a light mist descend from overhead pipes. Once again, rows of shelving supported bottles sprouting with fungi. This version was a brilliant white cascade of icicles brimming over each rim.

"Come on," Carys directed. She pointed to a field of stumps. Ken came to a halt and stared. Each stump had been sliced horizontally into discs and the discs restacked. Every layer supported a flush of sprouting mushrooms, popping out of the seams between the stacked discs.

"Stump inoculation," chirped Carys. "Edna helped with our fine tuning of the process. Reduces potential fuel for forest fires. Also grows great Nameko mushrooms." Carys reached over and took Ken's hand. "Come on, just a few more production techniques on our tour."

Ken clasped her hand happily. "Are you sure you can't show me a thousand?"

Carys beamed. "We haven't seen the Smokey Gilled Woodlovers yet. We grow those on sawdust blocks. And the shitakes. The ones we had for lunch? They came off inoculated logs. We stack them in towers."

Carys pulled him along. "We'll take a quick look at the maitakes growing on buried logs. Oh, and the turkey tails." Carys stopped and dramatically crossed her eyes. "Sorry, mushroom madness. We'll see the maitakes, and get you out to meet Edna."

"All warfare is based on deception."

Sun Tzu (c. 544 BCE – c. 496 BCE)

CHAPTER SIXTY-TWO

Sunday, mid-afternoon, Olympia

MEGA-STORE SHOPPING WAS a bore. Theodora picked out a dark red hair dye for Kurt. She found a basketball and went looking for a basketball shirt.

Theodora shoved the shopping cart past the women's apparel section. A pink hoodie in the Juniors department caught her eye. It radiated sweetness. Theodora selected one and tossed it into her cart. She could put her hair up into a ponytail and pass for a teen if need be.

Theodora stopped for a coffee at the drinks counter. She reached the last clean table at the same moment as a young mother burdened with an enormous diaper bag and a squirmy toddler. Theodora coolly said, "I believe this is my table." Cowed, the young mother shifted her child on her hip, and looked about anxiously until an older man signaled he was about to leave his spot.

Theodora sipped her coffee, ignoring the hard looks of a

pair of women at the next table. *Not my brat, not my problem*, she thought.

Her problem was getting a blood sample from Edna Morton, and, if possible, from her daughter, Angelena Anderson. She had identified M. Anderson of Ellison Loop as Milo Anderson, Assistant Professor at Summit College. She should go through this professor.

She could see Dr. Anderson, convince him of her credentials, and get him to tell his wife and mother-in-law that the blood samples were necessary. She could seduce Professor Anderson for access to the women. Theodora licked her lips. She'd have sex with a cobra if it furthered her plans.

Theodora sipped her coffee, pleased with her conclusions. She'd contact the Biology Department head professor by email. If she mentioned grant money, she might wrangle an appointment for the morning.

It would be best to chaperone the women to a professional lab for the blood draw, and have the samples sent by express courier to a DNA processing center.

Decision made, Theodora stood up. She ignored the nearby trashcan and left her coffee cup on the table. Clean up was not her concern.

"A friend is someone who will help you move. A real friend is someone who will help you move a body."

Unknown

Chapter Sixty-Three

Sunday, mid-afternoon, Edna's cabin, Kamilche peninsula

THE SUN WAS out in Edna's garden. Drewl leaned into the spray from the garden hose.

"He stinks," said Piper as she massaged in shampoo.

"Dogs often do," Grace told her, soaping from the other side.

Edna asked, "Are we ready for the power rinse?"

As the water carried the soapsuds off, Drewl gave a powerful shake, spraying his companions. Piper shrieked and dove in for more massaging under the stream of water. "Time for towels!" Edna instructed.

Piper dashed to the porch and came back with a stack of towels. As Piper and Grace went to work, Edna turned off the water and began coiling the hose. Over the chatter of the young women, Edna heard the crunching of gravel that signaled a car. A dark sedan came out of the woods and stopped. The passenger side door opened to reveal Carys Kidwelly.

"Edna!" Carys called. "I've brought a friend!"

A slender Asian man stepped out from the car. "Ken Ito," he said. "From N.S.A."

"Of course!" Edna beamed. "Come in. I didn't realize you knew Carys!"

"We've just met, but I'm looking forward to knowing Carys for years to come."

Edna smiled and shot a glance at Carys, who beamed a grin in return. Drewl, on the end of a leash held stoutly by Grace, came surging out to greet the newcomers. Ken knelt down to pet Drewl's wet head. "Bath time, big boy?"

"We just got him today," Piper gushed. "Isn't he beautiful?"

"He is," Ken agreed. He looked up at Edna. "I have a ton of questions for you. Do you have time now?"

Edna said, "Now is fine. This is my granddaughter, Piper Anderson, and our friend, Grace Mossler. Mr. Ito is from the National Shellfish Association."

Carys said, "It's Dr. Ito and he's with the National Security Agency."

Ken said, "Call me Ken. I am here on a National Security concern."

"National Security?" squeaked Edna.

"Yes. We have some concerns."

Piper blurted out, "Growing out feathers is not illegal. It's not!"

Ken's mind went blank. What feathers was she talking about? He answered, "Actually my questions are about Anatoxin-a rescue remedy made some years ago." Ken looked from Piper, whose eyes were huge to Edna, who looked unnerved.

"I'd love to hear about your feathers too," he ventured, "if you think there might be national interests involved."

“Grandmom, I’m so sorry! I screwed up!” Piper burst into tears and buried her face into wet Drewl’s neck.

“I’m so sorry,” Piper howled.

Drewl sat down stoically, leaning into Piper. Long strands of spittle emerged from his jowls as he supported the weeping girl. Grace leaned over to give Piper a hug.

Edna took a deep breath. For Piper she had to be calm. She made her voice pragmatic and level to ask, “Carys, you like this young man?”

Carys took a breath and replied, “Yes, I do. I know he’s a scientist. And…” she fumbled for words before carefully saying, “He can be amazed and still think at the same time.”

“Well, you had better come in for a cup of tea,” Edna said. “Piper, Drewl is clean for the moment. He doesn’t need a saltwater rinse.”

Piper rocked back on her heels and sniffed. She pulled a forearm under her nose. “Sorry,” she murmured. “I hate thinking about this stuff.” She said, “Gran? Is Drewl an indoor dog?”

Edna studied the pair. She turned to Grace. “What do you think?”

“He’ll be happier with his pack,” Grace said.

Edna’s eyes swept the group. “It’ll be a full house.”

"It is good to rub and polish our brain against that of others."

Michel Eyquem de Montaigne
(February 28, 1533 - September 13, 1592)

CHAPTER SIXTY-FOUR

Sunday afternoon, Edna's cabin, Kamilche peninsula

EDNA TOOK CHARGE in her kitchen. There was no turning back now. "Take a seat," she directed Ken and Carys, waving at the table. "Grace, will you get down mugs? Piper, your jeans are soaked. You can serve the brownies, after you change."

Edna filled a teakettle and set it on the stove. She turned to the big dog, sitting at edge of the kitchen, "Drewl, lie down right there." To Ken's amazement, the dog did.

"You just got him?" he asked.

"We suspect he had some training," Grace said as she set down a pair of mugs. "He seems very biddable."

Ken studied the stocky young woman. Her face betrayed no emotion. *There's more to this one than meets the eye*, he thought. That was confirmed when Grace said, "I thought the National Security

Agency dealt with collecting information from other countries. I didn't know you worked within the states."

From many years of playing strategic games, Ken knew when it was time to build an alliance. "You're correct. Carys will tell you I know very little about mushrooms. My Ph.D. was in population dynamics of yeast colonies."

Ken added, "When something came in the door that had fungus mentioned, it was directed to me. I can't say anything more than we are following another country's interest in a fungal matter. Normally we'd pass off local interviews to an FBI specialist, but their mycologist is on leave. They let me out of my cubicle to come learn a little more."

Edna poured out tea and passed Ken a honey jar. He declined the sweetener and wrapped his long fingers around the hot mug. He waited until Edna sat down in the tall backed chair before he continued. "I don't have any authority to force you to answer questions. Anytime you tell me to leave, I'll leave."

Piper came back down the hall, stopping to pet Drewl. Edna arched an eyebrow and Piper slid over to the sink to wash her hands.

Ken plowed on. "Please know I am very interested in your rescue remedy… and in any long term side effects you may have experienced."

Ken deliberately kept his eyes off Piper as she set down a plate of brownies and handed around napkins. "I am a scientist. I'm not trying to make money or become famous. If you have something biological happening, I'd like to know about it and I'd like to help."

Edna sipped tea before asking, "What do you think, Grace?"

There was a chime from her pocket. "Sorry," Grace murmured. "It's my phone. I'd like to see if it's Milo." She checked the text message. "It's from Dr. Berbera," Grace reported. "I can get back to him later." She felt a pang of guilt, as she should have contacted her department head. He wasn't going to be happy with her.

Grace laid the phone on the table and said, "Edna, there's your answer. I'm sure that Dr. Berbera wants to ask Milo about the Internet video. We already know that the world is seeing Lena. The video has gone viral."

Grace paused to accept a brownie from Piper. "Maybe you should talk to Milo and Lena first..." Grace's comment was lost to a heavy metal blast.

"Oh, dear." Edna blushed. "My phone! I'll be right back." She slid off the chair and walked out of the kitchen as she opened her phone. "Milo! We were just talking about you." The rest was lost as Edna moved to the front porch.

"Great brownies!" Carys enthused, earning a shy smile from Piper. Encouraged, Carys said, "Tell me about your dog," which unleashed a waterfall of information from Piper.

The tea mugs were empty, and the brownies reduced to crumbs by the time Edna returned. The chatter fell silent as Edna retook her seat.

"There's news," Edna told the quartet. "My daughter, Lena, now has some feathers too. She went to take a shower and, apparently, some video photographers took pictures of Lena through the window as she was about to shower. The men ran off, and Milo is waiting for a sheriff's deputy to arrive."

"Is Mom alright?" Piper was pale again.

"She is a bit rattled but she is with your father and will settle," said Edna. She then turned toward Ken. "Young man, Milo said to bring you in on what's happening to us. I was gone so long because he took a few minutes to look you up on his computer. I didn't quite catch everything Milo said, but he liked your publication list. He also had an online chat with a colleague of yours from Duke."

"He works fast." Ken was impressed.

"Yes, he does." Edna turned her head back toward Piper and calmly said, "We do have a bit of a situation here. Your mother is fine and she is with your father. She is upset about the peeping Toms, but she is fine. Meanwhile, I need you to check yourself, please."

Piper's brown freckles stood out like a Dalmatian's spots as her face paled to a translucent white. She pulled her T-shirt forward and looked down, and heaved a sigh of relief. "Nothing, Grandmom. I'm good."

Next to Piper, Grace wiped suddenly sweaty hands. Drewl stood up and walked over to rest his heavy head in Piper's lap as a tear rolled down her cheek.

"Please let us help. What's going on?" Ken asked.

Edna slipped off her overall straps, unbuttoned her camp shirt and dropped the shirt. Ken and Carys could see the brown and gray feathers sprouting above a white bra.

"Whoa." Ken and Carys spoke in unison.

"I had odd skin pores appear nearly thirty years ago," Edna told them as she re-buttoned her shirt. "It was after I used a great quantity of the respiratory rescue remedy on the neighbor's cows. I was pregnant with Lena at the time. I didn't really think much about the pores until a few weeks ago when suddenly they produced quills that unfurled into feathers."

"Your daughter has the same skin pores?" Ken asked.

"As does Piper."

"What's on the video?" Carys asked.

"Lena was at the park yesterday. She ran to save a little boy who was bicycling toward a truck. It was taped by some teens." Edna paused. "Lena is fast. Faster than humans normally are."

"Milo thinks she has changes in her muscle fibers," Grace contributed. "It is a remarkable video. She's a blur of motion."

"The muscular change you also attribute to the respiratory remedy?" Ken inquired.

Edna put her hands out, flat on the table as she considered his question. "I'm not sure what to think." She capitulated and added, "I can show you the recipe for the remedy. It calls for a wee brown mushroom that we don't see often. I don't think it is a named species, actually."

Ken raised his eyebrows. "Didn't you want to find out, and name it yourself?"

Edna laughed. "Too much trouble to do the documentation."

"Can you show me the mushroom?"

"No. It won't be out this fall. I only see it when we have a muggy late summer. It's a brown-spored, brown-capped, gilled mushroom in the genus *Conocybe*. Some *Conocybes* have a ring and can be poisonous. This one lacks a ring, although I wouldn't eat it. It has a faint violet stripe on the stipe and smells of tobacco. My mother called it "Witch's Friend." I've only seen it out four times in my lifetime and I'll be eighty-four in March."

"So you and your daughter now have feathers," Ken marveled.

"And Piper has some enlarged skin pores," Edna added.

"Your daughter's name is 'Lena'?"

"That's short for Angelena. She was so pink and white when she was born. She had these big blue eyes and such a sweet nature. My husband said she was our little Angel."

Ken stared at her. "Biological fuzzy logic!" he marveled. "My God, this may be fuzzy logic!"

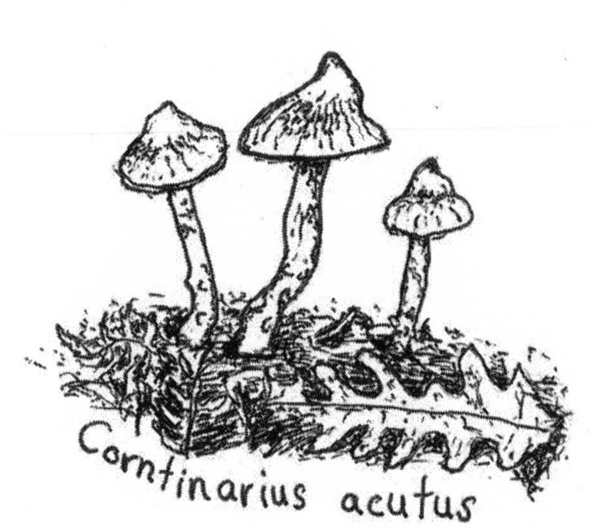
Corntinarius acutus

"Pay attention to your enemies, for they are the first to discover your mistakes."

Antisthenes (455 BCE – 365 BCE)

CHAPTER SIXTY-FIVE

Sunday afternoon, Channel 17 KBRN News Station

"ARE YOU OUT of your mind?" The newsroom producer shrieked into the telephone. "We can't use that! Try the pulp trade! She slammed the receiver down into its cradle and yelled, "Soo Min! On the double!"

On the other side of a slim partition, Soo Min rolled her eyes before she moved to her producer's side. "Yes, boss?"

Her producer was clutching her head with one hand and rummaging in a desk drawer with the other. Soo Min reached into her vest pocket and came out with a small bottle of ibuprofen. "Here you are."

The producer grabbed the bottle, snapped off the top and dumped out four pills. Soo Min's eyebrows rose. She'd never seen her producer take more than two. The producer glared at her and gulped down the tablets. "Soo Min, we are never, ever, ever under any circumstances hiring the Carlevaros again."

Soo Min sank down into a desk chair across from her producer. "What happened?"

"Those bozos knocked on the door of the blonde rescue lady. No one answered, so they take themselves around the side of the house, whereupon they find that they can shoot footage of the lady, naked, through her open bathroom window."

"No!" Soo Min gasped.

"Yes! Blondie screams, and they hotfoot it out of there. Now the Carlevaros are on the phone to me trying to peddle the footage. Can you spell 'lawsuit'?"

Ever practical, Soo Min asked, "Any 'No Trespassing' signs?"

"They said 'No'." The producer ran both hands through her already spiky hair. "Have you emailed the contract down?"

Soo Min shook her head. "I was about to."

"Don't send. Our official line is that we do not have a contract with the Carlevaros. Anybody wants to buy their stuff, it's their own lookout. If the lady makes a complaint, take her number and tell her I'll call back."

Soo Min nodded. Seattle would be dry and sunny in spring before the producer would return such a call. It was Soo Min's job to tap dance around complaints.

"Do you think they can sell?" she asked.

The producer threw up her hands, palms up to the dingy ceiling. "Naked woman? It could sell to somebody. Get this. Savio says the gal has feathers. Feathers!" The producer glanced up at the wall clock. "Call Maria and tell her she can have three for her protesters."

"Three minutes?" Soo Min stared. The rule of television broadcast was "for the end of the world you get two minutes, but only if you have great video."

Her producer glared at her. "It's a sunny Sunday in September. I got nothing. Tell Sports she can throw in middle school badminton for all I care."

"On it." Soo Min agreed. She'd also check the wire for late breaking news. Soo Min exhaled. This job was more exciting in theory than in practice.

Soo Min gave herself the treat of a stop at the ladies room. She wished she could see the footage that had Savio so excited. It was odd that he tried to peddle bathroom window shots to a reputable television station. He was a savvy guy. Were they missing some real news here? Soo Min glanced at her watch, shook her head, and went back to work.

"Tomorrow's sales require planning today."

Traditional sales tip for entrepreneurs.

CHAPTER SIXTY-SIX

Sunday afternoon, Mrs. Carlevaro's basement, Olympia

SAVIO DIDN'T CARE that KBRN news didn't want their footage. He'd only offered it out of a sense of honor. Vico understood. They'd been given the tip from Soo Min, and that meant KBRN got first dibs. Particularly since Vico liked Soo Min.

"Producer bitch?" Vico asked as Savio clicked off the phone.

"Totally." Savio rolled his desk chair over the worn yellow linoleum to his computer. "I don't think we can go mainstream."

Vico agreed. "Bathroom shots aren't for everyone. Good thing we're in the reverse produce business. Stuff that's too ripe this week gets less ripe next week."

"Go figure."

"You should link the blonde saves boy video to what we've got," Vico suggested.

"Good idea. We've got *"The Story behind the Save?"* Savio was typing.

"Fuck it, bro. The broad has feathers. It's gotta be *'Freak at the Park and in Private.'* Vico leaned over his brother's shoulder. "Try *World Day and Night.* They've got a mutant section."

"Boys?" came a voice from the top of the stairs. "You want a snack?"

"No, Mom," called Savio. "We're good. We got some new footage to sell."

"That's nice. Dinner will be at six. We're having cannoli."

"Thanks, Mom," the men chorused.

"Anything for my angels," said Mrs. Carlevaro.

Savio looked at his brother. "Maybe we should put one frame on your blog, and say we've got real live angel footage for sale."

Vico pursed his lips. "I could crop a bit down so you see the top of the breasts, the feathers and her face."

"Yeah. That could work."

"There's no time like the present."

Almost every coach or parent.

CHAPTER SIXTY-SEVEN

Sunday afternoon, The Kovacev home

RODGER RAPOSO PARKED his sedan well off the road, almost a hundred yards away from the driveway blocked by crime scene tape.

He strolled down the road, taking time to hook his badge on the outside of his blazer pocket. He stopped at the crime scene tape to speak to a young woman in uniform. "I'm Detective Raposo. I'm trying to locate one of our deputies, Don MacRae."

She said, "He's the one who called this in, right? Mason County?"

"That's right."

"Come on through. He's on the front porch with Sergeant Martinez."

Raposo sauntered down the long drive. An ambulance with lights whirling sat in front of a four-car garage. Two paramedics were bringing a wrapped body on a gurney down the steps. That, Raposo surmised, was Ms. Kaylee Kovacev.

MacRae was standing with his arms folded at the far end of a long porch, deep in conversation with an Olympia policeman dressed in dark blue. Rodger walked over, giving the two men time to register his arrival. Although he knew many on the Olympia P.D., he didn't know this sergeant.

Martinez acknowledged Raposo with a chin jab. "Detective. Just collecting your man's thoughts here." Raposo relaxed internally. Sergeant Martinez had used a pleasant tone of voice. It didn't sound like there was any territorial pissing happening.

Raposo looked at MacRae. "You okay?"

MacRae waggled a hand, so-so. "The door was open. She was inside. There were long stem roses on the floor. Lips cyanotic, like she'd had an allergic reaction, but as I was telling Sergeant Martinez, the entire west side of the house is a rose garden."

MacRae pointed toward the front door. "There wouldn't be a rose garden if a family member was deathly allergic. I was just telling him about Dr. Patel."

Raposo pulled a card out of his shirt pocket. "Be glad to ship you a copy of our homicide report on Dr. Patel, Sergeant."

Martinez handed over his own card after scribbling out a direct phone number. "I appreciate how your officer handled things. He backed off, called us, and waited for us to be on the scene."

A forensic technician in white overalls put her head out of the front door. "Sergeant, you may want to see this." Martinez strode off, leaving Raposo with Deputy MacRae.

"So," Raposo said casually, "You came over, found her body, backed off, but also managed to see what was growing on the side of the house?"

MacRae answered with a wintery smile. "It took them a bit to get here." He paused, and then said defensively, "I was careful."

"Fine. See anything that helps us?"

"Kaylee had a ripped earlobe. Long earring on the right

side, torn lobe on the left. Like somebody right-handed yanked the earring."

"Ouch."

"No kidding. I called our dispatch, and Marvin said he was the guy who took her call. Marvin said she sounded upset but she didn't ask for help. She just left a message for me to call her back." MacRae's gray eyes were haunted even as his voice was level.

"What the hell is going on?" mused Raposo. "I talked to Dr. Anderson. He had the long song and dance about two assholes filming his wife through the bathroom window, but when I asked to speak to the wife, she was unavailable." *Which was an error on his part*, Raposo thought, *I'll be back*.

"You think they're connected to Dr. Patel and Kaylee?"

"All my instincts say so. Patel treated Edna Morton, who is Mrs. Anderson's mother."

"And we know the M files were taken from Patel's computer."

"Yep. When I went out to talk to old Edna, she gave me the 'I'm just a dumb, sweet old lady' routine, when she's known to be sharp as a tack." Raposo gave the deputy his due credit. "Your suggestion to contact Kankakee churches panned out. Turns out our Army Ranger Otsoa had a sibling. A name I've heard before."

Raposo didn't finish. Sergeant Martinez hailed them from the door. "We've got a partial footprint in the master bedroom and a cat chewing on a passport. This may be a robbery."

Raposo and Deputy MacRae moved rapidly toward the open door. If Martinez was offering a look, they wanted to take it. They'd talk about Otsoa's family later.

"Know thyself."

Inscription on the Temple of Apollo at Delphi

CHAPTER SIXTY-EIGHT

Sunday nine p.m., The Haddad summer cabin, west of Olympia

KURT PUT HIS head under the kitchen sink faucet and rinsed away the excess dye. Once the water ran clear, he turned off the taps and began toweling his hair dry. "How's it look?" he asked.

Theodora studied him. "That dark red makes you look very different."

Kurt smirked. "It'll get me to Canada."

Theodora stroked his arm. "You'll help me finish here first?"

Kurt nuzzled her neck. "Yeah. Got a plan?" He reached down and cupped her buttocks, pulling Theodora in close.

She smiled up at him. "I always have a plan." She stepped back from Kurt's embrace and took him by the hand. "I thought we'd try the rocking chair."

Kurt grinned as she led into the cabin's living room. Theodora began laying out her plan as he undressed. "We'll watch the news tonight to see if there's anything more on Edna's daughter. I'll check the video posting for comments. Tomorrow morning I'll head into the college campus, and connect with Dr. Anderson."

Theodora gave a naked Kurt a slight push to seat him in the bentwood rocker. She briskly peeled off her shirt and dropped her slacks.

As she unhooked her bra, she added, "He's a scientist. I'll talk up how important it is to get blood samples and a proper genetic evaluation. If I'm confident and sincere, I can get him on my side to do the workup on Edna and his wife."

Theodora stepped out of her underwear and smirked when she saw Kurt's erection. "My, my. It looks like we've got Vlad the Impaler tonight."

She raised one leg and placed it on the arm of the rocker. Kurt guided his shaft into her as she moved her other leg up. The interlocked pair began to rock the chair, with Theodora thrusting herself forward and Kurt using his long legs to balance and push back. Their rocking action picked up speed.

Across the water of Oyster Bay, a retired physician was walking his aging Labrador in the dark. An odd, ongoing flicker caught the man's eye and he stopped to stare across the water to the Haddad's cabin. Hadn't Leo said that he and Jana were going to Paris and then to a niece's wedding?

The physician stopped to watch the flickering shadows from the Haddad's cabin. A light was on in the living room of the cabin. Something was moving. Could a family of raccoons be causing havoc? Why the light? Motion activated? Surely there wasn't a bear in the cabin. Jana was fastidious as hell. She would never leave food out. As the doctor ran through possibilities, the aging Labrador pulled on the leash. The old man gave into to the wishes of his dog. He'd walk over to Leo's in the morning, and see if animals had gotten into the cabin.

"I saw the angel in the marble and carved until I set him free."

Michelangelo di Lodovico Buonarroti Simoni
(March 6, 1475 – February 18, 1564)

Chapter Sixty-nine

Monday, The Anderson home

DAWN AT THE Andersons arrived with a tapping. The first two taps on the door were soft and timid. The next two were firmer. Then the doorknocker got into the spirit of door knocking and committed to a strong rat-a-tat-tat.

"Uhhh." Milo sat up in bed. He noticed that Lena was an unmoving log, buried in the blankets. The bedside clock read 5:40 a.m.

"Coming!" Milo shouted as he pulled his wrinkled khakis off the bedside chair. Yanking his pants on, he spied a navy T-shirt on top of the dirty laundry hamper and grabbed that too. It was rank. He didn't care. Early morning doorknockers deserved pungency.

"Who could that be?" came from the Lena log under the quilts.

"Maybe the sheriff? " Milo stalked out the bedroom and down the hall as the door knocking went into another round. Milo yanked open the door to come face-to-air above a short wall of a woman. She was no more than five-foot-two and surely tipped the scales at 240. Her long gray hair flowed over the shoulders of a dark purple caftan and down to large, puffy arms cradling a damp mound of white fur.

"I need to see the Angel," she said.

Milo blinked. "Excuse me?"

"I need The Angel." Tears began streaming down the woman's face with some droplets finding the grooves between her chins and disappearing down the crevices. "It's Sir Percival. My darling Sir Percival. He's seventeen and he's dying." She gulped and panted in distress before continuing with a shaking voice, "I can't lose him. I just can't!"

Lena came up behind Milo and slid around him to embrace the woman. "Is this Sir Percival?" she asked, reaching out to stroke the white fur.

The woman mutely nodded and heaved with sorrow. Finally she gasped, "The vet says he can't cure old age. I can't bear it. I lost Lady Blanchefleur, my Siamese, last year, and then, and then, and then," The woman took a deep breath and finished with, "My mother just died, and I just can't bear it."

"Shhh," Lena murmured. "You're not going to be alone. Didn't Percival have a son, the Black Knight?"

The woman in purple gulped and nodded, and then sniffed, weeping still. "I'm going to miss Sir Percival so much."

Lena slipped an arm around the woman's plump shoulders. "Nothing replaces those we have loved. But we do have room in our hearts to love more." Lena leaned down to rest her chin on the short woman's head. Lena said, "There's a Kitten Korner shelter not far from here. When you must bid adieu to Sir Percival, there will be an honorable knight and lady waiting there for you. I promise."

"You promise?"

"Yes, I do." In a practical tone she added, "They may be currently registered under a modern name." Lena straightened up and added, "There's a scripture that says 'Therefore I command you to be openhanded toward your brothers and toward the poor and needy in your land." Lena gave the woman a squeeze. "There are those who need you."

The tears began again in earnest.

Milo was done. "Where did you find out about us?" he demanded.

There was a sniff from the woman that Milo was beginning to think of as "Raining Mountain." She said, "I was online last night. I found you on *The Angels in Our Cosmos* site. It showed the Angel saving that little boy. The discussion forum gave your address."

Milo stared at her, stunned. "Are there others planning to stop by today?"

Raining Mountain nodded. "That's why I came so early. There's a van of Featherheads coming down from Tacoma this morning."

"Featherheads?"

"That's what we call those of us who choose to interact directly with the Angels of our Earth." Raining Mountain said, with some dignity.

Lena sent Milo an alarmed look. He snaked out a long arm and grabbed Lena by the elbow, hauling her toward the door. "Great. Best of luck with Sir Percival. We've got to go now." Lena put up no resistance. In fact, she sagged against the door once Milo had shut it firmly in the face of Raining Mountain.

"My God, what just happened?" Lena asked.

"You tell me, sweetie. What's with the scripture?"

Lena shrugged. "It just seemed like the right thing to say. She was so upset. People feel better when they can see the next step to take. That's all."

"I didn't know you knew any scripture."

Lena smiled up at him. "I don't work a job. I read a lot. I told you I was reading healing short stories."

"I didn't realize that it was Bible stories."

Lena's eyes twinkled. "You weren't interested."

"Ouch. Tell me this. How do you know there'll be a lord or lady at the cat shelter for Raining Mountain to adopt?"

"Oh, for heaven's sake. Use logic, Professor Anderson. There's always cats that need a home."

Milo drug a tired hand over his face. "Okay, I'll give you that one."

The telephone began to ring. "Don't answer it," Milo barked. "Let's get some breakfast and make a plan before the van of Featherheads arrive."

"That is the Lion's tail. Do not play with it."

Persian proverb

Chapter Seventy

Monday morning, Six-thirty a.m.
Apple Town Apartments

GRACE'S MORNING WASN'T starting any better. The coffee maker was farting out sad squirts of pale liquid, signaling it was a dying machine. She was out of milk and bananas. She was even out of toaster pastries. When her phone chimed it was all she could do to croak, "Hello."

"Glad you are a participating member of our department this morning, Ms. Mossler," said Dr. Berbera, the sarcasm slicing through Grace's pre-coffee fogged state.

"Dr. Berbera." Grace stuttered. "I am so sorry. I meant to call you last night. Golly."

"What do you know about Dr. Anderson this morning?"

Grace found she was standing at attention. "Sir, he should be at home. His wife was in the news and, uh..." Surely she shouldn't say anything about Lena and Edna's feathers. The fascinating Dr. Ito hadn't sworn anyone to secrecy, but was she supposed to share that a representative of the National Security Agency was in town and working with Milo's family? Grace stuttered another, "Uh, wow, sir. It was busy."

"Could you be more specific? Please."

"Dr. Anderson had reporters come to his house. They wanted to interview his wife about the Internet video." Grace gathered confidence and moved on with, "Mrs. Anderson is shy. She hasn't been well this year."

"Yes. I am aware. It's been unfortunate for the family," Berbera conceded.

"Well, Dr. Anderson's mother-in-law, Mrs. Morton, has been interested in getting a dog for some time, and she felt that the circumstances warranted getting a dog. I have a skill set with dogs, so I went with Mrs. Morton and Dr. Anderson's little girl to select a dog. That took a surprising amount of time. Most of the day, actually." Grace ended with a regretful note that often worked with her mother.

To Grace's great relief, Dr. Berbera softened. "I see. You found something for them?"

"Yes. An older Newfoundland. He's big and commands respect. He's a real cream puff, personality wise."

"Good. Well, getting back to business. Please do return my calls in the future."

"Yes, sir."

"Dr. Anderson did email saying he has a family emergency. I'm assuming his wife is not well. He asks if I can cover his nine-thirty class. I can do that. I was wondering if you have his lecture plans."

"Oh, golly. No. I know he was going to include material on birds this week. I'm a little muddled because there are two sections. We didn't end the week at the same spot."

"That can happen," Dr. Berbera rumbled. "I'll leave the birds to Milo. I'll talk about genetics and bring my nudibranch

PowerPoint. I'm sure you've heard about it – it's quite the popular lecture."

Grace's un-caffeinated brain froze. *What the hell was a nudibranch?* She fell back on the military brat's ace-in-the-hole-get-out-of-jail move. "What can I do to help, sir?"

"Pick up some bananas from Dining Service when you get to campus. Bring the bananas to class. The guy you want is Angus. You can't miss him. Red hair, utili-kilt. He runs the morning cash register at the breakfast bar. "

"Yes sir!" There was a red-haired guy in a kilt on campus? How could she have missed him? The day was improving.

"I've also received an early morning email from a Dr. Theodora Band."

"Dr. Band?" Grace's embryonic good mood evaporated.

"She's with the National Institutes of Health, and says there's grant money available. She wants to meet with Dr. Anderson this morning. I suggested she come in about 8:30. I can meet with her, and if she's dead set on meeting with Dr. Anderson, we'll have you escort her out for a meeting this afternoon."

There was nothing to do but to agree. As Grace clicked off her phone, she realized she needed reinforcements. She needed Aunt Esther.

"Luck is not chance, it's toil; fortune's expensive smile is earned."

Emily Dickinson
(December 10, 1830 – May 15, 1886)

Chapter Seventy-One

Monday morning, Eight a.m., Summit College

GRACE STABBED ANOTHER horrified look at the Civic's dashboard clock. It couldn't be eight already. She needed to get the bananas for Dr. Berbera and rendezvous with Aunt Esther, preferably before Dr. Band walked into the lobby of the Biology building at 8:30.

It was no morning to circle the campus in hopes of a close parking spot. She wheeled her car into a perimeter lot and swooped into an open slot.

Daypack on, Grace ran for the nearest sidewalk, leapt down a short flight of stairs and galloped for the dining hall, muttering, "He'll be easy to find. He's a redhead in a kilt." Berbera said Angus would be in a "utili-kilt." There was no time to research that word now.

Heaving for air, Grace took a right at the Physics building, and veered down a narrow gap between the Communications building and the library. She emerged at the far corner of the dining services building.

Eight a.m. was the crack of dawn for most college students. There were only two people in line for breakfast. Grace halted to gasp for air and to reconnoiter. The cafeteria line bent in a curve and she was too short to see the cashier. Grace grabbed a tray and slapped it on the steel tray rails. She hustled to catch up with a tall athlete who was loading his tray.

"Running late," Grace puffed.

"Go for it," the athlete said.

Grace pulled out around the tall one, raced forward a few more feet and came to a halt behind a petite co-ed carefully adding whipped cream to a hot chocolate.

"Excuse me, I'm just going to dash around you to pick up some bananas from Angus," Grace said.

"Angus! Oh, isn't he dreamy?"

Grace stared at the young woman, suddenly aware of her own sweating face and that she had chosen a faded, shrunken shirt to wear. There was nothing that could be done now.

"Sure," she said, and pulled out around the chocolate drinker.

Setting the tray back down on the rails, Grace grabbed a cold can of soda and zoomed toward the cashier.

Who had carrot-orange dreadlocks. Grace stumbled to a stop. The cashier's nametag labeled him as "Angus." Lean nearly to emaciation, Angus had a sharp, hooked nose, long knotted, orange locks that fanned over his shoulders and sparkling emerald eyes that seemed to rejoice in Grace's confusion. "Good morning!" he said.

"Hi. Ahh, I need some bananas. For Dr. Berbera."

Angus beamed. "The nudibranches lecture! Ah, fair lass, what a glorious day you'll be having to start your morning with nudibranches!"

"That's the first time I've been labeled 'fair'," Grace told him. "But I'm looking forward to it."

"And who are you, dark beauty of our rainy woods?"

"I'm Grace. I'm running late."

"Bolting with the bananas, are we?"

"Please."

"Berbera sent a text. I have them ready." Angus reached under the cash register stand to retrieve a quartet of yellow-green bananas. Grace's eyes dropped as he moved.

She saw that a utili-kilt was a kilt with pockets. Angus's utili-kilt was of green camo cotton duck. Grace was rather charmed by the confidence Angus must have to wear such a thing. However, the hoary yellow toenails extending a half-inch over the end of his sandals were not charming by any stretch of the imagination.

"No charge for the bananas. Bring them back after the show." Angus instructed. "A buck for the sugar water."

Grace paid for her soda, picked up the bananas and fled. Behind her, she heard Ms. Hot Cocoa coo a good morning to Angus.

"An interesting red-headed man but not MY red-headed man," Grace thought as she tried speed walking to the Biology building. To her great relief, Aunt Esther sat on a bench near the building's doors.

"Thank you for coming, Aunt Esther!" Grace sat down next to her aunt.

"Here to serve. What am I doing?"

"God. It's a lot of ground to cover, and I've only got a few minutes. Here goes. Your mushroom hunting pal, Edna Morton, has sprouted feathers."

"Feathers?"

"Shh. Not so loud. Yeah. Honest to God feathers. She has a triple row across the tops of her breasts and more now across the back. You don't see it when she has a shirt on. Her daughter,

Lena, also has had feather formation. The granddaughter, Piper, has some large pores in her skin, so she may be next. "

"Wow."

"It gets complicated fast. Lena also has some different muscle structure. She can run fast. Like bionic man fast. She saved a kid who was about to be run over by a pickup on Saturday. That's the good news. The bad news is that the incident was videotaped by some teens at the park and posted on online. It has over two million hits."

"So Lena's in the public eye, but the public doesn't know about Edna?"

Grace could have hugged Esther for being so quick. "There's more. Edna says her pores first appeared about thirty years ago when she was pregnant with Lena."

Grace popped open her soda and inhaled half of it. Then she couldn't speak because of the giant bubble erupting up her esophagus. There was nothing to do but belch.

"Sorry, auntie," Grace gasped. "This is my bad idea of a breakfast."

Esther made a shooing motion with her hands. "Move on," she said.

"Okay. Edna made up a respiratory remedy for colds, using salmon heads and some odd mushroom. She slathered some cows with it and got it all on her hands, where she thinks it was absorbed into her skin."

Esther nodded. "Salmon head soup is a Northwest traditional food for colds. Mushrooms could provide enzymes of some sort. Theory isn't proof. However, it is interesting."

Grace felt almost weak with relief. Esther could see the possibilities. "There's more. There's a guy here named Dr. Ken Ito. He's with the National Security Agency. I don't quite get what he's investigating, but he came out to talk to Edna about the respiratory remedy. I was there yesterday when he showed up. Edna told him about the feathers. He's got some ideas about how they're forming, and he's going to be working on that today."

Grace took a deep breath and plowed on, "Edna Morton went to a health clinic last week. She went in to see her doctor, a Dr. Patel – a guy she trusted. While he's starting to look at her, another doctor, a visiting doctor comes in. Her name is Dr. Theodora Band. She sees the feathers. Edna doesn't like Band. She says Dr. Band is "evil." I don't know if she is or she isn't, but Edna doesn't like the woman."

"I'd trust Edna's instincts."

"Me too. Anyway, Dr. Patel runs Dr. Band off and tells Edna not to worry. A few days later, Dr. Patel is murdered at his clinic."

"Murdered?"

"Yeah. Gruesomely. The TV news say an Army Ranger is a 'person of interest.' This morning the local news reported on the death of a young woman named Kaylee Kovacev. They think she was at home during a robbery. But get this, she was the receptionist for Dr. Patel."

"We don't know that this connects with Edna," Esther interrupted. "The medical people could be selling drugs or doing something else unsavory."

"True enough, but Edna's rattled by Dr. Patel's death, and she sure doesn't like Dr. Band. Yesterday I spent the day with Edna and her granddaughter Piper. We got them a dog. I stayed way too late last night talking over epigenetics with Dr. Ito and a fungal expert named Carys Kidwelly."

"I know Carys! She's very sharp."

"Good. I think so too. That brings me to this morning. I get a call from Dr. Berbera. Dr. Anderson asked him to take over his morning class – the one where I'm the warm body graduate student. I'm not sure what's up with Milo. It may be that he and Lena are staying out of the public eye. The scary thing is that Dr. Berbera mentioned an 8:30 a.m. meeting here with a Dr. Theodora

Band. He says she's with National Institutes of Health, and she wants to meet with Milo about handing out grant money."

Esther stared at her niece. "That's extremely odd."

"I thought so too. Normally they'd take applications, right?"

"Yes. There's a very specific vetting process. They don't hand out research dollars like peanuts."

"So I'm smelling a rat, and I've got to do the grad student thing at the 9:30 class."

"What do you want me to do?"

Grace put her palms together under her chin, like a child putting up a prayer. "I was hoping Dr. Mossler of the Yale School of Forestry could be accidently, on purpose, dropping by the department at 8:30. See if you could bump into Dr. Band and check her out."

"I see. With a heavy emphasis on 'Yale' in my every other breath?"

Grace tried to shrug nonchalantly. "If you got it, flaunt it?"

Esther laughed. "It has its uses. All right. I'll see what I can find out. I do know Yousef Berbera. It's not so far-fetched that I should stop in and say hello. Anything else?"

"If you can throw out some distractions, great. Dr. Berbera said that I might get drafted to drive Dr. Band out to meet Milo this afternoon. I'm not sure how to get out of that."

Esther nodded. "I'll see what I can do."

"Aunt Esther, I am so glad you came."

"Oh, it's nice to ride to the rescue. I can handle this."

Cortinarius alboviolaceus

"Draw water for the siege, strengthen your defenses!"

Naham 3:14

Chapter Seventy-Two

Monday morning, Eight a.m., The Anderson home

"THANKS, MOM. WE may be overreacting. I'll call you later with an update." Lena clicked off her cell phone, and gave a thumbs-up to Milo. "Mom says that they've had breakfast. She'll take Piper to school."

Milo leaned back in his desk chair. "I feel like Drewl is a relative already. I'm got seven emails from Piper with photo attachments."

"Oh dear. That doesn't sound like she spent much time on homework last night."

"We'll worry about that later. How does this look?" Milo picked up a sheet of paper from the printer tray. The text was in a large font. *It's an Internet Hoax. Go Away!*

"Very fierce. I certainly wouldn't go further."

"Yeah, but you're a sweetheart. Lena, are you sure you don't want to go spend the day at your mother's?"

Lena leaned against Milo's desk. She crossed her arms and looked down at her husband. She said, "I am trying to be pragmatic here. Mom has enough on her hands. She's eighty-three, and I've been leaning on her all summer. Today she's taking Piper - again. It's time for me to handle something."

Milo reached over to pry one of Lena's hands loose. He raised her hand to his lips and bestowed a kiss. "You're sounding firm. This could get challenging."

"We'll do this the same way as before. I'm briefly visible with no wings and unavailable for comment. You're lecturing about Internet hoaxes. You bore them to death, and we're good. A van full of ladies shouldn't be too scary."

"Yes, Ma'am. I'll put these up on the door. We've got the rope across the driveway, and the windows covered. That's not bad for an hour's work."

"I hate that we used the staple gun on the wood paneling in Piper's room."

"Sheets stapled over a window are not the end of the world. Besides, we used the lavender sheets. She might like the look."

Lena rolled her eyes. "Color me dubious. "

Milo pulled his beautiful wife into his lap and held her close. "We're not alone. Remember that. Dr. Ito will spend today looking into epigenetics. Grace is impressed with him so far, so that's a huge plus."

"You trust him that much?"

"I feel wary of the whole National Security Agency thing, but my contacts say he has some serious mental chops. Sounds like Carys Kidwelly likes him – a lot."

Lena smiled. "I was so jealous of Carys Kidwelly when I was a kid."

"How so?"

"I'd see her when we delivered chanterelles to her family's farm stand. She's all smiles and confidence. I froze whenever I was around her. I ached for a friend, but that didn't happen." Lena gave Milo a kiss on the cheek, "until I found you."

A knock on the door interrupted their embrace. Milo snatched the papers off the printer. "Stay here," he ordered.

Milo strode the length of the small house and flung open the door. A trio of women with beaming faces looked at him and said. "We're here for the Angel!"

A dozen more women were coming up the walk.

Milo could see over his visitors' heads. The driveway had a station wagon and three minivans lined up bumper to bumper with the last van halfway out onto the road. More women were exiting the minivans. The heavy rope he'd tied across the drive lay limply on the ground. He could see more vehicles turning off the main road.

Too late Milo realized that they had underestimated the number and mindset of the people coming.

The women pushed forward.

"Go Away! She's resting!" Milo shouted, throwing his arm across the opening.

"She's HERE!" a short one shouted. She stepped forward. Milo shoved her back. He slammed the door shut, and flipped the deadbolt latch.

Milo shouted, "I'm calling 911!" but when he grabbed up his cell phone it was already buzzing. "Hello?" he answered, grabbing his hair with his free hand. "No, Goddamn it, I will NOT do an interview. We have an emergency. Get off this line!"

Milo pushed the off button and strode down the hall, trying a second time for 911.

He blinked when he turned into the home office, because Lena wasn't there. He spied her toes behind his office chair. She was curled up in the kneehole of his desk.

Milo got down on the floor and patted her knee. He took a deep breath and concentrated on his phone, making his shaking fingers hit the 9, 1 and 1 and send. This time he connected.

"911. What's your emergency?"

"We need help."

"What's your emergency, sir?"

Milo blinked. What should he say? He stammered and said, "There's a mob on our front lawn. We live at 759 Ellison Loop"

"Is it a flash mob, sir?"

"A flash mob?"

"Yes sir. When people show up at the same time for a short demonstration. Sometimes they sing or dance."

"It's not like that."

"Are they violent or destroying property?"

"I don't think so." The women looked like matrons from a garden club tour. Milo decided now was not the time to describe the crowd.

"Why do you think they are there, sir?"

"My wife was in the news."

"Is she a celebrity, sir?"

"No. We're local people. Please. Send a patrol car."

"Yes sir, I will dispatch to your location. And sir?"

"Yes?"

"Be advised that we cannot provide ongoing security for a celebrity. If you feel your wife is attaining celebrity status, you may want to enlist a private firm to provide security."

"I understand. When will the patrol car get here?"

"Dispatching now. Estimated time of arrival is fifteen minutes."

"Thank you." Milo disconnected. He faked a confident face and said, "Fifteen minutes. Don't worry. We got the law coming."

Lena tried to smile, but couldn't. "They've only just arrived, and I already feel like a zoo animal. I think I may have misjudged my spine for this."

"You can stay there as long as you like, sweetie. But let me check something."

"What?"

"That gal with the cat this morning. She said she was a 'Featherhead,' and she read about you on the…Angels in the Universe site."

"*The Angels in our Cosmos*," Lena corrected.

Milo climbed up into the desk chair. "Let's see what they're saying." Milo typed, clicked, read and then murmured, "Well, shit."

He looked down at Lena and said, "Buses have been rented. The Vancouver, WA Featherheads and the Vancouver, B.C. Featherheads will meet here mid-afternoon."

"My God. Milo, what am I going to do?"

Hericum abietis

"Why has God given me such magnificent talent? It is a curse as well as a great blessing."

Albrecht Durer (May 21, 1471 – April 6, 1528)

CHAPTER SEVENTY-THREE

Monday, 9:30 a.m. The Anderson home

MILO'S PHONE RANG within seconds every time he turned on the phone. Lena was having the same problem.

"What about Piper's old phone? Lena suggested.

"Any idea where she stashed it?"

Lena and Milo began rummaging through their daughter's belongings.

"Lena, did you know Piper has a scrapbook on tattoos?"

"No, but, Milo, now is not the time."

"Right. Hey. Got it!" Milo found the old flip phone in the bottom drawer of Piper's pink desk. "Let's hope it still has some battery life." Milo punched in 9-1-1 and send. As the phone connection began to burr, Milo heard more rapping on the front door. He ignored it as he had all the previous hour.

"911. What's your emergency?"

"This is Milo Anderson on Ellison Loop. We requested a

deputy about an hour ago. No one's showed up. The crowd on our lawn is getting huge."

"Any injuries, sir?"

"No." Milo paced back and forth. "It's very upsetting. We can't get out of our house."

"Please hold, sir. I'll check on the unit dispatched."

Milo drummed his fingers on Piper's desk. Then, still holding the phone to his ear, he sat down in her pink chair and started up her computer. It took a few moments of one-handed typing to log onto his campus email. Milo swore. There were hundreds of emails.

Milo opened one email from a colleague. He scanned the message and clicked on the link. *The Angels in our Cosmos* site unfurled across the screen. Lena's picture was front and center.

"Sir?" said the emergency operator, "The deputies are unable to reach your location because of a traffic jam."

Milo said, "It's the same people who are holding us prisoner in our house. They're called 'Featherheads'."

"Featherheads?"

"I think so. Apparently a picture of my wife was posted on a website and these people think… " Milo couldn't say it.

"They think what, sir?"

Milo wiped his face with his free hand. "They think she's an angel. She's not. She has a funny skin condition."

"A skin condition, sir?"

Milo moved to the doorway of Piper's bedroom and slowly tapped his head against the doorsill. Maybe banging his head against the wall would help. "Yeah. A skin condition. When can the deputies get here?"

"I don't know sir. Are any of the Featherheads in the house?"

"No. We've locked all the doors and windows. The windows are covered. We can hear them moving around the whole house."

"Can you tell what the Featherheads are doing? Are any of them carrying weapons?"

Milo rolled his eyes. To Lena he said, "She wants to know if any of the Featherheads are carrying weapons."

Lena inched over to put an ear against the lavender sheet covering. "They're singing '*Nearer my God to Thee.*'"

"We really don't think they are armed or dangerous," Milo told the emergency operator. "They are just a... fan club."

"Fans can turn dangerous, sir. Please be advised that it is best if you remain indoors until our deputies can get there."

"Will do. Good bye." Milo clicked off and sighed. "The deputies are coming. Eventually." Milo motioned Lena to join him at the computer. "*The Angels in our Cosmos* have linked your feathers in the bathroom shot with the park video. It has gone turbo-viral."

Lena sank onto Piper's bed and wrapped her arms across her stomach. "Turbo-viral. Is that a real term?"

"It is now." Milo sat down next to his wife. "It changes things. You'll make the nightly news. Maybe for days. We're going to have to make some plans. Staying here is not going to be an option."

"What about Piper?" Tears streamed down Lena's face. "She's started making friends here. Where would we go that the Featherheads wouldn't find us?"

Milo rubbed her hands. "It's not just Piper. It's Edna too." He laughed in frustration. "And a giant dog. Something tells me Drewl is going wherever we go."

Lena wiped her tears away and sniffed. "We need to engineer an escape with two feathered women, a kid and a giant dog - with an old Subaru station wagon and without much money. It's a good thing you're smart, Dr. Anderson."

There was another round of rapping on the front door. It seemed that someone was assigned to rap every few minutes.

"Jesus." Milo groaned.

Lena managed a watery smile. "If angels really do exist, no wonder they don't show themselves. We are ready to love them to death."

"We must not say every mistake is a foolish one."

Cicero
(Jan. 3, 106 BCE – Dec. 7, 43 BCE - assassinated)

CHAPTER SEVENTY-FOUR

Monday morning, Olympia and beyond.

MONDAY MORNING WAS busy for many. On Ellison Loop, a retired physician whistled for Sutton, his aging Labrador.

The leash was snapped on. The old man and his dog ambled down the driveway and took a left onto the road. It was time to check the Haddads' cabin.

The planned walk would take man and dog around the very foot of Puget Sound, just as the tide was rising to cover the mud flats. It was a pleasant walk, with tall firs and cedars along the road, and sheep grazing in the fields of an organic farm.

Dr. Taggart only made it part way around Ellison Loop. There was a traffic jam. He stared in disbelief. In the four decades he had lived in the area, he could recall only an occasional party - and none of those on a Monday morning.

It was a massing of matrons. Vans and sensible sedans were

turning onto the loop. Other cars were carefully parked on each side of the road. Gray and dyed heads bobbed down the road as the women streamed toward a small home on the inland side of the loop.

Dr. Taggart recalled that the family was new to the street. He had met the girl, who had been keen to scratch Sutton's ears. Piper. That was her name. Surely Piper was in school on this third Monday in September.

Taggart came to a halt, studying the crowd. "Sutton, given the lemming-like look of the ladies, this must be a garage sale of fabric and craft supplies. Distinctly not our métier. Being wise fellows, I recommend we rapidly rally to the rear." Pleased with his powers of observation and his alliteration, he reversed his steps to walk Sutton another way. He'd check on the Haddad cabin later.

*

Not many miles away, an important series of rhythmic muscle spasms began. A week previously, an ingested earring had moved rather quickly through Sir Percival's esophagus and stomach and into his small intestine. The earring was made of long feathers, so progress through the twisting small intestine had been slow. It had been an uncomfortable passage.

There had been a particularly long delay for the earring when it arrived at the ileo-colic sphincter. Now the forces of peristalsis and a recent jarring car ride combined to orient the earring for passage.

Once past the internal sphincter, the earring moved rapidly through the ascending, transverse and descending colon. At long last, the undigested remains of the earring descended to the rectum.

Sir Percival roused himself with a leisurely stretch. He leapt down from the floral patterned sofa where he had spent the week resting. He stalked into the mudroom where he selected the middle of three pristine cat litter boxes. Stepping delicately into the box, Sir Percival circled to left, arched his back and left a deposit.

Sir Percival used his right front paw to cover the remains of the earring. He worked leisurely and did a thorough burial.

Satisfied with his results, Sir Percival stepped out of the box and made his way to the kitchen. He was hungry.

*

The third event unfolded on the East Coast. At the Homeland Security Advanced Research Projects Agency (HSARPA), a technician sent an email to Dr. Zebulon Szczepanski with a link to Lena's web video.

Dr. Szczepanski, known as 'Z' to his colleagues, had just microwaved his lunch. He scrolled through his emails as he waited for his noodles to cool. Once he launched the video, the noodles were forgotten.

He needed to find this woman. He needed to find her before Carlos Rivera at the Department of Homeland Security Chemical and Biological Defense Division found her. Carlos had landed funding for three programs recently and had four more in the pipeline. The man was a money-grabbing machine. He was also a mean-spirited, territorial shit who was rapidly building his own empire over at Chemical and Biological.

Z replayed the video clip again - and again. It was fascinating to watch the blonde's long legs pick up speed and become a blur. That was one gorgeous woman - and one very lucky kid.

Z saw where a second, expanded video was posted. He clicked on the link and saw more of the chunky young woman with a daypack running down the length of the parking lot, and the two men, one tall and fit, the other beefy and slower, all converge on the woman and boy sitting on the grassy turf after the bike had been crunched under the truck.

He replayed the video. The extended video could be used to

document distance. One of the cars was an older Honda Civic. Its dimensions would be easy to find. The approximate size of the boy's bike and the height of the incoming pickup could also be used as markers to determine the distance the runners covered. Once distance was established, the video time line would allow a viewer to calculate the speed of each person.

Some amateurs had already done some of this and had posted in the comments section. "Seventy two yards in 3 seconds = 49.09 miles per hour! World record for the hundred yard dash is 22.7 mph. Wow!""

That would have to be confirmed for Z to believe.

Who was the blonde? The middle school boys identified her as 'Lena Anderson.' Who, exactly, was that? Her level of speed could have military or homeland defense applications. Was she on a supplement? A special training regimen? Was this even real? Having middle school boys involved with the posting of the video put Z's bullshit meter on high alert. Was this an "eagle grabs baby" Internet giggle?

Z's email inbox dot popped up again. His technician had anticipated his interest in the rescuing blonde and had researched the woman further.

The Angels in our Cosmos? What the hell? Z couldn't believe what he was seeing. The same long blonde, but with feathers? Z shook his head. Hoax. It had to be a hoax. Still, there was something compelling about the rescue video.

He leaned in to study the still shot on *The Angels in our Cosmos.* The base of each of the feathers was wrapped tight in a keratin sheath – just as emerging feathers appeared in real life. If this was a hoax, someone was paying careful attention to detail.

Z's inbox dot popped up again. Carlos? Z opened the email and read "See the stuff from the west coast on the Angel Speedster? See attached links. What do you think? Carlos."

Z immediately typed back, "Got to be a hoax. A fun one, but hoax, for sure."

The inbox dot reappeared. "Agreed."

Z typed "feather development" into his search engine. It wouldn't hurt to learn more.

*

Edna dropped Piper off at school. As Piper joined the stream of students, Edna coaxed Drewl into the front passenger seat.

"I can't have you drooling down my neck, sweetie," she told him. "You sit up here and I'll put the window down. You can drool out the window."

Edna's cell phone rang with its heavy metal ring. At the same moment, a mother in a minivan tapped her horn impatiently.

Edna shut the phone off. She hated that ringtone. She'd have to tell Piper, in a nice way, of course, and have Piper install something else.

Edna pulled out of the school parking lot and signaled a left turn for the highway.

"Let's go to the woods, Drewl. It's such a lovely day."

Drewl put his head out the window and inhaled the smells of the Pacific Northwest.

Edna's face crinkled into happy wrinkles as she saw Drewl lean into the wind. Edna told him, "You are such a sweet old bear."

"The height of cleverness is to conceal it."

Francois de La Rochefoucauld
(September 15, 1613 – March 17, 1680)

CHAPTER SEVENTY-FIVE

Monday morning, Biology Department, Summit College

THEODORA WALKED INTO the Biology Department at 8:28 a.m. She wore a heavily starched lab coat over her outfit of dark slacks and royal blue sweater.

Her hair was pinned up in an elegant French braid, and she had reading glasses on a chain around her neck.

There were times when her petite build was not an asset. Playing the academic heavyweight was one of those times. To compensate for her youthful appearance, Theodora wore a mannish watch and gold stud earrings. The crowning detail, Theodora smirked, were the black oxford shoes with a narrow crepe sole. It was not a predacious look.

The desk dragon in the reception nook was near retirement age. Cool, gray and sophisticated, she took Theodora's name and telephoned Theodora's arrival into the inner sanctum.

"Dr. Berbera is expecting you. He'll be right out," she murmured back to Theodora.

The administrative assistant greeted the next arrival with a wide smile. "Dr. Mossler! How wonderful to see you!"

Theodora turned to see a dark-haired, middle-aged woman entering the waiting area. Dr. Mossler wore blue jeans and high top sneakers in bright green. She completed the outfit with a green plaid shirt and a multi-pocketed khaki vest. Theodora eyed Dr. Mossler's jewelry. There was a coral and turquoise heishi necklace of stunning workmanship and a thick cuff bracelet of intricately worked silver. This was an interesting woman.

Esther held out both hands to the departmental dragon. "Margaux! How good to see you." The assistant clasped hands with genuine goodwill.

"Yale let me off for sabbatical. I thought I'd pop in and see Yousef. I should have called." Esther's tone was light and happy.

"He'll want to see you!"

To Theodora's great irritation, Dr. Berbera emerged from his office and spoke first to the dark-haired woman with a warm, 'Hey, there, Esther!"

Theodora stifled her irritation at the momentary wait and came up with a gracious nod as Dr. Berbera said, "Esther, you should meet Dr. Theodora Band. She's with National Institutes of Health. Dr. Band, this is Dr. Esther Mossler from the Yale School of Forestry. Esther is a world renowned expert on lichens."

"You make me blush! And what is your field, Dr. Band?" Esther chirped.

"Medicine - with an interest in epigenetics," Theodora replied.

Dr. Berbera added, "She's here to meet with Milo Anderson about NIH funding some work here at Summit College."

"NIH? How interesting. I've held one of their grants and, I must say, your institution insists on good value for its money. We should talk later. We may have some colleagues in common."

Theodora didn't blink an eye. She couldn't back down from her lies now. If Uncle David ever heard that she had represented herself as a member of his agency, he'd be apoplectic. She should push ahead, and fast.

Theodora said, "Of course. We are particular with our funding. Dr. Anderson's in a special position."

"In epigenetics?" Esther plastered mild confusion on her face. "I thought Milo was an ecosystems chap."

Dr. Berbera clasped his hands together to produce a cheerful pop. "Our Milo is a multi-talented sort! Alas, Dr. Band, he has been called away with family this morning. I am to fill in for his nine-thirty class. You can tell me about your interests right now, or we could wait a few hours and see if Dr. Anderson can become available. One of our graduate students could escort you this afternoon."

Theodora frowned. "My schedule is tight but I could make this afternoon work. I'd be glad to go out to his home."

Esther leapt in. "Actually, I have the morning free. Dr. Band, I could show you some of our local flora, fauna and fungi. We might come across Dr. Anderson's mother-in-law, Edna Morton, who is very much a mushroom expert. I know some of the spots where she likes to collect. You could get some local exposure, and let Dr. Anderson have a few hours for his family first."

Yousef Berbera blinked in surprise.

Theodora couldn't believe her luck. She'd much rather find Edna first. She said, "I would appreciate such a tour. I'd love to meet a fungal expert." Theodora turned a smile on Dr. Berbera. "Why don't I go with Dr. Mossler? I can call you later to see if Dr. Anderson is in."

"That works. I know you are in outstanding hands with Dr. Mossler."

Eavesdropping outside in the corridor, Grace held the green

bananas to her chest and bit her lower lip in horror. Aunt Esther was taking Dr. Band on a tour? To see Edna?

She heard Aunt Esther say, "Let me go get a water bottle, and I'll meet you in the parking lot. "

As Esther exited the door, she grabbed Grace's elbow and towed her along. "Don't worry," Esther whispered. "I'll run her all over the Olympic Peninsula. There's not much in the way of mushrooms out yet. I'll go someplace other than Kamilche."

"Be careful, Auntie."

"I will be – Don't worry. A career in Higher Ed gives one long experience with tap dancing. Don't you have a class?"

"Going now." Grace fled for the classroom.

Inside the Biology Department's administrative lobby, Theodora said her goodbyes. Dr. Berbera escorted her to the corridor and shook her hand. He stood in the doorway and watched her stride down the corridor and out the front double doors. Only then did he turn to his administrative assistant.

"Margaux, what did you make of our visitor?"

Margaux arched an elegant eyebrow. "If she's with National Institutes of Health, I'll eat my ficus. A lab coat for an office visit? Dropping in unscheduled? We grovel to suits for money. The scientists have never come to us. But that's a beautiful woman. Do you suppose she has the hots for our Milo?"

Dr. Berbera snorted. "That one has ice, not fire, in her veins. I've got to get to class. See what you can find on Dr. Theodora Band."

"Of course. And, Yousef?" Margaux leveled her cool blue eyes at him. "Why would Esther Mossler take such an interest?"

Dr. Berbera stared at her. "Mossler. Margaux, we're getting slow. Isn't Milo's new grad student Grace Mossler?"

Margaux angled her head. "Yes. I hadn't made the connection."

Dr. Berbera rubbed his thumb across his chin. "I thought she was Navaho. Maybe she's a coastal tribe member?"

Margaux disagreed. "Grace's home address is in San Antonio."

"Well, Mossler isn't a common name. Have you seen the video of Milo's wife?"

Margaux nodded. "It's unbelievable. You have to think it's a hoax. No one runs that fast."

Dr. Berbera replied, "I'm not sure what the hell is going on. Grace spent yesterday helping Milo's family. If she is related to Esther Mossler, maybe she gave Esther a heads-up. It'd be great if the department can get some funding out of NIH. Maybe that's Esther's angle. She's muscling in so Yale gets dollars to research Mrs. Anderson."

Margaux tsked softly. "I'd hate to think that of Esther Mossler, but you are talking grant money. It's amazing what some people will do."

"When thou seest an eagle, thou seest a portion of genius; lift up thy head!"

William Blake
(November 28, 1757 – August 12, 1827)

Chapter Seventy-Six

Monday morning, 9:30 a.m., Biology of the Northwest Class, Summit College

THE STUDENTS FELL silent when Dr. Berbera strode up to the podium and said, "Let's go bananas."

"Back at the dawn of time, when I was a student at Berkeley," Dr. Berbera said, "We heard that bananas had a psychoactive substance in the peel called 'bananadine.' More than a few peels were dried and smoked before researchers at NYU showed that there are no intoxicating chemicals in banana peels."

Dr. Berbera reached out and took the small bundle of bananas from Grace, who was standing, as directed, on Berbera's right. Dr. Berbera presented the bunch with a flourish to the nearest student.

"Do pass these, please," he said. Grace moved up a step to make sure the bananas kept moving without mischief.

Dr. Berbera returned to his notes and spoke in quiet tones,

almost as if he were speaking to himself. "Bananas, are, of course, naturally radioactive. Bananas have a high potassium content, and the naturally occurring isotope potassium-40 which decays some 30 atoms per second. In fact, a truckload of bananas can activate a cargo Radiation Portal Monitor at a seaport screening site."

The pace of the banana passing increased.

"Bananas are high in iron, B vitamins, and they are a good food for those of us in the Pacific Northwest who get gloomy in the winter, because bananas contain tryptophan, a natural mood enhancer. Students undergoing testing are more alert and less stressed if they have recently consumed a banana."

Dr. Berbera added, "Students are also more alert in class if they have something to handle. But we, dear students, are interested in the banana today because of the DNA of bananas."

Grace didn't know where Dr. Berbera was going with his lecture. She could see the students were attentive. No one was texting.

Dr. Berbera said, "The DNA of this fruit that goes so well with your breakfast cereal shares a strong resemblance to our own DNA. There is a joke T-shirt that says, "You're 50% the same as a banana, so get over yourself."

"Bananas, like humans, do have the same sort of DNA. We do the same sorts of things with our DNA. Both the banana DNA and Yousef Berbera's DNA are made of adenine, thymine, cytosine and guanine. On the cellular level, both the green banana and myself are using the Krebs cycle, are exchanging things across cell membranes, and are aging. In my case, quickly." Dr. Berbera rubbed a hairy hand over his balding forehead, garnering some chuckles.

"So why aren't I green or yellow with a nice peel to protect my innards? It's not what you have, it is how you use it." That did get a laugh.

"I'm serious, folks. Whether it is DNA of a mouse, a banana, a rhino or a Yousef, the DNA has the same building blocks. You learned this in middle school biology."

"A human has forty-six DNA chromosomes in each cell. So does a guppy. And yet most of us feel we are superior to the average guppy."

More laughter. Grace saw the bananas were being passed without much horseplay. She moved up the stairs to be ready to pick up the bananas at the end of the last row.

Dr. Berbera continued, "Most people know that there are differences in the sequence of those building blocks, and they assume that is all there is to the story. But more and more, we are learning that it is the location of a gene on a chromosome, the action of nearby genes, the methylation of DNA which, in turn, changes which DNA is read or not read – all of these mechanics alter the outcome of what DNA does."

"Humans and guppies have 46 chromosomes. More specifically, we have 23 chromosomes, each with a partner that is silent or partially silent in expression. So we have 23 pairs of chromosomes. It is instructive to look at simpler organisms to understand what even a small collection of chromosomes can produce."

"Today I introduce you to the butterflies of the sea." Dr. Berbera pushed on a clicker and the room darkened. The screen behind him exploded in color. A turquoise and orange horned beast undulated across the screen.

"The Nudibranches. Also known as sea slugs. These are soft-bodied, marine mollusks of great diversity. These beautiful, simple creatures typically have only thirteen pairs of chromosomes. There are some three thousand species and they are all colorful carnivores."

"Nudibranch – note the hard "k" sound at the end – means 'naked gills' and those weird branching fans you see on the back of the animal are actually its lungs. In some species, the 'lungs' are feathery looking and circle the animal's anus."

Dr. Berbera brought up a picture of a tan creature covered with electric blue fringes."*Pteraeolidia ianthina*, one of the 'Blue Dragons.' The bristly tentacles at the front end are 'rhinopores' or the 'nose' that lets the nudibranch smell or taste the water. And those frilly tube collections down the back are called "cerata." They are digestive glands. Basically you are seeing the equivalent of the villi of your intestine inverted and attached down the outside."

"The defense mechanisms of nudibranches are legendary. One species, *Glaucus atlanticus*, is a specialist that eats jellyfish. When it encounters the stinging tentacles of the jellyfish, it nibbles off the tentacles, and passes the stinging cells, the nematocysts, through its own gut to its skin, armoring itself with borrowed weaponry."

Grace flicked her eyes across the auditorium. No one was moving. All eyes were on Dr. Berbera's slide show.

Berbera clicked again. This time the sea slug looked like a gently waving spotted plant.

"Nudibranches can also be cryptic. Here we have *Phyllodesmium longicirrum.* This nudibranch is solar powered. This animal will store algae in its skin and will consume the products of the algae's photosynthesis. From just a few centimeters away, this creature looks like part of the flora of the sea floor."

Dr. Berbera next click split the screen into two. The right half of the screen showed a white sea slug with bright pink dots. The left half of the screen displayed a navy blue slug with neon green dots. "The brilliant colors can signal that the nudibranch is toxic. These dramatic colors can also be protective. Many of these nudibranches actually match their food source."

"Let's talk sex." The next click showed circling pale yellow sea slugs, each decorated with purple stripes.

"*Hypselodoris whitei.* This is a mating pair. Nudibranches are hemoprohodites. Each of these individuals will impregnate the other. This species mates head to tail through a specialized opening in the neck. Each animal will extend its penis and insert it into the female duct of the other animal. Gives new insight to the romantic term necking, doesn't it?"

A wave of nervous laughter swept the auditorium.

Grace finally collected the banana bunch at the back of the auditorium. She leaned against the back wall and tried to enjoy Dr. Berbera's showmanship. He was doing a good job of illustrating how diverse life could become from the original design of a simple slug with relatively little DNA.

Tangerine, fuchsia, ruby, and chrome yellow animals came up on the screen. Some were zebra-striped, sapphire-streaked, tie-dyed, or sprinkled with dots like a decorated donut. Others came with frilly ruffles or sleek ribbon-like profiles. Dr. Berbera returned again and again to the very few chromosomes at work. Grace's head throbbed as the colors and shapes flipped by. She ached to know what Aunt Esther was doing.

Glaucus atlanticus

"An association of men who will not quarrel with one another is a thing which has never yet existed..."

Thomas Jefferson
(April 13, 1743 – July 4, 1826)

CHAPTER SEVENTY-SEVEN

Monday, 9:30 a.m., The Red Hawk Inn

KEN WOKE WITH a jolt. Carys! Where was she? Ken moaned and flopped over onto his back. He had dropped Carys off at the mushroom farm at midnight. She had smiled sweetly when he insisted on waiting until she had started her car. He had desperately wanted to follow her to make sure she got home safely. He had to be content with seeing her car take the on-ramp to Shelton.

Was it a good sign that she was now his waking thought? How many beautiful, young women have a subscription to *The Journal of Yeast Research*? Ken punched his pillow. At least one. One was enough.

Ken was in the shower when the bedside phone began to ring. He ignored it. He could not stop thinking about fuzzy logic.

DNA was too often seen as having "on" or "off" switches.

However, there were times when cell systems reached an important juncture where a range of possibilities unfolded. Sometimes – even most of the time – a predictable cascade of events would unfold. Occasionally the pinball of life would careen into another direction. Take fungal myceliums.

Ken smiled as that made him think of Carys. Then his brain leapt to fungal myceliums that consumed and transported nutrients through the root-like hyphae, then used those nutrients to grow more hyphae to keep the mycelium running. Every now and then there was something that triggered the development of the fruiting body – the mushroom.

Ken leaned into the hot shower spray, deep in concentration. For most mushroom species, it was usually a combination of moisture, temperature and light that sent the mycelium into fruiting body production. Once in a great while cellular biology struck off in unexpected directions. Why was it that a particular cancer would progress rapidly in one person and slowly in another? What triggered the occasional 'miraculous' cure?

Then there were the great mysteries of high school life. Why did one guy have the whiskers of a walrus in eighth grade and another guy remain smooth and soprano for another four years? Even then, everything was a 'matter of degree,' with one guy having biceps like hams and another being doled out walnuts. There wasn't an "all or none." There was a spectrum of possibilities and the more complex the system, the wider the spectrum of outcomes possible. Outcomes could be fuzzy, sloppy, variable and uncertain.

Ken poured a dollop of shampoo into his hand and went to work on his hair. Edna and Lena seemed to have something in their systems that sent their cellular chemistry cascading in a new direction. Placodes was the word used to describe the site in an embryo that gave rise to teeth or hair or feathers. What signal caused a placode to form? Why a feather? Edna was particularly interesting. Lena's placodes could have been nudged in a new direction while she was in utero. Edna? How did her cells change at age eighty-three?

Ken finished showering when he realized his fingers were pruning. He stepped out into a hotel bathroom fogged with steam. The hotel phone was ringing. Ken started toweling off and ran through his mental memory banks. The phone had been ringing off and on most of the time he had been showering. He may have missed as many as seven or eight calls. "Hyperfocus," he grumbled. At least this time it wasn't a fire alarm he'd been ignoring.

Ken took time to dress before answering the phone. He knew he tended to be unfocused when naked. Finally he picked up the phone.

"Hello!"

"Jesus, Ken. Where have you been?" Harry snarled.

"Sorry. Overslept. In the shower. What's up?"

"Try the biggest hoax since Piltdown Man. It's caught the eye of both Z and Carlos. You are about to be roped in."

Ken closed his eyes and swore. The rivalry between the two scientists was legendary. He did not have time for this.

He said, "So they are pawing the dirt and tossing their horns again. Why do we care?" Ken started scrolling through his cell phone messages as he asked. There were fifty. He flipped open his laptop and clicked on his email. There were two hundred messages. He groaned.

Harry was relentless. "We care because you are there, on the ground. Some dame in Olympia has sprouted feathers."

Ken suddenly couldn't breathe. How had Harry, Carlos and Z found out about Edna? Edna said she had only revealed her feathers to her family and Grace.

Harry barreled on. "Some lady named Lena Anderson in Olympia popped up on a Internet video running across a parking lot. Runs like the wind. Close to fifty miles per hour. That's a hundred yard dash in less than four seconds. There's more. She's also on a site called *The Angels in our Cosmos* where she's shown with feathers. Z says there's tremendous attention to detail. For a hoax, it's a doozy."

"And if it's not a hoax," Ken filled in, 'then every agency, including the military, is going to want a piece. The scientists will be looking at the feather development, and the military at the speed aspect."

"You got it, my friend. So, somehow, someway, our pal Carlos knew that you are out in Olympia."

"You're kidding me!" Ken sank down to sit on the edge of the bed. "How'd that happen?"

"My guess is that he picked up somewhere that you are our brightest biological guy, and he has some travel app that lets him know when and where you're traveling."

"He's spying on me?"

"Welcome to the world of Government. They don't call us Big Brother for nothing. But Z works the other way."

"Meaning?"

"He has a data base of government specialists by location. When he typed in 'Olympia' this morning, he got your name popping up, hence the call from Z."

"I work for you and NSA. What do you want me to be doing?"

"Check out the woman. Let me know what we've got, if anything. "

"Are we backing Carlos or Z?"

Harry sighed. "Honestly, I don't want to be around either one of those nutcrackers. I hate these turf wars."

"What would be in Mrs. Anderson's best interests?"

Harry sighed again. "That is a good question."

*

Three miles away, a dental technician pinned a paper bib around the neck of Detective Rodger Raposo. She said, "Dr. Trung will be right in."

Raposo leaned back in surrender. He had put off his dental work as long as he could. He had a thousand things to do, but today was going to be spent under the drill.

Seek and ye shall find.

Matthew 7:7

CHAPTER SEVENTY-EIGHT

Monday morning, County roads west of Olympia

ESTHER MOSSLER DROVE. Her brain sped through the options for local woodland trails. She needed to take Dr. Band to a place where it would seem possible that they would run into Edna, but it also needed to be a place where Edna was not likely to be this morning.

September showed western Washington at its best. The sun beat down through a clear blue sky to dance on the big leaf maples. The heat of August had turned grasses and ferns yellow and brown as the tall cedars and firs on the hills remained evergreen.

"So you know where to find Edna Morton?" Theodora asked.

"It's hard to say." Esther made her tone of voice nonchalant. "It sounds like you have several hours to fill before trying Dr. Anderson again. We might as well check out some Edna-centric sites."

Esther added, "It's been dry, so the best mushrooming hasn't begun. When the rains come there will mushrooms everywhere."

Esther reached a decision. She'd go out Delphi road to the McLane Creek nature trail. It was shady, cool and charming. The McLane trail had an hour-long hiking loop through forest and marsh with a short cut through the middle. The figure eight-like layout would give Esther good flexibility.

Theodora wanted no questions on the funding connections she had claimed, so she peppered Esther with questions until Esther slowed down to turn into the trail parking lot.

"There's two levels of parking," Esther told her. "On weekends it can be crowded. Today we should be able to park right next to the trailhead."

Indeed, the upper lot was completely empty. Esther exited the lot at the far end and took the winding road down to the trailhead lot.

As Esther turned the car around the last bend, Theodora gave a cry of glee. "Look! That's Edna's station wagon! I remember the bumper stickers!"

Esther stabbed on the brakes and stared with horror at the faded blue Volvo parked at the far end of the lot.

"Oh, my," was all she could muster. Of all of the hundreds of forest trails in the area, somehow she had managed to lead Dr. Band directly to Edna. One sticker on the station wagon read "There's always room for mushrooms," and another said "Moreliac." It was unquestionably Edna's station wagon.

Theodora bubbled with enthusiasm. "This is fantastic! We'll catch her by waiting."

Esther's brain scrambled for traction. "Ahh, why don't we take the trail? It will take us to the beaver pond. There's great visibility and some benches. We could sit and watch Edna come to us."

Please, dear God, Esther prayed, *let Edna see us*. Edna was a wood wise woman. She'd pay attention to voices floating across the water of the pond – Esther hoped - but mushroom hunting tended to cause one to focus on the ground. It was possible that they would come up on Edna while she was absorbed in her hunting. The left hand choice of the trail was the one to make. It would put Esther and Theodora out in the open.

Theodora slid out of the car and strode down the trail. Esther called after her to slow the pace.

"Dr. Band, the key to finding Edna is knowing how to hunt mushrooms." Esther deliberately walked down the path with a measured step. Theodora stopped and waited.

"Cedars don't do a great job of supporting fungus," Esther lectured. "Not for edible mushrooms. Douglas firs are better. Mushrooms are often cryptic, so it is good to go slow."

"Tell me about the poisonous ones," Theodora said. Her eyes lit with amusement.

"Well, there's some that you could serve for dinner that you could eat but would poison your guests," Esther offered. "Members of the *Coprinopsis* genus have a chemical called coprine. You are fine to eat edible *Coprinopsis* as long as you abstain from alcohol. The coprine interacts with alcohol. If your guests have the mushroom and a glass of wine, they could become very ill – even comatose. A nickname for the genus is 'tippler's bane.' "

Theodora's smiled with delight. "What's the mechanism?"

Esther gave a nod of approval for the question. "Coprine is an amino acid. It stops the metabolism of alcohol, so acetaldehydes build up, affecting the autonomic nervous system. It causes skin flushing, swelling and throbbing in the extremities, chest pains and even coma. It can be quite diabolical because the mushroom's effects can linger four or five days."

Esther stopped on the trail to examine lichens on a tree stump. She added, "One could serve mushrooms on Thursday and have a wine tasting on Saturday. It is unlikely that an ER physician would make the link."

"Really?"

"The giveaway symptom is a nasty metallic taste in the mouth. It's similar to the antabuse tablets given to alcoholics."

"Where does this mushroom grow?" Theodora's eyes were bright with interest. This was science she could use.

"*Coprinopsis atramentaria* is known as 'inky caps.' Look for a white mushroom that has black, dripping edges. It grows in grassy areas and on disturbed soils. After it releases spores, the mushroom starts to digest itself, so it rots from the edges out. You can use the black fluid for actual ink."

Esther wandered past the first bench on the trail. She wanted to get Theodora out on the boardwalk extension over the beaver pond. Edna had the best chance of seeing them there.

Esther pointed out a pileated woodpecker winging its way through the firs. She continued, "You should take a mushroom identification class. The auto-digesting rim is a feature of several mushroom species. As the rim disintegrates, the next level of spores is ripening and made available to be carried away by the wind. Not all the auto-digesting species are edible, and many are very similar in appearance."

Esther reached the boardwalk and briskly moved forward onto the wood walkway. Theodora followed.

Esther did her best to stomp along the boardwalk, hoping the noise would echo across the water. It did.

Theodora didn't seem to notice. "Tell me about other poisonous mushrooms," she insisted.

"There's several types of poisons," Esther told her. "The common names of some of the mushrooms are enough to give you goose bumps. There's 'Poison Pie, 'Deadly Parasols,' and the beautiful and famous 'Death Angel'."

It was odd, Esther thought. She shared Theodora's taste for the macabre.

Theodora smirked. She thought, *'Death Angel?' Who knew*

toadstools could be known for beauty? Theodora could hardly wait to tell Kurt. He could have his Christian fish motif. She could counter with deadly angels.

"Look, DOCTOR BAND!" Esther shouted. "A red-winged blackbird!" *Doctor Band* floated out over the water and echoed back to the boardwalk. Theodora looked about in confusion. There were dozens of blackbirds about.

"A male in breeding plumage," Esther stated confidently.

The two women stood on the platform, shading their eyes and looking out over the pond. The blackbirds whistled. There was a 'plunk' in the water. A beaver came swimming by, causing V's of ripples. Theodora stared at the beaver in fascination. She had thought of a beaver as a fat, dull rodent. This one powered through the water like an ocean liner. "He's magnificent!" she whispered.

Esther agreed as she used the moment of distraction to scan the far shore. Her eyes caught a small movement in the brush. It was Edna, and she was hurrying toward the parking lot. She carried a mushrooming basket and a leash connecting to an enormous black dog.

Esther's eyes flickered ahead to where Edna was traveling. There were thick ferns and tall thimbleberry bushes for a dozen yards. Then there was a bald spot in the foliage. That would be where Theodora would surely spot Edna across the pond.

The beaver dove under the water, and Theodora turned a happy face toward Esther. "That was amazing."

Esther smiled back. "Let's turn this way," she said, rotating to the other side of the decking. "Maybe he'll pop up on the other side." Esther could keep her face serene. The challenge was to slow her heart rate so her pulse didn't vibrate the arteries in her neck. Esther focused on a tall hemlock across the water and breathed deeply.

They stood, side by side for several moments. The beaver did not reappear. The sound of a car starting came floating across the water.

Theodora's face became a mask of fury while Esther sagged in relief. "We need to catch her!" Theodora ran down the boardwalk, yelling "Stop! Ms. Morton! Stop!"

Esther followed. She had the car keys. She could make sure that they didn't catch up with Edna. As Esther moved off the boardwalk and back to the trail, she decided that while Edna had escaped, she, Esther, had a new challenge. She really didn't like that flash of fury she had seen on Theodora's face. With a rising sense of unease, Esther began to jog down the trail after Theodora.

Did you hear about the fungus and the alga? They took a lichen to each other.

CHAPTER SEVENTY-NINE

Monday morning, McLane Nature Trail

THEODORA PACED BY Esther's car as Esther huffed into the parking lot. Theodora's eyes glittered with rage as she turned on Esther.

"Could we please hurry?" Theodora snapped.

Esther took a deep breath and picked up a stick. "No," she said. "We're going to do this." Esther took the branch and walloped a sword fern. She hauled back and walloped it again and again, sending up a cloud of brown spores. She spied another downed branch at the edge of the gravel lot. She picked it up and waved it at a shocked Theodora.

"Smack things!" Esther commanded. "Go for it!" Esther tossed her the stick.

Theodora snagged the branch as it came to her. She whirled and beat a dead sword fern until it shattered into fragments. Then she turned and beat another fern into a green mash. She whirled to her right and beat the stick against a log until the stick broke in two.

"There!" Esther laughed. "Now we're ready to make a plan."

The two women stood for a moment, grinning at one another.

"I do feel better," Theodora said.

"It's 'transference behavior.' You're transferring your annoyance." Esther said, "It's better to take out rage on an inanimate object that has no monetary value. You wouldn't want to do this," she said, pointing to the fern remains, "to a person or furniture."

"I'm familiar with the concept," Theodora admitted, "but I didn't realize someone like you would be… this way."

Esther smiled at her. "Someone like me? It's human nature to be angry at limitations."

Theodora nodded. "Where do we go to find Edna now?"

Esther shook her head. "Edna has a thousand spots for mushroom hunting. We're better off heading back to campus. Milo Anderson is the one you really wanted to see, right?"

Theodora took in a breath and exhaled. It didn't matter if she got her samples through Edna or through Dr. Anderson.

"You're right," she agreed. It was odd, but she found herself liking this short Yale professor. Theodora mulled that thought. She normally didn't like anyone.

Esther said, "It's only ten thirty. Let's take a moment and see if we can find what Edna was collecting."

"Look." Esther pointed to large reddish-brown shelf fungus, each the size of a dinner plate growing off a fallen log. "That's *Ganoderma*. Those have antibiotic properties and can be used on wounds. It's still too dry for many other species to be out."

"Rain triggers mushroom development?"

Esther nodded. "It's a factor. The mycelia of a fungus grows through the forest soil by the hyphae branching out and extending – like a plant's root system – although fungi are actually closer to the animal kingdom than the plant kingdom."

She continued, "The tip of the hyphae is a living interface between the world and the fungus. The cell wall at the tip is dynamic – it modifies itself according to conditions. Sections of the tip can signal mechanical strain. That strain activates enzyme activities and there is flow of building components to the root tip. It pushes forward, even through rock."

Esther added, "We don't know what triggers hyphae branching or fruiting body development. Is it an enzyme? Calcium? Oxygen gradient? What's intriguing is the notion that a cell may be responding to the extracellular matrix. What happens outside may trigger what happens within."

"What do you think might trigger new structure development in a mammal?" Theodora asked casually.

Esther met her eyes. "Good question. There's the entire field of Evolutionary Development that has come about in the last decade, asking the question of how do we get novel structures from existing genes."

Esther continued, "The field of epigenetics is exploding. How do genes interact with signals from the environment? What triggers changes that descend through following generations?"

Esther shrugged. "My best guess would be a molecular chaperone that helps in protein folding. In times of stress, chaperones can be overworked. That can result in the switching on of a previously cryptic genetic variation. Recently I've also heard quite a lot about DNA methylation."

Esther took out her car keys and pointed toward the parking lot. "Let's get back to campus. We can talk about the platypus on the way."

"The platypus?"

"Ten sex chromosomes and shares some genes with reptiles and birds."

"I'd like to hear what you know about bird genetics," Theodora replied. "Especially pertaining to the development of feathers."

Esther opened the car door and slid in, thinking rapidly. She'd wanted something charming and completely tangential to Edna's situation. Theodora had just boxed her in. Well, she was a Yale professor. She would pontificate on something.

"An old fox is not easily snared."

Romanian proverb

CHAPTER EIGHTY

Monday morning, 10:45 a.m. West of Olympia

EDNA'S HANDS SHOOK as she dialed the numbers on the lock. The lock did not yield. It had been several years since she had been through this gate. Edna closed her eyes and focused. She recalled the moment when the landowners had given her permission to collect mushrooms. Ah, there were the numbers. Their anniversary. This time the padlock opened.

Edna unwrapped the chain loop from around a robust fir and opened the metal gate. She rushed back to her Volvo, drove the vehicle past the gate and then emerged to dash back and lock the gate behind her. She drove down the dirt road and around a sharp bend to hide the car from the main road.

Edna still felt shaky. She opened the car door and invited Drewl out. "Come on, sweetie."

It was hard to know how much Drewl understood as he hopped out in an agreeable fashion. He seemed inclined to stay close to Edna, which she appreciated. She reached into the vehicle and pulled out a faded quilt and a daypack. Edna stopped and listened. She could hear cars whooshing down Delphi road. She heard bird song. No voices. No movements through the woods.

Chirping to Drewl, Edna moved along the dirt road until she found a break in the undergrowth. She took a left on a footpath and followed it until it opened out on a sunny clearing. She stopped to listen again.

Satisfied, Edna spread the quilt out at the edge of the clearing. She sat down, cross-legged, and opened the daypack. She pulled out four tuna fish sandwiches, wrapped in wax paper. Drewl sat at the edge of the quilt, attentive. As Edna began to unwrap the first sandwich, Drewl produced a long ribbon of spittle accompanied by a quiet, nervous shuffling of his front feet.

"Quite right. We're hungry." Edna placed the sandwich at his feet. Drewl reached out and gulped down the sandwich.

Amused, Edna fed him two more sandwiches. She told him, "That's enough. This last one has onion in it. It's not for you. It's mine." She poured herself a cup of tea from a thermos and unwrapped the last sandwich. Drewl watched her every movement until the sandwich was gone.

"All done. Here. Lie down." Edna patted the quilt beside her.

Drewl stretched out in the sun with a sigh.

Edna gave him a pat. "The best thing for us to do right now is to stay out of sight. Dr. Band doesn't strike me as a patient thing. God only knows what she's doing with Esther Mossler. We're going to trust that Esther can take care of herself."

Drewl rolled onto his side and leaned into Edna.

"You are absolutely right. We should have a nap." Edna took off her cardigan and bunched it into a pillow. She curled up next to the big dog and threw an arm over him. The sunshine played over the clearing as Edna and Drewl fell asleep. The silenced cell phone in her pocket vibrated. Edna was snoring and Drewl didn't care.

"The workman is known by his work."

Guild and Shop adage

CHAPTER EIGHTY-ONE

Monday morning, 10:45 a.m., The Haddad summer cabin

KURT LEFT THE cabin to retrieve his whetstone from his truck. He was surprised at the amount of traffic noise coming from Oyster Bay Road. He heard an unrelenting barking from two directions.

He carried the sharpening kit out to the deck. He didn't need the spotting scope to see the traffic backing up along Oyster Bay Road.

"WTF?" Kurt sat down in a deck chair and watched. He used the spotting scope to look across the water to Ellison Loop. The entire area was constipated with vehicles and people. There were circles of big women dancing on the Anderson's small lawn.

Across the road from the Anderson's, a large German Shepherd dashed around the tennis courts of a waterfront home, keeping up a steady stream of barking. He wasn't the only agitated dog. At the farm at the bend in Oyster Bay Road, a border collie yipped at the slow traffic inching by the farm gate.

Kurt grunted. It was good to know about the dogs. But what the hell was going on? He went into the cabin and turned on the television. It took a few minutes to find the Northwest Local News. There he learned that the weather would continue to be clear and unseasonably warm. Kurt turned up the volume and went into the kitchen to find some breakfast.

He came back into the living room with a microwaved breakfast burrito just as a news anchor said, "Do we have an angel in Washington? This footage of Lena Anderson of Olympia was posted online. Ms. Anderson saved a child from almost certain death. Let's watch."

Kurt took a bite of his burrito while holding his eyes on the screen. The news station had edited the Internet video down to the most dramatic ten seconds. Man, that woman was fast.

The news anchor came back on. "A photo of Ms. Anderson has been posted on *The Angels in our Cosmos* website that allegedly shows Ms. Anderson sprouting feathers." The screen changed to a photo showing Lena's face, shoulders and chest, stopping just above the nipples. Kurt stared at the screen, forgetting to chew.

"There is speculation that this may be the latest Internet hoax as the heroic Mrs. Anderson is topping the local morning Twitter trends. Angel fans are discussing her at #AngelWA. And now for Sports."

Kurt realized he had a full mouth of burrito. He chewed and swallowed and thought. He needed to talk to Theodora. This much news was not a good thing.

He took a savage bite of the burrito. He'd sharpen his knives. He'd look around for gardening tools. The 'Eco Loving Lawn Care' sign was already on the door of the truck. Kurt smiled as he wolfed the last bite of the burrito. He liked the little bunny on the sign.

*

Ten miles away, Deputy Ron MacRae stood frozen with a toothbrush in his hand. After eight days of work, he had been looking forward to this day off. He had meant to sleep until noon. Then his neighbor started his wood splitting. The constant thunk-thunk-thunk of the mechanical splitter had made sleep impossible.

After a few choice words, MacRae had given up the idea of sleeping in. He turned on the news out of habit. His ears caught "Lena Anderson" just as he uncapped some toothpaste. He stuck his head out of the bathroom and was transfixed by the news story.

As the newscast switched to Sports, MacRae began to brush his teeth. He needed to find Rodger Raposo.

*

Fifth grader Dylan Kushner hated worksheets. He particularly hated worksheets that said, "explain your answer," not because he was stupid, but because he couldn't write out an answer without Miss Phillips complaining about his handwriting. He'd made three efforts to please her during the first week of the term, and that was his limit.

When the worksheets were handed out, he excused himself to the boy's restroom. He had lifted his sister's smartphone from the kitchen counter that morning. Now was as good a time as any to check it out. It was so unfair how she got the good electronics.

He'd see if he could spend the next twenty minutes playing Tetris in the last stall and emerge in time for recess. Dylan snorted. *Live for the moment.* That was his motto. The next few minutes promised to be excellent. As he closed the door to the stall, he decided that it would be cool to check the Mariners standing. Dylan hit a browser icon. He'd try the ten a.m. Northwest News.

*

Margaux, Dr. Berbera's administrative assistant, stood up and stretched. She glanced out the window to the sunshine. If she wanted to spend Saturday mulching her garden, it would be smart to put in the mulch order early. She should check the weather forecast on the news.

"Avoid popularity if you would have peace."

Abraham Lincoln
(February 12, 1809 – April 15, 1865)

CHAPTER EIGHTY-TWO

Monday morning, 10:30 a.m. The Anderson home

"THURSTON COUNTY SHERIFF!" came through the door along with a loud rapping.

"Finally!" Milo strode the length of the small house and opened the door. "You guys took forever," he barked at the two men at the door. The pair was a near matched set with frowns and sweating faces.

"Take it easy, sir," one said. "There's a lot going on out here."

"Milo!"

With that tone of admonishment from his wife, Milo regrouped.

"Sorry," he apologized to the deputies. "It's been crazy."

"Step back!" A deputy turned to halt the women who crowded up the sidewalk to peer into the house.

Milo invited the deputies into the house. "Thank you. We're glad you're here. It's been nuts."

"We can see that. We've never seen this sort of congestion

out here. Sir, what is going on?" his voice trailed off as Lena came down the hallway.

The deputies stopped and stared. With the room darkened by window coverings, Lena's white blonde hair seemed to radiate a soft glow.

"The ladies seem to think I'm an angel," she said.

The slightly shorter deputy swallowed hard and asked, "Are you?"

Lena wrinkled her nose. "No. We think there's been some Internet hijinks with my image, and, well, people can be so hopeful."

"Desperate and idiotic, more like it," Milo grumbled.

"No arguments there, sir," said the taller deputy. "I think we've got close to three hundred people in the vicinity."

"I'm not a celebrity," Lena said with conviction. "People are just hoping that I am."

Happy shouts came from outside the house. One of the deputies opened the door and looked, his eyes moving upward as the sound of a helicopter registered. He shut the door and came back to say, "KIRI 3 helicopter. You're making the news."

Milo asked, "What can be done?"

"Several things," the taller deputy told him. "We can get people off your lawn and out of your driveway and we can get traffic directed away from the area. It is going to take a while. The whole loop is packed. We're going to need more officers and even then this won't be easy. Do you have any people that need to reach you?"

"Our daughter is at school," Milo replied. "She gets out about two thirty. And my mother-in-law and my graduate student are likely to be here later."

The deputy checked his watch. "Does your girl ride the school bus?"

"Yes."

"I'm going to suggest you call the principal. See if your daughter can get a ride home later in the afternoon. Can you get in contact with your other people?"

"Yes, I think so." Milo looked at Lena. "We should find the charging cord for Piper's old phone."

Milo turned back to the deputy. "Our cell phones are turned off for now. We're having constant calls. We've got an old cell phone of our daughter's."

"Okay. I'd like you to come up with a password that you are going to give to us and to your legitimate visitors. Think of something that is unlikely to be guessed by the public. We'll get a roadblock up. The only ones allowed in will be people with your password or people with proof that they live on this road."

Lena sighed. "Our neighbors are going to be so unhappy."

"Yes Ma'am. They are."

Milo looked at Lena. "Got a password idea?"

"Sure. *Mycelium*."

"Mycelium?"

Lena gave him a sour smile. "Mushroom growers always want the mycelium running, and running is just what we need to be doing."

Milo agreed. "Mycelium it is."

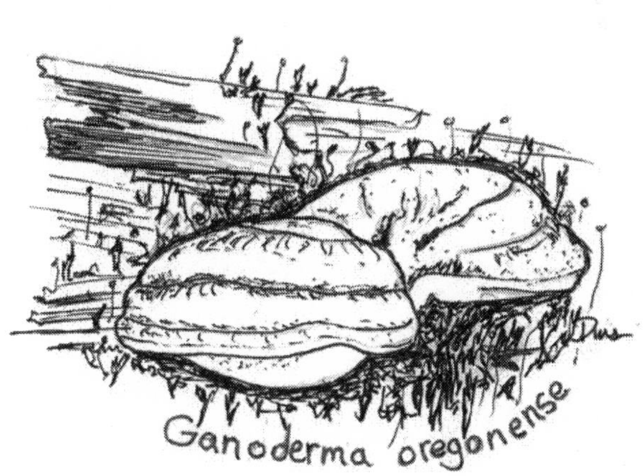
Ganoderma oregonense

Trending now…

Chapter Eighty-Three

Monday morning, 11 a.m. Summit College

GRACE WAS WILTING under a pounding headache. Dr. Berbera lectured all the way to the end of the class hour. Then he stayed on as students crowded around the lectern to buzz him with questions.

Grace tried to soak up the intervening minutes by checking the seats for left items. Finally she carried the bananas down to the front of the auditorium and tried to convey a polite patience.

Potential liberty seemed to show its face when the administrative secretary, Margaux, arrived at the top of the stairs with a cloud on her face and a computer tablet in her hand. She descended the steps like an incoming thunderstorm.

Dr. Berbera took her in with a sweeping glance and waved off the remaining trio of students. "Bureaucracy beckons," he joked.

It was not a new joke to Margaux, although she granted him a wry smile. "You'll want to see this," she said. She beckoned Grace over as well.

Margaux set the tablet on the lectern. "I went to check the weekend weather report on the news, and I saw a story on Mrs. Anderson. I think it may be the lead story on the eleven o'clock news."

There were several interminable minutes of mattress and car sale ads before the screen showed *"Breaking News."*

"We're following a breaking story in Thurston County," the news anchor began. "Mrs. Lena Anderson of Olympia allegedly rescued a boy from oncoming traffic on Saturday. She covered about seventy yards in a world record shattering 3 seconds."

"An amazing video of the rescue was posted online on Saturday night, followed by a posting on Sunday on the *The Angels in our Cosmos* website that allegedly shows Mrs. Anderson sprouting feathers. As you can see, the picture of the emerging feathers looks very real. These two events have angel fans everywhere buzzing. Let's go to Miranda in SkyEye for an update. Miranda?"

"Good morning, Allie. We're over the Anderson home, west of Olympia, where traffic is in a tangle. Angel fans from as far away as Vancouver, B.C. have driven down to meet with what they believe is an angel. Thurston County deputies have been directing traffic away from the neighborhood and are asking the public to refrain from visiting. As you can see, there are many who are not heeding the request of the Sherriff's office."

"Thank you, Miranda. Now we turn to Tufa who is in Lacey, where he is with a woman who has actually met the alleged angel. Tufa?"

"Good morning, Allie. I'm here with Nora Gillespie who tells us her cat, Sir Percival, was saved by Mrs. Anderson this morning. Ms. Gillespie, will you please tell us what Sir Percival experienced?"

The weeping mountain of a woman from early in the morning had transformed herself into a radiant hill of emerald green rayon. Snowy white Sir Percival nestled against her formidable bosom, with matching emerald eyes that stared unblinking at the camera.

"I just had to call in to tell you," Ms. Gillespie said. "This morning Sir Percival was on death's doorstep. I took him out to Mrs. Anderson. She stroked him. Now look at him!"

Sir Percival looked irked, disdainful and unquestionably alive.

"Is Mrs. Anderson a veterinarian?" asked the reporter.

"No. She didn't give him any medicine. She just stroked him and quoted a Bible verse." Nora Gillespie gulped air and continued; "She said 'Therefore I command you to be openhanded toward your brothers and toward the poor and needy in your land.' That's from Deuteronomy. I looked it up when I got home."

"Do you think Mrs. Anderson is an Angel?"

"Oh, Yes! Yes, I do! And her message isn't just for me, it's for all of us."

"There you have it, Allie. A satisfied customer."

"Thanks, Tufa. Viewers can join us at noon when Reverend Josiah Jefferson will be sharing a brief history of angels. Stay right with us. The weather for our Angel and angel fans, when we come back."

Grace stared at the screen, horrified. "Oh, my God," she whispered.

"Did you know about these feathers?" Dr. Berbera asked.

Grace stared at him in bewilderment. What should she say? She came up with, "Honestly, sir, I did not see Mrs. Anderson yesterday. I didn't. I was at the park when she ran to save the little boy, and that was incredible – but yesterday I was with her mother, Edna Morton, and her daughter, Piper and we went to pick out a dog."

Grace conveniently left out the evening with Ken Ito and Carys Kidwelly. She inhaled and went on. "Piper must be very upset."

"Hopefully, Piper is at school," Margaux observed, somewhat tartly. "Speaking of class, Yousef, remember you have a graduate seminar at one today. And Dr. Mossler called. She and Dr. Band are returning to campus."

Dr. Berbera gestured toward the computer tablet. "Now we know why Yale and NIH are here today." Dr. Berbera turned a frowning face to Grace. Her hopes of disappearing to return the bananas evaporated. "Are you related to Esther Mossler?" he asked.

"She's my aunt. I asked her to keep an eye on Dr. Band," Grace confessed.

She had Margaux and Dr. Berbera's full attention.

"Edna Morton had an encounter with Dr. Band last week. Edna went into a health clinic for an exam. I'm not exactly sure what transpired, but Edna doesn't like Dr. Band." Grace said.

Dr. Berbera checked his watch. "I need to make some calls and get some lunch. Ms. Mossler, you should attend the graduate student seminar at one. Be there. We'll discuss the news and evaluate the best course forward for our department and our employees, including Dr. Anderson. Bring your aunt, if you can."

There was nothing to be said but, "Yes, Sir."

"Are you in contact with Milo?"

"Not this morning," she answered truthfully. "I was going to check my messages now."

"I'll be very interested in hearing what he has to say." With that Dr. Berbera picked up his laptop and stalked out of the auditorium.

"Society is always taken by surprise at any new example of common sense."

Ralph Waldo Emerson
(May 25, 1803 – April 27, 1882)

CHAPTER EIGHTY-FOUR

Monday morning, 10:55 a.m., The Haddad summer cabin

DR. AND MRS. Haddad were organized people. There was a key on a cup hook next to the back door labeled "shed." Kurt took the key outside and unlocked a small garden shed. He found a rake, shovel, wheelbarrow, pruners, and garden gloves in two sizes, all clean and ready for use.

Kurt explored the shed. He took time to lift each gardening hat off its hook. Under the second hat, he found a ring of keys with a yellow foam oval attached. He studied the keys. "Boat fob," he decided. "Keys for padlock and ignition?"

He took the keys out into the sunshine and looked across the cove to Ellison Loop. The traffic was unrelenting. It looked like deputies had arrived to direct traffic. He should re-think lining up in the queue as a landscaper.

He stood still, keys in hand, and scanned his surroundings. He saw a footpath at the edge of the cabin deck that meandered to undergrowth on the right.

Kurt pushed past a huckleberry bush and set out on the footpath. The land sloped down abruptly. Kurt found himself almost twenty feet above the water. He kept on the path another dozen yards, and found he was looking down on a small roof. Nearby, a metal ladder was bolted to a towering fir.

Intrigued, Kurt climbed down the ladder. The little boathouse was ingenious. It was tucked into an inlet. Inside, a motorboat sat suspended over the water. The boat was cradled in a boat hoist with cables that ran over a pulley system connected to a wheel. Once the boat was steered into the cradle, even a child could turn the wheel and lift the boat out of the water. It was a clever way to keep the boat from being mired in muck at low tide.

Kurt balanced on a narrow dock walkway and leaned in to loosen the boat cover. The interior of the boat was pristine. Kurt worked the entire cover off and stepped back. A seventeen-foot SeaRay gleamed in the morning light.

He replaced the boat cover and gave the boat hull a pat. He climbed back up the ladder with a smile. He now knew a little something special about the Haddads. Someone, likely Dr. Haddad, liked hidden treasures.

Kurt checked his watch. It was time to call Theodora and give her an update on the circus across the cove. After that, he'd go through the cabin carefully to see what else Dr. Haddad had hidden.

*

"Sorry to disturb you, Sir, but this can't wait." Deputy MacRae was in uniform at the door of the dentist's cubicle.

"DankGdd" came from a supine Rodger Raposo. He pulled cotton batting out of his mouth. "I meant to say, 'Thank God.'"

Raposo massaged his upper cheek carefully. "She's not finished, but I am. Help me out of here."

MacRae extended a hand. Raposo got to his feet without adjusting the chair. He peeled the paper toweling off his front and dropped it into the chair. "Let's go."

"Don't you want to know what this is about?"

"No." Raposo grabbed his coat and strode out to the lobby. "Emergency!" he barked at the receptionist. "I'll call and reschedule later." Shoving MacRae out the door, he bolted for the deputy's sedan.

"Take time to deliberate; but when the time for action arrives, stop thinking and go in."

Andrew Jackson
(March 15, 1767 – June 8, 1845)

Chapter Eighty-five

Monday morning, 11:45 a.m. The Red Hawk Inn

KEN DECIDED TO acknowledge the knocking on his door. He had been at the computer for two hours, and it was time for a break.

He looked through the spyhole and was delighted to see Carys. Ken flung open the door and opened his arms. She walked into his embrace. He hugged back.

"I'm so glad to see you!" Ken pulled her into his hotel room. "I'm having commitment issues. It's very confusing."

Carys blinked. She sat down at the edge of the bed. "Commitment issues?" she asked carefully.

"Yes! We say a cell is 'totipotent' if it can divide and differentiate into any sort of tissue. But humans are only totipotent in the embryonic stage."

"Whereas fungi are always totipotent," Carys said.

"Yes! So why is it that fungi retain the ability to morph into different directions, and mammals don't? More specifically, why do Edna and Lena suddenly have feathers? And even if we had a mammalian embryo that produced feathers, what would cause that? What causes a cell to commit to a pathway?"

"I don't know," Carys replied, "But we count on a mushroom's plasticity in my business. We can take a sample of a fruiting body in the field and come back to the farm to inoculate a growth medium to get mycelial growth."

"Right. You can't do that with mammals. Sure, there's been a ton of cloning work done, but that's intense management of the cell in laboratory conditions. With Edna, this happened naturally."

He went on, "Fungal cells are not committed to a particular differentiated state the way animal cells are. The fungal cells can break their commitments and go a new direction."

Ken tore at his hair. "We know from gene sequencing that several organisms can each have a biochemical pathway that is so identical across the different organisms that we don't think the pathways came from parallel evolution. We think one group of cells recruits gene sequences from another organism."

"So you are thinking that Edna and Lena and perhaps Piper have somehow taken up a gene sequence from something else?"

"Yes! It's what makes sense to me."

"But since it's feathers, doesn't it make sense that they would have picked up a gene sequence from a bird?"

"That's the part that's making me crazy. All my instincts as a yeast man make me think that Edna's extreme exposure to fungi is important – but there's no way to know that or show that without…," Ken paused and sadly concluded, "Without Edna being at a lab."

"Where there are scientists taking samples," Carys finished.

"Yeah. Blood samples, skin samples, urine samples. Multiple, ongoing samples. For years." Ken sat down next to Carys on the bed. He slid an arm around her. She nestled her head on his shoulder. Ken propped his chin on her dark hair and held her close.

Ken said, "There's a couple governmental big shots in Homeland Security interested in Lena. I got a call from Harry, my supervisor. I'm supposed to check out Lena and report back. You know her, right?"

Carys said. "You haven't seen the news this morning, have you?"

"No. I've been thinking. What's up?"

"The world is on Lena's doorstep. That's why I'm here. One of the guys at the farm had the local cable news on this morning while he was washing up in the prep area. He came and told me because…, well, because he's a guy and he's always thought Edna's daughter is, as he says, 'beyond hot.' He knows I know Edna."

"Anyway," Carys said, "There are a couple hundred angel fans that are mobbing the Anderson's house. Lena's inside, not saying anything. There's helicopters overhead, traffic for miles. It's insane. There'll be a special report at noon."

"Any word on the news about Edna?"

"Not that I saw at eleven. I tried to call you, but you didn't answer. By the way, your voice mailbox is full."

Ken winced. "Sorry, I was thinking."

"I thought so. That's when I decided I should drive over." Carys picked up the television remote and clicked the television on. "It's on the Northwest local news channel."

The TV blared.

Angel Wings paper towels are the towels for you! An ideal balance of softness and strength at the price you love.

Stop by Glenn's Paintball Emporium in Tacoma! We

have a great collection of Angel Paintball collectibles. Come join the action! The finest paintball equipment in the Pacific Northwest!

"Looks like the advertising staff are good at their job," Carys said.

Ken didn't answer. His focus was on the screen.

"Welcome to Noon News Now. I'm Allie Sanchez. Our top story is Angel-mania unfolding in Thurston County. Angel fans from Portland to Vancouver, B.C. are descending on a home west of Olympia in hopes of seeing Mrs. Lena Anderson, an alleged miracle worker, who is credited with saving a small child from certain death and with reviving a dying pet."

"A photograph of Mrs. Anderson has been posted online, supposedly showing the lady with feathers, fueling the angel mania. We go now to Thurston County, where SkyEye is overhead. What can you tell us, Miranda?"

"It's popular, Allie. As you can see, traffic continues to stream down Oyster Bay Road in Thurston County toward the Anderson home. In the last half hour we have seen at least four adults carrying children down the middle of the road. That is dangerous, given the amount of traffic we're seeing. Thurston County deputies are out in force, directing traffic and dealing with the crowds."

"Any sign of Mrs. Anderson?"

"No. We've seen no one go in or out of the Anderson home."

"Thanks, Miranda. And now to Dr. Juliet Ma. Thanks for joining us this morning. Dr. Ma, have you ever heard of a person sprouting feathers?"

"Good morning, Allie. No, I haven't. There are those of us who can be hairy individuals, but we are humans, not birds. I think it is highly unlikely that Mrs. Anderson, or anyone else, has really sprouted feathers. Our hair and nails are an alpha keratin and feathers are a more complex beta keratin."

"Are you calling this Angel-mania a hoax?"

"It's hard to say just what is unfolding. It may be that Mrs. Anderson is a fast runner. However, it is possible, with today's technology, to engineer a video clip or a photograph to make any number of amazing things look possible."

"A Photo-shop Angel?"

"A distinct possibility."

"Why are so many people traveling to Thurston County to see this woman?"

"We are a hopeful, gullible species, Allie."

"Thank you, Dr. Ma. And now we have Reverend Josiah Jefferson with us for a brief history of angels. Reverend, thanks for joining us."

"Delighted to be here, Allie."

"What can you tell us about angels through history?"

"It's a huge subject, Allie. The idea of holy messengers dates back several thousand years. Interestingly, named angels in the Judea-Christian tradition are almost all male. Angels are also part of Islamic and shamanistic cultures. There's a fascinating excavation in modern day Turkey of a shrine that shows a human form with vulture feathers. The shrine dates back to 6,500 BCE."

"Did the vulture angel have a harp or a halo?"

"No, Allie. He did not. Harps and halos have been part of art for centuries. Halos on angels really took off around the eleventh century when Europe began a major angel-mania phase."

"Thank you, Reverend Jefferson. And now for the weather updates for our viewers and angel fans."

Carys hit the mute button. "Can you believe this?"

"No," Ken admitted. "My God, how did it get away from us so fast?"

"The age of the Internet."

"Carys, I've got to get over there to Lena. Christ. I blew it. I should have been there first thing this morning."

“I don’t see how any of us could have foreseen this,” Carys told him.

“Thanks, but foreseeing things is exactly why they pay me.” Ken shut his laptop and unplugged it. “Any ideas on how I cut through that crowd to see Lena?”

Carys smiled. “I came prepared. We’ll go out Highway 101 past the Oyster Bay exit and onto the Kamilche peninsula. I borrowed a shorty wetsuit for you and a waterproof bag for your gear.”

“We’re swimming?”

Carys gave him the double dimple grin. “Ever kayak?”

*

Noon, Twin Cedars School

As a long time principal, Mrs. Sheehan knew children always had the capacity to surprise her. It was a joy when there was a reversal of a downward trend.

Still, she did not expect to see Dylan Kushner come into her office with an arm around Piper Anderson. Both children were pale, with Piper looking frightened and Dylan very determined.

“It’s her mom,” Dylan said. “She’s in the news.”

"Too many cooks spoil the broth"

– too many people, too many times

CHAPTER EIGHTY-SIX

Monday, Noon, The Albatross and Eagle Bar and Grill, Mud Bay Road, west of Olympia

RODGER RAPOSO PROPPED his elbows on the bar and cradled his numb face in his hands as he watched the news. Next to him, Deputy MacRae shifted nervously. Raposo ignored MacRae until the news finished. He tossed a dollar into the tip jar and nodded to the bartender. "Thanks."

Raposo jerked his head toward the door. "Don, let's get out of here before some little old lady complains about your unit hanging out at the bar."

As the two men strode out into the September sunshine, an Olympia police car pulled up next to MacRae's Mason County sedan. Sergeant Martinez tabbed his window open. "Morning, gents."

"Morning, Sergeant. We're catching the noon news. What do you know about the jam out on Oyster Bay?"

"I know it's a total cluster fuck. It's Monday morning, for

God's sake. Who staffs up for a Monday morning? Sheriff's office is calling in deputies. Everyone's tired."

MacRae agreed. "I've worked eight straight. I'm not supposed to be here either. Here we are, anyway. We may have some connections to this."

"Related to Ms. Kovacev?" Martinez was all ears.

"Possibly," Raposo grunted. "Ms. Kovacev's employer treated the mother of Mrs. Anderson. An old gal named Edna Morton."

"Mushroom Edna? She's in this? That I would not have guessed."

"It's not clear just yet. We need to get out to the Andersons for a talk."

"Watch out for a deputy named Pendergast. He can be a real territorial prick. Sheriff moved him to days because of some anger management issues."

"Great."

"Yeah, we live to serve, except for the ones that don't." Martinez sketched a salute and drove off.

Raposo turned frosty eyes to Deputy MacRae. "I hate territorial pricks. Right now we've got Thurston County Sheriff and Mason County Sheriff with Olympia PD thrown in. Let's hope we don't get any more governmental agencies in on this deal. The last thing we need is more chiefs."

"Yes, Sahib."

Raposo laughed. "Come on. Let's get rolling."

"Speak softly and carry a cell phone."

Teddy Roosevelt, updated
(Theodore Roosevelt, Jr. 1858 – 1919)

CHAPTER EIGHTY-SEVEN

Monday, 12:30, Summit College

GRACE HOTFOOTED THE bananas back to Angus. She mumbled her thanks and grabbed an energy bar and a mega-caffeinated drink, ignoring Angus's questioning face. She made one more promise to herself that her next meal would be healthy, and charged back toward the Biology building. She nearly collapsed with relief when she saw her Aunt Esther sitting, once again, on the bench outside the Biology building.

"Auntie! I am so glad to see you!"

"I just parked Dr. Band with Yousef Berbera. Margaux gave me an earful, and I caught the 12:15 news re-run. Sounds like a lot is going on."

"It's unreal. Where did you go with Dr. Band?"

"Out to the McLane Nature Trail – where, believe it or not, we almost bumped into Edna. I managed to get Dr. Band out to the middle of the boardwalk. Edna heard us and took off in a hurry."

"How did Dr. Band take that?"

"Not well. She's scary, Grace. She's got a lot of banked fury, and she's intense. No wonder Edna steers clear of her."

Grace pulled out her phone. "I haven't checked messages in hours. The class went on forever, and then Margaux came in and showed us the cable news. I'm hoping there's something here from Milo."

Esther pulled out her own smartphone. "I'm afraid to look at my inbox."

The two round-faced women sat in the dappled shade and scrolled through their messages.

"Milo says they're surrounded. He says they've turned off their cell phones because of constant calls. He does have an old phone of Piper's that's working. He also asks for me to come out when I can, and the password to get past the roadblock is 'mycelium,' Grace said.

Esther replied, "I just sent a text to Edna, telling her I'm free of Dr. Band, and asking if she wants to meet. Uncle Raymond says the Andersons are on the news. You know, he can be a great asset if we end up needing logistical help."

Grace nodded. "Let me call Milo. I've also got a message from Ken Ito. He's the N.S.A. researcher who came out to Edna's with Carys Kidwelly. Ken says he and Carys are going to try to reach Milo and Lena by kayaking out from Kamilche."

Grace typed in the number for Milo and jumped up to pace while she spoke. Esther smiled as she watched Grace march away a hundred feet, then pivot and stride back, talking all the while. She did the same thing. So did Raymond.

Several minutes later Grace tapped the phone off. "Wow. Milo knows Ken is coming. The principal will drive Piper home later in the day. They don't know where Edna is. She's not answering her phone."

Esther said, "No answer yet from my text to her. Keep in mind that Edna is of an earlier generation. If she turned the phone off, it may be several hours before she bothers to check messages."

Grace sighed. "That makes me crazy. What's the point of having technology if you don't use it?"

"Perhaps a discussion for another time?" Esther stood up and grabbed Grace's elbow, propelling her down the walkway. "Dr. Band just went by the stairwell window. She will be exiting, I think." Esther pulled Grace up a small embankment, and the two women sank down into a bed of ferns behind a rhododendron. Theodora Band came out the door moments later. She was on her cellphone.

"No," Theodora said, "I disagree. I still think we can manage. Look, the department head is a stupid, hairy ape. I can get him to do anything."

Grace and Esther exchanged a shocked look. Yousef Berbera was hairy. Stupid? Not hardly. How had Theodora gotten that impression?"

"That's wonderful!" Theodora clearly liked something she was hearing. "That gives us some options, doesn't it? Definitely an asset."

Grace began to lean forward to hear more. Esther shot a hand out in warning. Theodora swung back toward the Biology building and said into the phone, "There's a graduate seminar here at one. Berbera invited me. My best bet is to dominate discussion. I'll see if I can get the hairy ape into a broom closet for a feel up. Anderson is overwhelmed. He's got to reach out for official support at some point, and I need to be it. Do me a favor. When you answer the phone, answer it "National Institutes of Health.' I'm going to give your number to the departmental secretary and invite her to check me out."

There was a pause as Theodora listened to a response.

Theodora said, "Yeah. That'd be great. Long time employee. Great researcher, blah, blah, blah. You got it." Theodora checked her wristwatch. “I’m going to grab some lunch. I’ll be back late afternoon.” Theodora ended the call and strode off toward the cafeteria.

Grace turned to Esther. “I do not like that woman.”

“I see your point. Are you part of this graduate seminar?”

“Yes. Dr. Berbera insists. He said to bring you, if you would come. He wants to discuss the news and how the department should respond.”

“That’s wise. If Lena’s popularity continues to grow, you can count that reporters will be here with questions about the family.”

“I wish we could reach Edna.”

*

In Washington D.C. it was mid-afternoon. Dr. Carlos Rivera was evaluating the news out of Washington State.

There were reports of crowds streaming into a rural neighborhood. That had to be people deluding themselves with the latest theory on messages from God.

It wasn’t the crowds that held his interest. It was his close scrutiny of the feather photos of Mrs. Lena Anderson that were now on several websites.

He enhanced one of the photos. It was clear that there were ‘goose bumps’ that looked to be in the early stages of feather production. The spongy wall of each papillae looked exactly as it should to protect and support the emerging feather. There were also keratin sheaths or ‘pin feathers’ jutting out above and below the feather rows.

Could they be real feathers?

Carlos checked his watch. No word from Ken Ito. Dammit. Ito should have checked in by now.

A red flag icon popped up in the corner of the screen. Carlos smiled. Zebulon Szczepanski didn’t know that his travel reservations were being monitored. Where was Z going now?

Carlos's fingers flew across the keyboard. Seattle? This afternoon? That was interesting.

Carlos checked the itinerary. Z was traveling on a direct flight. Carlos brought up a travel site. He could get on the same plane. Carlos looked up at the clock. He needed to buy the ticket now and get to the airport. No way was Z going to scoop him on the Angel.

"The journey of a thousand sites begins with a single click."

Update on a Chinese proverb

CHAPTER EIGHTY-EIGHT

Monday, 12:45 p.m., The Anderson home

MILO HUNCHED OVER his computer and rapidly scanned another scientific paper. Lena brought him a sandwich and a drink. He ignored both until she tapped his shoulder and pointed at the plate.

"Thanks, hon." Milo ran a hand through his hair. "My current best guess is that something like adenosine 3': 5' - cyclic monophosphate is activating the differentiation in your cells."

"That's a mouthful."

"It's called cAMP for short. It's known to activate enzymes – I found a paper that connects cAMP to the phase when a fungus moves from just being a mycelium to when it initiates a fruiting body. But differentiation is such a tricky business. It could be a peptide."

Milo paused to bite into the sandwich. He spoke with his mouth full. "And we can't forget that fungi are often symbiotic.

Because of the external digestion, the initiator may come from the symbiotic partner."

Milo chewed and swallowed. "You know, Edna's remedy may be a false lead. What about zinc fingers? Zinc is a known transcription regulator for polypeptides."

Lena sighed. "My geek translator mechanism tells me that you aren't figuring this out."

Milo popped the tab on a soda. "No kidding. Honestly, sweetie. We need things like a DNA analysis - and people who know how to look, where to look, and what it means when they see something. It would take me at least a couple years to get up to speed on it."

Milo gulped down some of the soda and burped. "Biochemistry was my worst subject. Speaking of subjects, how are your fans outside doing?"

Lena waggled her hand so-so. "No one's rapped on the door in the last hour. It looks like the deputies have everyone off the lawn."

Milo leaned back in his desk chair. He tried to look casual.

Lena knelt down on the floor next to Milo's desk chair. "I know what you're thinking. Where's my mother? I wish she would call."

"Hey, she probably found a supremo mushroom patch and doesn't even know it's lunch time."

"Like you wouldn't have known it was lunch time if a sandwich hadn't magically appeared."

"Yeah, there is that." Milo leaned over and planted a kiss on Lena's forehead. "What have you been up to this last hour?"

"Eating."

"Eating?"

"For some reason, I am just starved. I plowed through an entire frozen cheesecake, and then I made sandwiches." Lena said. "Nervous energy, I guess."

Milo reached down and took her wrist. "Let's check your pulse."

"My pulse?"

"It may be that your metabolism is rising."

"Milo, you're scaring me."

"Sweetheart, let's do some data collection. Pulse, respiration, weight. Then we'll know if anything changes."

"If I keep eating whole cheesecakes, of course there'll be changes. I'll pop out of my jeans."

Milo looked down at his watch. "Be quiet and let me count. Hey, maybe we could sell you in pill form. The Angel high metabolism diet plan."

Lena was not amused.

"Of all the animals, the boy is the most unmanageable."

Plato (427 BCE – 347 BCE)

CHAPTER EIGHTY-NINE

Monday, 12:45 p.m., Mrs. Sheehan's conference room

"IT'S GLOBAL WARMING." Dylan said.

"Would you shut up? If it was global warming, we'd all be sprouting feathers," Piper groused back.

"No. Man, I'm serious. I read a book about oxygen levels in the time of the dinosaurs. Get this, when there's a rapid change in oxygen levels, it can change speciation rates. There was this thing called the Cambrian Explosion. All of a sudden, you had hundreds of species instead of, you know, primordial ooze."

Piper stared at him.

Dylan plunked an elbow on the conference room table and started picking on a scab on his elbow. "So the oxygenation levels in the Cambrian Period were at thirteen percent and now we're at twenty-one percent. Birds didn't appear until, like, the late Jurassic, but the really efficient respiratory system that birds have already existed in theropod dinosaurs. They both have pneumatized bones."

"Cambrian Period? Pneumatized bones? Dylan, are you a nerd?"

Dylan shoved and tilted until he balanced on the back chair legs. "Just interested in stuff."

Piper looked at him in amazement. "Why were you so nasty to Joey?"

Dylan shrugged and picked at his scab while balancing on the chair. "He was being a moron. Pretending. It's not manly."

"He's a kid!"

"Yeah, but you gotta grow up." Dylan brought the chair down with a thump. "That's what they keep telling me. You know what? I'll bet we could get up in the ceiling. We put the chair on the table and climb up. Then we lift one of those ceiling tiles. We could crawl across and make our escape."

"Dylan! Not a good idea! We're supposed to wait here!"

Dylan shrugged again. "We're also supposed to be getting an education, and I want to know if the ceiling has duct work."

"If it does, it's made of metal, and that would clang a lot if you crawled through it."

Dylan looked at Piper with some dawning respect. "Good point."

In a desperate move to redirect, Piper said, "Tell me more about the evolution stuff."

Dylan stuck a finger up his nose and drew out a crusty booger, which he flicked onto the floor. "So," Dylan said, "The idea is that respiration drives bodies. When the atmosphere changes, we get different bodies happening. When oxygen is high, evolution stalls. When oxygen starts to drop, you get stuff that has to cope."

"But we're in Olympia. There are trees everywhere. There's tons of oxygen."

"Duh. We're also near the ocean. Warm water doesn't hold as much oxygen as cold water, so you get plankton die off as the earth heats up. Dead zones. No oxygen production. It's in the news. And you got clear-cut forests and forest fires. Less forest, less oxygen."

"I don't see how that gives us feathers."

Dylan leaned forward to put both elbows on the table. "Go back to the start. Paleozoic. Low oxygen and primitive life. You need gills to get oxygen out of the water. Lots and lots of gills. That's how you get segmentation – all those worms and trilobites. You also get a ton of mollusks because they pump water over their gills. Form follows function."

Dylan motioned with his hands. "Soon you get fishes, and then the oxygen levels around the earth go up. Stuff comes out of the water onto the land. You get scorpions with book lungs – the air just passes over these flat plates that were stacked like pages in a book. All those pages are surfaces where the oxygen gets taken in."

"Like gills on a mushroom," Piper mused. "Only there the air is taking the spores away."

"Only scorpions are way cooler because they have armor. The armor protects them, and it keeps them from drying out."

"Yeah, but mushrooms are smart enough to live in moist climates, so they don't need any armor."

"Mushrooms are smart?" Dylan hooted.

Piper's cheeks flushed deep pink. She was rescued from her embarrassment when a large woman entered the conference room with two sack lunches.

"Here you go, dearies."

"Thanks, Mrs. Miller," Piper said. Dylan said nothing.

Mrs. Miller set the lunches down on the table and turned away. Dylan stared at her as she pulled the door closed.

"Dylan! What's with you?" Piper hissed.

"She's so fat."

"That's rude!"

"Just saying. Is there a Mr. Miller?"

"I don't know. Why?"

"Cause if he's dead, maybe he suffocated with his face in her boobs. Her boobs are gi-normous."

"Dylan!"

"Just sayin'."

"Well, don't." Piper reached for a lunch sack. "Go on with the evolution stuff."

Dylan opened his lunch, took out a sandwich and bit into it. "Next we get the oxygen levels going way up and we get giant insects. Dragonflies the size of buzzards. Scorpions three feet long. Then, Boom! Permian extinction. Oxygen slides. Ninety percent of life croaks. Clouds of hydrogen sulfide everywhere. The whole planet stinks of rotten eggs. Stuff has to adapt."

Dylan ate and spoke at the same time. "After the Permian crash, we get the Triassic explosion. You get bipedalism. Things can run – fast! You get thumbs. You get modified hips. And the big enchilada? You get lungs."

Piper daintily opened her sandwich. "I get that I'm supposed to be impressed, but I don't get why."

"Two kinds of lungs." Dylan said, with a full mouth. "In-and-out lungs like ours that have crappy efficiency, and then you got your one-way lungs. Lots of the Triassic dinosaurs have the one-way lungs - they pull air into air sacs in their bones and abdomen. Then the air whooshes out, over the lungs. The blood goes countercurrent, picking up oxygen, dumping carbon dioxide. Massively efficient. Like 200% better than what we've got."

Dylan leaned his chair back on two legs and tossed his apple into the trash with an impressive arcing throw. "Cold-blooded dinosaurs in the Triassic because, man, it was hot. Then oxygen levels go up, and, whammo. The Jurassic. Dinosaurs rule. Warm-blooded dinosaurs then. You get true birds in the Jurassic. One-way lungs. And feathered dinosaurs from the Jurassic into the Cretaceous. You know why?"

Piper sat, spellbound, with her sandwich still untouched. "So they can fly?"

"No! The hydrogen sulfide! Duh! Keratin that makes up hair and feathers lets the body get rid of hydrogen sulfide. When you get high metabolisms, you get poisonous leftovers, and the body has to crap it out, or grow it out."

"Dylan, how is it you know all this? I mean, you're like a D student."

Dylan blew out breath that fluttered his lips and produced a loud buzzing fart sound. He said, "I like dinosaurs. Always have. The D's stand for dumb stuff they make me do." Dylan thumped his chair down. "The teachers hate me, you know."

"Yeah, but you're a jerk. Why are you so… difficult?"

"My Monday therapist says I'm oppositional. My Thursday therapist says I'm intellectually honest." He slapped his hands on the table. "I can't write worth a fuck. I think I should chop my hands off. If I had some new ones, that might help."

Piper looked at him in exasperation. "It's not your hands. It's in your brain wiring. It's called dysgraphia. Duh."

"Whatever. Ms. Phillips calls it laziness. She's supposed to know. Got any chewing gum?"

"No. It's bad for your teeth."

"I don't want the gum, stupid. I want some foil." Dylan pointed at a flashlight resting on top of a filing cabinet. "We use a strip of foil to make an arc across a battery. That gives us sparks. We make a fire, which gets us a fire alarm, and we're out of class for at least an hour."

"Why not just pull the fire alarm?" Piper couldn't believe she was saying this. Dylan's deluge of thinking was pulling her along with its relentless logic.

"Because if I do that one more time, I'm expelled. My parents' home schooling would suck."

"Um, we're already out of class. We could just wait here."

"Good point. Are you going to eat that sandwich?"

"If you're still hungry, you should have eaten the apple."

"The Red Delicious? It's red but it's not delicious. It's a crappy apple. Piper, you can't trust these people. If they'll lie to kids about the apples, they'll lie to you about anything."

"Strategy without tactics is the slowest route to victory. Tactics without strategy is the noise before defeat."

Sun Tzu (544 BCE – 496 BCE)

Chapter Ninety

Monday, 1 p.m., The Anderson home

LENA POINTED THE remote at the television. She wanted to be outside in the garden on this warm September day. She had a row of raised garden beds behind the house, and the tomatoes were finally ripening.

Every year it was a race between the tomatoes and the cold fall rains. This year the tomatoes were sprinting ahead. There was also the last of the basil to cut, and it was time to clean out the strawberry bed.

Today Lena didn't dare show her face. She had to stay inside.

Lena tried the news channel.

"Today all eyes are on the west coast, where…"

Lena changed channels. Surely that was a report on an earthquake or a quarterback with a knee injury, but she didn't want to see her house on the news. She watched a few minutes of a yoga show before chiding herself for her cowardice. She clicked back to the news.

"Joining us after the break is Lakmini Chakrabarti, an expert on hoaxes. Who establishes a hoax, how do they unfold, and why do we believe them?"

Lena sighed and changed to PBS.

"Join us tonight as we host geneticist Nicholas Andronikos on DNA regulation, and the evolving field of epigenetics, with particular emphasis on the role of DNA methylation on cancer development. Dr. Andronikos has led groundbreaking research on the role on modulating gene expression through nutrition. Now back to Life of Birds."

Lena tried a home decorating channel.

"It's only a few weeks until Christmas! Join us in our next segment as we show you how to make an adorable angel tree topper. We'll be using heavy starch on vintage handkerchiefs along with some light floral wire to give our angel glorious, three-dimensional wings."

In desperation, Lena clicked again. There had to be a nature show or fall storm somewhere.

"We welcome Javon Turner, author of "A History of Bizarre Humans."

Lena felt her eyes flood with tears. She swiped her eyes. She made herself sit down and turn up the volume.

"We are curious about people who look significantly different than ourselves, even though the vast majority of unusual looks stem from readily understandable changes in the genetic code. Take John Merrick, the 'Elephant man' of Victorian times. It's believed that he suffered from a simple change in an enzyme that resulted in overgrowth of skin, bones and muscle."

"'Tree Man' syndrome, in which there can be terrible growths of warts on the extremities, is caused by a mutation on chromosome 17. Specifically, the genes that regulate zinc distribution are modified. Human papillomaviruses thrive because the viruses can access cellular zinc."

"It's astonishing that a single gene being activated or inactivated can have such life altering results."

Lena felt rather than heard Milo's approach. "Anything good on the tube?" he asked.

Lena muted the TV. She said, "I'm not finding any escapist television. It's just not my day."

"I told you we should have gone for more than basic cable." Milo sat down on the sofa next to her.

Lena turned to him. "Well, I did see a kind of cool craft project to make an angel out of a handkerchief." She sighed. "I'm not surprised that I'm confused. What says the scientist?"

"I'm going around in circles. We need specialized help to understand this, which boils down to a university or a government agency. Which university? One with a medical hospital, I'm thinking, and those guys are going to be sample happy."

Lena shuddered. "I can't imagine living that way. Even thinking about an MRI, I have claustrophobia. And blood samples? No way!"

Milo stroked her hair. "Okay, on to governmental agencies."

"Not the National Zoo."

"Piper might like the otters."

Lena dropped her head onto Milo's chest. "I can't bear the thought of Piper growing up like a zoo animal. To be stared at by millions."

"Shh. Right now she's safe in Mrs. Sheehan's office. She's probably dying of boredom. We'll find a path forward."

Lena squared her shoulders. "I need to be doing something productive."

"Atta girl. What do you have in mind?"

"Trying to call my mother again."

Boletus edulis

"Tis foolish to fear what you cannot avoid."

Publilius Syrus (about first century BCE)

Chapter Ninety-one

Monday, 1 p.m., Graduate Student seminar, Summit College

GRACE SLIPPED INTO the seminar room, determined to take a seat at the back. She was out-maneuvered by Dr. Berbera, who was working with Angus to pull chairs into a half circle in front of a giant flat screen unit.

"Twenty seats," Berbera said.

More grad students poured in and Esther arrived, having conjured a cup of coffee in a ceramic mug from somewhere. Dr. Band strode in just before one.

Dr. Berbera wasted no time. "Please give your attention to the screen. I'll be showing the online footage of Mrs. Anderson at the park. We'll visit a website called *The Angels in our Cosmos*, where we'll see photographs purporting to be Mrs. Anderson sprouting feathers. Please hold your comments."

The video launched and Grace found herself holding her breath. She could watch the rescue footage a thousand times over.

She didn't like seeing her galumphing run at the end. Too bad those last seconds of the video had to be included. The feather photos that came next were bizarre. Some of the feathers were well developed, with a central rachis and equally balanced sides. Others were downy.

Dr. Berbera spoke. "We've got three issues: one, What's happening; two, Why? And three, How do we assist the Andersons? Let's start with 'What's happening?' Comments? Oh, and since this is our first gathering of the term, please give your first name and your field."

"Angus here. Microbiology. My first thought is that it's a hoax. To what end, I'm not sure."

"Grace, you're Dr. Anderson's student. What is your assessment?"

"I'm Grace, Zoology. The run is not a hoax. I was there, in the parking lot. That's me that you see at the end, carrying the backpack. I hate how I run."

That brought a chuckle from others.

"I was there, and Mrs. Anderson really did run that fast. She was exhausted afterward. I also think a hoax would be wildly out of character for her and for Dr. Anderson." Grace didn't want to give Dr. Band anything more to consider than that.

Esther waved a hand. "Esther here. Lichenologist. I think we answer the question 'what's happening?' by stating the obvious: a novel form of *Homo sapiens*, presenting with fast muscle fibers and feather development."

"And why?"

Esther nodded and continued. "We are learning that DNA is more than a blueprint. DNA has switches and knobs. The switches may be methyl groups that allow DNA to be read, or be halted from being read. The knobs are histones. The DNA wraps around histones and when the strands are loosened from around the histones, we have new areas of DNA available to be read."

Esther added, "It may be that each one of us already has the DNA blueprints to produce faster muscles or feathers."

Grace jumped in. "There can also be horizontal transmission of DNA between organisms at times."

A pale young woman with narrow, black-rimmed glasses snorted. "Emma here. Ecology. It sounds like you're saying we shouldn't sleep with a cat because we might wake up purring."

Grace refused to be baited. "Of course not. There's also determination. There gets to be a point where an organism is on the cusp of change. It can go down one path, such as fungal mycelia making more hyphae, or it can go down another path and start to produce a fruiting body. Cancer is another area where we don't know all the triggers."

A husky black man put a hand up. "Jason here. Biochemistry. I'm more interested in the 'How.' Is it an environmental impact on her system? If so, what sort? Temperature? Diet? Stress? And is it trans-generational? Are there other members of Mrs. Anderson's family? Any have changes?"

Grace had only a moment to put up her poker face. She'd better shut up before she said something that might alert Dr. Band to Piper's skin pores. Milo had enough on his hands.

Dr. Berbera swung his eyes to Grace. "You spent yesterday with the family. What can you tell us?"

"Ah, Milo's mother-in-law makes terrific brownies."

"I'm sure his daughter helped eat them," Dr. Berbera said with a smile.

"There's a daughter? Theodora asked.

Grace blanched. She wanted to kick Dr. Berbera.

Dr. Berbera was oblivious. He said, "Yes. Very cute eleven-year old. Students, this is Dr. Theodora Band from the National Institutes of Health. What is your thinking, Dr. Band?"

Theodora knew that this was where she began taking control

of the process. She said, "The entire family is of interest. We can talk theories all day, however nothing illuminates more than data."

Theodora was blunt. "Mrs. Anderson needs to be evaluated by a doctor - one who knows epigenetics. Samples are needed - from all family members. DNA analysis and close observations are imperative."

She finished with, "Clearly the public must be managed. It is imperative that the subjects – the family - are removed to a clinical situation, with limited access by the public, so that work can be done without the hoopla of fans. These people need to be shielded as work is done. I'm thrilled to be available and here at this time. It's an exciting time to be a scientist."

Angus jumped in. "I think we're all fascinated by biological plasticity, but these are also our friends. Surely no one should be making decisions without their input."

Theodora turned glacial eyes on Angus. "Mrs. Anderson is a virtual prisoner in her house at the moment. I assure you, she'll be grateful to be in the hands of professionals."

The room erupted in chatter as the dozen graduate students weighed in on what data was needed, and how it should be collected. Grace risked a look at Esther who made a calming motion with her hands. Grace nodded. Nothing would be decided here. The real work began when they got out to Milo and Lena. The task now was to sit and endure.

"The talented hawk hides her claws."

Japanese proverb

CHAPTER NINETY-TWO

Monday, 1:30 p.m., Oyster Bay Road, west of Olympia

DEPUTY MACRAE INCHED the Mason County sheriff's sedan forward.

"What a mess," Rodger Raposo grumbled. There was no point putting on lights or a siren. They were on a narrow winding road with ditches and trees along each side. There was no place for the heavy traffic to move over.

Traffic both ways was bumper to bumper. There were children dashing about, and one woman marched up the middle of the road with a brace of greyhounds.

"They need a manned roadblock a mile back," MacRae said. "With a turnaround. They've set the turn back point much too close to the home."

"No shit, Sherlock. What moron is running this?"

They had their answer ten minutes later. They pulled up to a road barricade and a sweating, beefy Thurston County deputy slowly ambled over to them. His nametag read "Pendergast." MacRae tabbed down the sedan's window.

"Afternoon, sir." MacRae began.

"Not your turf," Pendergast barked. "We're not open for sight-seers. Turn it around and vamoose." Pendergast stepped back, and motioned MacRae to turn the sedan around.

Rodger Raposo erupted out of the passenger side, slamming the door. "Give us a minute," he snarled. "Detective Raposo here. I'm head of an interagency team investigating a pair of homicides. One Mason County, one Thurston County. I need to speak with the Andersons."

Pendergast hooked his thumbs into his belt and thrust an imposing belly toward the detective. "Not happening. No one is to approach the house. No one."

"We're on a pair of homicides. Get your boss on the horn."

"He's gone to lunch. Be back in an hour."

"Well, for fuck's sake. We'll wait."

"Not here you won't." Pendergast turned his back on Raposo, and motioned again to MacRae.

MacRae called out to him, "We could set up a turnaround back at the cross street. Divert people back to the freeway. That would let you deal with all this better."

Pendergast stopped and stared, the sense of MacRae's offer slowly percolating through his brain. "Yeah. You do that."

MacRae turned the sedan slowly, braking once for Raposo to get back in. MacRae had the good sense to stay silent as they began the creep back up Oyster Bay Road. He could feel the fury rolling off of Raposo.

Finally Raposo spoke. In a mild voice he said, "I'll get that fat bastard out of law enforcement if it takes me a thousand years of trying."

"Yes, sir." MacRae drove on, navigating the oncoming crowds

carefully. "Congratulations, sir, on your promotion to the head of the interagency team."

Raposo chuckled. "Yeah. I thought I deserved a promotion. God, my jaw hurts. The numbing stuff is wearing off, and I'm becoming a sad pup."

"Do we have a plan?"

"Set up the roadblock further out, like you suggested. We'll be seeing traffic coming both ways, and there's some turnaround space. We'll hang out there until we catch the boss man coming back from lunch. A pain in the butt. The good thing is that the Andersons aren't going anywhere."

Deputy MacRae nodded in agreement. "Not unless they can fly."

"Angels can fly," Raposo said. "If that happens, we should sell tickets."

"Deliver me, oh Lord, from lying lips, from a deceitful tongue."

Psalm 120:2

Chapter Ninety-Three

Monday, 1:30 p.m., Mrs. Sheehan's conference room

"DYLAN, IT WAS good of you to befriend Piper," Mrs. Sheehan said. "You can return to class now."

Dylan shot a stricken look at Piper. Piper found herself saying, "Um, Mrs. Sheehan, actually we were wondering if we could go to the library together and research some, uh, genetics. For the Science Fair."

Dylan added, "We're looking to tie the new field of epigenetics to global warming. We're doing a poster."

Mrs. Sheehan peered down her nose. "I see," she said.

"We could share a terminal," Piper offered.

"We'll be super quiet," Dylan promised.

Mrs. Sheehan gave Dylan a direct stare. "I'll allow on the condition of superior behavior."

"Yes, Ma'am." Dylan told her.

Moments later, he and Piper rounded the corner from Mrs. Sheehan's office. The corridor was empty.

"Race ya." Dylan dashed off down the hall.

Piper sprinted past him and slid to a halt at the library door. "You call that best behavior?" she asked.

Dylan shrugged. "Comparatively, yeah. Man, you are fast!"

Piper put her nose in the air and hauled the library door open. "Yes. I am."

The librarian was in the picture book corner with a class of first graders. Dylan and Piper tiptoed to a row of computer terminals. They were all unoccupied. "Fourth grade's on a field trip," Dylan suggested.

Piper sat down on a wheeled chair and sucked in her lower lip. She typed in "bird genetics" and scrolled down the results.

Dylan sat down at the next terminal. He typed in "Scam of the Day." Moments later he nudged Piper. "Look at this," he hissed.

Piper stared at his screen. *"Help our Angel in Need?"*

"Crowd funding. They've raised five thousand dollars in the last hour."

Piper read through the solicitation. "Lena Anderson, The Angel of Washington, is being besieged by mortals who do not have her best interests at heart. Help us raise funds for an Angel Refuge on the Hawaiian island of Moloka'I, long a welcoming destination for those needing shelter. Our Angel Refuge will house our Angel in tropical serenity and with holistic security."

Piper scrunched her face into a frown. "They are doing this for my mom?"

"No, you dolt. It's a scam. They say it's for your mom, but I'll bet it's going to go to some lard ass who inhabits the dark web and surfaces to feed on opportunity."

"You don't know what this someone looks like," Piper argued.

"Building a web scam isn't an aerobic activity," Dylan retorted.

"Anyway, the thing is, your mom's name is being dragged into this sort of thing."

Piper's face scrunched again, this time with tears welling in her eyes.

Dylan socked her in the arm.

"Hey!" she bleated.

"Shh. Don't wuss out on me. Get mad. And then get even."

*

Down the hall there was a tap on the door of Mrs. Sheehan's office. She looked up and smiled at her sister. Mrs. Sheehan said, "Mary Margaret, thank you for coming. We seem to have a situation unfolding."

Mary Margaret O'Reilly sat down in a chair across from the principal's desk, plunking down a large canvas bag at her feet. "The Andersons. The traffic is unbelievable. They are prisoners in their own home."

Catharine Coreen Sheehan agreed. "I'm to take Piper home this afternoon. I'd like to offer the Andersons some options."

"Do you have a destination in mind?"

"Not yet." Mrs. Sheehan opened a desk drawer and pulled out a rolled map. "I thought we'd begin by planning a departure from the neighborhood."

Mary Margaret O'Reilly reached down into her canvas bag. "I brought my address book."

"Good. Let us begin."

"There is nothing more difficult to carry out, nor more doubtful of success, nor more dangerous to handle, than to institute a new order of things."

Niccolo Machiavelli
(May 3, 1469 – June 21, 1527)

CHAPTER NINETY-FOUR

Monday, 2 p.m. Near the Anderson home

CARYS HAD THE expertise to keep the double kayak from coming to grief. Ken did his best to follow her instructions.

They beached the kayak on a shallow band of gravel downslope of a pseudo-Victorian home. Carys produced a length of polypropylene rope to secure the kayak to a tree.

"Sometimes a high tide will surprise you," she told him. "Better safe than sorry."

Ken Ito tried a bowlegged walk on the beach. He was sweating inside the neoprene shorty wetsuit while his exposed legs were popping with goose bumps. He didn't like having thunder thighs that rubbed.

They scrambled up the slope with their gear bags and waved to a lanky white-haired man on the deck of the big home. He had one hand on the head of a white-muzzled black Labrador. "Afternoon," he called.

"Hi!" Ken called back. "May we park our kayak down below for a few hours?"

"Alright. Going to the craft sale?"

"Excuse me?"

"There's a hell of a crush at the end of the loop. I was guessing it was a sale of some sort."

"You've got a… ah, budding celebrity down there. I'm Ken Ito. This is Carys Kidwelly."

"No kidding. I'm Will Taggart. This is Sutton."

"Yeah. We're friends of…" Ken stumbled for a moment. He'd never met the Andersons.

Carys broke in with, "Mrs. Anderson. We're friends with her mother, Edna. We're going down to see if we can help."

Dr. Taggart gave a quick nod. "It looks like they could use some help. I was going out for a walk, but after looking at that mess, I changed my mind."

Ken said, "It may be crazy for a few days."

"This has to do with the helicopter that's been buzzing around?"

"Possibly. Have you seen the local news?"

"On television?" Dr. Taggart looked pained. "I'm retired. I ignore the world to the best of my ability. I guess I could go watch the news if it's landing in my lap."

"This time it might help," Ken told him.

Carys asked, "Do you mind if I step behind your garden shed and change into my shore clothes?"

"Dear lady, you can take off clothes anywhere on my property."

Carys gave him her double dimpled smile and disappeared behind the shed.

Dr. Taggart looked at Ken. "Bet you're wanting to change too. Might as well come up on the deck and use a lawn chair."

"Thanks."

"Before I go watch the travesty that is called 'news', tell me, young man, just what the hell is going on."

"Short version is Mrs. Anderson saved a child from being run over." Ken said. "Some people think she's an angel. A real angel."

"No kidding."

Dr. Taggart let them stash their gear bags under his deck. "When you come back, please bang on the door and give me a report," he told them. "I'd like to know when the coast might clear."

Ken slid his cell phone out of a zip bag and asked, "Got a number to share? I can shoot you a message."

Dr. Taggart recited his phone number and added, "Let me know if I can help. They're a quiet family. Cute kid."

Ken and Carys had an easy walk down Ellison Loop until they came within a hundred yards of the Anderson home. A sheriff's deputy stood at a barricade. "No access, folks," he called.

"Hi. I'm Dr. Ken Ito with the National Security Agency. This is my colleague, Carys Kidwelly. We are going to see Dr. Anderson."

"Sorry, sir. There is no passage past this point."

"We were given the word 'mycelium'," Ken added.

"Ah. Very well." The deputy motioned them forward.

Moments later, Ken rapped on the front door of the Anderson home. There was no response.

"Dr. Anderson!" Ken bellowed. "Ken Ito here!"

A curtain twitched and Ken waved. The front door opened and Milo gestured them inside. Milo shut the door before taking time to shake hands. "Glad to have some reinforcements," he said.

The house was gloomy from the covered windows. Lena's hair glowed like a ghostly halo when she stepped into the hall.

"Visitors?" she called.

"Carys," Milo called back, "and Ken Ito."

Lena came down the hall with the grace of a gazelle. Ken tried not to stare. No wonder she was labeled as an angel. She was taller than he had expected.

"Hi, Carys," she said softly.

"Hey. This is Ken."

Lena put out a hand. "Nice to meet you."

Ken shook her hand and tried to act normal.

She smiled down at him. "Not the best of circumstances. I suppose you need to see the feathers."

Interesting, thought Ken. She doesn't say 'my' feathers. She says 'the' feathers. Out loud he said, "Yes, please."

Lena unbuttoned her plaid cotton shirt and slipped it down off her shoulders, revealing a peach colored bra and a striking row of white feathers that overlapped blue feathers. Smaller feathers overlapped to cover her sternum. The blue feathers shone turquoise at one angle and royal blue at another. Bands of black and white accented each tip of the longest feathers.

"Wow." Even after seeing Edna's collection, Lena's feathers were a surprise. Edna's feathers were shades of gray and brown. Lena's were bright and iridescent.

Lena agreed as she re-buttoned the shirt. "Wow. That's what we keep saying."

Ken turned to Milo. "My guess is epigenetically activated genes on existing DNA, or horizontal gene transmission from another organism."

"Agreed. But what's the activator? There's dozens of possibilities." Milo looked exhausted.

"And it's multi-generational." Ken mused. "With the color patterns differing between your wife and Edna."

"I've been telling Lena that we need to be working with someone who does DNA analysis."

Ken shot a worried look at Lena. "Could we sit down with you? This is, as you know, turning into a big deal. Among other things, there could be an interagency turf war about who gets to do this science."

"Crap," said Milo.

"Would you like some tea?" asked Lena.

Carys laughed. "Now there's a gender split in response." She smiled at Lena. "I'd love some tea," Carys told her. "By the way, where is Edna?"

"We don't know," Lena said. Her voice wobbled as she added, "She seems to have her cell phone turned off."

*

Five miles away, Edna woke herself with her snoring. "Oh, my!" she laughed as she stretched. "Drewl, there are few things less attractive than a snoring grandmother." Drewl lay with his head on his paws. His heavy tail made a happy thumping at her address.

"You stay here, Drewl. I need to find a bush." Edna stood up, and Drewl raised his head. Edna put an open palm toward him. "Wait," she said.

Drewl took the direction, although his eyes followed her as she partially disappeared behind a huckleberry bush. A few minutes later she returned.

"Where were we? Oh, yes, avoiding that horrid Dr. Band. Drewl, I should check in with Lena." Edna drew out her cell phone. "Thirty messages? Good heavens, Drewl. What did we sleep through?"

*

The graduate seminar was winding down. It had been a rollicking debate – one that Grace would have adored if she wasn't so worried about the Andersons and so unnerved by Dr. Band.

Grace saw an unhealthy glitter in Dr. Band's eyes whenever she argued a point forcefully. When Angus elegantly argued that a local physician and Summit College biologists could appropriately assist and manage a research project, Dr. Band shimmered with rage.

Grace cut her eyes to Esther, who raised one eyebrow in a fashion that confirmed that she was in agreement with Edna's assessment. Theodora Band was volatile.

Dr. Berbera oozed charm and respect. He stood chatting with Dr. Band as the students left.

Grace shouldered her daypack. Her skin prickled when Dr. Band placed a hand on Dr. Berbera's arm.

"Thank you, so much, for allowing me to sit in," Theodora purred. "We are at such an exciting time. I look forward to working closely with you."

"Let's exchange cell phone numbers," Berbera murmured back. "So we can be in close contact."

Grace and Esther fled the classroom, passing Margaux in the hall.

"Gack," Grace whispered to Esther. "Berbera and Band?"

"Gack, indeed," Esther agreed. "What next? Out to see Milo and Lena?"

"Yes, please. I need a few minutes to grab a book Milo wants from his office."

"I'll wait on the bench," Esther told her.

Inside the classroom, Margaux took a position against the wall, doing her best to fade into the whiteboard. She shouldn't have worried. Theodora Band swept out without so much as a glance in Margaux's direction.

Dr. Berbera motioned Margaux over.

"What have we learned?" he asked.

"I called the number Dr. Band gave me. A man answered. There are male receptionists, but I'd have to say they are still rare. I asked some questions. The fellow was full of glowing words about Dr. Band. 'Fine researcher, great record' that sort of thing. But, Yousef?" Margaux hesitated. "It sounds small..."

"Margaux, I trust your instincts."

"When he first answered, he said 'National Institute of Health.' "

"And?"

"It's plural. National Institutes of Health. We use the singular all the time or just say NIH, but a receptionist for the organization should be using the correct name."

"Ah," said Dr. Berbera. "An astute observation."

*

Detective Raposo was in rough shape. His jaw was pounding. He checked his watch. 2:30 p.m. "Brooke's last class just finished. I'm gonna call and ask her to haul me back to the dentist," he told MacRae. "I gotta get something done with this tooth or I'm no good on the job."

Deputy MacRae gave a quick bob of agreement as he motioned yet another vehicle to turn around. "We've got other problems, boss."

"Such as?" Raposo was already tapping his girlfriend's work number.

"We set up here to kill some time until that supervisor came back from lunch, but he's not showing. Technically, I'm a Mason County employee working overtime in Thurston County. That's a problem without the chief's approval."

MacRae put up a crisp hand to halt a minivan driver who had been approaching with some enthusiasm. When the van halted, he stalked up to the driver's window. "Slow down, Ma'am," he lectured. "This is a residential area. Only through traffic is for residents."

"I'm on my way to see the Angel of Washington," a hefty heart faced woman with perm destroyed hair replied. "My grandson is ill with leukemia. I have to see her."

MacRae held firm. "I'm so sorry to hear about your grandson," he said, "but indications are that there's not an angel. It's a media hoax. You need to turn here and go back to the freeway."

MacRae stepped back. He had now had a variation of this interaction many times in the last hour. People left with various signs of dismay or anger on their face, but they did leave.

Not this one. The lady put the van in park and burst into tears. "I have to see her," she wailed. "He's dying. He's our beautiful baby boy and he's dying. I have to see her."

MacRae flung a look at Raposo, who was talking on his cell phone. No question that the detective needed to get back to the dentist. And, he, MacRae, needed to get back to his day off. He sure as hell didn't want to arrest this sad lady.

MacRae decided it was time to punt. The difficult woman could be Pendergast's problem.

He turned back to the van. "Ma'am, I'm from Mason County. I'm helping with the traffic. Tell you what. I'll get dispatch to request a Thurston County deputy up here. You can pull over to that driveway and wait."

"Thank you. God Bless You. Thank you. Thank you." With a river of tears streaming down her face, the woman inched the van forward. MacRae went to his patrol car and began the process of finding Pendergast's worthless ass.

"An item in motion remains in motion."

Isaac Newton
(December 25, 1642 – March 20, 1727)

CHAPTER NINETY-FIVE

Monday, 3 p.m., west of Olympia

ESTHER AGREED TO travel in Grace's ancient Civic on the off chance that Drewl would need to be transported.

"I could keep him overnight," Grace said as they sped down the highway. "I'd have to pay a pet deposit if I kept him longer."

"It's hard to know what they are going to need," Esther replied. "Shielding from the Dr. Bands of the world, for a start. It's too much to hope that they are going to be left alone."

"Ken Ito is there, and that should help."

"Tell me again what Milo said about the crowds."

Grace slowed as they rounded a bend in the highway. "He said that the deputies had put up roadblocks, and that they moved people off the front lawn."

They came up to slow moving traffic once they exited onto Oyster Bay Road. Cars, vans, pickups and motor homes strung out in front of them. Traffic inched forward. Grace studied the traffic in front of them and then, bored, used her rear view mirrors to study the traffic piling up behind them. After a moment, she sat up straight.

"There's someone in a black car who looks like Dr. Band. It's about six cars back."

"Are you sure that's her?"

"Pretty sure. Shit."

"What?"

"Edna just exited the freeway."

"She's behind Dr. Band?"

"Several cars behind her." Grace's hands were suddenly wet with sweat.

"Honk the horn," Esther directed. "Focus attention on us."

Grace started pounding the car horn with enthusiasm. The driver in front of her extended a middle finger. Another driver took up honking. The traffic inched forward toward a sheriff's car that was partially across Oyster Bay road at the junction of a cross street.

A lean, orange-haired deputy was waving traffic off Oyster Bay and onto a cross street. Grace suspected the street led back to the freeway. A pot-bellied officer was interviewing a driver in a van pulled off to one side. Once in a while a car was waved on, past the pair of parked sheriff's sedans.

Grace gave up on the honking as she came close to the deputies. As the two cars ahead of her were waved through, the potbellied deputy turned away from the parked van and came over to the middle of the road.

She rolled down the window and tried to apologize. "Sorry, sir, my auntie is not well."

"Listen, Pocahontas, we don't need your attitude," said the pot-bellied deputy.

Grace froze. Pocahontas? What sort of racist crap was this? Grace sought the deputy's nametag. Pendergast.

"Mr. Pendergast, that was unnecessary," Grace began in icy tones.

The lean deputy stepped up. "Ma'am, we're turning aside all sightseers. If you're not a resident, please turn to your right."

MacRae. This guy's name was MacRae. Good. She could use a witness.

"Our apologies for honking," Grace said to him. "We're on our way to see the Andersons. I am his graduate assistant. I was told the password is 'mycelium.'"

Pendergast crossed his arms above his ample belly and snorted. "Yeah, right, you're a graduate student."

"Pendergast!" MacRae barked. "I'm leaving now. It's up to you to keep the traffic moving." With that MacRae stalked off. He got into one of the sheriff's units and pulled out onto the cross street, scattering gravel as he picked up speed.

Pendergast looked down at Grace and said, "Pull it over there, missy, and park it."

Grace shot a look at Esther, who sat, grim-faced, in the passenger seat. There was nothing to do but comply. She pulled over to the right and parked on the shoulder next to the mini-van.

Deputy Pendergast ambled back to his sheriff's sedan. He got in and spoke on the radio for a while. With no one stopping traffic, the cars that had been lined up behind Grace began surging down Oyster Bay Road. Theodora's black Lexus went by at a good clip. Several vehicles later, Edna's faded blue station wagon made leisurely progress down the road.

Deputy Pendergast emerged from his unit and began a slow walk to Grace and her Civic.

"What a jerk," Grace grumbled.

"Well, we were honking," Esther said. "Although, I do agree, he's a jerk. It's too bad the other guy didn't speak up." Esther began digging in her daypack.

"He lacked the courage. Did I tell you that Edna read my

palm? She said I was going to marry a red-haired man. Not that one, I'm sure."

"We'll worry about that another time," Esther said. "Here. Give him my card."

Grace made a point of keeping both hands on the steering wheel while she pinched Esther's card between her thumb and forefinger.

Deputy Pendergast stopped outside her car window and poked his belly aggressively in her direction. "Let's see some ID, sugar."

"My aunt's card," Grace said. "And I'll need to get my license out of my daypack." She was rummaging in her pack for her wallet when the deputy cleared his throat. "You gals go on down the road. Lay off the horn." With that he tucked Esther's card in his front pocket and retreated.

Grace turned an owl look on Esther. "What was on that card?"

"That's the one that says I'm a special representative to the Governor of Washington. I'm doing some lichen specimen collection for a big pharmaceutical company. Sometimes it helps to have some support from the governor's office when I want to go onto privately held lands."

"Okay, then." Grace reversed the car and turned back onto Oyster Bay Road. Both Edna and Theodora were out of sight.

Grace flicked a look at the rear view mirror. She saw the big deputy open the passenger side door of the van that was sitting on the shoulder. That was odd. Had she ever seen a police officer get into a stopped person's car?

Grace didn't dwell on the oddity. There was too much traffic whizzing both directions on the narrow road.

As Grace took the gentle curves of the road, she surmised that the road would be empty most weekday afternoons. The housing was sparse, with large swaths of woods, fields and marsh opening up on either side of the road.

They finally took a sharp bend in the road and came up on another traffic jam. Again cars crept forward to do another interview with another deputy.

Grace frowned. "See that green pickup? Dr. Band was right in front of them. I don't see her now."

Esther agreed. "But there's Edna's station wagon. I wonder where Theodora got to?"

"What do you make of her?" asked Grace.

Esther sighed. "Ambitious. Smart. Heartless. *Academicus commonalis.*"

Grace laughed. "Aunt Esther, I can't tell you how glad I am that I've met you. It is amazing to have a relative that reminds me of me."

"I love you too, dear child." Esther peered through the insect spatter on the Civic's windshield. "The one I'm having a hard time figuring out is your department head." Esther rolled her eyes. "He was flirting with Dr. Band. I do believe he is married."

"No on that point. Divorced. Or divorcing."

"Hmm. Well, I don't know where he fits in."

"Every one sees what you appear to be. Few really know what you are."

Niccolo Machiavelli
(May 3, 1469 – June 21, 1527)

CHAPTER NINETY-SIX

Monday, 3:30 p.m. The Haddad summer cabin

THEODORA PULLED UP to the cabin and felt the tension of the day seep out of her shoulders. She hadn't realized that she had driven with a tight grip on the steering wheel until she uncurled her fingers and set off a small wave of aches.

Kurt came around to the edge of the deck and waved. "Margaritas," he called.

"God, you're saving my life," she called back. She followed him around to the back deck where he had a pitcher of margaritas out on the patio table. The table and deck chairs sat in dappled sunlight as long shadows reached across the lawn. Theodora threw herself into a chair with a moan of relief. "We should get a cabin."

"Yeah. This is nice."

They sat in silence, sipping the margaritas and looking out over the water. To the left there was a break in the shoreline trees where they could see the traffic stopping and starting on Oyster Bay Road as people inched up to the sheriff's barricade.

"It's been like that most of the day," Kurt told her. "Traffic eased off between one and close to three. It's picked up again in the last half hour."

"They had another roadblock just off the freeway," Theodora told him. "They were turning people back. I wasn't sure what I was going to say to get through. Then they pulled out the sheriff's sedan just a few cars ahead of me, and I sailed through."

"There's no sailing through that," Kurt gestured with his glass. "But I do have an idea to try." Kurt set his glass down on the patio table. "We need to be careful, Teddy. Have you thought through just what you're trying to accomplish here?"

Theodora sipped her drink and licked the salt off her lips. "It's gotten more complicated," she admitted. "Originally I thought it was just a case of getting control of the old lady. Then we figured out her daughter may be even more interesting. I was thinking it was just a case of talking them into giving blood samples and having a lab do a workup. I was going to plan from there, depending on the lab results."

"But the publicity on this," Theodora waved a hand toward the traffic, "is nuts. I spent part of the afternoon at a graduate seminar. It's clear that everyone is interested and opinionated. I made some progress with the department head. Next I need to get in with the Andersons, fast, or someone else will."

Kurt sat and thought for a moment. "It's not smart for me to cross the roadblock," he told her, "not even as a landscaper. A deputy might ask me for my driver's license."

"Is that what they're doing?"

"I think so. Take a look with the spotting scope. It looks like they're chatting with each driver. My guess is that they're looking to see who is a resident."

"There's a computer inside. We could do something like a bill."

"Ahead of you there. I found a power bill for the Haddads. I scanned it into their computer and did some changes. I printed off a copy with your name and an address further down Oyster Bay."

Theodora grinned. "Clever!"

"Yeah. I'm thinking I could ride in the trunk of the Lexus and you could drive past the roadblock. You could let me out down the road and I could hike in to the Andersons. Check out the lay of the land. Hey, guess what I found in the back of Haddads' closet?"

"Clothes?"

Kurt gave her a lazy smile. "That. A gun cabinet. The key was on the shelf under a shoe box."

Theodora refreshed her margarita. "Guns?"

"Two rifles and a handgun."

"Sweet."

Kurt's face turned somber. "Teddy, I think you need to sort out exactly what you want. If I were in charge of that lady, I'd be moving her out tonight or first thing tomorrow. I wouldn't be surprised if the traffic triples tomorrow."

"We should watch the evening news." Theodora got up from the deck chair and sat down in her brother's lap. He stroked her hair and kissed the top of her head. She turned her face into his shoulder. "I love dancing on a high wire," she told him. "Having everyone think I'm one thing while I know I'm another."

Kurt gave her a squeeze. "I know. It's fun. How far can you take it? What can you make them do?" He gently closed his hand around her breast and gave the nipple a small pull. "Can you make them want you and fear you at the same time?"

Theodora threw back her head and arched her body. "Can you make them hate you, but be too terrified to move?" she murmured.

"That too," Kurt agreed. He slid his hand up under her shirt. "What happens," he asked, "tomorrow?"

"Depends on what we find out tonight," she said. "If I can

gain control of them, and can direct the research, then this gig could go on for years." Theodora snuggled into Kurt's chest. "But if I can't have them, then no one gets them. We'll slice, dice and move on."

"Sounds reasonable."

"I have a surprise too," Theodora whispered in his ear. "I learned something at the seminar."

"Oh, yeah?"

"Uh-huh. Lena Anderson," Theodora said, "Has a daughter. Eleven years old. She should be there tonight."

"No man is an island, entire of itself; every man is a piece of the continent, a part of the main."

John Donne
(January 22, 1572 – March 31, 1631)

CHAPTER NINETY-SEVEN

Monday, 4:30 p.m., Oyster Bay Road

PRINCIPAL SHEEHAN BROUGHT the school van to a smooth stop in front of the sheriff's sedan. "Good afternoon, Alan," she said to the deputy who approached the driver's side window.

"Hi, Mrs. Sheehan. I take it you have business in the neighborhood?"

"Yes. This is Piper Anderson. I'm delivering her home to her parents. I believe the password is 'mycelium.' "

"That's the open sez a me," the deputy agreed.

Mrs. Sheehan darted a quick look at Piper, who sat quiet and pale in the front passenger seat. "Don't worry, Piper. These officers are here to make sure everything is safe."

Piper bit her lip and gave an almost imperceptible nod. "I know. It's just the traffic. I've never seen so many cars out here."

Piper turned a worried face toward Mrs. Sheehan. "My mother doesn't like crowds. She's very shy."

"And you are tired. It's been a long day." Mrs. Sheehan did not add that there were many hours yet to go. She turned the van down Ellison Loop and drove past the No Trespassing signs at the edge of the Anderson lot.

She parked the school van behind an old red Civic, which was parked behind a faded blue Volvo. Piper gave a cry of relief.

"That's Grace's car and my Grandmother is here! Drewl should be too." Piper scrambled out of the van and raced up the sidewalk.

Mrs. Sheehan took her time, setting the parking brake and gathering her briefcase before stepping out of the van. As she did so, she flicked her eyes at the shoulder high huckleberry bushes that lined the far side of the lot. She called, "Dylan Kushner, you can come out now."

There was a thrashing in the bushes. Dylan emerged holding a wilting bunch of black-eyed Susans.

"Are those for Piper?"

"No!" Dylan looked appalled. "For her mom. I thought she could use some cheering up."

"I see." Mrs. Sheehan studied Dylan for a moment. "Do your parents know you're here?"

Dylan nodded. "Absolutely."

"What did you tell them?"

Dylan suddenly found the trees behind Mrs. Sheehan to be very interesting. "Ah, you know. Helping a friend." There was a pause. "Study group," he added.

Mrs. Sheehan drew her lips into a firm line. Dylan threw prevarication to the winds. "I gotta be here," he told her. "Amazing stuff is happening here. Don't send me away." He looked up into her eyes and pleaded, "I can do things you can't. I can climb trees, crawl under stuff. You might need somebody my size. I could be important."

"So, to borrow a phrase from history, 'He will win whose army is animated by the same spirit throughout all its ranks.' "

Dylan's eyes went wide with delight. "Absolutely!"

Then he asked, "Who said that?"

"Sun Tzu, a great general. You'll learn more about him next year in world history." Mrs. Sheehan motioned him forward. "Let's go in. We'll see what the Andersons have to say."

*

The little house was crowded. Ken Ito sat at a laptop computer on the dining room table. Milo and Carys flanked Ken. Grace and Esther also leaned in to see the screen. They ignored the newcomers.

Lena sat with Edna on a blue sofa in the living room with Drewl at their feet. Piper was on the floor, scratching Drewl's ears as Dylan and Mrs. Sheehan came in the front door. Lena waved at them.

"We seem to be having a party," Lena said.

Dylan proffered the wilting bouquet to Lena. "I'm Dylan. Sorry about the playground stuff."

Lena eyed him carefully. "Thank you," she said. "Welcome to our home."

Duty done, Dylan turned to Piper. "That's your dog?"

"My Grandmom's. His name is Drewl. He's a Newfoundland. We just got him yesterday."

"Man, he must make piles the size of platters."

Edna laughed and said, "It's good to see you, Catharine," to Mrs. Sheehan.

"Thank you, so much, for bringing Piper home," Lena added.

Mrs. Sheehan sat down in a small, upholstered chair, with her backbone erect.

"It was my pleasure," she said. "I would like to address the group, if you don't mind."

Lena said, "Please do. We could use some direction."

"Ladies and gentlemen," Mrs. Sheehan's voice filled the space, and then left a dramatic pause. The computer-centered group all looked up.

"Good afternoon. I'm Mrs. Sheehan. This is Dylan Kushner. I am the principal at the local school. More importantly, I may be your transport to your next destination."

Milo ran a hand down his face. "Hi, Mrs. Sheehan. Sorry, we were caught up in some stuff. I'm glad you're here. This is Ken Ito of the N.S.A., and you know Carys, I think." Carys gave a cheerful wave. "And you met my graduate student, Grace. This is her aunt, Esther Mossler."

"Dr. Mossler and I are old friends," Mrs. Sheehan beamed. "Dr. Anderson, would you please bring me up to date? I can tailor my assistance to your needs better if I have a clear picture."

Milo exhaled. "In a nutshell? We've known for some time that Lena has fast muscles, and that was captured on Saturday on an Internet video. Since then Lena began sprouting some feathers. We don't know where the feathers came from or why, but we do know that the public is aware of this development. Some of the public are attributing angelic attributes to her."

Edna discreetly coughed.

"Um, yeah. Edna also has some feathers. In fact, hers appeared first."

"Have you heard of calcium channels?" Milo asked

"Actually, yes," Mrs. Sheehan said. "They move messages from nerve cells to the body. I was reading recently that autism and ADHD may have roots in the calcium channels of brain cells." She paused. "And some people take calcium channel blockers for blood pressure problems."

"Right," Milo agreed. "I picked calcium channels because

those are the best known. Our cells have all sorts of ion channels – for sodium, for calcium, for potassium. They are basically these little tunnels that ions move down- either into or out of the cell. The tunnels are teeny. Just an atom or two wide and most of the channels have 'gates' that are built according to directions from our DNA. A bunch of disorders, like cystic fibrosis, come from DNA mutations that affect channel gates – and most neurotoxins work by shutting down gates or jamming gates open."

Milo took a breath to plunge on, then hesitated. "Sorry, I was about to riff on why I think Lena's muscles are so fast. I'm starting to think it may have originated with calcium channels. But I'm striking out on the feathers. I suspect it's DNA activation, just as gate keeping of calcium channels can be. A small change with large consequences."

He finished with, "We're on a frontier. People are going to be interested. Lots of people."

Milo leaned back in his chair and waved a hand to the people around him. "We've got lots of brain power, and I'm sure we could get more. But we need time and, honestly, some very specific testing and expert help. We suspect that DNA methylation has a role, possibly from fungi. It may take years to suss out which enzymes acted and why."

Dylan looked over at Piper and whispered, "Does your family talk like this all the time?"

Piper nodded.

"Cool." Dylan settled in with his back against the sofa as he caressed Drewl's ears.

Mrs. Sheehan leaned forward slightly. "As I suspected, you need time and space, which you do not have here. We can anticipate larger crowds tomorrow as the media and the Internet continue to spread information about these developments."

Mrs. Sheehan added, "I spent some time this afternoon with

my sister, Mary Margaret. We developed a plan to evacuate your family unit from the area."

Piper interrupted, "Does that include Drewl?"

"Of course. Pets are often considered members of the family unit." Mrs. Sheehan squared her shoulders. "Mary Margaret is finalizing some details, and, if we call her, can arrive this evening with pizza."

"Score!" Dylan grinned.

Ken furrowed his forehead. "Just how are you going about this? Carys and I had to kayak over from Kamilche to get in. You're proposing to get three very distinctive adults, a child and a remarkably large dog out of what has become a cul-de-sac, all under the noses of the highly interested public?"

Milo put a hand up, stopping Ken's questions. "Mrs. Sheehan and Mrs. O'Reilly can do it. Trust me, if anyone can, they can. They could have organized the invasion of D-Day on the back of a napkin."

Mrs. Sheehan blushed a becoming pink. "Thank you. However, the point of tomorrow's operation is to avoid conflict." She swept her open hand toward the group. "Mary Margaret and I can organize the evacuation. We are working to get you access to transportation. You need to decide a destination, which should be shared on a need to know basis. I do not need to know."

Mrs. Sheehan directed a look at Dylan. "Because of the passionate crowds, this could become dangerous. We should send you home."

Dylan sat up from his slouch. "No! No! I want to help! Mrs. Sheehan, please. I'll go crazy if I miss this. If I'm in class tomorrow… my head will explode."

Mrs. Sheehan looked down at him with stern regard. "It is possible that you could be of assistance."

"I'll do anything."

"Will you wear a wig to look like Piper?"

"Sure!"

"Will you take direction?"

"Absolutely."

"Will you give me your solemn oath as a gentleman and a scholar that you will graduate from high school and apply to college?"

Dylan blinked. "That's seven more years."

"And college is another four."

"I'm going to join the French Foreign Legion when I start to shave."

"I see." Mrs. Sheehan said calmly. She added, "The price of admission to this mission is a commitment to education."

Dylan's eyes darted around the room, looking for a way out.

"She's got you boxed," Milo laughed. He stretched his long arms out over his head. *God Bless Mrs. Sheehan*, he thought. He needed a break from his own worries, and she had just delivered one.

Ken Ito was just as amused. "Dude, it gets better. Middle school is the worst. After that you can pick classes."

Lena, who was sitting on the sofa, reached down and put a hand on Dylan's shoulder. "Your assistance would be greatly appreciated," she said.

Dylan looked up at her and capitulated. "I'm in. Tell me what to do."

"A man arrives as a novice at each stage of life."

Nicolas Chamfort
(April 6, 1741 – April 13, 1794)

CHAPTER NINETY-EIGHT

Monday, 5 p.m., The Carlevaro home

FOR VICO AND Savio, Momma came first. It was easy to say and live that vow because most of the time Momma Carlevaro was as healthy as a horse. Today was a rare exception. She had been carrying a load of laundry up from the basement when she twisted her knee.

Despite two tablets of ibuprofen, a cup of tea and an intense prayer of petition, the knee ballooned to a doughy, mottled mass by mid-morning. By the time Savio and Vico were up, it was clear that Momma needed to be seen by a doctor.

Which took hours. Momma couldn't remember where she had stored her Medicare card. "Some place safe," she insisted. Vico finally found it taped to the inside of the medicine cabinet door, where the constant moisture variations of the bathroom had turned the paper card into a fragile wafer. Then there was the slow transition to the car. Momma was never speedy, even at the best of times, and this was definitely not the best of times.

Getting to the clinic, waiting to be seen, getting Momma to x-ray and back to the doctor's cubicle sucked up the entire afternoon. Savio sweet-talked a receptionist into changing the channel on the waiting room television from cartoons to the local news.

Savio and Vico alternated between sitting with Momma and following the day's events. When Momma was finally released at five o'clock with a prescription, a padded knee brace and instructions to rest, the Carlevaro brothers were exhausted but informed.

Getting up the stairs at the house wasn't as bad as Vico thought it would be. Momma was floating away on the painkillers. She was thoroughly enjoying the attention of both of her sons.

"Such good boys," she giggled. "Such good boys." They got her to her bedroom, slipped off her shoes and tucked her into bed.

Vico said, "You rest, Momma. We'll take care of dinner."

Momma Carlevaro sat up as if she'd been electrocuted. "Not in my kitchen!"

"No, Momma. We'll order in Chinese."

"Alright." Momma sank back onto her pillows and was almost instantly asleep. Savio gently pulled a quilt up over her shoulders, and the brothers crept out of the room.

"We gotta take care of Momma," Vico started.

"Shh. And the way we do that is we get some pictures to sell. We know where the angel lives. We know what she looks like. This thing is the hottest thing we'll ever get. Tomorrow we gotta be out there and ready to pull out all the stops."

"What about Momma? You know the minute we're outta the house, she's gonna be on her feet."

Savio thought for a moment. "Let's call Aunt Rina. She could come stay with Momma."

"Good thinking. Aunt Rina loves a crisis."

"She likes you better. You call. I'll order the Chinese. Then we need to get our gear together. We need to be there before first light."

The brothers tapped knuckles and went to work.

*

"Z", a.k.a., Dr. Zebulon Szczepanski of the Homeland Security Advanced Research Projects Division, slid his overnight bag out of the overhead bin of the jet. He was in no hurry. He permitted himself a wry smile as he acknowledged his heart was pounding.

Carlos Rivera of Chemical and Biological Defense had taken the bait. Z had been ready. He had booked an economy seat at the back of the plane. He had heard Carlos preferred the front of the plane and Carlos did not disappoint. The tricky part had been getting through airport security and onto the plane without bumping into Carlos.

Carlos helped by staying engaged with his laptop. Once through security, Z sat down behind a wide pillar at another gate until the flight was called. He boarded first, making himself amble casually behind Carlos, who sat staring at his screen.

Z spent the long flight hunkered down in the last row of the plane.

Now they were both in Seattle and the next trick was to pick up a rental car without converging. Z stopped at an airport shop and bought a hideously expensive Mariners baseball jacket and a matching cap. He pulled off the tags and slipped on the gear.

"When in Rome," he muttered as he began to match the airport crowds.

Z wove through the airport crowds to get to the car rental desk. No sign of Carlos. If all went well, Z thought, he should be on the Anderson's doorstep in ninety minutes.

"It is impossible to transmit speech electronically. The 'telephone' is as mythical as the unicorn."

Professor Johann Christian Poggendorf, 1860.

CHAPTER NINETY-NINE

Monday, 6:00 p.m., The Anderson home, Olympia

THE ANDERSONS AND their supporters crowded into the living room.

All eyes were on the television. A reporter was interviewing a professor from the National Laboratory of Ornithology.

"Dr. Ifrit, is there any chance these feathers are real?" the newscaster asked.

"It's highly unlikely," answered the balding professor. "Here at the lab, we have long been pioneers in the field of evolutionary biology. There's been a great deal of work in understanding the evolutionary phenomena of mutation, adaptation and speciation. As chair of Genetic Architecture, I can honestly say I have overseen hundreds of scientific papers, and I have never seen anything that hints of a mammal sprouting feathers."

"What a blowhard," Milo groused.

"Shhh," Lena admonished.

"If such a thing were to occur," the professor continued, "I'd put my money on horizontal gene transfer."

The professor pushed his glasses up on his nose. "There's been many cases demonstrated of gene transfer in bacteria. We also know that the genome of a pea aphid includes genes transferred from fungi. However, that is a far cry from a transfer between birds and mammals."

The professor leaned forward in his chair and said, "Birds are so different. Their digestive tract, their respiratory system, their reproductive systems are all enormously different than mammalian systems. Birds, for instance, don't pee."

The reporter laughed. "They don't pee?"

"No. No bladder. The kidneys empty into the intestine. They excrete uric acid in a semi-solid form, known to us all as bird poop."

The professor smiled. "And, of course, birds lay eggs and have beaks instead of jaws with teeth."

"Crocodiles have jaws with teeth and lay eggs," the newsman countered.

"Ah, yes. But crocodiles are reptiles." The professor held up a hand, "These are big topics. There are interesting exceptions. For instance, the famous platypus lays eggs, but also nurses its young. It has a bill and no teeth, but it has hair, not feathers."

The professor added, "Its lesser-known cousin, the echidna produces milk, but has no nipples. The male echidna also has a four-headed penis. Biological oddities abound."

"Why don't you think it's possible for this 'Angel of Washington' to have feathers?"

"It's so… far-fetched. Biologists and physicians have been looking at the human body for thousands of years. We've never seen anything like this."

"Wait a minute," the newsman responded. "What about the art through the ages that shows angels? Isn't it possible that there were earlier versions of feathered people, and that they were known to their communities?"

The professor shrugged. "We also have many who believe they will win the lottery. Fiction abounds."

"Some people do win the lottery!" Piper yelled at the television.

"Shh," Lena admonished.

"We were reading up on DNA today," the reporter said, "It sounds like we all have a great deal of DNA that's not in use. It used to be called 'junk' DNA. Now scientists are saying it's not junk. Is there any possibility that we have the DNA to make feathers but it isn't active?"

"In a word, no. We have all sorts of DNA that stays wrapped up and may only be expressed for a short time in the life of a creature. Most of our genome is associated with regulation – when will something start or stop."

Professor Ifrit looked straight at the camera. "The traffic cop," he said, "is a carbon with three hydrogens. It's called a methyl group. It attaches itself to the cytosine in our DNA and directs action. Embryonic germ cells are usually un-methylated. By the time we're born, about 80% of our cytosine sites are methylated. We're learning that times of stress can reprogram methylation."

The professor took a breath and plowed on. "We are learning that DNA can respond, directly, to changes in the environment. This is the entire field of 'epigenetics.' It may be that what happened to Grandpa has a direct effect on who you are and how you function."

"However," he grumbled, "Activating a higher blood pressure or skewing a family toward weight gain is a far cry from sprouting feathers."

"You don't think this Angel of Washington is real?"

"No. I don't. If she is, she has another problem. That of 'koinophilia.' That's a biological term that refers to the fact that no creature wants to pick a partner who is terribly peculiar. The chances of such an odd bird - if you will, reproducing, are slim to none."

At the Anderson's house, Lena gasped, but Piper hooted, "Hah!"

"Thank you, Dr. Ifrit. That was Dr. Ifrit of the National Laboratory of Ornithology. After the break..."

Milo hit the mute button. "No National Laboratory for us. I'd smack that smug twit on Day One."

Carys spoke up. "Edna and Lena don't need hospital support. They're healthy. The challenge at a university will be the egos involved."

"The same is true of government agencies," Ken said.

Esther disagreed. "Ego is part of human nature. And any department, team or agency can start out one way and change over time – for better or for worse. What you need is a destination with the resources to help you sort things out, but where you retain control."

"So this is a dominance exercise," Grace said thoughtfully. "Where can Lena go where she is in control?"

*

Carlos picked up the keys to his rental car and checked his watch. It would take about an hour and a half to get to the Andersons.

"Possession is nine tenths of the law," he murmured. "First one wins." He turned from the rental counter and looked for a security guard. He found a young woman in a blue uniform.

"Evening," he said to her. "I was in the men's room just after I deplaned, and I saw a man open his suitcase. He had two bags of white powder." Carlos lied smoothly. "I just saw him again. He's right over there, wearing a Mariner's jacket and cap."

"Thank you, sir," the young officer replied. "We'll check into it."

"No problem can withstand the assault of sustained thinking."

Voltaire (November 21, 1694 – May 30, 1778)

CHAPTER ONE HUNDRED

Monday, 6:30 p.m., The Haddad summer cabin

THEODORA'S LEXUS SAT in the dense shadows of the cabin. Kurt popped the trunk open and studied the trunk space. "I'll fit," he said. He loaded a dark daypack that held the Bionic ear unit, binoculars and a water bottle.

"It's another hour before dark," Theodora said. "Are you sure now is the time to go?"

"Yes. The deputies are going to expect people to be getting home from work, so you'll be part of the regular traffic. And having a little light will help me get into position."

Kurt knelt down and double tied his bootlaces. "I wish I had night vision glasses."

"Something for tomorrow?" Theodora mused.

"Possibly. Honestly, Teddy, I think tomorrow's going to be insane out here."

"Let's do this. I'll drop you off and find a place to wait.

Message me if you think I should show up at the Andersons this evening."

"Okay." Kurt stood up and began folding his long frame into the trunk of the car. Once he was in, Theodora shut the trunk.

She drove out of the long driveway and turned onto Oyster Bay Road. She merged with the long line of traffic that inched up to the barricade near Ellison Loop. When her turn came, she gave the deputy a friendly smile.

"What's going on, officer?"

"You've got a budding celebrity in the neighborhood. Are you a resident, ma'am?"

"Yes, I am. Let's see, my driver's license has my old address." Theodora made a production of looking through her purse.

"Oh, here. Here's my utility bill." She produced the faux document with a happy flourish.

The deputy barely looked at the bill. He waved her through, already focused on the next vehicle.

Theodora drove down the road to the second entrance of Ellison Loop. She turned onto the loop and found a pull out near a small apple orchard. She parked and liberated Kurt from the trunk. He unfolded, stretched and looked about.

"Good spot," he grunted.

"I'll wait here for you."

Kurt moved off down the road. Theodora watched him until he disappeared into the understory in the woods between two homes. She knew he'd circle up into the trees to descend behind the Anderson home.

*

It was almost seven o'clock before Mary Margaret O'Reilly and her daughter, Cassie, arrived at the Andersons with a tower of pizzas. They parked on the street and came up the driveway with a sheriff's deputy.

The pizzas were greeted with cheer. The deputy waited until everyone had a paper plate and slice in their hands before he spoke. "Do you have plans for tomorrow?"

Thirty yards away, Kurt Otsoa adjusted the volume on the Bionic Ear. He was curled up next to a swath of sword ferns. The thick understory of ferns and huckleberry was a reconnoitering dream. The spongy moss underneath was almost as comfortable as a mattress.

The conversation in the Anderson home was coming through clearly. Kurt smiled at the perfection of his placement.

Inside, Milo paused, mid-chew, to answer the deputy, "We'll depart tomorrow. Early."

"Good," the deputy replied. "We're racking up significant overtime. We can't sustain this level of support. It's on all the news feeds that we're turning away visitors. Hopefully that will discourage visitors."

The deputy threw a sympathetic look to Lena. He said, "I strongly suggest that you leave as early as you can. We're following the news and the twitter feeds. It sounds like we are on the front end of a great wave of interest in Mrs. Anderson."

"Thank you," Lena said softly. "I can't imagine what today would have been like without your help."

The deputy dipped his head. "Glad to assist. We'll shut down the roadblock about midnight this evening and start up again in the morning about six."

"Understood." Milo told him.

The deputy declined a slice of pizza and departed.

Mrs. Sheehan dabbed her lips with a napkin. "Mary Margaret, are we ready to begin?"

Mrs. O'Reilly stood up and opened the one remaining pizza box. Inside was a large, laminated map of the neighborhood, a stack of index cards, a yellow T-shirt and a woman's wig. She put the map out on the table, and everyone crowded around. Mrs. O'Reilly began to speak.

Outside Kurt adjusted the volume down on the Bionic Ear. This speaker's voice carried.

"As you see here," Mrs. O'Reilly began. "We have one road into the neighborhood. Our challenge is to evacuate three adults, one child and one dog, all without garnering the attention of fans or paparazzi."

"Paparazzi." Lena shuddered.

"We'll start with Dr. Anderson, because, well, he's the easiest. At eight a.m. the Evergreen Bike Club will bike down Oyster Bay Road. There will be fifteen cyclists, all wearing the club jersey. Milo, prior to eight a.m., you will hike up behind your house and descend, here."

Mrs. O'Reilly pointed to a home further up Ellison Loop. "You will enter the garage of the Malek's, where Mrs. Malek will meet you and give you her son's club jersey and bike shorts. Tyler is close to your size, so it should fit. Tyler has also agreed to loan you one of his bikes. The cycling club will arrive at the Malek's at approximately 8:15. You will join the group. Fifteen cyclists will arrive, and sixteen will depart. You will peddle out to the Inland Market store where I will meet you and transport you to your downtown destination. One of the cyclists will have his truck there to pick up Tyler's bike."

Milo stared at her. "That's brilliant. No one ever counts cyclists."

Up on the hillside, Kurt silently agreed.

"Next," continued Mrs. O'Reilly, "Edna and Drewl. This evening I recommend that the family pack suitcases and load them in Edna's station wagon. Don't overpack. We can ship items to you later."

Mrs. O'Reilly stopped to take a sip of water. "Edna, you and Drewl will take the station wagon to your home this evening. You will find my husband has installed a rope across the road with a No Trespassing sign. We really are not expecting any trouble in that direction as you have not been in the news."

There was a frozen moment of silence. Mrs. Sheehan gave a delicate cough. "Edna may be of interest soon."

Mrs. O'Reilly's eyes swept the group. "I see. As soon as tomorrow?"

"It's possible," Ken Ito said carefully.

"Very well. We'll stick with this plan at the moment, which is for Edna and Drewl to remain at her home throughout the day. At six in the evening, Raymond Mossler will arrive in his work van."

Esther, sitting on the sofa, reached down and patted Grace's shoulder. "White van, no windows, labeled "Raymond's Plumbing," she whispered.

"Indeed," acknowledged Mrs. O'Reilly. "Raymond is well known in the area. You, Edna, and Drewl, and the suitcases will be transported in the van to our rendezvous location."

She paused, in thought, and said, "I think I shall call Tron at Tron's Tree Trimming and see if he can put some equipment on the road near Edna's during the day. That would stop traffic coming in."

Ken stared at her. "My God, you think of everything."

"Yes. That's my job. The notecards are for all of us to record phone numbers. Everyone will program numbers into their cell phones. You will also keep a card of contact names and numbers on your person as a backup hard copy. It will be important for us to be in communication tomorrow. We don't need a dead battery to be a show stopper."

Young Cassie O'Reilly, plump in a pink shirt that contrasted violently with her rusty brown hair, piped up with, "P to the Seventh. Proper prior planning prevents piss poor performance."

"Indeed," said her mother. "Cassie, would you please speak to Piper's evacuation protocol?"

Cassie stood up from the floor, where she had been stroking Drewl. She crossed over to the dining room table and pulled out the yellow T-shirt and the woman's wig.

"These are for you," she said, thrusting them at Dylan. "Do not screw up, or I will use every power in my repertoire to make your life a living hell."

Dylan accepted the items without objection.

*

Up on the hillside, Kurt frowned. He couldn't tell which person the speaker was addressing or what was being shared. He shrugged. The important thing to learn was the family's reunion point and ultimate destination.

The sun had set and the woods were dark. Kurt froze as he heard the ferns behind him rattle. Moments later a short, hefty woman came within inches of Kurt. He could smell her sweat and hear her rapid breathing as she thrashed her way forward.

Kurt stilled, looking down, so his face would not reflect the moonlight. As the woodland wanderer pushed on, Kurt cut his eyes sideways and got a fleeting look at the woman's heart-shaped face. As she struggled down the hillside, her silhouette showed wild corkscrews of hair.

The woman tripped out of the ferns and onto the Anderson's back lawn, where she paused and heaved for air. After a moment, she moved forward and took position outside a pair of glass patio doors.

Kurt couldn't see much more than her bulky outline. He surmised she was putting an ear to the glass.

*

Inside, Cassie O'Reilly was enjoying her moment as a manager. "Aunt Catharine will pick you up tomorrow morning in the school van and take you to school," she said to Piper. "You've seen this T-shirt, right?"

Piper nodded. "Camp St. Agnes? Sure. Lots of girls wear them."

"So, Mom and I went over the camp roster and identified thirteen girls from Grades 3 to 7 who have shoulder length brown hair and who have this summer's T-shirt. I called them this afternoon."

Cassie continued, "At two p.m. tomorrow, we will all gather in the cafeteria and have everyone part their hair and braid it like you wear it. Everyone will wear a camp shirt."

Cassie permitted herself an excited grin. "When school is dismissed at 2:40 p.m., there will be eight mothers in mini-vans in the front parking lot. All the girls will depart the school at the same time and load into the mini-vans. Aunt Catharine will direct traffic so that all the mini-vans depart as a caravan."

"Wow," Piper said. "With Dylan, that's fifteen of me."

"The vans," Cassie went on, "Will drive to the State Capital complex where all of you will take the 3 o'clock tour of the Capital building. The Capital rotunda has a State Police security presence, so we are thinking it is unlikely that anyone will approach the tour group."

Cassie was on a roll. "At 4:30 p.m., the tour concludes. Dr. Anderson will meet with us in the hall behind the rotunda. Piper, you and Dylan will peel off with your Dad and stay the next hour at the art display in the Secretary of State's office. You'll change to dark T-shirts. The administrator knows you are coming. She closes the office at five. She'll drop you at the public library. When it closes at seven, you find some dinner at a downtown café and then walk over to the marina."

Mrs. Sheehan gave a regal nod, "Good job, Cassie. Excellent attention to detail."

"Which takes us to Mrs. Anderson," Mrs. O'Reilly said.

"Please, call me Lena."

"Yes. You are the most challenging to extract. However, we do have a plan."

"Little by little, the bird makes her nest."

Haitian proverb

CHAPTER ONE HUNDRED ONE

Monday, 8:45 p.m., The Anderson home

MRS. SHEEHAN LAID out the details for Lena. She was almost finished when a staccato rapping on the door made everyone jump. Milo frowned and signaled to Lena. She pulled a colorful afghan off the back of the sofa and draped it over her head and torso like a psychedelic burka.

Milo opened the door a crack.

"Good evening," came from a tall, dark-haired man. "I'm Dr. Carlos Rivera of the U.S. Department of Homeland Security. I'm with the Chemical and Biological Defense Division."

Milo said, "We don't want to talk now."

Carlos persisted. "I strongly suggest we have a conversation. I can call in further authorities, but I'd rather just talk."

Inside the tiny house, Ken Ito murmured, "Damn!"

Milo sighed. He opened the door and Carlos stepped inside.

Carlos surveyed the room, committing people's faces and

positions to memory. Grace noted the raking gaze and adopted her best dumb-looking face.

Lena peeked out from under the afghan. Carlos reminded her of a sharp-shinned hawk, all lean muscle and efficient aggression.

Before Milo shut the door there came a shout.

"Hold on!" Another tall man, this one with light brown hair, came barreling through the door. "Don't listen to him. He's trouble."

"And you are?" Mrs. Sheehan asked.

"Dr. Zebulon Szczepanski. It's easiest if you call me 'Z'. I'm also with the Department of Homeland Security. I'm with the Advanced Research Projects Agency. We're the proper group to investigate and support research on any new biological development."

"The hell you are!" snapped Carlos.

As the two men launched into argument, Grace said, "Come on, kids. Bring Drewl." She stood up and walked past the dining room table, reaching in to grab the blank index cards. Mrs. O'Reilly caught her eye and gave a nod.

Grace led the way back to Piper's room.

"Who are those guys?" Piper asked.

"Alpha males having a pissing match," Grace replied. "Let's get these cards done. No matter what, it'll help to have numbers on everyone."

"I've got my mother's number and Aunt Catharine's," Cassie offered, pulling out her cell phone.

"I've got my folks, and Grandmom and you." Piper added.

"And I've got my Aunt Esther's."

Dylan leaned against the doorframe. "Not for me. My handwriting stinks."

Grace proffered a pencil and card. "Can you go ask Dr. Ito and Carys Kidwelly to write out their numbers for us?"

Dylan disappeared down the hall. The volume of the shouting in the living room increased.

Grace and Piper went to work at a small desk. Cassie pulled a book from a shelf and used it as a support as she also carefully copied out phone numbers.

Dylan was back a few minutes later, with a smirk on his face.

Grace eyed him suspiciously. "When my little brothers have that shit-eating grin, I know something is up."

Dylan smirked. "After I got the numbers, I got down on the floor and crawled under the table. I tied their shoelaces together."

"Whose shoelaces?"

"The guys that are yelling. Get this, Mrs. Sheehan saw me and she just smiled."

Dylan recited phone numbers for Ken, Carys, and Raymond's Plumbing.

"You don't have to write them down?" Piper was amazed.

"Nah. Total recall." Dylan tapped his head nonchalantly.

Grace smiled. Male strutting behavior emerged early in some.

"What's a Weismann barrier?" Dylan asked.

"Wow. Where'd you hear about that?" Grace responded.

"Part of what they're shouting about."

"It's this notion that cells get their direction from their DNA. Then scientists found an enzyme, called reverse transcriptase in some retroviruses that seem to pick up some of the DNA of one host. When the virus moves to a new host, it carries and inserts that DNA in the next host."

Grace looked at Dylan, not sure how much further to go with her explanation. He looked at her steadily. "Got it," he said.

She said, "It's part of how HIV infects people. And HIV can move to the next generation"

"Ah," Dylan scratched his ear. "So it has genetic engineering applications."

"You're eleven?"

"Twelve. Got held back a year. But the Internet," Dylan shot back. "Does not age discriminate."

*

Up on the hillside, Kurt gave up. There were just too many people and too many conversations going on in the Andersons' home. He folded up the listening device and slid it into the daypack.

He checked down the hill before he stood up. The woman with the corkscrew hair still sat next to the glass patio door. Kurt moved smoothly to his feet and picked his way up through the trees. Once he reached a deer trail he lengthened his stride and moved over the hill, silent as a cloud.

It took only minutes to reach Theodora. She sat in the driver's seat, working on her laptop. Kurt opened the passenger side door and slid in.

"I got Wi-Fi out here," Theodora told him.

"Modern world. That house is packed. I can't even tell you how many people are in there."

"Should I go for a visit?"

"Not a good idea. Two guys from Homeland Security showed up. They're having a turf war."

"Damn. I didn't need that."

"Before they showed up, some women were making plans to get the Andersons out of the house tomorrow. The good professor is biking out with a bunch of cyclists. Granny Edna is going to be at her house tomorrow, but they'll have someone with her."

Theodora's eyes narrowed. "And the other two? The blonde and the kid?"

"The kid goes off to school and from there to the rendezvous point. Get this, the blonde strolls out of the house tomorrow at dawn, comes up over the hill, like I just did, and down to one of the waterfront homes. She gets picked up by a boat at midday."

Theodora smiled. "We've got a boat."

"Yep. Even better, the family meets up tomorrow night at Swantown marina. Your pal, Dr. Berbera?"

"Yeah?"

"Meeting them with his RV."

"We know where they're going and how they're getting there. Excellent."

"What do you want to do?"

Theodora thought for a moment. She said, "Homeland Security I should avoid."

She turned to face her brother. "Wouldn't it be just really tragic if the Angel of Washington had her throat slit tomorrow morning?"

"You want me to do the blonde?"

"Yeah. That'd leave me Granny and the kid. They'll be in shock. I could ooze in and comfort them."

Kurt thought for a moment. "I think her husband will do the morning walk through the woods with her. I could take him too." Kurt ran his tongue over his teeth. "Yeah. That's good. Let's go back to the cabin. If I'm going to be back here before daylight, I need to get some sleep."

*

Back at the Andersons', the woman with the heart-shaped face and the corkscrew hair leaned against the patio door. She prayed for the wellbeing of her grandson. Then she wept.

"Dreams are true while they last,"

Alfred Lord Tennyson
(August 5, 1809 – October 6, 1892)

CHAPTER ONE HUNDRED TWO

Monday, almost midnight, The Anderson home.

"I WISH I WAS like Grace." Lena lay in bed, next to Milo.

"Like Grace? She'd think that was funny."

"No. I'm serious. She keeps moving forward. She's unflappable."

"Oh, I think she flaps inwardly. She just knows how to soldier on."

Lena sighed. "I don't. I want to run away."

"Fight or flight. We all have those reactions to stress. Sometimes flight makes damn good sense." Milo rolled over and put his hand on his wife's stomach. "It's going to be alright."

"Where are we going to go, Milo? I mean, I get our three-ring circus plan to get out of the neighborhood, but then what? How far are we going to get in Yousef's RV?"

"Shh, shh. Grace and Ken are working on that."

Lena drew in a soggy breath.

"Shh. Don't cry. Talk to me. What worries you the most?"

Lena laughed. "That I can't turn off my brain. One minute I'm thinking that my mother will never make it living away from her cabin. Then I'm thinking she's a heck of a lot tougher than I am. The next minute I'm worried that we've forgotten something important to Piper. Like, did we pack her swimsuit? And the dumbest?"

"What?"

"It's bugging me that there's a beef tenderloin in the freezer. It's for your birthday. I was going to cook it with porcinis. I got the beef on sale, and it still cost a fortune."

Milo smiled in the darkness. "I love you," he said as he pulled his wife closer.

*

On Kamilche Peninsula, Edna was up and working. Her long afternoon nap had refreshed her. She didn't sleep much at nights these days anyway. She cleaned out the refrigerator, and then she sat down and wrote out detailed directions to her most favorite mushroom patches.

Edna finished the location list and fixed a cup of tea. She took the mug and sat down on her old orange sofa with a leather bound book. She opened it and read *The Journal of Sara Louisa Funderburk, 1702-1705* that was written in elegant script.

Edna turned to a passage that she knew well.

December 15, 1702

I did not know I would ever see this day. The goode Reverend Green will examine the excommunication of our dear friend Martha Corey. Her death weighs heavy on my heart. She should never have been hanged, for she was, in every manner, a most Devout and Kind Christian.

It has been ten years since Martha was taken from us by the vicious and crazed persons of Salem towne. Every day is a day of Shame for I did not speake, though I knew what crazed the girls. I knew the rye had in it the creeping rotte that produces the fire of Saint Anthony.

I did not speake for the Wildness of the People would have surely destroyed me. Examination of my body would not yielde the witche's teats but the bird's downe.

I weep for my good friend, Martha. I castigate myself for my oddities and my weakness.

Edna closed the book. She was certain that the genetic toolbox had been opened many times before. Ken Ito should see this.

She retrieved another leather bound volume from her bookshelf. She had so much history of odd women and medicinal mushrooms. It shouldn't be lost. She should share them. When things were settled. When Piper was older. No. That kind of thinking led to trouble. She was eighty-three. The time was now. The books had to have a safe harbor. She shouldn't leave them here.

At her feet, Drewl's feet twitched as he dreamed of a paddle in a lake.

*

Five miles away, Deputy Don MacRae tossed and turned in his bed. He should have handled Pendergast better. He'd been so tired and so angry, that leaving the roadblock had seemed the best choice at the time. Now he was thinking of what he should have said, and what he should have done when Pendergast had harassed that dark-haired girl.

*

Tucked away in his loft bed, earphones on to dampen the sound of the cries that came from his sister, Dylan Kushner dreamed of vultures, cannons and war.

"This is the forest primeval. The murmuring pines and the hemlocks, Bearded with moss, and in garments green."

Evangeline by Henry Wadsworth Longfellow
(February 27, 1807 – March 24, 1882)

CHAPTER ONE HUNDRED-THREE

Tuesday, 5 a.m., The Anderson home

THE DAWN AIR nipped. Fall was arriving with a chill.

Milo slipped back inside the front door. "No one in the driveway. Yet."

"We should have had the deputies stay the night," Lena replied.

Milo disagreed. "The department is small. We're not the only folks to have problems."

"I know. I'm nervous to leave Piper. I'll be all right. You stay."

"No way. We'll pop over the hill to Crystal Kastenbaum's, and then I'll hotfoot it back here. Won't be ten minutes, total."

"Crystal terrifies me."

"Shh." Milo pulled his wife into a hug. "Everything terrifies you. Then you decide to be brave, and you are."

They stood tucked in together, for more than a minute. Lena pulled free. "I'll get my jacket."

Moments later, the pair stood at the rear patio door of their small home. Lena wrapped a scarf around her head while Milo put his hand out onto the finger groove of the patio door and slid the door open.

A body fell into the house.

Lena shrieked and leapt back. The body came to life, with arms flailing.

"Oh. Sorry! Sorry!" came from the rotund body. She struggled to her knees and stood up. Lena and Milo looked down on a short woman with a heart-shaped face and a head of hair permed into corkscrews.

"You spent the night out there?" Lena asked.

"Yes. I have to talk to you. I just do." Tears came in rapid spurts. "I've never had such a compulsion in my life, but I know I'm supposed to be here." She wiped her eyes. "I am so embarrassed. I've never done such a thing - but I am terribly desperate."

"I'm not an angel," Lena said softly. "I'm a woman with an odd genetic condition."

"I know. I listened last night. Those two guys sure got to shouting. I know you are leaving today. My grandson is dying of leukemia. He's just a toddler. Somehow I know I am supposed to talk to you."

Milo interrupted. "Sorry, but we've got to get going."

Lena disagreed. "I need to get going. You stay here with Piper. This dear lady and I can go through the woods together. She can tell me about her grandson on the way."

Milo started to object, but Lena cut him off. "She's the perfect beard," she said flatly.

Milo paused. Once in a while Lena was clearly Edna's daughter with a vein of pragmatic country toughness. When that pragmatism appeared, the ethereal Lena took backstage.

Milo looked down at the curly haired woman. Anyone looking

for Milo and Lena would know that this short woman was certainly not Milo. Time was passing.

"Walk fast," he said, and kissed his wife goodbye.

Up on the hillside, tucked into the fern bank, Kurt smiled as he packed up the Bionic Ear. He'd much rather have Angel and Little Curly walking through the woods.

Kurt pulled a knife out of his leg sheath. This, he exulted, was when he felt most alive. Sex was great. Hunting was better.

He should do the blonde first. She was fast. The Curly Head he could catch. He'd let the two move past his hiding spot. He'd fall in behind them. The trick would be to be noiseless. He couldn't let the stiff branches of the salal thrash against his pants.

Kurt drew in the early morning air, full of fall smells. Perfect for a hunt. Kurt felt his adrenaline levels pick up as the women moved his way.

How could a man be a serial killer? Kurt shifted the knife in his hand, feeling its most excellent balance. Easily. In truth, how could a man deny himself this glorious satisfaction?

Kurt rose to his feet, giving his blood a chance to feed his knees. He should challenge himself. Could he follow the women all the way across the hilltop? He should wait until they could see the house that was their destination. He should strike just as there was a moment of relief in their minds.

*

Lena and her companion moved up the trail. "I'm never up this early," Lena whispered. "Isn't it beautiful?" The morning light was giving shape to the treetops. Off in the distance a bird called.

"The forest primeval," agreed her new friend.

"How did you get past the police barricade?" Lena asked.

"Ohh, boy. You really don't want to know. Let's just say I performed a personal service."

Lena turned her head to look down at her companion. "Oh, dear."

"Yeah. Guy named Pendergast. Once he was happy, he radioed ahead and had me waved through. I parked my van at the other end of the loop and hiked over this hilltop."

"Tell me about your grandson."

The short woman said, "His name is Benjamin. We call him 'Benjie.' He's such a sweet boy. He's been sick a long time. We didn't realize it."

Tears came once more. "He's always slept a lot. A low energy kid."

The woman stopped and took in two ragged breaths. "We laughed about that," she sighed and said, "and we said how great it was that he was tired all the time."

The woman took in another shaking breath. "My daughter and son-in-law have older twin girls. Oh, God."

"Shh. Shh." Lena stopped and put her arm around the woman's shoulders. "You didn't know. "

"We should have. A woman at the park said Benjie was too bruised. I got so mad at her. I told her she was a busybody. But she was right. A baby shouldn't have bruises."

"So when did you figure out something was wrong?"

"Last week. He was coughing, and his little lymph nodes were all swollen. He passed out. I was there when it happened. I called 911. They sent an ambulance out and we all went off to the Emergency Room. We got the diagnosis a few hours later. It's bad."

Kurt slipped out behind the women once they moved past.

The dawn light came through the trees, making a descending march to the soil. Kurt could make out the leaves on outstretched huckleberry bushes even as the center of the bushes remained dark.

Kurt frowned as Lena took the lead. He wanted her first. Now he'd have to do the short one from the rear to get to the Angel.

As the trio neared the top of the hill, Kurt slowed and slid behind the trunk of a large cedar tree. Instinctively he knew the women would stop for a breather before descending to the road.

"It's funny," Lena said, "My daughter comes up here all the time, but I don't – and I should. Well, I should have."

"Don't worry, honey. You'll be back."

Lena laughed. "Here you are, with all your worries comforting me."

"Well, in my case, I know the doctors want to help Benjie. I couldn't tell you who to trust between that pair that were screaming at your place last night."

Behind the cedar, Kurt flexed his grip on the knife handle. He could help. A little throat slash, and Lena's worries would be over.

"We're going down the hill to that house," Lena said, pointing.

"The mansion?"

"Yes. The owner has a very scary pair of Dobermans named Jack and Jill."

"Jack and Jill?"

"Too funny, isn't it? Our organizers called Crystal last night. She's supposed to be up and looking for me."

"And then the boat guy comes later for you."

Lena laughed. "Sounds like you heard it all."

"Yeah. I think I did."

The women began the descent. Kurt moved closer.

Lena stumbled.

Kurt gripped the knife. There was a rustle in the bushes down the slope. Kurt paused.

Lena righted from her misstep and stepped forward. The

morning dawn now lit the bushes around her. There were just a few feet of underbrush between Lena and the road.

Kurt inhaled, ready for the dash and slash.

A bright light flashed.

Two men popped out of the bushes, cameras hoisted high.

"Run!" screamed the little woman.

Lena transformed into a blur as her friend ran at one of the photographers. The little woman delivered a vicious knee to the crotch. The photographer grunted and went flailing into the bushes.

The second photographer ran after Lena's blur, with his camera flashing.

Across the road, a full-bosomed woman opened her yard gate to the blur. The matron slid her arm forward, pointing at the photographer. Two slender Dobermans came sprinting across the road.

Kurt marveled at the speed and focus of the Dobermans. They ignored an old man and fat Labrador who were emerging from the next driveway.

The dogs honed in on the standing photographer like heat-seeking missiles. They grabbed his arms and began to pull. He went down, screaming.

"Jack! Jill! Come!"

The two dogs let go of the photographer and raced like paired rockets back to their home gate. The matron cooed as the dogs came in. Lena had already disappeared within the colonnaded door.

Savio Carlevaro came limping out of the woods to meet up with Vico. The Carlevaro brothers retreated down the street.

The short, curly-haired woman emerged onto the road where the dog walker beckoned to her.

Dr. Taggart and Sutton, the dog, ambled over to speak to

Lena's defender. "I'm Will," he said. "That's quite a knee you got there."

"Thanks. Is she safe? The Angel?"

"Yes. Crystal got her in, and Crystal will watch her like a hawk. I'm supposed to stroll down the street and call to tell Dr. Anderson what I see."

"My van's that way. Could we walk together?"

"Sure. I'd rather you had some company in case those paparazzi come back. Ah, what's your name Miss?"

"Miss? Goodness, I haven't been a Miss in years. I'm Celeste."

"Celeste. Are you a friend of the Andersons?"

"No." The little woman reached out and stroked Sutton's ears. "I've got a sick grandbaby. Yesterday when I heard about this Angel I had to come. It was the weirdest compulsion."

She added, "I spent the night leaning against the Andersons' patio door. Now that's obsessive."

"Or ordained."

Celeste laughed merrily. "I sincerely doubt that."

Up the hill, Kurt lay still behind a swath of sword ferns. He breathed deeply, striving to return his heart rate to normal. Paparazzi with their cameras changed things.

Kurt returned his knife to its sheath.

There still was a chance to get the blonde when she went out on the boat. Kurt thought a moment. The Anderson family was reuniting at the Swantown marina this evening. At an RV.

It might be easier to do the child. Theodora could comfort the parents. It was an idea worth exploring.

"Always mystify, mislead and surprise the enemy if possible."

Stonewall Jackson
(January 21, 1824 – May 10, 1863)

CHAPTER ONE HUNDRED-FOUR

Tuesday, 6 a.m., Apple Town Apartments

GRACE BARELY SLEPT. She was on the computer before dawn. She had just these early morning hours to find a destination for the Andersons, while Ken Ito completed the complex preparations needed for the Andersons to transit, transplant and survive.

Grace stood up, stretched and went into the kitchenette to microwave more instant coffee. It was horrible stuff. There was no time for a grocery store run now. Grace leaned her forehead against the kitchen cabinet and fanaticized about an IV full of brewed caffeine. "Focus," she muttered.

Grace filled her mug with water.

'Microclimate,' she mused. "We need someplace that has Internet service or Milo will go mad. It needs to have space and solitude, or Lena will be miserable. And mushrooms? How important were mushrooms to Edna?

Grace stirred dehydrated crystals into her cup, staring at the different colored swirls the instant coffee made as it dissolved into the water.

Water. Water would keep Drewl happy. It could also be a barrier to people. A little water discouraged visitors.

A castle with a moat? Too rare, too expensive. Most were tourist attractions anyway. An island? Better. Where did one find an affordable island? The San Juans were expensive. Hawaii more so.

Edna was healthy. She was in her eighties. Would she need health care?

Grace shook her head. "Natural spot with services, all for low cost. Yeah, right."

She sipped the instant coffee. It was ghastly. Only her high school chemistry partner, Nuri, could drink coffee like this.

Grace set the coffee mug down with a thump. Nuri! He was in the perfect location. Grace left the mug on the counter and ran to her computer.

*

Ken Ito hadn't slept. When his cell phone rang, he leapt on it. "Harry?"

"Yeah. Look, you gotta get your people outta that house. Carlos has a Special Forces team out of Fort Lewis coming your way. Sounds like he's going with 'possession being nine tenths of the law.'"

"Our gal should be on her way."

"Don't tell me. What I don't know, I don't have to lie about." Harry coughed. "And you don't want to know what it took for me to learn this."

"I'll owe you forever."

Harry snorted. "Damn straight. You got worse problems too. Either Carlos or Z finds out you got greater loyalty to the

Andersons than to the good ol' U. S. of A., and your career will be toast."

"Well, I've been thinking about teaching some math at a community college."

"Whatever floats your boat. Keep in touch."

Ken clicked off his phone and looked across the room to Carys Kidwelly. "Not exactly how I envisioned my first night with you," he said.

She gave him her double dimple special and said, "Good things are worth the wait."

"There is that."

Ken brought his phone to life and soon reached Milo. "You've got to get gone," Ken told him. "An Army unit is headed your way, probably to take protective custody."

Ken said, "Good," and hung up.

"What did he say?" Carys asked.

"Mrs. Sheehan has picked up Piper. Milo's about to hike over the hill to pick up the bike."

"This is when the day gets interesting."

Ken picked up Carys' phone. "Yeah," he said. "This is where things could go wrong."

*

Theodora's cellphone rang at seven in the morning.

It was now full light. Theodora could hear the crunch of a car on the gravel as Kurt pulled up in the driveway of the cabin.

Theodora took her chiming phone over to the window of the cabin. She could see Kurt look up at her as he climbed out of her Lexus. He was shaking his head 'no,' which told her hadn't been able to get to Lena.

Theodora answered her phone. "Hello."

"Yousef Berbera here. I hope I'm not calling too early."

"Oh, no, I'm delighted to hear from you." Theodora's voice oozed warmth.

"I need to shake the bugs out of my RV later today. I'm loaning it to some friends this evening. If you're interested in learning a little bit about the area, I could show you around this afternoon."

"How lovely. I'd like to meet your friends. Where will we be going?" Theodora ladled more warmth into her words.

"We could see Mima Mounds, and come back to town for dinner. I've got to drop off the RV at Swantown later this evening. Want to come along?"

"I think that's an excellent idea," Theodora purred.

"All is flux. Nothing stays still."

Plato (427 BCE – 347 BCE)

CHAPTER ONE HUNDRED-FIVE

Tuesday, 7 a.m., west of Olympia

"THANKS FOR PICKING me up." Dylan slid into the back seat of the school van. "What?" he barked at Piper.

"Never heard you say 'Thanks' before. Surprised, that's all."

Dylan slammed the van door shut. "I'm in. Let's go."

Piper looked at the dark house behind Dylan. "Your parents don't mind you helping us today?"

"My parents are potheads. They don't even know what century we're in."

"Dylan!" Mrs. Sheehan warned, flicking her eyes at the rear view mirror. "Dylan's parents are attorneys with a mission. Dylan's sister has been very ill."

Dylan was surprised by her summary. His face of astonishment was briefly held. He slouched back in the seat and said, "My sister has polyarticular juvenile idiopathic arthritis. She hurts all the time."

Dylan turned toward Piper and said, "Marijuana gives her some relief."

Dylan aimed a savage kick at the back of the front passenger seat. "My parents think they need to test each batch before they give it to her." Dylan crossed his arms and added, "They spend their days and nights stoned. I take care of me."

"They've done a great deal to change laws and mindsets so ill children can get relief," Mrs. Sheehan said.

Behind her, Piper sat still. Dylan's bullying of Joey made sense in an odd way. Piper blinked back tears. She didn't want to leave Olympia now.

*

At eight a.m. Detective Raposo strode into the Mason County Courthouse. He glanced at the clock on the wall and turned down the corridor that led to the small courtroom. With luck he would testify by nine and be on his way by nine-thirty.

Today he would talk to both Andersons. He'd bring Edna Morton in for a grilling if he had to. He could feel, to his bones, that she was connected to Patel's murder. And Kaylee Kovacev's. Somehow Edna fit into the picture.

Raposo's cell phone beeped. He read a text message from Don MacRae. "Ready."

Raposo tapped back, "Court now. Will call after."

He could see Judge Peters coming down the corridor from the other direction, shrugging on her gown as she walked. The fabric billowed in and the judge crashed to the floor.

Raposo moved to help her up. "Twisted my ankle," the judge gasped.

The detective helped the judge limp to a nearby bench. She sank down onto it, grimacing. "I should have had my robes shortened. Stupid to think higher heels were the solution."

The judge looked up and made eye contact with Rodger.

"Detective Raposo, will you get the bailiff? We're going to need to delay court an hour."

There was nothing to do but comply.

*

Milo's legs burned. His chest ached. He put his head down and pedaled for all he was worth. Christ. These people were insane. He was fourteenth in the group of cyclists and was certain that the two gals behind him were hanging back just to be kind.

It was hard to be grateful when one was struggling for air. Milo was grateful anyway. He knew Lena was safe with two Dobermans at her feet.

"They're quite sweet," she'd said on the phone.

Piper was away with Mrs. Sheehan. He knew that Mrs. Sheehan would guard Piper with all the shrewdness and power she had. No worries there.

He hadn't had a chance to talk to Edna. Milo kept pushing. No time to worry about Edna now. Funny, he had driven this road a million times and had never noticed that there was a slight incline. It seemed like Everest to his tortured thighs.

A trio of Army trucks came into view. The trucks barreled down the road with scary authority. There was an efficient slowing as the trucks neared the cyclists. As soon as the cyclists were past, Milo could hear the trucks accelerate.

Too late, suckers, Milo thought. He pedaled harder.

*

Vico sat in the sword ferns across the road from the Kastenbaum waterfront home. "My neck hurts," groused Vico. "You'd think my nuts would hurt more, but it's my neck that's killing me."

"Shh." Savio said as he dropped down next to his brother. "Sound carries. We're the only ones who know the Angel is down at this end of the loop."

"What'dja find out?"

"Lotta people at the Andersons home. Get this. There's a preacher on the lawn saying that the Angel is here to smite those in gay marriages."

"Lotta smiting to be done then."

"There's no one left at the house." Savio gestured across at the mansion. "The Angel is here. The rest of the family does a bunk. We stay here, and we get the pictures. Could you manage the video camera?"

"No way. Not with this neck."

"We'll stick with the still cameras. She's got to come out sometime."

"For you know I have plans for you,"

Jeremiah 29:11

Chapter One Hundred-Six

Tuesday, Noon. Oyster Bay from the Kamilche Peninsula side

BY NOON THE tide was near its peak.

"You get the middle," directed Esther. "Raymond will sit in back and steer."

Aunt Esther eased off the dock and into the front seat of a bright red canoe, while Grace's Uncle Raymond held the canoe steady.

Grace paused as she looked down into the canoe. It looked a long way down. She felt absurd. Uncle Raymond had insisted she wear a life vest. Esther had draped her in a button-covered black and red wool blanket and plopped a woven lampshade on her head. At least the hat looked like a lampshade to her. Uncle Raymond had also given her a flat drum the size of a pizza pan.

"I'm not sure how I'm supposed to get all this down into the boat," she said.

"Well, for starters, never call it a boat," replied her Uncle

Raymond. "If you call it a boat again, we have to throw you overboard, and have you swim under the canoe. Then you say 'it's a canoe,' and swim under it again. And again. And again. Then we pull your wet self out and let you back in the canoe."

"Got it. It's a canoe."

"So set the drum and beater down on the dock. Then sit down and dangle your legs over the edge."

Uncle Raymond coached her into the canoe. He ignored her one nervous squeal that escaped when her weight transferred from the dock to the center of the canoe. She decided she liked her uncle.

He handed her the flat drum and the beater. Grace laid the pieces across her lap.

"Stay with your body weight centered in the canoe," he told her as he slid in. He picked up a paddle with fluid grace, and a few moments later, Esther did the same. The two paddlers sent the canoe surging away from the dock while Grace clutched the gunnels of the canoe.

"The next low tide is not that low," Raymond called from the back. "You've got to watch the tides when you go up into the bays, or you can get stuck on the mud flats. Oyster Bay turns into two hundred acres of mud at low-low tide. It won't get that low today."

After that reassurance, the canoeists fell silent. Grace felt surprisingly comfortable. The button blanket defeated the chill of the fall day. The lampshade hat shaded her eyes.

Grace could see small moving blocks on shore that she knew were cars. They seemed irrelevant. A seal popped his head up and watched the canoe go by.

"You should come with us on an ocean canoe," her uncle called. "We'll do some training in the spring. I could show you."

"I'd like that," Grace called back

A pair of gray birds floated by, their long white and black necks snaking an S curve.

"Grebes," Esther said.

"We'll stop paddling when we round the bend into Oyster Bay," Raymond suggested. "We can start up the drums then. The tide will carry us down the bay. At that point we just want to be as loud as possible. Local color."

"We should chant something," Esther called back.

"Yeah. Let me think." Raymond dug his paddle in and sent the canoe sliding forward. "How about, 'No government without representation'?"

Esther used the tip of her paddle to send a spray of water back at her brother.

"Okay, Okay. We'll do something traditional."

*

Kurt used the spotting scope to survey the far shore. "There's a tour bus." He straightened up and turned to Theodora and said, "If it were me, I'd be getting her off at high tide."

Theodora stretched like a cat. She knew she'd be at the Swantown marina in the evening when the Anderson family reassembled. She was content to let the morning pass.

"What about Granny Edna and the girl?" she asked.

"I don't think anyone is left at the house," Kurt told her.

He took another look through the scope. "Ahh. Red canoe. These guys are the distraction. They'll come down here and make some sort of scene. While that's happening, the Angel steps off the dock at that house with the Dobermans. She gets into a boat and disappears."

Kurt looked again at the traffic on Oyster Bay Road. "Two television trucks. Yeah. We're about to have a diversion." He stood up and made a decision. "I'm going out on the SeaRay."

"You think you can do her on the water?"

"We'll see."

*

Lena wound a scarf around her head. She reached down and fondled Jack's ears. "You are such a good dog," she told him.

Lena turned to her hostess, "Thank you, Crystal, for having me."

"Oh, my pleasure, honey. I should have had you down ages ago." Crystal Kastenbaum reached over and patted Lena's arm. "You have my number. You let me know if you need me."

"Just keep the photographers away!" Lena told her. "Those guys scare me."

Crystal leaned back in her Queen Anne chair, folding her arms under her impressive bosom. "I think I know that pair. They've given their poor mother fits for years. You don't worry about them. I'll deal with those knuckleheads."

Lena grinned. She stood up and took Crystal's picnic hamper from the gleaming kitchen counter.

Lena peered out the patio door. She could see Joe Harbo's oyster boat coming across the inlet.

Lena waited until Joe had his boat nudged up against the dock. She waved a good-bye to Crystal and stepped out onto the deck. She carried the picnic basket in one hand and tried to move in a casual way – just a person out for a lunch on the water.

Lena walked to the end of the dock, where Joe offered her a hand as she stepped down into the oyster boat. "Good morning, Joe," she said softly.

Joe ducked his head in sudden shyness. He pointed to a padded toolbox in front of the wheelhouse.

"That's a good spot," he said.

As soon as she was settled, Joe put the boat into reverse and cleared the dock. He turned the wheel and steered into the inlet.

Lena stared at the water. The waves that had been slapping at the dock had hesitated. In the space of just a few moments, the water went from slapping to bobbing. She was seeing the turning of the tide.

That, she thought, *is a good sign.* Off in the distance she could hear drums. *Give 'em hell, Grace*, Lena thought with a smile.

She was suddenly hungry again. She called to Joe, "Want a sandwich?"

"You go ahead," he told her. "I'll eat after we're behind Squaxin Island."

*

Kurt opened the cruiser up once he was away from shore. The little powerboat could move.

It was a good thing he'd launched the boat when he did. He had exited Oyster Bay and looked up the shoreline just in time to see the oyster boat leave the mansion dock.

That had to be the Angel leaving.

The fact that it was an oyster boat gave Kurt some pause. Milo Anderson he could take. But an oysterman? The oystermen spent hours on the water hauling oysters, shell and spawn. Most of them were built like gorillas. Territorial of their oyster beds, they often lacked any dainty objections to violence. It'd be foolish to rush in.

Kurt eased off the throttle. For now all he needed to do was keep the oyster boat in sight.

"I'll wait," Kurt said to the wind. "Let's see what the day brings."

"For man is born into trouble,"

Job 5: 7

CHAPTER ONE HUNDRED-SEVEN

Tuesday, Four p.m. West of Olympia

BY LATE AFTERNOON Rodger Raposo was in a swearing mood.

After Judge Peters postponed court an hour, the bailiff saw an unmarked package in the men's room. There was nothing to do but clear the building. It took two hours for the building to be secured. It was after lunch before Detective Raposo testified, and even later before he collected Deputy MacRae.

They drove out to Kamilche Peninsula to talk to Edna. Raposo was ready to get a full story from her.

That didn't happen. An enormous vehicle was lodged across both lanes of the rural road. The truck had "Tron's Tree Trimming Service" emblazoned on the door.

"Sorry, man," said a pony-tailed worker in orange overalls. "We've called for a part. It's coming from Seattle."

Snarling, Raposo executed a three-point turn and headed back for the highway, only to run afoul of heavy traffic near the Oyster Bay exit.

It was close to four before Raposo and MacRae finally made it to the Anderson home. This time Raposo tore a strip off the young deputy manning the barricade and was let through. Pendergast was nowhere in sight.

Neither were the Andersons. There was a steady stream of would-be pilgrims knocking on the front door. Some sat on the grassy lawn, and others took pictures.

Raposo and MacRae walked around to the back patio. There they found a short, plump woman sitting at a patio table sharing coffee from a thermos with an older gentleman in a plaid flannel shirt and jeans. A white-muzzled Labrador snoozed on the patio flagstones.

Raposo recognized Will Taggart. It had been fifteen years since Dr. Taggart had tripped up Rodger in a courtroom. Rodger had made a medical assumption, and Taggart had made hay with it. Those things one didn't forget.

"Good afternoon, young man," Dr. Taggart said.

"Good to see you, sir," Raposo meant it. "We're here to speak with the Andersons. Any idea where they might be?"

Taggart had a great poker face. The little woman didn't. She flinched at the question.

Raposo moved in. "This is important. We're working on a double murder investigation. A good man named Dr. Neeladri Patel had his throat cut last week. His office secretary, a young woman named Kaylee Kovacev, was found dead in her parent's home."

The curly-haired woman threw a worried look to Dr. Taggart.

Raposo continued, "We think there is a connection between those two deaths and Edna Morton, the mother of Mrs. Anderson. There is someone very violent out there. We need to stop him. Mrs. Morton and the Andersons may need our protection."

Will Taggart looked across the patio table to his companion and nodded.

The little woman said, "I know where they will be later tonight."

Raposo didn't like what he heard.

*

"No, Uncle. It's too high for him." Grace stood at the back of Uncle Raymond's van, looking at Drewl's nervous shifting of weight. The old dog was hesitating to obey Raymond's direction to jump in the back.

"Wait," Grace ordered. She looked around and then grabbed a picnic cooler and set it behind the bumper. She pulled over Edna's suitcase, making a two-step staircase.

"Kennel," she directed. Drewl clambered up the makeshift stairs into the van. Grace sagged against the bumper. Every muscle she had ached. They had paddled and drummed for over an hour before beaching the canoe for a break. She'd taken Esther's place at the front of the canoe on the way back. The afternoon filled up with moving and logistics.

"Here," said Edna, coming down the path. She thrust a sandwich at Grace. "Eat something."

Drewl leaned forward from the van's interior, put his head over Grace's shoulder and… drooled.

"This is for you," Edna told him. She handed the dog a tuna fish sandwich that he devoured in two gulps.

Grace bit into the sandwich. She felt better instantly.

Ken Ito and Carys Kidwelly came down Edna's walk, each with a suitcase in hand. "This is it," Ken said.

"I'm having qualms," Grace said.

"Me too," Ken agreed.

Ken turned to Edna and said, "It truly has been an honor to meet you. I don't know when or if I'll see you again."

Edna smiled. "I've seen Carys' hand. I'll be seeing you again." Then she sobered. "That's assuming this evening goes as planned."

*

"Kurt, believe me, this professor is crazy," Theodora hissed into her cell phone. "He wanders around these piles of gravel talking about vernal pools, nebkhas, pocket gophers and earthquakes."

Her afternoon excursion with Yousef Berbera had descended into the field trip from hell. Clouds scudded in, threatening rain. The wind had picked up in the last hour as Dr. Berbera continued to wander through acres of gravel mounds, talking all the while.

Theodora had finally escaped, claiming a need to tend to nature's call. She knew it was only a matter of moments before Berbera latched onto her again, insisting that she share the wonder of one more forb or burrow.

"Well, I'm fucking freezing," Kurt snarled back. "It's cold out here on the water."

"Where is the Angel now?"

"Having a fucking tea party in a fucking sun room," Kurt ground out. "They hung out behind a big island until the clouds moved in. Then the boat goes over to a dinky waterfront house, and they unload. The Angel goes up to a coffee klatch."

"You can't take a party of ladies?"

"Not when their husbands are down at the dock working on gear. There's three of them, and they are the size of houses."

Theodora realized she had never heard her brother sound so frustrated. *I can use this*, she thought.

"She deserves it," she told him. "Whatever you decide to do, she deserves it. We know she has to end up at the marina tonight. Get the boat over there. Get something to eat. I'll meet up with you and we'll do things right."

"Fucking Right." Kurt agreed.

"Hey, Theodora?" came from a distance. "We're in luck! There's a late blooming *Dodecatheon hendersonii*. It's spectacular!"

Theodora tapped her cell phone off and stomped on a nearby patch of flowers. She yelled, "Be right there!" as she ground the blossoms under her heel.

"Scattering is easier than gathering."

Irish proverb

CHAPTER ONE HUNDRED-EIGHT

Tuesday, Seven p.m., Downtown Olympia

"YOU GOTTA PLAY to your strengths." Dylan crammed a handful of French fries into his mouth and added, "You can run."

Dylan sat with Piper and Milo Anderson at a rundown café not far from Swantown marina. Dylan may have matched Piper in shirt and braids, but his actions were all male. He grabbed the ketchup squirt bottle and powered out a cup of ketchup onto his next pile of fries, then slurped down half a Pepsi while continuing to grind on the current mouthful.

Milo was amused at his own domestication. He had forgotten what it was to be a middle school guy.

Piper averted her eyes from Dylan's masticating potatoes with a frown. "I can fight," she reminded him. "I cleaned your clock."

"You got the drop on me." Dylan scooped up another fistful of fries. "I totally did not see you coming. You're still a girl."

Milo jumped in before Piper could. "Dylan, you keep that

attitude and you will continue to get your clock cleaned. However, Dylan does have a point."

Milo put his hand on his daughter's shoulder. "You are fast. We all bring our disposition to confrontation. There's fight and there's flight. I think you have some flexibility, Piper. You can fight if you have to. For tonight I am going to ask you to run if anything unusual happens. Not that I think that it will."

Piper shrugged an agreement.

"Here's what's going to happen," Milo said. "We're going to finish dinner. You can have dessert. We're not in a rush. Dr. Berbera is supposed to drop his RV at the marina about nine. We'll hike over there and hang out in his RV."

"A camper van?" asked Dylan.

"It's a big bus with all the conveniences of a home – even a TV. Grace and Grandma are up in Shelton. They're headed out to the mushroom farm so Edna can deliver her library to Carys."

Milo hesitated. He didn't understand why Edna had been so adamant on that point. She had insisted that her collection of family journals had to go to Carys. Today. When life got back to normal, he was going to have a talk with Edna.

Milo exhaled. Normal was a long way off.

"Okay, so we're at the marina. We're hanging out. About ten tonight, the tide will be rising, and Joe Harbo will bring Mom over." Milo looked at Dylan. "Best behavior?"

"Yeah." Dylan looked down at the lettuce leaf that was all that remained of a double cheeseburger. "We're good."

"Grace will arrive with Edna and Drewl. Then Grace takes Dylan home."

"Where are we going?" Piper asked.

"Grace has something in the works." Milo picked up the menu. "Let's look at desserts."

Dylan started to say something. Milo gave him a hard stare and jerked his head at Piper.

Dylan dipped his chin in acknowledgement and said, "I could go for the Mother Lode sundae."

"That's five scoops of ice cream," Piper gasped.

"So?"

*

"Retreating so soon?" Carlos asked as Zebulon Szczepanski put his computer in the trunk of his rental car.

"Retreat or return to sanity?" Z snapped. "The Andersons are gone. Good luck to them - one more bizarre biological hiccup in a world of biological spasms. I'm not spending my agency's time and money on smoke. Back to the plodding world of plodding, persistent science for me."

"I know where they're headed."

Z folded his arms and leaned against the car. "Yeah?"

"I had a tap put on Ken Ito's phone."

"Christ, you're a bastard, Carlos."

"True. The Andersons split up. They're meeting again tonight at a local marina. I'm going to be there. Want in?"

Z studied Carlos for a long moment. "Why the sudden invite?"

"Oh, brotherhood in science. We should be better friends."

"The Army pulled out, didn't they? You got no backup!"

"Something better came along."

"Be specific."

"One of the Rangers put me in touch with a half dozen guys with a little firm that specializes in security."

"Rent-a-Ranger. Mercenaries."

"That's harsh, Z. Very harsh. Think of them as motivators and protectors. But you can see why I need you to come along."

"No, I don't see."

Carlos thumped the car hood in frustration. "I think outside the box. I push the boundaries. Hell, I piss on boundaries all the time. I get results. But I don't terrorize little girls and grandmothers. Ito's right to protect these people. Unfortunately, his vision is small."

Carlos gestured out into space. "Ito thinks they can drive down the road in a big old RV, and nobody's going to notice them when they stop for gas and a hot dog. The only place this feathered woman is going to be safe is on a military base or in a federal research facility."

"Under your control."

"Sure. Why not? Someone's got to be in charge. Why not me?"

"Why do you need me?"

"Another scientist. Talking to Ken Ito, and to the Andersons. Running isn't the answer. They need a destination. A destination we can offer."

Carlos allowed a wry smile to emerge. He said, "I also could use you to make sure my Rent-A-Rangers stay in line. I don't want anyone hurt. There's a kid, her grandmother and her civilian parents. We don't need things to get out of hand. We also can't have them loose on the road. It's dangerous for them. Plus it does nothing for science. Calm heads must prevail."

Carlos knew his man. Z folded. "What do you want me to do?"

"Choose only one master – Nature."

Rembrandt Harmenszoon van Rijn
(July 15, 1606 – October 4, 1669)

Chapter One Hundred-Nine

Tuesday, Nine p.m. Downtown Olympia

"WE COULD GO down to Capital Lake and see the bat flight," Yousef Berbera said. "There are several species that are still foraging. It's a tremendous sight."

"Thank you for a wonderful and educational afternoon," Theodora told him, "Dinner was delicious, but now I'm supposed to meet my brother. Aren't you supposed to be meeting your friend?"

"Yep. I'm late," Yousef said cheerily. "Often am. Well, I had a wonderful time too."

"Ta!" Theodora slid out of the passenger seat of the RV and descended the steps out of the bus. She gave a cheery wave as Berbera pulled off in the big rig.

Theodora stalked to her car, tapping her cell phone as she went. "15 min," she texted.

"Good," came back.

Theodora opened the trunk of her car and tossed in her daypack. Kurt was right. It was cold near the water. She pulled out the pink hoodie and slipped it on. A look of innocence wouldn't hurt.

*

Raymond's van swayed, and Grace clutched her knees as she sat on the metal floor in the back. Drewl swayed with her, as did the short tower of suitcases. Grace couldn't remember the last time she had been in a vehicle without a seatbelt. She tried hard to not think about her high school physics class and the mathematical formulations on force. Uncle Raymond had been a prince today. It was no fault of his that his work van wasn't meant for family relocations.

"Sorry!" Uncle Raymond called back. "Squirrel in the road. He's safe."

Edna, in the front passenger seat, started talking about squirrel stew. Raymond asked her which mushrooms she would recommend.

Grace blinked her eyes, trying to get some moisture moving in eyes sandy from exhaustion. What a day. She'd discovered an uncle, arranged an evacuation, moved a library and even learned to paddle her own canoe.

She liked Dr. Ito. She liked how he thought. He'd heard her suggestion, and then moved forward, taking it to an improved level with speed.

The next few hours were critical. There had been so many phone calls. Some on Ken Ito's phone. Some on hers. Many on Carys Kidwelly's. *And where was Dr. Band?*

*

Milo felt exposed standing on the asphalt. He was relieved when he saw Yousef Berbera turn into the marina parking lot at fifteen minutes after nine.

The parking lot had scattered clusters of vehicles, testament to the number of people who resided on boats at the marina. There was an openness that unnerved. The few working street lamps caused the clusters of vehicles to cast dark pools of shadow.

As soon as Yousef pulled to a stop, Milo had a hand on each child and propelled the pair across the empty section of the parking lot to the bus.

"I'm going already!" Dylan objected.

"Welcome aboard," Yousef said as he propped open the door. "Two girls?" he asked.

"Piper's friend, Dilys," Milo answered. "She'll be with us for a bit. Grace will take her home."

"Hi Ladies. There's some video games you can try." Dr. Berbera motioned Piper and Dylan up the stairs.

Piper and Dylan scrambled aboard and began exploring. Yousef stepped down onto the asphalt. "Keys," he said. "Extra set in a magnetic box under the front bumper.

"Thanks," Milo said. "I can't tell you thanks enough."

"Welcome. I didn't get out at all this summer, so it was just gathering dust balls. I have a winter field season in Arizona. She's yours until then."

"Hopefully we only need a few days."

"What's the plan?"

"Grace shows up with Edna. A friend is bringing Lena over on a boat. Then we load up and head out."

"And after that?"

Milo chose his words carefully. "Get out of town first. Get away from the crazies. Take some time to think. You'll have to cover my classes."

"We can do that. Talk to Personnel when you can. Maybe you can take a semester sick leave. It'd be good to have you back."

Milo took in a shaky breath. "We'll see. At this point, who

knows?" Milo changed the subject to something safe. "How do you get home?"

"I'll ask Grace for a lift. If not, I'll call a cab. Right now I'm going to check the bat flight and see if Angus has had any bright ideas this afternoon. Angus is one of the sharpest students I've ever had - he lives in a boat off the G dock. Want to come?"

"Angus lives on a boat? Didn't know that." Milo checked his watch. "We've got half an hour. I would like to hear what Angus has to say. Biochem is not my strength. Let me get the kids."

But Piper refused. Dylan had already found the game console and controllers and was showing Piper the first level of something violent.

Piper spoke while pushing buttons on the controller. "You go, Dad. It's just half an hour. We'll be fine."

Milo hesitated.

Piper's character took a fatal hit. She groaned as Dylan laughed.

"You'll get it," Dylan told her. "Restart."

Piper looked up at her father. "Dad, we'll shut the door. I'll honk the horn if someone shows up. We won't let anyone in. You've been, like, looming over me." Piper's eyes rolled, and she hunched her shoulders forward. "No one is interested in me. We'll be fine."

"We should stick together. I'll hang out with you."

"Dadddddd. Go. I mean, I just need to… breathe a minute. I mean it's not like Grandmom is ever going to play this with me." Piper scowled. "I don't want to stand out on the dock getting eaten by mosquitos while you talk about science stuff, like, forever."

Milo studied his daughter. Piper glared at him. He caved. "Okay. We're just down at the G stairs. The ramps are in alphabetical order."

"Dad, I know. It's fine. We'll stay here, and we can run from A to G if we have to."

"Check before you open the door to anyone. If you don't know who's knocking, don't open it."

"Sure, Dad. We'll be careful."

Milo stepped out of the bus and pushed the door closed. "Clouds coming in," he said. "We might not see many bats."

"One way to find out," Dr. Berbera said cheerfully. "You never know what's out there unless you look."

Kurt, crouched nearby in the shadow of his truck, agreed.

"There is danger in both belief and unbelief."

Phaedrus (15 BCE – 50 CE)

CHAPTER ONE HUNDRED-TEN

Tuesday, Nine-thirty p.m. Swantown Marina Parking Lot

RODGER RAPOSO AND Don MacRae pulled into the parking lot at the Swantown Marina at half past nine.

"Down at the end. There's a Class A RV," MacRae said. "Only one. That's got to be the rendezvous point."

"The mom is supposed to come in around ten." Raposo clicked off the headlights of the sedan and said, "Let's do a little lookie-loo." He slowly drove the car down the lot.

"Stop!" MacRae barked.

Raposo hit the brakes. "What have you got?"

"Dark Lexus with a Kankakee High School window sticker."

"Good catch." Raposo pulled the county sedan into a parking spot. He and MacRae exited their unit carefully, closing the doors with a quiet click. They checked out the Lexus. "Engine's warm," Raposo noted.

MacRae produced a pencil flashlight and turned it on. He

peered into the car. "Laptop case in the foot well, passenger side," he reported.

"Huh. You'd think someone would lock that in the trunk."

"Coming back soon, maybe?"

MacRae clicked off his light as a van came up the service road to the parking lot. "Raymond's Plumbing. He's a Shelton guy. What he's doing this far east?"

"Clogged boat toilet?" Raposo mused.

The van pulled up near the A stairs. A slender, dark-haired man got out.

"That's Raymond," MacRae said.

Raymond went around to the back of the van and opened the doors. A stocky young woman and a big black dog hopped out.

"Wow. That's an elephant." MacRae said. He stuttered, "The dog, I mean." The young woman took the dog over to a grassy patch underneath a street light.

"I know her," MacRae said. "She came through the roadblock. She's Professor Anderson's graduate assistant."

"Ah. We are at the right place."

"How do you want to handle this?"

"Let's leave the unit here and take a little stroll. When we get close, we'll find a spot to sit and watch."

*

Milo and Yousef Berbera were already down the staircase that led to the floating G dock. A high mesh gate barred the way.

"I'm not sure about climbing over this," Milo said. "This is no night for me to get arrested."

"Nah. Just a minute." Dr. Berbera trilled out a cry like a squeaking door.

"Pacific Loon?"

"Angus says I'm definitely one."

There was silence for a moment. A head popped up out of a sailboat two slips away. "Dr. Loony?"

"Yo! Angus! Can you let us in?"

"Be right there."

Milo checked his watch. "I don't want to be gone too long."

"Sure," Yousef agreed.

Angus came down the dock. He pulled a key out from a string around his neck and unlocked the mesh gate. "Welcome. What's up?"

"Dr. Anderson is leaving town soon. Thought we'd look at your bats coming in and pick your brain a bit."

"I've been thinking all afternoon. Deep stuff. I've got some ideas."

*

Theodora found Kurt crouched behind his truck twenty yards from the RV. She knelt beside her brother.

"A lot of traffic, Teddy," Kurt whispered.

"The sedan was probably a boater," she whispered back. "The van's a plumber. What's happening on the RV?"

"Two girls. The professors left them to go look at bats."

"Could you do two kids?" Theodora smiled in the dark. "That could be a rush."

"Yeah. But that RV is one way in, one way out. Good for me to trap them in, bad for me if someone comes in from behind. How long is a bat watch?"

"Trust me, that pair of professors are going to be gone a while. They're probably having a lecture-thon right now. Bat diet, bat digestion, bat anatomy, bat flight, bat psychology…"

Kurt snorted. "I get your point. Good." He said, "Time to make a choice. I do the girls or I do the Angel. Then, Teddy, I'm out of here."

"Fair enough. I like the high wire, Kurt. I'd like to manage the feathered bitches if I can. You know, mix a lot of terror and a little science. I've got this."

Theodora pulled a syringe out of the tunnel pocket of her hoodie. "The Nembutal you picked up. It's enough to put someone in a coma."

Theodora shifted her weight and restored the syringe to her pocket. She whispered, "If the Angel gives me any crap, I'll give her a wallop. I can always say she was getting hysterical."

"And you'll also have Grandma."

"Yeah. I can manage her."

"So I'm doing the kids."

"Works for me."

Kurt put out a hand and drew his sister in for a kiss. "Might not see you for a long time."

Theodora stroked his face. "Love you."

"Love you too. Go get yourself some birds."

Theodora stood up. She did a quick survey of the parking lot. She studied the van. She didn't see anyone. There was no need to be seen by the plumber. She'd cut across the parking lot, go down the C stairs and walk up the main pier walkway to the A dock.

Kurt got ready. He wouldn't use the pistol tucked in the small of his back. A knife would be much more entertaining. He pulled on two pairs of nitrile gloves and unsheathed his dagger.

"All warfare is based on deception."

Sun Tzu (544 BCE – 496 BCE)

CHAPTER ONE HUNDRED-ELEVEN

Tuesday, Nine-forty-five p.m.
Swantown Marina Parking Lot

KURT SLID ALONG the side of the bus. He could hear the video game blasting. *It's fun when they start happy*, he thought.

At the door of the RV, he ran his fingers along the seal. Not bad, but no match for a knife blade slipped under the rubber gasket. Kurt eased the blade in and pried gently. The door gave enough for his fingers to slide in. He curled his fingers in and began to pull. There was no halt. The door wasn't locked.

Would the dome light come on? With luck, it wouldn't. Kurt pulled further.

The dome light flicked on. Kurt pulled the door wide and came up the steps as fast as he could.

The girls were a dozen feet back in the vehicle, facing the door as they sat at a dinette table with game controllers in their hands. The kids saw him come up the stairs. The children looked at him with wide eyes and open mouths. In unison, their controllers came down on the table with a clunk.

Kurt strode forward with a grin. He held the knife, blade up in his right hand. "Scream and you die," he said.

He smiled. "You're cute." The kids sat frozen as Kurt leaned over them. "Twins, almost," Kurt said in a conversational tone. "Cute little birds. Wonder which one of you has feathers?"

His hand shot out to grab the hair of the closest girl. Dylan's wig came off in Kurt's hand.

Dylan dove for the floor, screaming, "RUN!" Dylan shot both feet up into Kurt's left kneecap, scoring a strong hit. Kurt grunted as pain shot through his leg.

Piper scrambled up off the bench and crawled straight across the table, swinging her feet down behind Kurt. He reached for her, grabbing air as Piper ran for the front of the bus.

Kurt pivoted to grab Dylan. Dylan was already crawling away down the aisle. He got further traction with one toe and pushed forward and away from Kurt's long reach.

Piper reached the front of the RV. She smashed a hand down on the center of the steering wheel, sending out a short horn bleat. It was a miniscule garbled toot, not nearly the blast she intended. There was no time for more.

Piper charged down the stairs, out the open door and into the night.

Kurt swore and lunged after Dylan, grabbing him by one foot. Kurt pulled Dylan back, while changing his grip on the knife. He'd skewer the brat with a stab to the kidney.

Dylan dug his fingers into the carpet.

Kurt pulled him closer.

Dylan rolled and kicked Kurt's kneecap again. Kurt hissed, but hung on. Dylan rolled to the other side, pulling Kurt with him. Dylan was now a foot further up the RV aisle. An under sink curtain fluttered with the commotion. Dylan could see the bases of aerosol cans in the gap between the curtain bottom and the toe molding that held the cleaning supplies in place.

Dylan clawed through the curtain and seized a can. He flipped over, ignoring the pain in his foot as Kurt held on. Dylan slapped the top of the canister and shot a stream of cleaning foam into Kurt's eyes.

Kurt recoiled from the foam. He kept his grip on Dylan.

Kurt pulled Dylan down the carpeted aisle by the foot.

Dylan jammed his free foot against the wall. Kurt was stronger. As Dylan slid down the aisle, he spied something metallic and narrow laying at the edge of the carpet next to the dining nook.

Kurt paused in his pulling to cough and shake away some of the foam from his stinging eyes.

Dylan erupted from the floor to plunge a kebab skewer through the underside of Kurt's chin. Kurt screamed as the skewer slid through and emerged from his cheek just below his left eye.

One strong twist and Dylan was free. Dylan scrambled to his feet, leapt up onto the dinette table and slid down the table and past Kurt like a sure-footed squirrel. Dylan raced down the aisle to grab the knee-wall of the entrance. He swung down the stairs without touching a foot to a step.

Rodger Raposo and Don MacRae heard the small horn warble. They saw Piper come flying out of the RV. She made a blue blur as she sped across the parking lot toward the plumbing van that sat in a pool of light.

"Whoa." MacRae whispered.

Moments later another runner came out of the RV, this one also a child. The second kid was moving with legs flashing and arms pumping, looking like a kid in trouble.

MacRae broke into a run, heading for the RV. Raposo followed. A tall man left the RV and ran toward the access road. The runner crossed the road, slid under a three rail fence and disappeared into a vast yard of shipping containers.

The officers stopped at the RV. "We won't catch him," Raposo called to MacRae. "Let's check on the kids."

They turned and jogged to the plumber's van, where they found a tear-stained Piper clinging to her grandmother. Raymond had an arm around the shoulders of a white-faced and heaving Dylan. Grace and Drewl completed the huddle.

"He had a knife," Piper said. "He's tall. Red hair. He had a knife."

"He was going to kill us," Dylan gasped. "He grabbed my hair and the wig came off."

"We'll find him," MacRae said. "Don't worry. We'll track him down."

Raposo didn't waste any time asking why a twelve-year-old boy was wearing a wig. "I'll call in Olympia P.D.," he said. "See if we can get a unit with a dog over."

"Please," Grace interrupted. "No cops. Well, no more cops. Mrs. Anderson is going to be arriving very soon. Our whole reason for being here is to get her out of town quietly. If you start calling in people, it won't be quiet at all."

Don MacRae squared his shoulders. "We could take a look at the yard."

Raposo stared at him. WTF? MacRae made eye contact with Raposo. "We can take a look," MacRae repeated.

Raposo saw the dark-haired young woman nod hopefully. He looked around the rest of the group and made an assessment. Three adults. Raymond looked tough. Two kids old enough to take direction. A big dog.

"Where's Dr. Anderson?" he asked.

"He went with Dr. Berbera to talk to a biologist who lives on a boat," Piper told him. "Down the G stairs, I think. He'll be back in a few minutes."

"Deputy MacRae and I'll take a look in the container yard. You stay here – together. And Miz Edna? You and I need to talk."

Edna had to nod an agreement. She pulled Piper in close and whispered, "Don't worry. It's just a few minutes more."

"Watch out for the unexpected mushroom."

Sicilian proverb

CHAPTER ONE HUNDRED-TWELVE

Puget Sound near Olympia

LENA'S AFTERNOON HAD been lovely. It had been a grand respite to have an afternoon tea with Daylene and her sisters.

The talk had been of stenciling and scrapbooking. The conversation turned to knitting, quilting and gardening. Lena found she excelled at making sympathetic noises as complaints were shared about grinding transmissions, shrinking pants and independent-minded children.

At three in the afternoon, Little Joey clattered off the school bus and joined them. He gave Lena a hug when he came in.

As the evening shadows arrived, Daylene packed monstrous sandwiches and a thermos of coffee to take along.

Daylene also insisted she take a heavy quilted barn coat, saying, "You won't believe how cold it gets on the water."

Lena took the coat gratefully. Soon she boarded the boat, once again with a scarf over her hair and a picnic basket in hand.

Joe took the boat along the inlet with an understated confidence. They inspected his territory, slowly and carefully.

It was after nine before the gloaming faded into dark. Joe turned on the port and starboard lights, and killed the engine. They floated, drifting southward. Lena drank in the quiet magic of the water.

"I could live out here forever," Lena said.

"Yep."

Lena smiled as she accepted a mug of coffee. "Thanks, Joe. For everything. I feel like today was a gift. It's hard to think about living somewhere else."

"Where will you go?" Joe asked.

"I don't know. I don't really care. If my family is together, and we're safe, that's all that's important. Grace said it's isolated, and I like the sound of that."

"Yep."

They drank coffee in silence. Joe checked his watch and grunted, "Time to go."

Lena poured the dregs of her cup over the railing and returned the cup to Joe. She sat down on a toolbox in the front of the wheelhouse, drawing Daylene's heavy barn coat around her.

Daylene was right. It was getting cold. Besides the needed layers, the coat had the warmth of friendship in it. Lena crossed her arms and tucked in her hands. She could hardly wait to see Piper and Milo again.

*

Grace saw the boat lights in the distance. "That's them," she said. She looked down the parking lot. There was no sign of Milo and Dr. Berbera. The detective and the deputy had not come back.

Grace made a decision.

"I'll take Drewl down to meet the boat," she said. "To make sure everything's okay."

"Hang on," her Uncle Raymond said. "Go prepared." He reached into the back of the van and pulled out a two-foot pipe wrench. "Just in case."

Grace transferred the leash to her left hand and hefted the pipe wrench in her right. It was heavy. "Probably drop this on my foot," she muttered.

"Probably," agreed her uncle.

Grace and Drewl went down the sidewalk to the top of the stairs. She looked out on the Sound. The boat lights came closer, with the shape of the boat's wheelhouse emerging from the dark.

Grace moved towards the metal gate at the top of the stairs. Every staircase was locked to casual visitors. She glanced down at the dock, hoping to see a resident boater with a key to share. There was no one.

She needn't have worried. As she reached the gate, she saw that someone had slapped duct tape over the latch and the strike plate. A notecard was duct-taped to the gate that said, "Party! A-10. Sat. 8 'til ?"

Given that it was now Tuesday night, it seemed the revelers weren't much on cleanup tasks.

Grace opened the gate. She took Drewl across the gate threshold and down the A stairs. The old dog surged down the steps. He seemed energized by the nearness of the water.

Grace walked Drewl to the end of the A dock where she saw two low dinghies lashed to the end of the dock. The next dock over was clear. Joe would dock there.

Grace stopped near the dinghies. She could walk all the way back and then out the next dock, but the *Darling Daylene* was already pulling in. Grace decided to wait where she was.

Joe stopped the *Darling Daylene* within inches of the B dock. Lena stepped off and waved cheerfully. Grace waved back.

Drewl leaned forward, tightening the leash.

Grace looked down at Drewl. She followed his intense gaze out past a row of covered motorboats.

A slender, small woman in a pink hoodie came striding down the B dock toward Lena.

"Mrs. Anderson!" Theodora called. "I'm Dr. Band. I'm here to help you." *I've got her*, Theodora thought. *There's no place she can go.*

Lena came to halt. She looked around wildly.

Grace was forty feet away on the parallel dock. Lena swung her eyes back to the walkway. Dr. Band was rapidly closing in. The dock was narrow. Could she push by Dr. Band?

Lena began backing up. She looked over her shoulder to where the *Darling Daylene* was reversing away from the drop off. Joe could keep her safe. Lena pivoted back towards the boat. Joe was looking away, concentrating on the reversal. He finished the backup and put the boat into drive.

Grace saw Dr. Band pulled a syringe out of her pocket and charge after Lena.

Grace waved the pipe wrench up in the air and yelled, "Stop! Stop!"

Joe didn't hear her.

Lena launched herself off the dock in a frantic attempt to reach the boat. She hit the cold water with a splash. Lena tried to scream. Nothing came out.

Lena pushed down on the water, struggling to keep her head above the wake of the *Darling Daylene.* Finally, she got a stroke started and began to swim after the *Darling Daylene.*

The heavy barn coat, such a friend when dry, was now a deadly liability. Each arm lift was a struggle.

Theodora didn't hesitate. She put the syringe crossways in her mouth and dove in after Lena, swimming easily. *Got you now, mutant bitch.*

Drewl whined and leaned forward.

Grace didn't stop to think. She unsnapped the leash, threw her hand forward and yelled, "Drewl! Fetch!"

The big black dog launched out over the water.

*

At the other end of the marina, Milo Anderson had a prickle of unease. Lena should be here soon.

"I should head back," he said to Berbera and Angus.

Angus nodded and walked with Milo back to the dock gate. Angus took the key necklace off and inserted the key.

The men heard Grace's voice belting out over the still marina as she shouted, "Stop! Joe! Stop!"

Angus turned the key.

The key stuck.

Milo rattled the door, swearing.

Angus gave the key a ferocious twist.

The key snapped off in the lock.

"Those who were my enemies without cause hunted me like a bird."

Lamentations 3:52

CHAPTER ONE HUNDRED-THIRTEEN

Tuesday, Ten p.m. Swantown Marina

THE WATER WAS frigid. Lena struggled to breathe. She thrashed in the wake of the *Darling Daylene.* The water-logged barn coat made each stroke an effort. She didn't dare stop to shed the coat. Dr. Band was right behind her.

Theodora was breast stroking easily, keeping her head out of the water with the syringe still in her mouth. *You have to go slow in cold water*, she thought. *Swim too fast and it's hard to get enough air.* It was too bad that Lena had run, but no matter. She'd smack her with the syringe and claim the Angel was hysterical.

Whether the Angel lived or died was of no concern. The important thing was to have control. She, Theodora, would be the decider. Lena dead would be a well-milked tragedy. Lena alive would be a patient in need of management.

Theodora felt a small wave as Drewl hit the water to her left. Theodora was surprised as the dog triangulated to where the swimmers were headed. Joe Harbo finally looked back. He cut the power to the engines. The *Darling Daylene* began to drift back toward Lena.

Lena was white and gasping as she fought the water, the coat and the cold.

Her pace slowed. Lena stopped. She had to get out of the coat.

Lena fought the coat. If she could just get one arm out, the second arm would be easy. The wet quilted lining of the coat adhered to her long-sleeved shirt. Lena tried to float on her back as she peeled and shoved the coat away from her sleeve.

Theodora came gliding up with a powerful frog kick. She reached up to take the syringe from her mouth.

Theodora reached for Lena.

Theodora was yanked back. Drewl had hold of the pink hoodie and was towing her back to the dock.

Theodora wallowed and rolled. The pink sweatshirt slipped up and covered her face. She fought the wet cloth as Drewl ploughed through the water pulling her back to Grace, a canine tugboat extraordinaire.

Theodora clawed the cloth off her face with one hand. She still had the syringe. Could she stop the dog?

Drewl paddled onward, oblivious to peril.

Theodora twisted. She rolled over in the water and plunged the needle into Drewl's neck.

*

Across the marina, Milo rammed his shoulder into the mesh door. It held.

Angus swore. He kicked off his sandals and stuck his toes in the chain link. He hoisted and went over the top. Angus landed with an "oof" and sprinted down the walkway.

"Here," said Yousef. He held out cupped hands.

Milo put one foot up into Yousef's hands.

Yousef hoisted and Milo straightened his leg. He perched, belly button to fence top for a perilous moment, then swung a leg over the fence. He ignored the pain of the wire top that poked into his crotch.

Milo swung down to the other side of the fence. He staggered up to the dock staircase and ran after Angus.

*

Grace set the pipe wrench on the dock, preparing to help Drewl and the doctor out of the water. She wasn't sure what was in the syringe that Dr. Band had used, but it surely was nothing good.

Grace climbed down into one of the dinghies lashed to the end of the dock. She picked the inflatable dinghy with wide, rounded sidewalls, thinking it was less likely to capsize as she worked to get dog and people out of the water. It had a diver's ladder at one end.

"Here, Dr. Band. Let me help you." Grace wasn't at all sure that she wanted to get Dr. Band out of the water. A cheerful tone was the one to take.

"Get him off me," Theodora snarled.

Then again, maybe not, Grace thought. "Give," she instructed, and Drewl let go of Theodora's hoodie.

Grace grabbed Drewl by the collar and heaved. Drewl scrabbled with his paws on the dive ladder. He came up out of the water and into the dinghy, bringing gallons of water on board.

"Good dog."

Drewl shook mightily, soaking Grace further. The syringe came flying out to roll on the floor of the dinghy. Grace stared at it. Before she could move to pick it up, she heard Dr. Band.

"For Christ's sake, get me out of the water, you stupid bitch."

Grace turned to Theodora who was struggling to grab onto the round sidewall of the rubber boat.

"There's a ladder," Grace pointed. Theodora began to make her way along the dinghy side, fury radiating in every motion.

Grace decided to leave the dinghy to Dr. Band. Grace pulled herself up onto the dock and called to Drewl, who seemed to be invigorated by the swim. With no hesitation, he jumped up onto the dock.

Grace saw Joe Harbo tossing a line and bumper out to Lena.

Lena grabbed the rope and Joe began drawing it in, hand over hand with quick efficiency.

Grace got to her feet, picking up Uncle Raymond's pipe wrench as she went. Afterwards she thought this action was simply the result of a lifetime of training from parents who liked tidy floors.

Grace heard Milo shouting, "Lena!" and saw the shapes of two runners flashing between the gaps of the boats along the docks. The man in front had long locks bouncing with each stride. The hair gleamed bronze under the parking lot lights. Grace exhaled. Angus and Milo. She also saw the tall deputy and the Mason County detective come racing down steps and through the unlatched gate. Reinforcements were coming.

A flicker of motion came from the left. A tall man emerged from behind a boat prow near Grace. He must have come down the stairs behind her. His hair gleamed maroon in the subdued lights of the marina. His left cheek hosted a hole that glistened with bloody wetness. He looked down at Grace and grinned. He pulled a black pistol from the small of his back and extended his arm toward pale Lena who was halfway up the stern of the *Darling Daylene*.

Grace leapt forward, swinging the pipe wrench. She screamed "LOZEN!!!"

"It is indeed a desirable thing to be well-descended, but the glory belongs to our ancestors."

Plutarch (45 – 120 CE)

CHAPTER ONE HUNDRED-FOURTEEN

Tuesday, Ten minutes after Ten p.m. Swantown Marina

THE PIPE WRENCH connected with Kurt's right temple just as he pulled the trigger. A shot cracked out over the water as Kurt crumpled. Within moments, there were figures on the dock, next to Grace, next to Kurt's body, and next to a screaming, thrashing Dr. Band, who writhed at the edge of the dinghy.

Grace sank to her knees in relief.

"Miss. Put down the wrench."

Grace stared at Deputy McRae. He repeated his direction. Grace let the pipe wrench go and it clattered on the dock. McRae stooped over Kurt's body. He pulled on a disposable glove and gently removed the gun from Kurt's hand.

"Did I kill him?" she croaked.

"Yes, Ma'am. I believe so."

Grace crawled to the edge of the dock and vomited.

Deputy McRae moved to her side and stayed until she finished. Grace blinked at him, then rocked back on her heels. "Lena? Is she alright?"

"Yes, Ma'am. She's on the boat."

Grace saw Joe Harbo bring the *Darling Daylene* to the end of the dock. Soon Lena was transferred off the boat and into Milo's embrace. Lena was shivering uncontrollably as Milo picked her up and made his way down the dock walkway.

Grace started shivering too. *Shock,* she thought. *I'm no good at bashing people.*

Angus came out to Grace. He peeled off his heavy wool sweater and offered it.

Grace felt tears welling up. She sniffed and nodded. With Angus's help, she stood up and slipped the sweater on.

Angus was barefoot. Grace stared down at his feet. His toenails were trimmed. His feet were long and graceful. They were beautiful.

Grace saw Detective Raposo grab the screaming Theodora Band. He manhandled her with an easy competence. Theodora was pushed into plastic handcuffs as tears streamed down her face.

"Is Dr. Band under arrest?" Grace asked.

Deputy McRae said, "She's a person of interest. She's being restrained for everyone's safety."

Grace blinked back tears. "Wow. I don't know what to think." She swayed a bit and Angus reached out to steady her.

The deputy turned to Angus and said, "Sir, step back. I need to speak with this lady a minute."

Angus nodded. "Sure. Let's get her sitting down."

Grace moved to the side of the dock. She sat down with her legs dangling over the pier edge. Drewl moved in. He pushed his wet body against her. Grace dug her fingers into his thick hair and choked back tears.

Angus gave her shoulder a pat and then stepped back as the deputy knelt down next to Grace.

"Dr. Band hit Drewl with a syringe," she told him. "It's in the bottom of the dinghy. Drewl shook it out."

"Is he okay?"

Grace looked at Drewl who looked back at her with clear-eyed serenity.

"I think so. He has a thick ruff."

"I'll look for the syringe in a minute. Where did you learn that word?" he asked.

"What word?"

"When you swung the pipe wrench. You yelled 'Lozen,'" he told her.

"Lozen? That's something my mom says when she's mad. I asked her once what it meant. She said it's a word for being furious. She didn't know what language."

"Lozen was an Apache woman warrior," McRae told her. "She fought with Victorio and Geronimo. She was skilled, brave, smart and ferocious. She was an amazing woman."

"Oh." Grace tightened her grip on Drewl's pelt. "Wow."

McRae's short hair glinted a light ginger red in the dim light of the marina.

"You like dogs?" McRae asked.

"Yes," Grace told him. "Yes, I do."

"There is nothing so powerful as truth – and often nothing so strange."

Daniel Webster
(January 18, 1782 – October 24, 1852)

CHAPTER ONE HUNDRED-FIFTEEN

Tuesday, Ten–thirty p.m. Swantown Marina

DREWL DIDN'T WANT to get into the RV. He put on the brakes and refused to move. Angus and Raymond joined arms behind his rump and heaved as Edna called him up the stairs. Drewl finally scrambled up and took up a position under the dinette table.

Raymond and Angus made quick work of moving the family suitcases from Raymond's van into the bottom of the RV.

Lena, now in dry clothes, had regained some color. She sat with Piper and Edna at the RV table with Drewl crowding in at their feet. Lena clutched a cup of hot cocoa in one hand and had her other arm around Piper.

Milo stood on the asphalt, speaking with Sergeant Martinez from the Olympia Police Department while an ambulance sat in the parking lot with flashing lights, ready to remove the body of Kurt Otsoa.

Finally Milo shook hands with Sergeant Martinez and came over to Grace. "Thanks," he said. "Thanks for everything!"

"Sure! Let me know when you get there."

"Will do!" Milo pulled her into a quick embrace, which pleased Grace no end. He climbed up the steps and closed the door to the RV.

Within moments the RV moved off.

"Where are they going?" asked Rodger Raposo.

"I'd like to know too," said Dr. Berbera.

"Ah, maybe we don't want to know," offered Angus.

"It's not for general publication." Grace drew in a breath and added, "But Milo said I should tell you. They go first to Portland. Tomorrow they travel by private jet to Palmyra Atoll."

Dr. Berbera laughed. "Perfect."

"Yep. Visitors have to get a permit."

"Where is this?" Detective Raposo asked.

"About a thousand miles south of Honolulu," Angus told him. "Private island group with a big lagoon. Owned by a nature group in partnership with the U.S. Government. The paparazzi and fans will have a hard time getting there. How'd you come up with that idea?"

"I know a biologist there," Grace replied.

She turned to Dylan. "We need to start saving some bucks. We could go see Piper."

"Do they have a school?"

"I don't think so."

"Good. I'll go."

Grace laughed. "It's hot," she told him. "There's snorkeling. Sharks. Manta Rays."

"Awesome."

Dr. Berbera yawned. "Come on, Dylan. Let's ask Raymond to get us home. The exciting stuff is all over."

Grace turned to Angus. "Thanks. Thanks for everything. Can I get the sweater back to you tomorrow?"

"Sure. Are you going to be alright for tonight?" Angus's eyes moved over her face with concern.

Grace smiled at him. "I'm good. I need to talk to the detective. See you tomorrow?"

"Sure." Angus sketched a wave and moved off.

Grace waited a few moments before speaking to Detective Raposo, who was waiting patiently. "Am I going to be arrested? For…" she couldn't say 'murder', so she finally said, "attacking that guy?"

"Kurt Otsoa? No. We need to wait until the Olympia PD finish processing the scene and they will have more questions for you. Eventually there will be an inquest. We'll ask you to testify. I'll testify too. We believe Otsoa is responsible for the death of a local doctor, and possibly for the death of a young woman as well."

Raposo added, "We got a call today from a woman who saw Otsoa's picture on a news bulletin. She says he was her rapist. We'll be digging into Mr. Otsoa's past with some diligence to see if anything else connects. He may have a long history."

Don MacRae drove up in a dark sedan. Grace fell silent as the lanky deputy exited the car and joined them.

"Dr. Band has been booked into the Thurston County jail. And, Miss, I owe you an apology."

Grace looked up at MacRae. "About?"

"I shouldn't have left you to deal with that jerk at the roadblock yesterday. He was out of line, and I didn't stop him. I am so sorry about that."

"Thank you for saying that," Grace said. "That helps." She exhaled. *Three redheads in one evening. I killed one, but the other two…*

Grace shook her head. She'd have to think about this tomorrow. She was beyond exhausted now.

Rodger Raposo interrupted her muddled thinking by saying, "It's late. Let me check with the guys down on the dock and see if they are willing to talk to you tomorrow. Seeing as how Don and I were on the scene and are witnesses, that might be okay."

"Thanks." Grace was near weeping with exhaustion. She rallied to ask, "What happens to Dr. Band?"

"We believe she is Otsoa's sister. She'll stay in custody tonight. We'll be in court when she's arraigned and argue against a bond."

"Tell her what Dr. Berbera said," Don MacRae urged.

Raposo grimaced. "Your department head is convinced Dr. Band has what he called 'a complex antisocial personality disorder'. He said, 'I work in academia. Believe me, I know the signs."

"Great. My chosen field," Grace muttered.

*

As Grace was collecting her thoughts at the Swantown marina, an unmarked van arrived at the Olympia Yacht Club. The van was parked in heavy shadow that almost covered the exit of four muscular men and two lean men.

Ken Ito was watching. He called and waved. "Dr. Rivera! Dr. Szczepanski! Over here!"

Carlos and Z came out of the shadows, frowning.

"Sorry, you missed the action," Ken told them.

"What do you mean, we 'missed the action'?" Carlos snapped.

"The Andersons convened at the Swantown marina about an hour ago."

"Swantown?" Carlos asked

Z started to laugh. "We're at the wrong marina."

"Yes," Ken agreed. "The Andersons have departed."

"What is their destination?" Carlos demanded.

"Someplace outside the continental United States. He smiled.

"Edna traded directions to her favorite mushroom patches to a Hong Kong CEO for use of his private jet."

Z snorted. "Carlos, you've been bested by a little old lady."

Ken said, "The family will be given a chance to regroup and research their biology. They will retain control of the research process and will give samples when and where they see fit."

"You put this together this afternoon? I'm impressed," Carlos said sourly.

"It was touch and go," Ken admitted. "We used a lot of different phones."

Lights flashed behind Carlos. The burly men near the van darted into the shadows, scattering like cockroaches.

"What the hell?" Carlos barked.

"That's a pair of brothers named Savio and Vico. They just documented your van and your guys. They've been working as paparazzi. This afternoon a friend of their mother's, a Mrs. Kastenbaum, convinced the brothers to go into wedding photography. I believe she said a great deal about nice paychecks and pretty bridesmaids. But before they switch careers, I asked them to come down to get pictures of your team. For insurance purposes."

"Insurance for what?" Carlos snapped.

"Insurance so the Andersons have some time and no complications from Homeland Security. I'm sure our senators would be interested to know how your agency funds are being spent in Washington State."

"It's our job," Carlos argued. "That woman's biological changes may have huge implications for our nation."

"Or it may be just one more oddity like the Elephant Man or the Indonesian Tree men," Ken retorted. "Milo Anderson is a scientist. Give him some time. He'll share what he learns."

"And his wife gets some life with dignity," Z added. Z tapped Carlos on the shoulder. "Give it up. You were worried about that. Ken found a path. And there's another bonus."

"Yeah?" Carlos growled.

"It wasn't me that beat you to the project."

Carlos managed a half smile. "There is that." He eyed Ken. "This isn't over. My memory is long."

"I don't doubt that." Ken Ito replied. "I'll be around."

Carlos rolled his shoulders, and stretched. Then he turned to Z. "We should buy the guys a beer."

"They're not going to be happy. Better make it a lot of beer."

"Poor is the pupil who does not surpass his master."

Leonardo da Vinci
(April 15, 1452 – May 2, 1519)

CHAPTER ONE HUNDRED-SIXTEEN

Twelve weeks later - January

"WHAT DO YOU think of Arizona?" Piper asked. She was on Skype with Dylan.

"Beyond awesome. Dr. Berbera showed me how to classify scorpions. Tomorrow we're taking students to a rattlesnake den. And guess what?"

"What?"

"Dr. Berbera's taking me to talk to a scientist in Seattle about my ideas on global hydrogen sulfide levels triggering feather development. It may connect to some work they are doing."

"Not bad for a D student," Piper teased.

"Yeah." Dylan grinned back at the screen. "How's Drewl?"

"He's better now the trade winds have arrived. He spends a lot of time on the veranda. He has a big bed in the shade, and Grandmom has her lounge chair out there too."

Piper giggled. "Grandmom goes out there with a book. She

says she's catching up on family history, but then there's a lot of snoring. We all go out for a swim in the lagoon after dinner. Drewl likes that a lot."

"How's your mom?"

Piper rolled her eyes. "Fine. Apparently I am going to have a sibling in late May."

"Whoa."

"I said we could name it 'Budgie,' and Mom got mad."

Dylan burst out laughing. "You've been infected with my attitude."

"Yeah. I think so."

*

Rodger picked up the phone on the first ring. "Raposo," he grunted.

"Will Taggart here."

"Ah, Dr. Taggart. What can I do for you?" Rodger leaned back in his desk chair, intrigued.

"I've been talking to my friend, Celeste. You remember her – she was with me at the big who-hah in September.

"Yes sir. Short lady. Curly hair."

"That's my Celeste," Dr. Taggart agreed. "The thing is, she has been telling me how she got past that roadblock. Seems there is an officer who, ah, will take a personal favor from a lady, to, ah, well."

Dr. Taggart stuttered to a stop. Then he rallied to say, "The guy's name is Pendergast. He works in law enforcement. And the son-of-a-bitch shouldn't be."

Raposo touched his bloodhound bobble-head dog. The toy bounced into motion. "Dr. Taggart, I would really like to talk to Ms. Celeste."

*

Grace tabbed the car fob to lock her cousin's van at the airport lot.

It was odd to acquire an extended family. Family was arriving from all over for Esther and Alasdair's wedding.

Grace was looking forward to meeting her cousin Jason. And it wasn't just Jason on her pickup list. Grace checked the time on her phone. Her family should be near the baggage claim.

When she found them, her brothers were taller, her mother grayer, and her father slimmer than she remembered.

"Oh, Honey, you look fabulous!" her mother gushed.

"New haircut! Aunt Esther insisted."

"She as bossy as ever?" her father was smiling as he spoke.

"She's good at getting things done," Grace admitted.

"Are we going to meet this boyfriend?" her father asked.

"Yeah, Dad. You are." Grace smiled. "I think you're going to like him."

"A redhead?"

"Yeah, Dad. A redhead."

DHS
Geastrum saccatum

Acknowledgements

I HAVE LEARNED it takes the love and support of family, many friends and a few kind strangers to get a story to The End.

I'm grateful to authors Jim Lynch, Simon Winchester, Michael J. Sullivan, Robert Dugoni and Kari Aguila for demonstrating the art of being a gracious professional writer. I have learned important things from each of you.

Many thanks go to my family and friends. I'd be lost without you.

Thanks to Steve King of the Oyster Bay Book Club for slogging through Version One of this book. You are a gentleman and a scholar even as you enjoy playing the rascal.

Rosalie Martens found more than one idiotic error. After seven or eight drafts, I wasn't sure which was up and Rosalie pointed the way home. Thanks, mate!

Thank you to Chris Herrera and Carolyn Bumford of the South Sound Mushroom Club for cheerfully looking at a few of the sections that mention mushrooms. Thank you to Gregg Bennett, D.V.M. for discussing cat digestion with me. Any errors in taxonomy or anatomy are mine, not theirs.

It has been a great pleasure to work with illustrator Duncan Sheffels. I also deeply appreciate the work of the Damonza.com book design team.

I am humbled and deeply grateful to The Angels who helped the story cross the finish line. My special Angels are Forrest Rice, Mary and Roger Anderson, Ed and Laura Tang, Sandia and Bing Tang, Bridget Carragher, Nalini Nadkarni and Nat Wheelwright, Mark Worcester, Joy Gray Grover, Terry Sickelbower, Stephen King, Gloria Temple, Janine Bogar and Robert Payne, and Ruth Duvall.

Critical support came from Truffle fans, including Deb and Randy Steele, John King, Mark Iler, Nancy Pestal, Jen Tunnell, Molly Schloss, Tricia Gray, Sarah Rice, Lon Davidson, Andrew MacMillen, Kari Aguila, Judy Oliver, Rinae Perron, Janet Bryant, Marie Zimmermann, Carol and Jim Rainwood, Sally and Gregg Bennett, Laura Stephenson, Cindy Levy, Janet Brislawn and Maria Reidelbach.

In addition to the Angels, Truffle lovers and inspirational writers, there are the Mountain men of Riceland. Cliff, Forrest, Paxton and Newton, thank you for being there.

Made in the USA
Columbia, SC
05 July 2018